TEMPLE COMMANDER

POWER ASCENDING: BOOK FIVE

PAUL J BENNETT

AND SO IT BEGINS...

A bowsprit came into view as a large, two-masted warship rounded the eastern end of Constance. It was much slower than the ship they pursued, but the ballistae mounted on its deck could wreak terrible damage if they got close enough. Understanding the threat, the *Sprite* kept a sufficient distance between them to avoid an engagement. Their new southerly bearing looked like a safe course for escape.

"This is all so frustrating," noted Charlaine. "To have them so near yet be unable to close."

"It won't be long now." Danica turned to the south, scanning the horizon. "There," she said, pointing. "Do you see it?"

In the distance, another ship was closing, this one similar in size to the *Valiant*.

"Is that the *Vanguard*?" asked Charlaine.

"It is. You know your ships."

"It was an easy guess. What other ships have we with a triangular sail, other than *Valiant*?"

"If I have my way, there'll be many more like her." Danica chuckled. "I considered re-rigging the *Vigilant*, but it's too difficult to get out of Grazynia's hands."

"I knew *Vanguard* was supposed to be fast, but I never imagined she'd be so sleek. I bet she could even outrun this ship."

"It's quite possible. We built her to the same specifications. You might say she and the *Valiant* are sister ships."

"Quite fitting," said Charlaine, "considering they both belong to the order. Are you looking at building more of the larger vessels?"

"Not in the immediate future," said Danica. "The new shipyard at Temple Bay isn't adequate for a hull of that size. We have the five ships Halvaria donated to our cause, so there's more than enough for now."

Charlaine laughed. "Donated?"

"Well, captured. It amounts to the same thing."

ALSO BY PAUL J BENNETT

INTO THE MAELSTROM

MIDWINTER MURDER

THE BEAST OF BRUNHAUSEN

A PLAGUE ON ZEIDERBRUCH

First Edition: March 2023

ePub ISBN: 978-1-990073-47-2
Mobi ISBN: 978-1-990073-48-9
Smashwords ISBN: 978-1-990073-49-6
Print ISBN: 978-1-990073-46-5

DEDICATION

To my wife, Carol, who gave me wings to let my imagination fly.

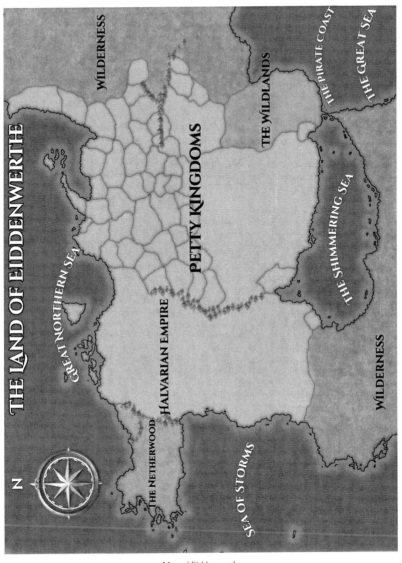

Map of Eiddenwerthe

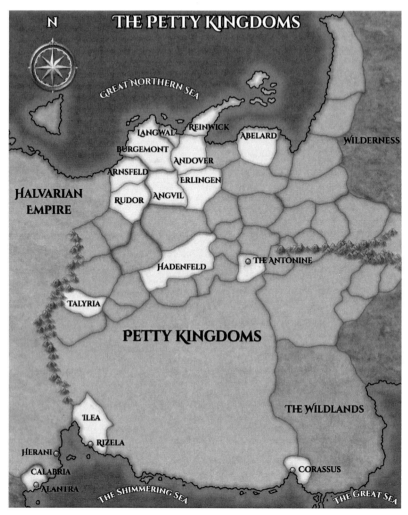

Map of Petty Kingdoms

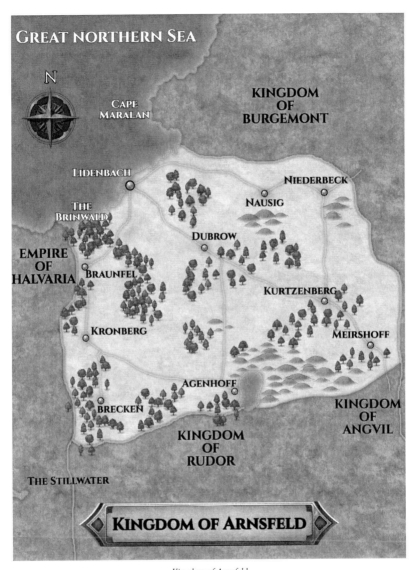

Kingdom of Arnsfeld

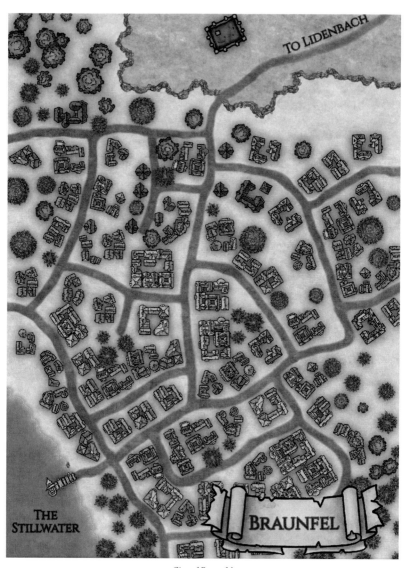

TO LIDENBACH

THE
STILLWATER

BRAUNFEL

City of Braunfel

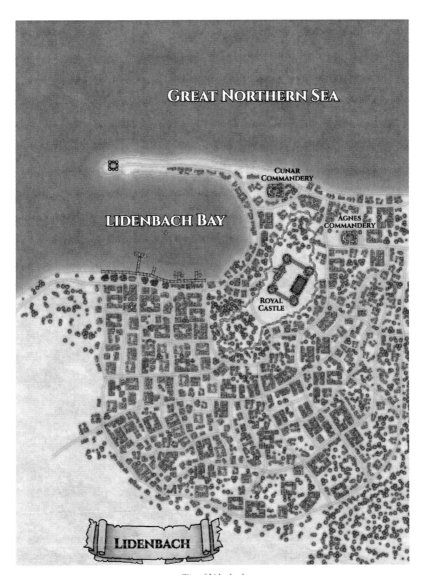

GREAT NORTHERN SEA

CUNAR COMMANDERY

AGNES COMMANDERY

LIDENBACH BAY

ROYAL CASTLE

LIDENBACH

City of Lidenbach

1

PURSUIT

SUMMER 1102 SR* (SAINTS RECKONING)

The bow dug deep, sending water cascading over the *Valiant's* foredeck. Charlaine clung to the rail, her eyes glued onto the ship in the distance. It had taken months to track down the *Sprite*, and they'd finally located it, only to be confounded by the fast sailer. She glanced at Danica, who seemed far calmer than she would have expected.

"They're getting away," said Charlaine.

"Not yet, she's not. She may be fast, but that doesn't mean she can outrun a net."

"Meaning?"

Danica's smile was most curious. "Those Halvarian ships we captured have proven useful these last four years, don't you think?"

"They have. Is that why you're smiling?"

"The island of Constance lies to the north, while Amity is to the south, which means they can only go east."

"Unless they choose to turn and seek battle with us."

"True, but I'd wager the presence of our Temple Knights would be a huge factor in dissuading them from that course of action. I only hope our timing is spot on."

"If something's going to happen, it better be soon. The *Sprite* will be out into open water before long." The enemy vessel began turning to the south. "What's this?"

"It appears they've spotted something," said Danica. She stood on her toes as if doing so would somehow improve her vision. "There she is, the *Fearless*."

A bowsprit came into view as a large, two-masted warship rounded the eastern end of Constance. It was much slower than the ship they pursued, but the ballistae mounted on its deck could wreak terrible damage if they got close enough. Understanding the threat, the *Sprite* kept a sufficient distance between them to avoid an engagement. Their new southerly bearing looked like a safe course for escape.

"This is all so frustrating," noted Charlaine. "To have them so near yet be unable to close."

"It won't be long now." Danica turned to the south, scanning the horizon. "There," she said, pointing. "Do you see it?"

In the distance, another ship was closing, this one similar in size to the *Valiant*.

"Is that the *Vanguard*?" asked Charlaine.

"It is. You know your ships."

"It was an easy guess. What other ships have we with a triangular sail, other than *Valiant*?"

"If I have my way, there'll be many more like her." Danica chuckled. "I considered re-rigging the *Vigilant*, but it's too difficult to get out of Grazynia's hands."

"I knew *Vanguard* was supposed to be fast, but I never imagined she'd be so sleek. I bet she could even outrun this ship."

"It's quite possible. We built her to the same specifications. You might say she and the *Valiant* are sister ships."

"Quite fitting," said Charlaine, "considering they both belong to the order. Are you looking at building more of the larger vessels?"

"Not in the immediate future," said Danica. "The new shipyard at Temple Bay isn't adequate for a hull of that size. We have the five ships Halvaria donated to our cause, so there's more than enough for now."

Charlaine laughed. "Donated?"

"Well, captured. It amounts to the same thing."

"I'm sorry I haven't had more time to visit. I hear the settlement is coming along nicely."

"It is," said Danica. "The toughest part was recruiting the shipbuilders. Once we made it clear we wanted their families to join them, things moved quickly."

Having spotted the *Vanguard*, the *Sprite* began turning back to the west.

"It appears you shall get that fight after all," said Danica. "I suppose the *Sprite's* captain felt he had a better chance against us than potentially taking on two ships at once." She turned aft to order the Temple Knights to prepare, but they were already donning their helmets in anticipation. There were only six of them, yet their plate armour was almost impervious to anything a pirate was likely to carry.

The enemy vessel turned into the wind, causing it to slow considerably. It was always a risky manoeuvre, for if they didn't do it correctly, the ship would lose its momentum, quickly becoming dead in the water. The *Sprite*, however, navigated the turn with an expert hand and was soon heading straight towards the *Valiant*, although at a significantly reduced speed.

Danica ordered her own ship to take in sail, slowing to prepare for boarding. Sister Celine removed the tarp covering the arbalest and loaded a grapnel. The five remaining sisters moved to the railing on the port side, taking up crossbows and preparing to unleash a volley. There would only be time for a single bolt each, for once they closed the distance, they would draw swords and board the enemy vessel.

The *Vanguard* changed course, following the *Sprite* as it clawed its way westward. Being a less nimble sailer, the *Fearless* reduced sail and maintained its course, its presence acting as a deterrent should the enemy attempt to flee eastward.

Arrows flew from the enemy, a volley proving wildly inaccurate in the pitching waters of the Great Northern Sea. Celine let loose with the arbalest, the grapnel sailing across the distance to bounce off the enemy's deck and careen into the railing on the far side. Sailors rushed to take up the slack on the rope and hauled away, pulling the *Sprite* towards them.

At this point, the enemy had two choices: either cut away the rope or embrace it and attempt to board.

Charlaine shook her head. As had happened too many times in the past, the pirates decided to fight. Had the *Valiant* been a ship from one of the Petty Kingdoms, they might have stood a chance, but the Temple Knights of Saint Agnes were not the typical seaborne warriors employed by the kingdoms littering the coast.

As the *Sprite* pulled closer, it was easy to see the men clustered by its railings, eager to come to grips with their foe. Crossbows sang out, taking down three of the pirates, and then the enemy ship's hull came alongside, bumping up against the *Valiant*. The impact sent people scattering on both ships, many falling to the deck.

Having secured herself against the expected impact, Charlaine drew her sword and rushed down the deck, ready to fight off any attacks.

Someone on the *Sprite* threw down a boarding ramp while his crewmates tossed their own grappling hooks, eager to ensure the two ships remained locked in place.

Charlaine waited for the spiked ramp to dig into the railing, then rushed across it, ready to deliver holy vengeance upon the enemy. A sailor blocked her way, but the swing of her sword soon took him down. She advanced, dropping to the *Sprite's* deck, her blade seeking any who resisted.

A sword careened off her helmet as her own weapon took a man in the chest. He staggered back, mesmerized by the blood staining his shirt, then slumped to the deck. An axe crashed into Charlaine's forearm, denting her armour and knocking the blade from her hand. She withdrew, seeking some space to draw her dagger, but then her foot slipped on the bloodied deck, sending her crashing to her knees.

A shape pushed past her, followed by another as the Temple Knights of Saint Agnes fought their way onto the enemy vessel.

Charlaine looked around, but the fighting was over. Three men lay dead and another five wounded, but they held no desire to continue, for they'd dropped their weapons.

"That was nice and quick," came Danica's voice. "And not a single injury to our own knights." She looked down at Charlaine. "You're not wounded, are you?"

"Only my pride."

Danica helped her to her feet. "You know, we have knights to do all the fighting. You didn't need to be the first across."

"I was trying to set an example."

"Of what? Being impetuous?"

Charlaine smiled. "You know, I would take that as an insult from anyone else."

Sister Vivian pushed a man forward, forcing him to his knees. "This is the captain," she said. "I found him hiding below."

Charlaine looked the fellow over. He was rail thin, sporting a face with a very patchy beard. "You're the notorious Captain Booker?"

"The very same," he replied. "Captain Elgar Booker, at your service."

"I was expecting someone taller."

"Sorry to disappoint."

"You're remarkably calm for somebody with a death sentence hanging over them."

Booker shrugged. "It was bound to come to an end eventually. I made my bed, and I'm not afraid to lie in it. I am curious, though. To which port are we headed?"

Charlaine looked at her companion. "That's your choice, Admiral, although I doubt it makes much difference. The penalty for piracy in any of the Petty Kingdoms is death."

"We'll bring him with us to Korvoran," said Danica. "We need to get you back to the commandery there anyway." Danica turned to Sister Vivian. "See that he's properly bound before you take him aboard *Valiant*. We'll hand him over to the authorities once we're in Korvoran."

"Aye, Admiral," the knight replied, hauling the prisoner to his feet and marching him off.

"The *Sprite* is a fast ship," said Charlaine. "Will you take her into the fleet?"

"No, she's too small, although I suppose she might do for running dispatches."

"Have you the crew for her?"

"A ship like that would only require a handful of men. I'm certain we can scrape together enough to put her into service. Of course, I'd put a sister knight in charge."

"I'm sure there are many to choose from," said Charlaine. "You might even consider putting a Mathewite in charge."

"Why would I do that?"

"The Temple Knights of Saint Mathew are respected everywhere. Not even the Halvarians would attack a ship flying their flag, especially when it's not a ship of war."

"That would make us reliant on another order."

"And we aren't now? I might remind you they look after our sick and wounded, and we know we can trust them to keep the location of Temple Bay secret. It's only a suggestion, of course. You're the admiral."

Danica chuckled. "And you're the Temple Captain of Korvoran. Technically, I still report to you."

"You know as well as I that's only an administrative convenience."

"True, but one of these days, the order will reassign you, and there's no guarantee your successor would look at things the same way."

"Nonsense. I've been here for almost five years. If they were going to reassign me, they'd have done it by now."

The *Valiant* sailed into Korvoran Harbour with little fanfare. As usual, the sisters secured the ship, then posted a guard to keep onlookers at bay. The *Sprite* had sailed ahead and now lay tied to the dock alongside the spot reserved for the order's ships.

Charlaine stepped ashore to find Sister Marlena waiting for her, not an unusual occurrence, given her position as the Temple Captain's adjutant. Still, something in her stance gave the impression there was news of some sort.

"Well?" said Charlaine. "Why the long face?"

"There are dispatches from the Antonine."

"We get messages from there all the time."

"True," replied Marlena, "but one is marked urgent."

"Then we best return to the commandery and see what's so important." She was about to head down the dock, then thought better of it. "Danica?" she called out. "I need to speak with you about something. Come to my office when you get a chance, will you?"

"Of course. I'll just see to the *Valiant's* restock first."

Charlaine made her way into town, accompanied by her aide. "Anything else of interest happen while I was gone?" she asked.

"A couple of replacements came in, but Leona has them well in hand."

"And the duke?"

"More congratulations from his court. It appears sweeping the sea of pirates has been good for trade."

"So, no bad news for once?"

Marlena smiled. "I'm afraid you're not getting off that easily. Somehow, he discovered we've been stealing some of his shipwrights."

"We didn't steal them, merely hired them away. Besides, the duke doesn't maintain his own fleet."

"I think he's just annoyed that we didn't ask him first. Speaking of shipwrights, how did the *Vanguard* fare?"

"Quite well. She's a fine addition to the fleet."

"Will we build more?"

"I think so, although that would be the admiral's decision, not mine. Any more problems with the Cunars?"

"No," said Marlena, "which concerns me. Ever since their new captain arrived, they've grown quiet. They don't even bother showing up at court anymore. It's as if they're withdrawing from the world of politics. Did you know they reduced their garrison here?"

"They've been shrinking their garrison for the last four years. I'm surprised they haven't pulled out completely."

"And if they do?"

"That's hardly our concern, unless you're suggesting we make up the numbers?"

"Is that even possible?"

"I don't know," said Charlaine, "and in any case, only the grand mistress can make a decision like that." As they rounded the corner, the commandery came into view. "Ah. Home, at last. It'll be nice to put my feet up."

"There's still that dispatch to read," said Marlena.

"Don't remind me. It's probably another warning about fraternization outside of the order."

"I doubt that would be marked urgent."

"Good point."

.   .   .

Charlaine sat behind her desk. Most Temple Captains passed the bulk of their time in a room such as this, but she found it much more engaging to spend time amongst the sisters. After all, this was a fighting order, and to her mind, the most effective leaders led from the front.

The letter sat there, daring her to open it. "Ah, well," she said. "I can't keep putting it off."

She used her dagger to remove the seal before carefully unfolding it. Inside was a two-page letter, written in a fine hand she recognized as belonging to Sister Nicola, the grand mistress's aide.

The message was of immense interest, and Charlaine read it twice before finally putting it down. She rose from the chair, walking over to the windows facing west where the setting sun hung over the city, casting long shadows in the streets.

The door opened, revealing Marlena. "I brought you some dinner, Captain."

"Thank you. Put it on the desk, will you, and then please inform Leona I wish to see her."

She heard the door close but remained where she was. She'd spent the better part of five years here in Korvoran, and she would miss it dearly.

Charlaine had no idea how long she stood there, mulling things over until the door opened, revealing Sister Leona.

"Come and sit, Sister," she said. "There is much to discuss."

"Am I in trouble, Captain?"

"Not at all. Why would you think that?"

"You must admit, it's not every day I get summoned to your office."

Charlaine chuckled. "No. I suppose it isn't, but let me put your mind at ease. You are not here to be punished for some transgression of the rules."

"Then why am I here?"

"You'll find out in a moment. We're just waiting for the admiral to join us."

"She's here?"

"She will be shortly. I saw her coming down the street." Charlaine turned from the window to where her food sat on her desk, likely cold by now. She sat down, looking at her treasurer. Leona's leg was missing from the knee down, but her injury hadn't prevented her from contributing to the order's welfare.

Marlena opened the door. "The admiral's here, Captain."

"Good. Come in, both of you. We have things to discuss."

Charlaine waited as they entered. "I received word from the Antonine," she began. "I've been promoted to Temple Commander and reassigned."

"To where?" asked Danica.

"Arnsfeld. Do you know it?"

"Yes, though I've never been there myself. I believe it's one of the westernmost Petty Kingdoms. If I'm not mistaken, it borders Halvaria."

"It does," said Charlaine. "And that's one of the reasons I'm being sent there. It appears the Temple Knights of Saint Cunar have withdrawn from the area."

"Surely, you jest?" said Leona. "They're the only thing keeping the empire at bay."

"The grand mistress is well aware. I am to take command of the commandery there and those in the neighbouring realms. We're increasing our presence to compensate for the deficiency."

"Any word on your successor?" asked Marlena.

"Yes. She left the choice up to me, and I've decided to promote you, Leona, making you the order's senior representative in Reinwick. You're more than ready for the role."

"And what of me?" said Marlena.

"Don't worry. You're coming with me. I'll be dealing with the court of Arnsfeld and need your expertise." She turned to Danica. "As for the fleet, I shall prevail upon you to deliver the two of us to my new command."

"Of course. Will we be maintaining a presence there?"

"That is for you to decide, but at the very least, you should take the opportunity to learn more about Arnsfeld's defences. I suspect it won't be long before the empire takes advantage of the Cunar's withdrawal."

"So, it's true, then?" said Leona. "The Temple Knights of Saint Cunar are falling apart?"

Charlaine held up the letter. "According to this, they're reassigning their forces to better reflect a defence in depth in the event of an invasion."

"This is terrible," said Danica. "It also puts the Petty Kingdoms in a very precarious position."

"I agree, but we must work with what we're given."

"When do you want to leave?"

"I'd like to be out of the harbour by week's end. Can you arrange that?"

"Of course."

"Good," replied Charlaine. "In the meantime, I must put my affairs into order."

"You should alert the smiths guild," said Danica. "They'll need to know where to send the correspondence."

Charlaine nodded. Since her arrival in Korvoran, she'd been using the guild's messenger service to deliver important and confidential information instead of trusting the Church's couriers. Her time in the Antonine had revealed traitors in her order, and she'd spent the intervening years building up a network of trusted confidantes.

"I shall talk to Barbek," she said at last, "and trust that he can make the appropriate arrangements."

"If I am to command here," said Leona, "have you any special orders?"

"Yes. Trust your instincts. There may come a day where we can no longer remain neutral in the affairs of the Petty Kingdoms."

2

ON THE WAY

SUMMER 1102 SR

Charlaine stepped aboard the *Valiant* and then turned, taking one final look at Korvoran. The city had been her home for the past five years, and it was hard to think she must now leave it behind.

"You'll miss it, won't you?" said Danica.

"I shall, but at the same time, I'm looking forward to getting to know Arnsfeld."

"I hope you don't mind, but I arranged to transport your horses aboard the *Barlowe*. The *Valiant* is much too small a ship for them."

"That's fine. I doubt we'll be needing them straight away. Any idea on how long they'll take to catch up?"

"A bit, I expect. Captain Dulworth wants to make stops along the way to buy and sell cargo."

"Oh? He's not just shipping other people's goods?"

Danica laughed. "No. He found out there was more to be made speculating."

"And how's that working for him?"

"Well, he's not ready to retire just yet, but he has made some improvements to his ship."

"Excellent," said Charlaine. "It's nice to see trade flourishing. That's a testament to the good work you and the fleet have been doing."

"I shall accept the compliment, though I would claim there's still work to be done. The sea east of Reinwick is much safer than when we started this endeavour, but the coast to the west? Well, that's an entirely different matter, which is why I'm taking two ships to deliver you to your new assignment."

"Two? But I thought you said the *Barlowe* would make stops along the way?"

"I did," said Danica, "but the *Vanguard* will accompany us."

"Not the *Vigilant?*"

"No, I'm leaving Grazynia in command of the region while I'm away. Besides, Nadia needs a bit more experience commanding her own ship, and what better way to learn than by an extended sea voyage?"

Charlaine moved aside as Marlena and two other knights carried her belongings on board.

"Looking forward to a little reading?" asked Danica.

"Every commander is expected to know the contents of those three books." She lowered her voice. "Truthfully, most of it's useless, but there is a smattering of wisdom to be found on occasion."

"Perhaps you should write your own book?"

"I would need the time for such pursuits, and I have a feeling I'm about to be very busy."

"I'm a little concerned," said Danica. "You're going into a potentially hostile environment with very few allies."

"Marlena will be with me, and I'm sure the fleet won't be too far away."

"Speaking of the fleet, I've been thinking about what you said."

"I've said a lot of things," said Charlaine, chuckling. "What, specifically, are you referring to?"

"If our ships are to have a presence to the west, we'll need to secure permission to re-provision at a port."

"And you feel Lidenbach is the best option?"

"I've been talking to some merchant captains here."

"And?"

"They tell me it has a natural harbour and shipbuilding facilities."

"Shipbuilding? Does that mean Arnsfeld has a fleet?"

"I don't know," replied Danica. "My understanding is they build mostly trade vessels, but a cog is a cog, whether it's used as a merchant or warship."

"I shall bear that in mind when I visit their king."

"Speaking of which, what do you know of the fellow?"

"Very little. The grand mistress admitted they had sparse information on the area. Until now, nothing was of interest to our order there save our normal promise to protect women."

"I suppose that all changed once we received word the Cunars had withdrawn. Do you truly believe this whole 'defence in depth' thing, or has the order been compromised in some fashion?"

"After what we witnessed in the Antonine," replied Charlaine, "I'm leaning towards the latter, but regardless of the reasons, someone has to take up the responsibility of ensuring people's safety, and I don't see any other order stepping up to assume that burden."

"Perhaps we should send more knights? I could ship them from Temple Bay?"

"And strip the fleet of its Temple Knights? I think not. I've been promised additional sisters. We'll just have to pray they arrive in time to avert any potential disaster."

"You believe it's that bad?"

"I won't know for certain until we get there," said Charlaine, "but I doubt the grand mistress would give me this much authority if the situation weren't dire."

"You were made a Temple Commander. How much more authority can you hold?"

"I was permitted to name my successor here in Korvoran. Have you ever heard of such a thing?"

"No, never."

"Nor I, which only emphasizes how bad things have become. The grand mistress obviously didn't want anyone interfering in our plans."

"Because she didn't name your successor?"

"Remember," said Charlaine, "there were those in the Antonine who saw us as a threat."

"You mean Temple Commander Hjordis? But she failed, surely?"

"She did, but that doesn't mean her influence didn't spread, and even the best of us does not live forever."

"What are you trying to intimate?"

"Eventually, they'll replace the grand mistress, and when that happens, there's no guarantee her replacement will feel the same way we do."

"Then we must do all we can while we're still able," said Danica.

The *Valiant* set out from Korvoran, accompanied by the *Vanguard*, making excellent time as they headed up the east coast of Reinwick, for the weather remained fair for the first few days of sailing.

They rounded the peninsula, and then contrary winds forced them to claw their way down the west coast. The ships weathered it well, but the crew was exhausted by the time Gossenveldt came into view.

They rested in port overnight before setting out early, seeking the coast of Langwal. Charlaine came up on deck to find Danica staring off to the south.

"Trouble?" she asked.

"Not at all," replied the admiral. "I was just taking in the view."

"Haven't you sailed these waters before?"

"I have, although admittedly not for a while. The last time I was here was back in ninety-nine, when I took Ludwig and his new wife to Burgemont."

"That feels like ages ago. You know he has a son now."

"Does he?"

"Yes, Frederick."

"Will he have more, do you think?"

"That's hard to say, but I doubt it. Charlotte had a difficult birth. I don't imagine he'll be eager to see her go through it again."

They remained silent, staring out at the coast as they sailed past.

"That could have been your son," Danica finally said. "Tell me, do you regret losing Ludwig?"

"We each have our own paths to tread. In Ludwig's case, he had the responsibility to continue his line. I don't begrudge him that or the happiness of taking a wife."

"That's not what I asked. Don't you sometimes wish you had children of your own?"

"But I do, don't you see? The entire order is my family now." Charlaine looked at her companion. "And what of you?"

"I feel the same way. I never had a sister growing up, but if I did, I'd like to believe she would have been a lot like you."

"Now you're just trying to butter me up for a promotion."

"No, I'm serious. You're the closest thing to a real sister I've ever had."

"I feel the same, but we'd best change the subject before we both start tearing up." Charlaine cleared her throat and turned to stare northward. "Aren't we close to those two islands?"

"You mean The Eyes? Yes. They're just on the horizon, though admittedly, they're not much to look at. I've heard smugglers and pirates like to hide amongst the inlets there, but I doubt they'd trouble us. Who in their right mind would take on a Temple ship, let alone two?"

"I see a ship."

"Yes. The lookout spotted that first thing this morning."

"Do you think she's shadowing us?"

"More likely sailing in the same direction, but we'll keep an eye on it to make sure."

"Perhaps we should move closer. If these waters are as unsafe as you say, they might be placing themselves in danger?"

"That's a good point, but I wouldn't want to delay your arrival in Arnsfeld."

"I think it worthwhile to keep people safe, don't you?"

"Very well. I'll alter course."

Danica gave the command, and the *Valiant* veered north. The *Vanguard*, spotting their change, reduced sail and kept their distance.

As they drew closer to the ship, Charlaine could make out more details. In design, it was very much like the longships of old, with a single square sail and a side tiller. It had a wide beam shorter than the *Valiant* but struggled to keep a straight course despite the favourable wind.

Only two people were aboard—a man and a woman, by the look of it, although it was difficult to tell for sure at this range.

Danica leaned on the railing. "Who are you?" she called out.

"The *Cygnet*," replied the man. "Out of Vilnitz."

"You're a long way from home."

"We're on our way back from Gossenveldt, but we ran into some trouble."

"Pirates?"

"No, our tiller broke. It's making it very difficult to keep on course."

"Lower your sail," said Danica, "and we'll come aboard and see if we can be of assistance."

"And you are?" the man called back.

"The Temple Ship *Valiant*, out of Korvoran."

"Thank the Saints," said the woman. "Our prayers have been answered." Moments later, they began taking in the sail.

Danica brought the *Valiant* alongside, keeping just enough distance to avoid bumping into one another. They lowered the ship's boat, and Danica, Charlaine, and two sisters rowed to the stricken vessel.

"Greetings," the man called out. "My name is Sandro Ripley, and this is my wife, Nadine."

"I'm Danica, and this is Temple Commander Charlaine. May we board your vessel?"

"Of course," said Sandro, "but watch your step. I'm afraid there's not much room to move around."

Danica stepped onto the ship's deck. "This is a lot of cargo for such a small ship. Aren't you afraid you might tip it?"

"The *Cygnet* can bear the weight as the wide beam makes it quite stable."

"The waves here seem to indicate otherwise."

"We normally sail much closer to shore," offered Nadine, "but without the tiller, the wind blew us out to sea."

Danica made her way aft to inspect the damage, leaving Charlaine to ponder their cargo. "What is it you're shipping?"

"We brought silver, copper, and tin to Gossenveldt," said Nadine, "along with linens from back home. We then used the funds to buy up these finished goods."

"Such as?"

"Candlesticks, cups, lanterns, you name it. Luxury goods, mostly, targeting the wealthy."

"And does that make you a decent living?"

The woman shrugged. "We've seen better days. The prices have fallen considerably these last few years, as you can probably tell by the condition of this ship. What about you? Is your ship heading to Vilnitz?"

"We're on our way to Lidenbach. Do you know it?"

"Aye. We've traded there once or twice, but I hear there's little profit to be made there these days."

"Why would that be, do you think?"

"Couldn't tell you, and to be honest, we're about ready to give up shipping altogether." She looked around at her small ship. "Look at the *Cygnet*! It's not as if it gives us much protection against the weather."

Danica returned from examining the tiller. "The wood looks rotted. I imagine the salt water hasn't been kind to it."

"So that's it?" said Sandro. "We're out of luck?"

"Not quite. We can fashion a new one back on the *Valiant*, but it'll take a bit."

"And what do we do in the meantime?"

"With your permission, we'll tow you until we can complete your repairs."

"Won't that slow you down?"

"It will, but it's our sacred duty to help those in need."

"Yes, it is," added Charlaine, glancing westward. "Though I wonder what those dark clouds portend."

"We're south of one of The Eyes," said Danica. "We'll tow them there and take shelter from the coming storm in an inlet."

"And what of pirates?" asked Nadine.

"Don't worry. Our ships are more than capable of dealing with any threat that might materialize."

The evening found them sheltered in a small bay, barely large enough to fit the three vessels. The rain came at midnight, but it was light, and the clouds passed well before sunrise.

At first light, Danica had three of the *Valiant's* crew aboard the *Cygnet*, installing the new rudder on its starboard side. The Ripleys were thankful and promised to make a donation to the order upon their return to Vilnitz.

Danica accompanied them until the coast of Burgemont was in sight, then took both the *Valiant* and *Vanguard* farther out to sea. Charlaine watched as the *Cygnet* disappeared from view. "An unusual ship to take on the open sea."

"That was all we had centuries ago."

"If the design is that old, why is it still used?"

"It's not about the design, but the cost. A ship like the *Valiant* here would easily cost ten times the *Cygnet*."

"And those large Halvarian warships?"

"Too expensive for my tastes, and that's not including the gold leaf we removed from the larger vessels."

"So, you're saying the Halvarians have lots of coins to waste?"

"Yes," said Danica, "and it saved us a tidy sum when we captured them."

"At least we had the people to crew them."

"We did," said Danica, "but it's stretched us to the limit."

"Because we don't have enough knights?"

"Knights aren't the problem—it's the sailors. There are enough sisters to form the fighting complement, but it takes an experienced crew to work the ship. I thought about training our knights for such work, but it defeats the purpose of having them aboard in the first place."

"Sounds like you'll need to recruit more sailors for any future ships."

"We will."

"Perhaps you'll find some in Lidenbach."

"Only time will tell."

"How much farther have we to sail?"

"Around the coast of Burgemont," replied Danica, "then we're there, although I must warn you, that will put us dangerously close to Halvarian waters."

"And if we encounter their warships?"

"You tell me. We're not at war with them. So as long as they don't threaten anyone, I suppose we'll have to leave them alone. That doesn't mean we won't keep an eye on them, though. You and I both know they can get up to all sorts of mischief."

With the storm's passing, the skies cleared, and they were blessed with fair weather for the remainder of their journey.

Once they were off the coast of Arnsfeld, the number of ships in the area increased, although most were small fishing vessels. Danica steered well clear of these boats, not wishing to interfere with their catch.

The city of Lidenbach was nestled within a natural harbour with no defences, just a jut of land around it where someone had taken great pains to build a signal tower to mark the harbour's position.

They sailed *Valiant* around this arm to see a city spread along the shoreline, but of more immediate concern was the presence of a ship bearing the flag of Halvaria. The immense vessel was easily the size of the *Fearless*, the empire's flagship at the Battle of Temple Bay.

Danica had left the *Vanguard* at sea, well out of sight of the harbour, but now she wondered if it would've been better to keep it close at hand. Rather than sail up to the docks, she anchored in the bay, then ordered the ship's boat to be made ready.

Charlaine approached as the admiral supervised the lowering of the ship's boat.

"Well," said Danica. "We're finally here."

"Anything of interest?"

"Not that I can see, but there's likely plenty more city behind that hill over yonder."

A large castle dominated the hill, giving it a commanding view of the bay, where buildings similar to those in Korvoran clustered along the waterfront, though not as many. Even the docks appeared to be a less-grandiose version of Reinwick's capital, indicating much less sea trade found its way here.

Of all the things to see, the Halvarian ship stood out the most, its stern detailed with copious amounts of gold leaf.

"That's no merchant," said Danica. "In fact, I'd say it's the same design as the *Fearless*."

"Yes," added Charlaine, "which confirms it's no provincial ship. I wonder if it has a full complement of warriors?"

"Hard to say. We're currently at peace, so there's a decent chance not."

"*Conqueror*. An interesting name for a ship, wouldn't you say? Not exactly the most welcoming name for a diplomatic expedition."

"What makes you think it's here for diplomacy?"

"Why else send a ship of that stature? I wager the price of that gold leaf alone would buy out half this city. I exaggerate, of course, but not by much."

A few men clustered around the aft end of the Halvarian vessel, the *Valiant* having drawn their attention.

"It looks like they've taken an interest in us," said Danica.

"I wonder what its purpose is here."

"Intimidation, perhaps?"

"That would be my thought. The question is, what are they trying to enforce?"

"We know the empire likes to cause dissent prior to an invasion. Could that be the case here?"

"I hope not," said Charlaine, "or my tenure as the regional commander will be very short."

Marlena appeared at the railing. "I hate to interrupt, Commander, but there's something I think you ought to see." She pointed at a large cog entering the bay.

"By the Saints," said Danica. "She's huge. I don't believe I've ever seen such a large ship!"

"The *Triumphant* was larger," said Charlaine, "but that was a warship."

"How much cargo do you think that thing could carry?"

"Easily twice as much as the next largest ship. Whatever they're bringing to trade, there's a lot of it."

The great ship slowed until it finally dropped anchor.

"Well," said Danica, "at least they're not unloading warriors."

"Yes, but imagine how many it could carry if they set their minds to it."

"Quite a few, I wager, but I think it's a poor sailer."

"What makes you say that?"

"It lacks sufficient sail for its size," said Danica. "I imagine it would wallow in rough seas. We could easily outpace it."

"Let's hope it doesn't come to that. I don't much fancy the idea of trying to board a ship with sides that high."

"I'm with you on that."

"I'm sure the giant ship is most interesting," said Marlena, "but I must remind you we're here on a mission."

"Yes, of course," said Charlaine. "Admiral, will you join us ashore?"

"I would be delighted."

3

LIDENBACH

SUMMER 1102 SR

Charlaine stepped onto the wooden dock, noting how it groaned beneath her weight. The other two followed, freeing up the ship's boat to return to the *Valiant*.

Marlena wrinkled her nose, drawing her cloak tighter against the chilly morning air. "Something stinks."

"Rotting fish," said Danica. "Someone's abandoned their catch."

"Why would they do that?"

"Perhaps they fell ill? In any case, we should get going to the commandery."

"Any idea where that is, precisely?"

"There's an easy way to find out," said Charlaine, moving farther up the dock to where an old woman sat, fixing a net. "Excuse me. Could you tell us where we could find the Saint Agnes commandery?"

The woman looked up at them, spat on the ground, and then resumed her work. Charlaine wondered at the scornful reaction but felt it best to seek out her fellow sisters for answers.

"Not the response I'm used to," she said as she stepped onto the cobblestone streets of Lidenbach.

"This is most unusual," said Danica. "Do you suppose someone is trying to discredit our name?"

"You mean like the Halvarians? I suppose it's possible."

"If you'll pardon my saying so," offered Marlena, "it's far more likely this is a result of the Cunars leaving. These people likely feel abandoned by the Church."

"If that's the case, then we'll have a difficult time trying to put their minds at ease."

"How are we going to find the commandery?" asked Marlena.

"We'll start by climbing that hill. It should give us a good view of the city, and as we know, a commandery has a rather distinct appearance."

They made their way through the streets of Lidenbach, garnering much attention from those they passed.

"Odd," said Marlena. "These buildings are quite run down."

"A sign of hardship," said Charlaine. "I'm guessing the city has seen better days."

"Because of the condition of these houses?"

"Not only that. If you recall, that couple on the *Cygnet* said there was little profit to be made here. That seems to indicate a general lack of coins hereabouts."

"Yet there are businesses here," offered Danica.

"True," replied Charlaine, "but none appear busy."

"How long do you think this has been going on?"

"Quite some time, I imagine. At least long enough for people like the Ripleys to hear of it."

"The harbour has seen better days if that dock is any indication."

"You noticed it too?" said Charlaine.

"I could hardly miss it. I thought my boot would go right through the planks."

"Yet the harbour here is large. It should, by all rights, be packed with ships. You're the expert in such things—any ideas?"

"Nothing solid," replied Danica, "although it wouldn't surprise me to learn the Halvarians are somehow involved."

"Come now," said Marlena. "I realize the empire is our enemy, but you can't blame them for everything."

"What else could cause this?"

"The king might've taxed his subjects into poverty, or maybe there's a preponderance of storms off the coast, scaring away merchants?"

"She makes a good point," said Charlaine. "It might be best not to dwell on the subject until after we've gathered some details. In any case, we still must find the commandery so I can—" A woman shouting at something up the street interrupted her thoughts. Following the voice, she noticed a small crowd gathered, but their presence blocked her view of the affair.

"Something's happening," she said. "We'd best go and take a look."

As they advanced up the street, an angry man's voice echoed off the buildings.

"What's going on here?" shouted Charlaine. She pushed through the crowd to where a woman stood, her back to a storefront, facing off against three men holding cudgels. At the sight of the new arrivals, they all turned.

"Who are you?" one of the men demanded.

Charlaine was surprised that he'd failed to recognize the trio as Temple Knights but then remembered their cloaks concealed their scarlet cassocks.

"I am Sister Charlaine deShandria, Temple Commander of the Order of Saint Agnes. What is your business here?"

"Not that it's any concern of yours," replied the taller of the three, "but this woman failed to live up to her part of our business arrangement."

"And what arrangement might that be?"

"This man," the woman insisted, "demands I pay him, else he'll damage my property."

Charlaine moved in, placing herself between the storekeeper and the trio of thugs. "Is this true?"

The tall one smiled, his grin revealing a mouthful of broken teeth. "It's common for merchants to contribute towards the community fund. Now, stand aside and allow us to conduct our business. This is none of your concern."

"You there!" came a woman's voice. "Stand down." Six Temple Knights of Saint Agnes rode through the crowd, pushing the onlookers to either side.

The one leading the patrol flipped up her visor, revealing an aged face that bespoke of years of experience. Her eyes locked with those of Charlaine. "New recruits are to report to the commandery, not throw their weight around on the streets of Lidenbach."

"This woman is in trouble," replied Charlaine.

"Her distress is none of your concern. Stand aside, Sister, or I shall be forced to discipline you."

Danica snickered. "She thinks we're recruits. I don't know whether to be flattered or insulted."

"I am Temple Commander Charlaine deShandria, the new head of this region. Your name?"

"Sister Johanna. Sorry, Commander. We received no news of your appointment."

"Is it not the sworn duty of our order to protect women?"

"It is."

"Then why would you not seek to intervene in this matter?"

"Our commander has issued orders to the contrary."

"And your commander is?"

"Temple Commander Nina."

Charlaine stared back in astonishment. "Did you say, Nina?"

"I did, Commander."

"By any chance, did she serve in Ilea?"

"She did, as commander of a detachment," replied the knight.

"Am I missing something?" asked Marlena.

"She was the captain of our first posting," replied Danica. "That doesn't bode well for what we're likely to find at the commandery."

"Do not speak ill of your superiors," warned Sister Johanna.

"This," said Charlaine, "is Admiral Danica Meer. You'd do well to remember that."

Sister Johanna tried to hide her embarrassment at her mistake by snapping at those in her command to remain quiet. A moment later, she cleared her throat, turning back to her new superior. "What would you like us to do, Commander?"

"I want two knights stationed here to see to the well-being of this establishment. These men are to be arrested and turned over to the authorities."

"Begging your pardon, Commander, but the king's men won't take them."

"Pardon me?" replied Charlaine.

"The king's soldiers will not take them into custody."

"Why not? Are they not sworn to uphold his laws?"

"I am not an expert in such things, Commander. You'll need to ask Commander Nina."

"Then send two sisters to see them off with a stern warning to never again threaten this business, or any other, for that matter."

"And the rest of us?"

"You will escort us to the commandery."

"Very well." Johanna issued orders to the other Temple Knights.

"This is proving to be very interesting," said Danica. "Perhaps I'll keep the *Valiant* close at hand for the foreseeable future."

"And by 'interesting', you mean?" asked Marlena.

"She means," said Charlaine, "that our job here likely became a lot more complicated."

"Captain Nina might have changed," offered Danica. "Anything's possible."

Sister Johanna led them through the streets of Lidenbach, passing by the Royal Castle before turning left to skirt the edge of the great hill upon which it sat. Once they reached its northern extremity, and turned east, the commandery came into view.

In design, it was nearly identical to that of Korvoran, save for a slightly different pattern to its doors. Traditionally, the captain's office would face westward, though the regional commander's room would take precedence in this case.

They arrived to find no guards posted, necessitating one of Johanna's knights to dismount and open the door to the centre courtyard. Charlaine left their escort, entering the building from the alleyway that granted access to the horses. Danica and Marlena followed, struggling to keep pace with their commander.

Their brief trip through the commandery raised the eyebrows of those stationed there, but none saw fit to challenge the individuals marching past as if they owned the place. They only stopped when they stood before the commander's door.

"Where's the guard?" asked Marlena.

"Good question," replied Danica as she knocked on the door.

"Who is it?" came a familiar voice.

"The new regional commander," replied Charlaine.

"What nonsense is this?" Someone pushed a chair back, scraping the floor, and then footsteps approached. The door opened, revealing Temple Commander Nina. Grey now tinged her brown hair, while dark shadows lay beneath her eyes and lines etched her face, but there was no mistaking her stern countenance. She stood there, mouth agape.

"Commander Nina," said Charlaine. "I'm here under orders from the grand mistress. I'm to assume command of the region."

"I've received no such commands."

Charlaine turned to Marlena, who'd already dug through her satchel to find the necessary documentation. She took the scroll, offering it to Nina. "These are your orders, Commander."

A look of resignation flooded Nina's face. "You'd better come in while I read this over." She sat behind her desk.

Charlaine entered the room, noting its fine furnishings and elegantly laced curtains. A commander, or captain, for that matter, can decorate how they wish, but it was unusual to see such an overt display of wealth. It begged the question of where the funds came from to pay for such extravagant tastes, but she kept such thoughts to herself.

"This says I am to report to the Antonine," said Nina.

"That is correct."

Nina raised an eyebrow. "I was unaware my next assignment was any of your business?"

"The grand mistress herself informed me of it, Commander."

"Oh? Privy to the order's internal workings now, are we?"

Charlaine remained silent.

"Well, it appears my days in this rat-infested city are at an end. For once, the future looks bright." Nina's forced smile did nothing to hide her anger. "I assume you'll want to address the sisters?"

"There's no hurry if you want to say your farewells?"

"That's unnecessary. However, I have several administrative details to see to before I relinquish command of this region."

"I understand completely."

"Tell me, will you replace my captains?"

"I don't know," said Charlaine. "That largely depends on what I find here. However, the order will be increasing its presence in Arnsfeld."

"I take it you have armour and horses?"

"Our armour is aboard the *Valiant*, and our destriers will be here in a week or so."

"It is a poor knight who doesn't travel with their mounts."

"My orders stressed that I should assume command as soon as feasible. I thought it best to favour a quick arrival over making an impression."

"Shall I assign someone to give you a tour of the commandery?"

"I doubt that will prove necessary," said Charlaine. "Unless the layout of this place differs from others somehow?"

"Not at all. Tell me; is there anything else you would like to know while I'm still here to answer your questions?"

"What of the other orders?"

"The Cunars, as you are no doubt aware, abandoned their commanderies."

"And the Mathewites?"

"There are lay brothers within Lidenbach, but very few Temple Knights to my knowledge."

"To your knowledge? Are you suggesting you didn't bother to enquire?"

"Why would I? Their order's activities are of no interest to us."

"They are our allies," said Charlaine. "They, like us, help to protect women."

"In times of war, yes, but we don't possess the numbers needed to patrol the streets properly."

"So what do you do?"

"Our very presence oft times acts as a deterrent to would-be criminals. Thus, we send out daily patrols to make our presence known."

"Yet those same patrols refuse to intervene when trouble threatens?"

Nina stood, her nostrils flaring. "Do not lecture me on my duty. We possess no power here or permission from the king to arrest criminals even if we wanted to." She forced herself to take a deep breath. "In time, you'll see what a hopeless situation we are in, here in Lidenbach."

"Hopeless?" said Danica.

"Yes. The people of Arnsfeld barely tolerate our presence, and the king would prefer to see us gone from this land."

"Surely he'd want us to counterbalance the threat of the Halvarians?"

"You would think so, wouldn't you?" said Nina. "You should try raising that issue with His Majesty, assuming he even agrees to see you."

"Are you suggesting you carry no influence at court?"

"That's putting it mildly. Ever since word came of the Cunars' abandonment, we've been publicly ostracized. The king refuses to send his own warriors to keep the darker elements of society at bay. Quite honestly, it's enough to make one cry."

"I'm sorry to hear that," said Charlaine. "I had no idea things were so dire. What was it like before the brothers left?"

"The influence of the Church on matters of state has been dwindling for years. I'm surprised we didn't join the exodus ourselves." Nina looked around the room. "I would be lying if I said I would miss this place. It had its charms initially, but I'll be glad to be rid of it. Do you know how they mean to employ me back in the Antonine?"

"I'm afraid not."

"Ah, well. I shall go where I'm needed, although it would be nice to receive an assignment where I could make a real difference for a change."

"How long do you need to hand over your command?"

"A day, at the most, I would imagine. I'm sure we can find you rooms here in the commandery while you wait."

"That's quite all right," said Charlaine. "We'll remain aboard the *Valiant*."

"Very well. I shall send word once I've vacated my office."

"What of these decorations?" asked Danica. "Do you wish to take them with you?"

"And carry them all the way to the Antonine? No, consider them a gift. You may deal with them as you see fit. Now, if you'll excuse me, I have much to do."

Dismissed, they made their way out to the street.

"Well," said Danica. "That was not what I expected."

"Are you suggesting it went better than expected?" asked Marlena. "Or worse?"

"At this point, I'm not entirely sure."

"Was she like that in Ilea?"

"No. In a sense, she was worse. Back then, she didn't care about anything other than her own position."

"And now?"

"It appears all her attempts to make changes were rebuffed." Danica turned to Charlaine. "I don't envy you. It sounds like you'll have a hard time of it."

"So it would seem, yet I can't help but feel there's more to this place."

"Meaning?"

"Nina suggested the king was uninterested in enforcing his own laws. Does that sound reasonable to you?"

"You mean, regarding the king, or Nina's claim?"

"Either or both, if you like."

"Well," said Danica, "an illness might explain the king's indifference to the plight of his subjects. Or perhaps he's recently lost his wife or child? Grief can have far-reaching implications."

"And Commander Nina?"

"I think she feels slighted by her superiors, yet she was promoted to Temple Commander. She was either very effective, like you, or possesses some powerful friends."

"Couldn't she be both?" asked Marlena.

"Yes," said Charlaine. "I suppose she could. We remember her as an ineffective leader, but our memory is tainted. Perhaps she's learned to thrive since her reassignment?"

"You'll find out soon enough. You'll have access to all her logbooks when she hands over command. That should give you a good idea of what they've been up to for the last few years."

"Assuming she's kept them up to date," said Danica.

"I remember her as a stickler for details," said Charlaine. "And if I recall, she constantly kept notes back in Ilea. If anything, I'd expect those logs to be very thorough."

"So what do we do now? Return to the *Valiant*?"

"It's only mid-morning. Can you think of nothing better to do?"

"I can," offered Marlena.

They both looked at the adjutant. "Well?" said Charlaine. "I can't read your mind."

"I propose we return to the *Valiant* and change into plainer clothes."

"To what end?"

"It would serve us well to get a better idea of how this city is organized, and our cassocks would make us stand out."

"There is some wisdom in that," said Charlaine. "We could walk around the city without drawing undue attention."

"Yes," said Danica, "but what else is there to see? It's not as if we could enter the Palace without the king's permission."

"True, but we could see what remains of the Cunar commandery."

"To what end?" asked Marlena.

"The grand mistress promised us more knights."

"And?"

"What better place to house them than a commandery."

"But it's a Cunar commandery."

"I fail to see why that matters. The layout of all the Temple Knight commanderies is identical."

"I suppose that makes sense, but that being the case, why visit it at all?"

"To ascertain what condition it's in. Doubtless, the walls and doors will be in decent shape, but we must be mindful of other things."

"Such as?"

"Beds, tables, chairs, not to mention the state of its kitchens."

"Good point," said Danica. "How long until the extra knights arrive?"

"My orders don't say."

"Which means?"

Charlaine shrugged. "They might take months, or they could arrive before the end of the week."

"Then I suppose we'd better make equipping it our top priority."

"And how do we pay for all that?" asked Marlena. "It's not as if we have any wealthy patrons here in Lidenbach."

"Then maybe it's time we found some," suggested Danica. "I can start by making enquiries down by the docks. Perhaps we'll get lucky and find a merchant willing to sacrifice some of his ill-gotten gains."

"And if we don't?"

"Then I shall take the matter to the king," said Charlaine.

"Speaking of the king, why do you believe he won't enforce his laws?"

"I suspect he has his reasons, although what those would be is anyone's guess."

4

ABANDONED
SUMMER 1102 SR

Marlena stared at the wide-open door. "This doesn't bode well."
The entrance to the old Cunar commandery revealed a
passageway strewn with discarded clothing, broken furniture, and scraps of
paper. Charlaine moved in cautiously, scooping up a letter as a gust of wind
disturbed the rest.

"Anything of interest?" asked her aide.

"These look to be orders of some sort. It appears the Cunars left their
home in some haste." Charlaine perused the paper. "It's a patrol schedule.
Certainly not the type of thing they should've discarded carelessly."

"But they abandoned the place. What does it matter that they left such
things behind?"

"Every Temple Captain has specific instructions on how to shut down
their command, should it prove necessary. The doors are to be locked, and
the contents secured. In addition, they should have destroyed any correspondence left behind."

"Could these notes have been accidentally lost?"

"Perhaps, but we should make an effort to gather them. If nothing else,
it'll give us some idea of how they operated here."

"I'll close the door," said Marlena. "That, at least, will stop this incessant
wind from blowing them all over the place."

There turned out to be almost twenty pages, although some were in
worse shape than others. Marlena dutifully tucked them under her arm.

"Where shall we start?" she asked. "The stables?"

"I think the captain's office might provide more answers, don't you?"

Treading the halls of this abandoned commandery was an eerie experience, as the layout was identical to theirs back in Korvoran. Here, however, disturbing signs indicated something was amiss, for although it was common amongst the Cunars to hang their banners in the upper halls when not carried into battle, there were at least three abandoned here, an unforgivable sin within any order of Temple Knights.

"How do you account for this?" asked Charlaine, staring at one such flag.

"Could their rush to leave have been so hasty as to avoid their duty?" Marlena moved to the closest door, opening it to reveal a barracks room with furniture broken and unusable, fit for little more than firewood. A shutter that used to open onto the courtyard was broken in half, with the other side off its hinges, lying on the floor. "Such destruction."

"It seems they didn't want anyone else using it."

"But the doors are all intact."

"Yes," said Charlaine, "but they're thick oak, made to be defensive positions in case of an attack. I doubt they'd be easy to break. I suspect we'll find more of the same as we explore. I'm afraid it will be expensive to get this place up and running again."

"I don't understand why they would do this?"

"We all think of the Cunars as a highly disciplined order, but recent events paint them in a different light. I believe this is an indication of just how low they've sunk."

"Couldn't someone have come in after they departed and destroyed all of this? After all, they left the door wide open."

"To what end? If they wanted firewood, they could have just carted it away. And the furniture in this place could have fetched a tidy profit if it were still intact. No, this seems more intentional."

"What if Halvarian agents were responsible? They bear no love for the order."

"True, but if that were the case, wouldn't they have taken those papers?"

"Was this a regional command?"

"Not to my knowledge," replied Charlaine. "Their commander is based out of Burgemont, but I'm not aware if that still holds true."

"Do you think their other commanderies look like this?"

"I shouldn't like to speculate at this point. Let's find the captain's office, shall we? Perhaps we'll discover more of those papers."

They made their way upstairs, stopping at three more rooms along the way, but they all told the same story: the destruction of furniture and damaged shutters.

The captain's office proved a surprise, for whoever had commanded here had seen fit to install a heavy desk made of shadowbark, possibly the most expensive wood on the Continent. It was undamaged, which was not surprising, considering its robust construction, but its drawers were open and devoid of contents. Even the curtains were removed, although a rickety-looking armour stand remained off to one side.

Charlaine moved to look out the window. "There's a clear view of the bay from here, and we're only a block or two from the docks."

"Are you suggesting we make this your regional command?"

"Not until we get more knights, but it's worth looking into."

Marlena moved to stand beside her, taking in the view. "I can see *Valiant* out in the bay."

"Yes, but of more interest are the Halvarian ships, particularly the *Conqueror*."

"Why so?"

"It's most unusual for a warship of that size to sail into port without an invitation. Many might consider it an act of war."

"Do you think it's here at the king's behest?"

"We'll know more once I meet with him."

"And when are you to do that?"

Charlaine chuckled. "Let's get settled in first, shall we? We've yet to officially take office." She was about to say more, but something out the window caught her attention. "It appears the *Valiant* is sending a boat towards the docks. How about we head down there and see how Danica fares?"

They left the commandery, making sure to close the great doors behind them. The docks were easy to find, and before long, they were watching the ship's boat as it rowed up to the pier.

"Didn't expect to see you here," said Danica. "Any luck with the commandery?"

"That's a discussion best left for later. You?"

"I made some enquiries concerning the presence of a shipping guild, but the trade here looks to be unregulated." She paused to reach into her cassock. "I also have a letter from Temple Commander Nina for you."

"And they took it out to you?"

Danica shrugged. "They thought you'd gone back aboard the *Valiant*. The messenger seemed surprised you weren't there, but I assured her I'd deliver it into your hands."

Charlaine took the letter and broke the seal. "It appears she's vacated the commandery."

"That was quick."

"I assume she was eager to be on her way."

"Still," said Danica. "I would've thought she'd at least formally pass over the command."

"I might remind you we had no such welcome in Korvoran."

"True, but if you recall, that was different. They sent you to make up a shortfall in command, whereas Nina was a regional commander. Surely that accounts for something?"

"We can complain all we like, but that won't see things sorted. Better to put this behind us and get on with our assignments here."

"Our?" said Danica. "Does that mean you want the *Valiant* to remain in the area?"

"The *Vanguard*, too, if that's all right with you. I suspect the Halvarians are up to something, and it would be nice to have some eyes I can trust out at sea."

"You could always hire some local fishermen?" offered Marlena.

"I doubt I could expect them to give an honest account, particularly after the reception that woman gave us when we first arrived."

"True," said Danica, "but that makes me wonder what the king will make of having *Valiant* in port. I doubt the Halvarians will like it."

"I'll be sure to put that at the top of my list when I meet him. In the meantime, I must now assume command of the region."

"Mind if I tag along? It wouldn't hurt to have an ally."

"What do you call ME?" said Marlena.

"Sorry. I should've said an additional ally. I hope you'll forgive me."

"Of course, Admiral."

Charlaine smiled. "Then come along, you two. There's work to be done."

They returned to the Agnesite commandery to see three sister knights guarding the doors, a far cry from their first visit. At Charlaine's approach, two of them stood at attention while the third disappeared inside, no doubt to inform the Temple Captain of their approach. She must've been close by, for mere moments later, the guard returned, followed by a short woman with streaks of grey running through her red hair.

"Commander Charlaine," she said. "Welcome to the Lidenbach commandery. I'm Temple Captain Bernelle, and this is my aide, Sister Octavia. I'm sorry I wasn't here to greet you earlier, but Commander Nina had me busy elsewhere."

"Nothing serious, I hope?"

"A minor misunderstanding with a local horse breeder. You may rest assured it's all been settled."

"Glad to hear it. May I introduce my adjutant, Sister Marlena, and Temple Captain Danica, Admiral of the Fleet."

"Pleased to meet you," said Bernelle, then turned to Charlaine. "We've been expecting your return. I hope you don't mind, but I took the liberty of ordering the knights to assemble in the courtyard. I thought you'd like to address them."

"Most definitely. Lead on, Captain."

The building was a hollow square, with a courtyard in the centre, where the entire company had assembled, resplendent in their cassocks. Captain Bernelle ordered them to attention as their new commander made her way to stand in front of them.

"Sisters," began Charlaine. "We find ourselves in unprecedented times. The Temple Knights of Saint Cunar have abandoned the region, and we've been called in to take their place. Now, I know what you're thinking: we lack the resources to assume the task, but the grand mistress has assured me reinforcements are on the way."

She paused, using the moment to search the faces staring back at her. They were eager for news, yet what else could she tell them? Charlaine had no idea how many Temple Knights the Antonine would send or when they'd arrive.

"As regional commander, my duty is to ensure those under my command are ready and able to respond to any threat that might present itself. To that end, when you are dismissed, proceed to the armoury immediately. I want to see each and every one of you back here in full armour and weapons as quickly as possible. Is that clear?"

A few mumbled responses drifted towards to her.

She raised her voice. "I said, is that clear?"

"Yes, Commander!" came the reply.

Charlaine turned to Captain Bernelle. "Is this everyone?"

"All except for two in the infirmary."

"Injured?"

"A slight fever. Nothing contagious as far as we can tell."

"I shall make a point of visiting them later. Dismiss the company so they may don their armour." Charlaine turned, walking over to where Danica and Marlena stood watching.

"Dismissed!" called out Captain Bernelle.

The Temple Knights hurried into the building, eager to don their armour.

"Anything we can do?" asked Danica.

"As a matter of fact, yes. While this lot gets dressed, I'd like you two to inspect the stables. You know what to look for."

"And if we find anything amiss?"

"Unless it affects the well-being of the horses, you can tell me later in my office. There's no sense in discussing such things in front of anyone else."

"And you?"

"I'll be having a chat with the good captain here."

Charlaine waited for them to disappear into the stables before waving the captain over. Bernelle walked stiffly, uneasy in the face of her new commander.

"Do you have a patrol roster?" asked Charlaine.

"Yes, Commander. Back in my office. Shall I fetch it for you?"

"Not at the moment. I'm not so interested in names as I am in how you carry out the patrols."

"I send them out in groups of six, each led by a senior sister."

"And how many times a day?"

"Only once, Commander."

"Yet there's an entire company to call upon."

"Your predecessor didn't wish to cause undo hardship on the population of Lidenbach."

"And how, might I ask, did our patrols cause hardship?"

"Ever since the Cunars left, there's been a lot of animosity towards us."

"And were any steps taken to overcome this?"

"None that I am aware of, Commander."

"Did you or Commander Nina ever spend time at court?"

"I believe the commander was in the king's presence at the Midwinter Feast last year."

"Do any patrols go outside the city limits?"

"No, and even within the city, we follow prescribed routes."

"You can expect that to change."

"And in the meantime?"

"Cancel any further plans for today," said Charlaine. "I shall be evaluating the sisters' fighting abilities."

The captain stiffened. "My knights are more than capable of holding their own in battle, Commander."

"I'm sure they are, but if I'm to lead them, I want a full understanding of their skill levels."

"Are we expecting battle?"

"We are a fighting order. We must always be prepared for it."

"You didn't answer my question."

Charlaine smiled. "You're right. I didn't."

Just then, Danica came out of the stables.

"Well?" said Charlaine.

"No problems, so far. Marlena is looking closer at the food stores, but I doubt there's anything worth worrying about."

"Have you a smith?" asked Charlaine, turning back to Captain Bernelle.

"That's a delicate matter," replied the captain. "The current smith has given us a low priority."

"Why's that?"

"He claims his other, higher-paying customers are more important to him."

"Then we'll need to find another."

"No others are willing to take us on," said Captain Bernelle.

"We shall see about that."

The captain wanted to know more but restrained herself, instead watching the courtyard, awaiting the return of her knights. Marlena soon reappeared, nodding to indicate all was well.

The Temple Knights trickled back, forming up in their previous places. To Charlaine, it took far too long before the company was fully assembled, and she made a mental note to add it to the growing list of changes she would institute.

She considered talking to each knight but had to remind herself she was no longer a captain. Instead, she turned to Captain Bernelle. "Have the company go through their sword drills. I'm curious to see how they perform."

"Yes, Commander." The captain gave the order, and the knights paired off.

Charlaine wandered through the courtyard, noting those who looked nervous. "I'm guessing many of your charges recently joined the order."

"Yes," replied Bernelle. "How did you know?"

"They have yet to learn to vary their tactics. It makes their attacks very predictable."

A group of sister knights paused their practice, turning to watch their new commander.

"Perhaps you could do better?" blurted out a tall, blonde-haired knight.

"What's your name?" snapped Danica.

"Sister Enna."

"Tell me, Sister, are you in the habit of being so informal with your superiors?"

The knight's cheeks flushed. "No, Captain. Sorry… Commander. I meant no disrespect."

"For your information," continued Danica, "the commander has seen more than her fair share of battles."

"She has a point," said Charlaine. "It's one thing to complain about their drills, quite another to offer them an alternative."

"Then allow me."

"You left your armour back aboard the *Valiant*."

Danica faced the knight and smiled. "You have training swords, don't you?"

"We do," replied Enna.

"Then go and fetch a couple, and I'll show you how we fight aboard ship."

The knight hesitated, seeking her captain's approval.

"Don't look at me," said Bernelle. "You got yourself into this. Quick, now, before you earn extra duties."

The knight ran off to retrieve the weapons. Having heard the exchange, the rest of the company backed away, allowing room for the demonstration.

"Are you sure you're up to this?" asked Charlaine, keeping her voice low.

"What kind of question is that?" replied Danica. "I've spent the last few years chasing down pirates. You think a recent recruit will be a challenge?"

"Don't make a mockery of her. We're trying to teach, not punish."

"Understood."

Sister Enna returned, tossing a wooden sword to Danica. The admiral swung it a few times, getting used to the weight before she took a firm stance. "Ready?"

Without another word, her opponent rushed forward, sword overhead, ready to come crashing down. Danica parried it easily but kept a defensive posture instead of counterattacking. More blows rained down, the attacks repetitive and easy to predict.

"You've learned the drills well," the admiral said, "but in the real world, you'll need to adapt to changing circumstances." Danica waited until after Enna's next attack before striking with a series of quick jabs, which had the desired effect of driving back her opponent before she slammed the blade's edge against a vambrace with an audible thud.

Frustrated, Sister Enna again struck with a wide, swinging arc from her right. Danica stepped close, holding the sword top and bottom to block the attack, then elbowed the sister in the chest, knocking her to the ground.

The admiral stood over her opponent and held out her hand. "You possess great potential but must learn to control your temper."

Enna took her hand and got to her feet. "My apologies, Admiral."

"There's a lot of strength behind your blows, but vary your attacks. Don't worry. In time, it'll all become second nature to you. Who knows, one day, you might even serve aboard the fleet? Saints know we're always looking for more volunteers."

"Volunteers?"

Charlaine stepped forward, addressing the entire company. "From time to time, we recruit Temple Knights to join their sisters aboard the fleet ships. Such a duty is difficult, and not everyone can qualify, but should anyone be interested in volunteering, you are to forward your name to your captain."

"What qualifications are you seeking?" asked Enna.

"At sea," replied Danica, "we use crossbows for ranged attacks. We must also ensure those interested possess a good sense of balance and a strong stomach."

"Strong stomach?"

"She means," said Charlaine, "that you don't get seasick."

"Yes," added Danica. "Though, in truth, no one knows that until their first voyage. Tell me, are there any crossbows here?"

"No," replied Captain Bernelle. "We consider their use beneath a knight."

"Not anymore," said Charlaine. "At least not for those fighting at sea."

"I'll arrange for some to be sent from the *Valiant*," offered Danica. "It would be interesting to see if anyone here has any natural talent for them."

"I think we've seen enough sword practice," said Charlaine. "Time to move on."

"To what?" asked the captain.

"Why, to riding, of course. Saddle up the knights."

"How many?"

"All of them."

"Every single one?"

"You can leave a pair of sentries to guard the commandery, but I want everyone else ready to ride as soon as possible."

"And what of yourself? You have no horse."

"True, but there are two knights in the infirmary and two more on guard duty. By my reckoning, there should be at least four spare mounts. More, if you have extras."

"Will your entire party be riding out?"

"I should get back to *Valiant*," said Danica. "But I'll see to those cross-bows. Is tomorrow morning soon enough?"

"That would be fine," replied Charlaine. "Marlena, in my absence, I'd like you to inspect the barracks." This brought a chorus of groans from the company.

"Anything, in particular, I'm looking for?"

Charlaine smiled. "You know, the usual."

Marlena had been her aide for years, long enough to know it would be only a cursory examination. Such attention was not intended to punish, merely to ensure the sisters kept their rooms clean and tidy.

"Very well," Marlena replied. "I'll have a list of names waiting for you upon your return."

. . .

That evening, Charlaine stood in her office, staring out the window at pinpricks of light illuminating the city, making it look like hundreds of fireflies had descended upon the streets of Lidenbach. "Beautiful, isn't it?"

"Yes," replied Marlena, "but deceptive. From all accounts, Lidenbach is a city of danger at night."

"Where did you hear that?"

"From the sisters. They say no person in their right mind walks the streets once the sun goes down."

"Then we should endeavour to put an end to such fears." Charlaine looked out at the distant castle. "The king is a mystery to me, but that's something else I must change if we are to make a difference here."

"And so we are to change things wherever we go?"

"Why be here if we cannot effect change? Don't mistake my concern for dreams of glory. I seek only to better the lives of those within the Petty Kingdoms." She turned to face her aide. "Tell me, what are your first impressions of this commandery?"

"Captain Bernelle appears to know her business, but I sense Commander Nina's approach constrained her."

"That was my thought too. And our sister knights?"

"They're nervous, as they should be, upon receiving a new commander."

"And what did you make of their capabilities?"

"I'm a simple knight," replied Marlena, "not a captain."

"Nonsense. I wager you have more battle experience than all of this company combined. Now, come. Tell me the truth as you see it."

"There is a good core but far too many neophytes. We need to give them more real-world training."

"That will come in time," said Charlaine. "We can't make them better overnight."

"So, what's your plan?"

"You and I get to create a new patrol schedule tonight."

"Tonight? It's already late."

"So it is," said Charlaine, "but we must strike while the forge is hot."

"Really? Are you ever going to let go of the smith inside you?"

"Of course not. It's part of who I am."

Marlena moved to take a seat. "All right. Where do we start?"

"With two patrols a day, morning and afternoon. I want them to be highly visible, but they must vary their route each day. There's no sense in doing all of this if we only keep a few streets safe."

"Do we stick with six knights per patrol?"

"No, let's increase it to ten, at least for the foreseeable future. Once the townsfolk grow accustomed to our presence, we can begin nighttime patrols." Charlaine moved to her desk, pushing the ink and quill towards her aide. "You'd best record this; it's likely to get complicated."

"Very well." Marlena took a moment to write down a few words. "Any preference as to who's on the first patrol?"

"Yes. I want at least two experienced knights on each, but I'll leave it up to the captain as to names. We'll also need to send a detachment to secure the Cunar commandery, and they'll have to be relieved."

"Three shifts?"

"Yes."

Marlena finished making her notes. "That wasn't so difficult."

Charlaine laughed. "We've only just begun."

5

KEEP YOUR ENEMIES CLOSE

SUMMER 1102 SR

"This is it," said Marlena. "Jules Morel, Master Smith, or so the sign says. Are you sure you want to meet him?"

"Of course," said Charlaine. "He's the smith under contract to support the order. We didn't come all the way here, only to stare at his sign. But let's not tell him of my background, at least for now."

"Why ever not?"

"I'd like to see how he treats his customers, not a fellow smith."

They entered the smithy to the sounds of hammering. The workshop was reasonably small, not an altogether unusual sight for such a trade, yet it felt crowded. Two youths in their early teens bustled around the place while an older man with a strong resemblance to them examined a dagger over by a workbench. At the sound of the door opening, he looked up.

"Can I help you, Sisters?"

"I take it you're Jules Morel?" said Charlaine.

"I am. Are you in need of my services?"

She moved closer, holding out her hand. "I'm Temple Commander Charlaine, the new regional commander for the Temple Knights of Saint Agnes."

He extended his own, and she clasped it, pressing her thumb into the space between his finger and thumb while he merely shook her hand.

"Is there something you're looking for?" he asked.

"I came to see the quality of your work."

"You could've done that back at your commandery."

"I could have," said Charlaine, forcing a smile, "but then I wouldn't have an excuse to get out of my office." She looked around the workshop. "I see you make armour as well as weapons."

"Yes, though there's not much demand for it these days."

"Why is that?"

"The king's men no longer require my services."

"But you still provide weapons, I presume?"

"I do, but competition has driven down my prices. Still, it pays to be able to tell people you make weapons for the king. I suppose it's the price of doing business."

"Have you a sample I might examine?" asked Charlaine.

He put down the dagger and wandered to another table cluttered with various weapons. "What kind of weapon are you interested in?"

"A serviceable sword?"

He dug through the pile and pulled one forth, holding it up. "How about this one?"

"That will do."

Morel moved closer, passing it to Charlaine, who took it, examining the handle first. The work was serviceable, but it was odd to see a blade with such little adornment. She swung it around experimentally before returning it to him.

"Well?" he asked. "What do you think?"

"Is this a good example of your work?"

He smiled. "Of course. Nothing but the best for my customers."

"In that case, the order will no longer require your services."

"What? Why?"

"The sword is unbalanced, and if these imperfections on the blade are any indication, it would likely be very brittle. Not the type of weapon I would trust in battle."

The smith sneered. "You're sister knights, for Saint's sake. It's not as if you'll ever need to fight."

"And that is precisely why you're unfit to be in our employment. Come, Marlena. Our visit here is finished."

They stepped outside, leaving an astonished Morel sputtering in their wake.

"Are you sure that was wise?" asked Marlena. "He has a contract."

"A contract that is invalidated if he supplies us with useless weapons."

"But that leaves us without a smith."

"Not for long, it doesn't. You forget, I have the name of a master smith recommended by Barbek."

"And where do we find this fellow?"

"Bay Street. I believe it encircles the dock."

"Then let's be off," said Marlena, "before Master Morel starts yelling obscenities."

The workshop of Master Boris Skellen was of a similar size to Jules Morel, but whereas Morel's was disorganized, that of Master Boris was immaculate, reminding Charlaine of her own father's smithy.

Inside, a tanned, older man with a closely cropped beard and white hair looked up from some papers. "Can I help you?"

"Are you Master Skellen?"

"I am. What can I do for you?"

Charlaine stepped forward, offering her hand. "My name is Temple Commander Charlaine deShandria, of the Temple Knights of Saint Agnes."

He shook her hand, clearly surprised when she pressed her thumb into the space between his finger and thumb. "You're a guild member?"

"I am. I worked in my father's smithy back in Malburg."

"You must've been quite accomplished to be admitted to the guild."

"I was reckoned a master smith before I joined the order."

"Then you are more than welcome. Are you here on business, or is this a social call?"

"I came here on the recommendation of a good friend, Barbek Stoutarm."

Skellen's face lit up. "Now, there's a name I've not heard for years. How is the old rascal?"

"Quite well. He has his own workshop in Korvoran these days. As a matter of fact, he's under contract to the order there."

"Ah, now we get to the truth of the matter. No doubt you want to procure my services."

"I do, providing you're not too busy."

"I've worked for Temple Knights before."

"You have?"

"Yes, the Cunars, but they left unexpectedly. I hope you're not intending on doing the same?"

"I can assure you we're here to stay."

He pursed his lips. "There's only one problem."

"And that is?"

"Your order will already have a smith under contract."

"Up until earlier today, we did. A fellow by the name of Jules Morel. Do you know him?"

"I'm familiar with his work."

"And?"

"It can be good, but its quality is inconsistent. I fear he takes too many shortcuts. He's not a guild member, so it's of no concern to us that you cancelled his contract."

"In that case," said Charlaine, "I wish to engage your services."

"Wouldn't you like to see a sample of my work first?"

"You would hardly be a guild member if the quality wasn't there."

"How much work can I expect?"

"There's currently one company here in Lidenbach, but it will soon increase to two. Naturally, the sisters all have weapons and armour, but I'm sure we'll need replacements from time to time, not to mention more specialized weapons."

"Specialized?"

"Yes. Swords are fine for patrolling the streets, but if we are to fight in battle, we shall need something capable of penetrating armour."

"So, axes, maces, and hammers? That sort of thing?"

"Precisely."

"And here I thought you were going to ask for something difficult. What about armour?"

"Are you capable of making plate?"

"I specialize in weapons, but I could recommend a few of my fellow guild members who can fulfill that requirement."

"And your price?"

He smiled. "If you'd agree only to engage guild members, we can offer you a discount—say ten percent?"

"Agreed."

"That's it? No haggling?"

"I prefer to be direct. Besides, I don't mind paying for quality—the life of a Temple Knight may depend on it. I'll let you know what we need regarding weapons once I've had time to settle in."

"I shall look forward to hearing from you."

"By the way," said Charlaine, "this is my aide, Sister Marlena. She'll be acting on my behalf."

"Pleased to meet you, Sister."

"And you," Marlena replied. "I trust you won't have any issues dealing with a woman?"

"It is unusual, especially after dealing with the Cunars, but I'm not one to complain." He chuckled. "I shall warn you, however, I'm prone to strong language from time to time."

"You obviously haven't heard us training inside the commandery."

He laughed. "Now that comes as a surprise. I always believed the sisters of Saint Agnes to be prim and proper."

"And they are," replied Marlena, "but we are Temple Knights, not lay sisters, and one can hardly be polite in the midst of battle."

"Your point is well-taken."

"Then we shall trouble you no more this day," said Charlaine. "Good day, Master Skellen."

Danica leaned back, nursing her ale. Vivian sat across from her, her gaze wandering over the crowded tables in the Broken Oar. Patrons chugged back cheap ale and chatted away at full volume.

Having eschewed their cassocks for more common garb to blend into their surroundings, they now sat silently, listening to the nearby conversations.

"Can I buy you ladies a drink?"

They looked up to see an older gentleman, his weather-beaten face highlighted by a scraggly beard and greying hair.

"And you are?" said Danica.

The fellow tipped his hat. "Captain Guillermo Carvahlen at your service."

"An unusual name for these parts."

"Indeed, it is. I am Calabrian by birth, though I've not been home for many years. I captain the *Sapphire*, a merchant that sails in these waters."

"Perhaps it is we who can buy a drink for you? Will you join us?"

"That's mighty kind of you." He took a seat.

"Ale?" asked Danica. "Or maybe something a little stronger?"

"Ale is fine, thank you." He waited while she held up her hand, calling over the server.

"I don't believe I've seen you two in here before," the fellow continued. "And I make it my business to visit the Oar whenever I'm in town."

"We're from the *Valiant*," replied Danica. "Are you familiar with it?"

"Strange name, that. There's a pirate hunter that sails farther east by that name."

"That's my ship."

"Oh? And what brings you here to Lidenbach? Not piracy, I hope?"

"No, at least not yet. Why? Are there any operating in these waters?"

"None that I know of. Of course, there are always rumours of missing ships, but we usually blame that on poor sailing. The Great Northern Sea is harsh to those who don't take it seriously."

Danica glanced out the window. The view of the bay at this table was good, one of the reasons she'd picked it, but of particular interest was the overpowering presence of the *Conqueror* tied up on the quay outside.

"Big, isn't it?" noted Guillermo. "They say it's the largest warship afloat."

"I don't know about that," replied Danica. "I've seen the *Triumphant*, and she's even bigger."

"The *Triumphant?*"

"Yes, the Holy Fleet's flagship, down in Corassus."

"You must have travelled a great deal. Corassus is a long way from here."

"You yourself claimed to be from Calabria. That's even farther by sea unless you know a way of dragging your ship across land?"

He chuckled. "I can see I didn't give you enough credit. How long have you been a captain?"

"A few years." She nodded towards the *Conqueror*. "Enough to know there's more to a warship that size. I am curious as to why it's here in port."

"There's no mystery there. It showed up some time ago, bearing an envoy from the Halvarian Emperor."

"Is that loathing I discern in your voice?"

"It is, and I'll make no secret of it. I already lost my home to that serpent; I'd hate to see this place under their thumb as well." He leaned in closer, lowering his voice. "I did hear someone destroyed their fleet several years ago, although regrettably, that was down on the Shimmering Sea, not up here. They say it was a catastrophic loss."

"It was," said Danica. "I was there."

"You were at the Battle of Alantra?"

"Along with other sister knights, yes. Does that surprise you?"

"You just look so young."

Danica laughed. "You're not the first to say that, nor will you likely be the last. In any event, that was a few years ago, and I've honed my skills since then. You should meet the local commander here; she's Calabrian too."

"Oh? What's her name?"

"Charlaine deShandria."

"deShandria? Are you certain?"

"Yes. Why? Do you know her?"

"No," he replied. "At least not in person, but I recognize the name. There was a Tomas deShandria who was an advisor to the queen."

"That's her father."

Guillermo shook his head. "Will wonders never cease? To think I should hear tell of his family all the way up here, in the north."

A server deposited an ale on the table.

"What else can you tell me?" asked Danica. "About the Halvarians, I mean."

"Where should I start?"

"How about the *Conqueror*? Any idea how many men it carries?"

"You would likely have a better idea than me. Besides, the crew seldom leave the ship, and on those rare occasions when they do, they're accompanied by guards."

"Where do they go?"

"From what I understand," replied Guillermo, "they only come ashore to arrange provisions."

"And the envoy?"

"Lord Corbin comes and goes as he pleases, although always with at least six heavily armed guards."

"What's your definition of heavily armed?"

"Chainmail mainly, though his captain wears plate armour when he sets foot ashore. Of course, I call him captain, but he may be something else: an admiral or maybe a governor?"

The captain paused for a moment and smiled. "You're asking a lot of questions about the fellow. You're not planning on having him meet up with an accident by any chance? Because if you were, I'd be more than willing to lend a hand. It's the least I could do after what they put me through."

"How about that cog out there? You know, the gigantic one in the middle of the bay?"

"Ah, that's the *Leviathan*. A fitting name, don't you think?"

"What does she carry?"

Captain Carvahlen shrugged. "To be honest, I don't know for sure, but I have my suspicions."

"Which are?"

"I travel the northern coast, buying and selling for profit. It's served me well over the years, but lately… well, let's just say some things are too good to be true."

"Meaning?"

"I like to buy low and sell high."

"Naturally," said Danica. "That's how you make a living."

"True, but even I don't like how cheap things have become here."

"I'm not sure I follow?"

"Believe it or not, furniture is always a popular trade item, especially amongst the wealthy, but the prices here are far too low. I don't see how a carpenter could make anything at these prices. Even things like buckets are selling for a mere pittance when I know the raw materials alone would cost more. Something is wrong here, and I believe the Halvarians are to blame."

"And by extension, you mean the *Leviathan*?"

"It would make sense, wouldn't it? What would drive down the prices?"

"Competition?" offered Vivian.

"Exactly. The kind of competition that there's no hope of undercutting."

"So then, how do the Halvarians do it?"

"Slave labour would be my guess; either that, or they deliberately sell it for less than the cost of making it."

"What would be their point?"

"Easy," said Guillermo. "They want to ruin businesses. The empire thrives on chaos, and the best way to promote that is to put honest people out of work."

"I don't understand," said Vivian. "Couldn't people just refuse to buy these cheaper products?"

"That's a fine idea in theory," said Danica, "but if funds are short, what choice have they? Cheap goods are better than none at all."

"But surely it would take more than one ship to do that?"

"It would," said Guillermo, "but bear in mind, the *Leviathan* isn't the only vessel of that size which has deigned to stop here. It's just the only one presently in port." He downed the rest of his ale, then looked at his new companions. "I don't believe you told me your names?"

"Danica Meer, Admiral of the Fleet, and this is Vivian."

"Admiral?"

"Does that surprise you?"

"I suppose it shouldn't. I heard there was someone young in charge. I just expected... well, to be honest, I don't know what I expected. In any case, I thank you for the drink. You can find me at the *Sapphire* if you want to talk more. You can't miss it—it's the one with the Calabrian flag flying from its mainmast."

"Are you sure that's wise with the Halvarians so close?"

"What are they going to do? Attack me in a neutral port? I don't think so. In any case, that's my burden to bear, not yours. I shall bid you a good day, ladies."

He wandered off.

"Well," said Vivian. "That was quite illuminating."

"It was," replied Danica, "but now my day has become all the more complicated."

"In what way?"

"I need to report this to the commander."

"Shall I accompany you?"

"No," replied Danica. "You'd best get back aboard *Valiant*. Ensure you keep everyone on alert. I wouldn't put it past the Halvarians to try damaging the ship, especially with what we did to that fleet of theirs."

. . .

Marlena opened the door. "The admiral is here to see you."

"Send her in," said Charlaine as she put aside her notes.

"I hope I'm not interrupting," said Danica.

"Not at all. Pull up a chair."

"I ran across a Calabrian merchant this morning."

"A Calabrian? Here in Lidenbach? He's a long way from home."

"He is and bears no love for the Halvarians."

"That's to be expected," said Charlaine. "I assume you learned a few things?"

"I did. It seems the *Leviathan* is not the only ship of that size to visit."

"Oh?"

"Yes. Apparently, the empire is flooding the market with cheap products, driving people out of business."

"They're likely trying to sow the seeds of discontent. It wouldn't surprise me to find out they're hiring people to fire up the populace. We must be sure to keep an eye out for such things."

"I also discovered Lord Corbin, the Halvarian envoy has been here for some time."

"And by some time, you mean?"

"A few months, at least. Long enough to ingratiate himself with the king, although I'm not sure how that helps the empire. I'd have thought it better to build up opposition to the king rather than support him."

"I imagine the plan is to control him," said Charlaine. "We know they've used some despicable tactics in the past. It would come as no surprise to see them repeated here."

"What do you think their plan is?"

"I suspect a rebellion of some sort. If they can get the local populace to rise up against the king, the empire could move in to assist, all in the name of keeping the peace."

"And how do we stop that?"

"That's a good question," said Charlaine. "I suppose the first step would be to learn more about King Stefan."

"And how do you propose to do that?"

"I've already secured my invitation to attend court."

"Really? How did you manage that?"

"Simple," said Charlaine. "I sent a letter asking to pay my respects."

"It was far from simple," added Marlena, appearing at the door. "It took half the afternoon to compose."

"Ah," said Danica. "The truth emerges."

"Yes," replied Charlaine. "And the reply came back right before you arrived."

"And when is this momentous occasion to occur?"

"Tomorrow. Care to tag along?"

"Ordinarily, I would, but I want to keep an eye on the *Leviathan*."

"To what end?"

"I intend to follow her when she leaves port. Don't worry. Once we're clear of the bay, I'll signal the *Vanguard* to take our place. She's watching from afar."

"Anything else I should know about?"

"Yes," said Danica. "There's a report that a well-armoured man, possibly the captain of the *Conqueror*, was seen in the envoy's presence. You might want to learn more about who he is, if you get a chance."

"I'll be sure to make that a priority." Charlaine reached for her goblet, taking a sip. "This Calabrian merchant could be useful to us. It might be best to cultivate a friendship."

"That was my thought as well. By the way, he knew of your father."

"I suppose that shouldn't come as a complete surprise. My father was a noble, even if it was in the last few years of the realm. Did the merchant mention anything else?"

"Not that I recall, but if I see him again, I'll press for additional details. Who knows, perhaps we can recruit others to keep their eyes on the empire?"

6

KING

The Royal Palace was nothing to inspire awe, paling in comparison to that of the Duke of Reinwick, although admittedly, it looked as if it had been here for centuries. The court itself consisted of little more than a large hall in which a few well-dressed and, no doubt, influential people wandered around.

"Well?" said Charlaine. "What do you make of it?"

"Not quite what I expected," replied Marlena.

"In what way?"

"It looks dreary as if all the colour has been banished."

"The people wandering around are fashionably attired."

"Yes, but only in dour, sombre colours. There's also surprisingly little jewellery on display. They say the king sets the tone for his court; do you think this was all Stefan's idea?"

"Quite possibly, though I know little about the king." Her gaze wandered over the crowd, and she smiled. "It seems luck is with us."

"Meaning?"

Charlaine nodded towards an individual. "It appears a fellow Temple Knight is in attendance."

"I took him for a lay brother. Why isn't he wearing his armour?"

"Let's go and find out, shall we?"

The man turned to greet them as they approached. "Temple Commander Charlaine, isn't it?"

"You have the advantage of me, Brother."

"My apologies. I am Brother Gatan, Temple Knight of Saint Mathew."

"How many of you are there here in Lidenbach."

"Only a small contingent, six, to be precise. Our only duty is to guard the Temple of Saint Mathew. Not that it requires much to make people behave themselves."

"Even a small presence is a blessing," said Charlaine. "There are few enough Temple Knights in these parts of late."

"I assume you're referring to our brothers, the Cunars. I'm afraid I'm not permitted to speak of such things," he said in an overly loud voice, then leaned in and lowered his voice. "The king is much displeased by what he sees as their abandonment of Arnsfeld."

"Is that why you're not wearing your armour?"

"It is. Yourself?"

"Sister Marlena and I thought it best to present a more modest appearance before His Majesty. We don't want to antagonize him."

Gatan nodded. "Yes. That's probably a wise move."

"What can you tell us about the king?"

"He is generally a cautious man. As such, he's not one to make spur-of-the-moment decisions. When you meet him, I suggest you be as diplomatic as possible."

"Why is that?"

"He is caught between the threat of the empire and his desire to rule this land without their influence. Such pressure can be a hard burden to bear."

"I shall be mindful of that."

"Might I ask where you come from?"

"Reinwick," said Charlaine.

"If I recall, there were rumours of a battle there a few years ago. Were you involved in that?"

"I had the honour of commanding our forces."

"Wasn't it at sea? Not the sort of thing we're used to hearing about in these parts."

"There was also a land engagement. The Empire of Halvaria set up an illegal stronghold on Reinwick territory."

"I'd be fascinated to hear more, but I'm afraid someone's trying to get your attention." He pointed behind her.

Charlaine turned to see a servant waiting patiently. "Yes?"

"His Majesty demands your presence," the man replied.

"Then lead me to him."

She followed him across the room to where King Stefan stood waiting. He was not an imposing figure, being short of stature, and she estimated him to be in his mid-forties, but the pallor of his skin seemed to indicate ill health. As she met his gaze, she noted one cloudy eye, yet more evidence all was not well. If truth be told, he was the last person one would expect to be the ruler of a Petty Kingdom. In stark contrast, the tall man beside him sported a neatly trimmed beard and hair to match—the very image of a commanding individual.

Charlaine halted, bowing before the king. "Your Majesty," she began. "I bring greetings and salutations from the Temple Knights of Saint Agnes."

"Sister Charlaine, isn't it?" said the king.

"Temple Commander Charlaine, Majesty. I have the honour of commanding the entire region on behalf of my order."

"I see. And what constitutes your definition of region?"

"I command all Saint Agnes's Temple Knights stationed within the realms of Arnsfeld, Burgemont, Angvil, and Rudor."

"Impressive," said the tall man, "though that says little of their actual numbers."

"Lord Corbin is correct, of course," said Stefan. "I often find impressive titles are given out when attempting to make up for a deficiency in other areas, don't you?"

Charlaine refused the bait. "It is not my place to question such things, Majesty, merely to obey the commands of my superiors."

"And does that include eventually abandoning my kingdom as your brother order did?"

"I assure you we are here to stay."

"You say that now, but then again, so did the Cunars when I pressed them on the issue."

"I cannot speak to that, sire, only reassure you such is not the case with us."

Lord Corbin's wry smile spoke volumes. "Yet you can't guarantee that, can you? I mean, the grand mistress of your order could change her mind, couldn't she? And if that happened, then you'd be forced to obey her commands." He turned to the king. "You see, Majesty? These Temple Knights are duplicitous folk, seeking to placate your fears even as they strive to undermine your rule by abandoning you in your time of need."

"With all due respect to Lord Corbin," said Charlaine, "he is in the exact same position. Were his superiors to order him home, he would abandon your lands, though you might be better off for their absence."

"Watch your tongue, dog, or I'll cut it from your mouth!"

"Enough," pleaded the king. "I asked the Temple Commander here in good faith, my lord. I will not see blood spilled in my home."

"This woman's reputation is known to us," said Lord Corbin. "Vessels under her command attacked our ships like common pirates."

Charlaine turned back to the king. "His Lordship fails to mention those vessels carried warriors ready to invade Reinwick."

"That's a lie!"

"Then please enlighten us, my lord," said Charlaine. "What was the purpose of having so many warriors aboard your fleet?"

"To protect our interests against corsairs such as yourself."

"Amusing," said the king. "However, the animosity between you two is of no concern to me, provided you behave yourselves in my presence."

"Of course, Majesty," said Lord Corbin. "I apologize for my zeal, but it's only natural when in the company of such despicable knaves."

"I also apologize, sire," said Charlaine. "Is there any way I might make it up to you?"

"I'm not sure what you're suggesting?" replied the king.

"Perhaps Your Majesty would like a tour of our commandery?"

"To what purpose?"

"To show we harbour no ill intent. The commandery has no secrets, Majesty, only good intentions."

"Good intentions?" said Corbin. "Hollow words. The king needs something tangible, Commander, not empty promises." He paused a moment, and then a sly smile creased the corners of his lips. "What about your ships?" he asked. "Are they to prey on Halvarian vessels in these waters?"

"Ships?" said the king. "I heard nothing of ships?"

"The commander has failed to mention the presence of one of her warships in the bay. The *Valiant*, isn't it?"

"Is this true?"

"It's true," replied Charlaine. "I came here aboard the *Valiant*, but it's a small vessel more suited to tracking down cutthroats and pirates than engaging in battle."

"Yet it took on our fleet," said Corbin, a look of triumph creasing his lips.

"It did and defeated them, though it wasn't the only ship present." She turned towards the king. "If Your Majesty wishes, I would be pleased to give you a tour of the *Valiant*. It, along with other ships of the fleet, have been very active in reducing pirates in the waters to the east of here."

The king appeared pleased until Lord Corbin leaned in closer. "I would advise against it, Majesty, especially with your declining health. It might be tempting fate."

"Then perhaps," added Charlaine, "Your Majesty might appoint someone to visit the ship on your behalf?"

The king scanned the room, his gaze stopping on a young woman. "Perhaps I'll send Rebecca. She would enjoy something like that."

"Hardly a task for a woman, let alone a princess," said Lord Corbin.

"I disagree," said Charlaine. "As our order is sworn to protect women, who better to tour the *Valiant* than one of Royal Blood?"

"Then it's settled," said the king. "I shall have someone contact you to make arrangements."

Lord Corbin did not look pleased but kept his thoughts to himself as he turned and nodded at a man dressed in plate armour, standing a few feet behind him.

Charlaine took in the fellow's features, committing them to memory. Was this the captain of the *Conqueror*, or someone else even more important in the hierarchy of whoever commanded Halvaria?

"You are dismissed," said the king.

Charlaine bowed, then withdrew, careful to remain facing him. King Stefan did not notice, for he was already making his way towards a door.

"You appear to have made an impression," came a voice.

She turned to see a man of average height, dressed in blue robes, a distinction that set him apart from the other guests' subdued colours. Even more remarkable was the ornate cane he held, a slightly glowing red gem topping it.

"And you are?" she asked.

"My apologies. I am Ashan, court mage to His Majesty, King Stefan."

"Ashen?"

"No," he said, "Ashan." He emphasized the second part of his name. "It is an unusual name in these parts, but I assure you it's quite ordinary where I come from."

"Which is?"

"Kouras, one of the Kurathian Isles."

"You're a long way from home," said Charlaine. "How did you come to find yourself in Arnsfeld?"

"I joined a merchant ship in my youth and travelled the Continent. Eventually, I realized I possessed the potential to wield magic, so I sought someone to instruct me in the art of pyromancy."

"An interesting story, but it still doesn't explain how you ended up here."

He smiled, revealing a perfect set of teeth. "That is a tale that would take far longer to tell."

"It seems there's nothing else to occupy my time at present."

"Very well. After mastering Fire Magic, I made a name for myself, spending several years in the employ of various rulers of the Petty Kingdoms. But, by and large, they only used my services when war necessitated it. As you can imagine, that led to very few offers of long-term employment, so I made my way here, to the very borders of Halvaria."

"To seek employment with the empire?"

"No, no, no. Have I not made myself clear? I am here because it's in King Stefan's best interest to employ me as a deterrent."

"You must think very highly of yourself," replied Charlaine.

"Why would you say that?"

"Surely you realize the empire would not flinch at the presence of only one mage, even a powerful one."

"You make an excellent point. If I'm being truthful, it was the argument I used to convince the king to hire me, but I never, for a moment, thought I'd actually have to use my magic in battle."

"Yet the history of the empire says otherwise."

"I'll admit," said Ashan, "Halvaria has a history of expanding its borders at the expense of others, but I don't see that happening here, at least not in the short term."

"What makes you say that?"

"Why risk invasion when you already control the king?"

"Are you suggesting King Stefan is under the empire's influence?"

"You've seen Lord Corbin's actions first-hand. How can you doubt it?"

"And how long has that been going on?"

"The Halvarians have been chipping away at the king's resolve for years now. Corbin is not the first envoy to grace this court, nor do I believe he'll be the last."

"What's their interest in Arnsfeld?"

"Who can say for certain?" said Ashan. "It lies on the border of the empire, so I suppose, from their point of view, it represents a potential invader, but there's no way Stefan's meagre forces would be considered a threat to anyone, let alone Halvaria."

He shook his head. "I'm afraid you wasted your time coming here, Commander. You bring too little, too late to be of any consequence."

"I'm not so sure," said Charlaine. "But I thank you for the insight, all the same."

"It was my pleasure. Perhaps we'll meet again? I should very much like to learn more about you." His face lit up with a smile, but he didn't wait for an answer, instead heading off towards someone else.

"Who was that?" asked Marlena, coming to stand beside her.

"A Fire Mage by the name of Ashan."

"He's handsome."

"Yes, and he knows it. No doubt he thought he could charm me."

"Does that make him an enemy or an ally?"

"Who knows, perhaps both?"

"Now you're talking in riddles," said Marlena.

"Then, for the moment, let's consider him someone who's neither good nor bad."

"So, neutral, then?"

"Yes, until we know more about him."

"I don't believe I've ever met a Fire Mage. What was he like?"

"A little smug, but that's common amongst the more accomplished mages. More important, however, was what he wanted."

"Why must he want something?"

"Why else be at court?" replied Charlaine.

"You don't trust him?"

"I don't necessarily distrust him, but I've yet to see any evidence of where his loyalties lie."

"That's Larissa Stormwind's fault."

"Are you suggesting I distrust all mages because of her?"

"It stands to reason. She betrayed the Duke of Reinwick, not to mention attacking our ships. You wouldn't be the first to take offence."

"But to blame all mages for the treachery of one? I think you underestimate my character."

"I didn't mean to," said Marlena, "but you seem a bit suspicious of his motives, especially when you've only just met him."

"I suppose I am, yet I can't quite understand why."

"May I make an observation?"

"Of course. You may always speak freely. You know that. The last thing I want is an adjutant who can't think for herself."

"That mage is a good-looking fellow."

"I'm not interested in that."

"I didn't mean to intimate you were, but people like that are used to influencing others easily. I think that's the part of him you dislike."

"Perhaps you're right. I've always abhorred the arrogance that much of the nobility exhibits, and I suppose that would include him."

"He's a noble?"

"No," said Charlaine, "but he's a court mage, which means he likely spends most of his time amongst the wealthy and powerful. It would be nice to meet a noble who showed some humility for a change."

"I doubt they can help it. Nobles are invariably in positions of power, which tends to encourage decisiveness, wouldn't you say?"

"There's a big difference between being decisive and being rude."

"Ashan was rude?" asked Marlena.

"No, not at all. In fact, he was very polite."

"But?"

"I can't help but have the feeling there's something dangerous lurking behind that smile."

"He's a Fire Mage. That seems to be the very definition of dangerous."

"True," said Charlaine, "but I'm not talking about his magic. Call it a gut instinct, if you like, but there's something disturbing about him."

"So… someone to keep an eye on, then?"

"I think that would be best, don't you? I'm not suggesting we order people to shadow him, merely keep our eyes and ears open to anything he might be involved with."

"I'll ensure I mention that to Captain Bernelle. Anyone else here we should be watching?"

"Yes, actually," said Charlaine. She nodded her head towards someone in the crowd. "Do you see that fellow over there with the plate armour?"

"The one with the envoy?"

"Yes. I'd very much like to know who he is. Danica suggested he might be the *Conqueror's* captain, but I wonder if he could be something else."

"Why is that?"

"Lord Corbin never mentioned him by name, but there was something in the envoy's behaviour suggesting he needed approval from that fellow."

"All this from one meeting? You've been observant."

"I can't help it," said Charlaine. "We're in a dangerous position here, and I must do all I can to aid in the success of our mission. I need to know who all the players are at court to ensure our survival."

"Players? You make it sound as if we're in a theatre."

"In a sense, we are. Look around you. Everyone here is playing a part, putting on a face, if you like, to impress the king. Our job is to discover what lies behind those stony expressions and determine who's a threat."

"Have we no allies? What about Brother Gatan? Not that he could be of much use to us, from a military point of view."

"The value of allies is not always measured by how many swords they bring to bear, or in this case, axes. There's no reason to believe we can't trust the Temple Knights of Saint Mathew. The entire history of our orders has been one of cooperation and support."

"True," said Marlena, "but how do six of them help us here?"

Charlaine smiled. "What is the dominant temple in Lidenbach?"

"That's easy—the Temple of Saint Mathew, the same as everywhere else in the Petty Kingdoms."

"Yes, and as such, they wield tremendous influence."

"The Holy Fathers do, but you're talking about five or six knights."

"Yes, but those knights will be familiar with the Church hierarchy in these parts."

Marlena mulled it over. "So, you're suggesting, what? That the Holy Fathers tell their flock we're here to help?"

"Now you understand."

"That could take months."

"Agreed," said Charlaine, "but winning over the hearts of the population is the key to our long-term survival. Do that, and the king will have to accept our presence."

"How do you know he won't simply order us out of Arnsfeld?"

"Without provocation? I doubt even the king would do something that bold. Besides, Brother Gatan described him as a cautious man. Does that sound like the type of person who'd do such a thing?"

"That doesn't mean the empire's envoy won't cause problems. If he's anything like those we fought in Reinwick, he's already plotting ways to discredit us."

"Then we must be on our best behaviour."

7

PRINCESS

SUMMER 1102 SR

Charlaine rode through the gates of the commandery and into the courtyard. She dismounted, keeping a tight hold on her horse. The beast had proven temperamental on every patrol she had accompanied, and she found herself missing Stormcloud. Charlaine looked across the courtyard to see Marlena exiting the building.

"Commander," her adjutant said. "You have a visitor."

"Oh? Did I forget an appointment?"

"No. She arrived unannounced."

"Now you have me intrigued. Who is it?"

"Princess Rebecca."

"And she's here to see me?"

"Of course," said Marlena. "Who else would she be here to see?"

"I invited her to tour the *Valiant*, not the commandery."

"Can't she do both? Or are you afraid we're not up to a visit?"

Charlaine chuckled. "After all the work we did getting this place into shape? Not at all." She turned to one of the knights who'd accompanied her on patrol. "I hate to do this, but I'm afraid I require you to see to my horse as I'm needed elsewhere."

"Of course," replied Sister Enna.

Charlaine watched her disappear into the stables. "Here I am insisting each knight take care of their own horse, and what am I doing? Exactly the opposite!"

"It can't be helped," said Marlena. "It's your duty as Temple Commander to welcome important visitors."

"Very well. Let's see what Her Highness wants, shall we?"

They quickly made their way through the halls to see Sister Johanna standing by the door to Charlaine's office. "I took the liberty of serving Her Highness something to drink, Commander."

"Thank you. Please remain here to ensure no one disturbs us."

Charlaine stepped inside, expecting a young girl, but instead, a composed young woman stood in her office, her hair tied up in an elaborate series of braids intertwined with golden thread.

The princess turned from where she was staring out the window. "It's quite a view you have from here."

"It is, Highness, although some might say it's better to the north."

"I've never been inside a commandery before."

"Would you like a tour?"

"Perhaps another time," said Princess Rebecca. "I'm here on another matter."

"Please feel free to elucidate."

"I fear my father's soul is in immortal danger."

"Why do you believe that?"

"A king who loses his kingdom will never reach the Afterlife. He'll be doomed to roam the Underworld forever, atoning for his sins."

"What makes you think he's going to lose his kingdom?"

"I know my father. He's fallen under the influence of Lord Corbin. I fear the kingdom's days are numbered."

"I understand your fears," said Charlaine, "but how would that even come to pass? Your father must have an heir?"

"He does—my husband, Lord Handrik, Baron of Braunfel, yet Father won't heed his counsel."

"A sad state of affairs, to be sure, but I'm curious why you brought this to me."

"I needed someone to talk to."

"You could've done that at the Temple of Saint Agnes. The Holy Mother would be pleased to hear you out."

"True, but she wouldn't have been able to do something about it. On the other hand, you have a reputation as someone who gets things done."

"I'm sorry," said Charlaine. "Are you asking me to take action against the Halvarians?"

"I am."

"And what is it, exactly, you expect me to do?"

"That's just it; I don't know. This is all new to me, yet I realize if I don't act, the good people of this realm will suffer. Lord Corbin wants this kingdom in the name of his emperor. We, however, must find some way to thwart his plans."

"It's hard to halt those plans when we don't know what they are."

"I believe I do. It has something to do with my husband's lands."

"Can you be more specific?"

"Braunfel lies to the west, astride the Stillwater River that separates our kingdom from that of Halvaria. At one time, a contingent of Temple Knights of Saint Cunar was stationed there, but since their withdrawal, the empire has grown bolder."

"Bolder?"

"Yes. Several times, the Halvarian authorities have crossed into Braunfel to arrest purported criminals."

"But they have no jurisdiction there, surely?"

"That does not prevent them from doing so," said Rebecca. "My husband has tried to prevent such tactics, but it only increased the incursions."

"Have you brought this matter to your father's attention?"

"Yes, of course, but Father refuses to condone any action that might lead to conflict with the empire, lest it makes matters worse."

"They're invading your land; how much worse can it get?"

"There's been no bloodshed yet, but I fear it is only a matter of time."

"Have any other barons experienced similar problems?"

"If they have, they've seen fit to keep it to themselves, and small wonder why—my father refuses to hear of such things."

"He won't listen?"

"He lives a life of fear. To his mind, it isn't so much a question of if the empire will absorb us, but when."

"Was he always like this?"

"He was never a decisive man, but as he's aged, he's become less willing to take chances."

"You mentioned the Temple Knights of Saint Cunar. How long ago did they leave?"

"Close to a year and a half," said Rebecca.

"And just to be clear, these incursions began shortly thereafter?"

"Yes, they did. Why do you think that is?"

"The empire feeds on the weak. With the Cunars gone, there's no longer anything acting as a deterrent."

"My husband has warriors."

"I have no doubt, but they are obviously insufficient to prevent the incursions, or you wouldn't be bringing this to my attention."

"Can you help?"

"I'm not sure what I can do at the moment. We have our hands full in Lidenbach."

"Could you come and visit us and see for yourself what's happening?"

"I can do that, though not for some weeks yet. I still have much to do here."

"I'll be returning home at the end of summer. Might I prevail upon you to provide an escort?"

"You have no warriors of your own to safeguard you?"

"I do, but I'd feel safer knowing Temple Knights protected me."

"You mentioned Braunfel was on the border. Is the town on the river, by chance?"

"It is. Why?"

"Just trying to get an idea of the lay of the land. Have you any docks?"

"Are you suggesting we take a ship home?"

Charlaine smiled. "It wouldn't be the first time *Valiant* has sailed upriver."

"But that would put you into Halvarian waters, wouldn't it?"

"Not quite. Assuming the river is the border, both sides have the right of navigation. Is there much river traffic?"

"A few merchant ships sail upstream, but they're small, little more than boats."

"That, at least, means the river is navigable, not to mention deep enough for ships to traverse."

"So, we'll sail aboard your ship?"

"It's not my ship to command, but I'll discuss the matter with the admiral. In the meantime, can I entice you with a tour of *Valiant*? I'm sure you'd be more than welcome aboard if I sent word."

"Yes. I'd like that. Thank you."

"I'll have my aide make the arrangements."

"Then, while we wait for an answer, might you show me to your chapel? I should very much like to pray, assuming that's allowed to outsiders."

"Of course," replied Charlaine. "We welcome anyone who follows the teachings of Saint Agnes."

They rowed out to the *Valiant* later that afternoon. An early morning rain had given way to a cloudless sky, and the seagulls were loud as the ship's boat took Charlaine and Princess Rebecca out to the ship.

Danica greeted them as they climbed aboard. "Welcome, Highness. You do us a great honour."

"Thank you," the princess replied as she took in her new surroundings. "To be honest, I expected something a little larger, more akin to that." She pointed at the *Conqueror*.

"The *Valiant* might be small, but she's the fastest ship on the Northern Sea. Well, her and her sister ship."

"She has a twin?"

"Indeed, Highness. The *Vanguard*. We built her to the same specifications as *Valiant*."

"Do all your ships begin with the letter 'V'?"

"No, only our pirate hunters."

"So, you have other ships, then?"

"We do," said Danica. "But those are more traditional ships of war."

"Have you anything to rival the *Conqueror*?"

"We do indeed. Three of them."

"And what are their names?"

"Furious, Formidable, and *Fearless*."

"Such serious names. Are you sure they aren't Halvarian?"

"Originally they were, but we renamed them."

"Just how large is this fleet of yours?"

"I prefer not to say," said Danica, "but we have sufficient ships to transport our Temple Knights wherever they're needed."

"And will you eventually bring them all here, to Arnsfeld?"

Danica looked at Charlaine before answering. "I suspect the commander would be better able to answer that."

"Don't you command the fleet?"

"She does," said Charlaine, "but much of what she does with it depends on the region's politics. It could mean war if the entire fleet were to descend on Lidenbach."

"For simply sailing into these waters?"

"The empire wouldn't take kindly to its presence here."

"Yet they have their own fleet, do they not? Surely the presence of a few ships would be no threat to them?"

"Not in a military sense, but politically, it might cause problems for your father."

"Perhaps that would be better for us all? Will you sail to our aid if war does come here?"

"That's a difficult question to answer," replied Danica. "I'd like to say yes, but it would depend on a great number of details."

"Such as?"

"Where the enemy attacked, what numbers they had under their control, where we thought they would strike next, which doesn't even include things like the tides or weather. All in all, there's much to consider before putting Temple Knights ashore. We'd also need to decide whether they might be better deployed against an enemy fleet."

"It appears you've given this much thought," said Rebecca.

"I'm an admiral, Highness. That's my duty."

The princess moved towards the bow, stopping to look at a tarp covering something large. "What's this?"

"An arbalest," said Danica.

"That's like a crossbow, isn't it?"

"It is, although on a much larger scale and made entirely of metal."

"And its purpose?"

"We use it for a variety of things. We can grapple with pirates, puncture hulls, or even damage sails using special bolts, although admittedly, those last two take considerable time."

"Perhaps you'll give me a demonstration at some point?"

"Most certainly, Highness, though not within sight of the Halvarians. We don't want to give away all our secrets."

"Have they nothing similar?"

"They have ballistae and catapults, but our arbalest is Dwarven-made."

"Which means?"

"Have you no Dwarves in Arnsfeld?"

"None with which I'm acquainted," said Rebecca, "though, in truth, I seldom frequent places where they might be found. Why? Is that significant?"

"A Dwarven master smith named Barbek Stoutarm created the arbalest."

"Should I know that name?"

"No," said Charlaine, "but suffice it to say our ships are the only vessels equipped with such things in these waters. It gives us a tactical advantage."

"Yet the Halvarian ships are much larger. How would a small ship like *Valiant* fare against such opponents?"

"We captured two of them at the Battle of Temple Bay. Our strength lies in our Temple Knights."

"And how many of those do you carry?"

"Our normal complement is only six, but in times of trouble, we carry more."

"And they operate this entire ship as well as fight?"

"No," replied Danica. "We carry a regular crew, experienced men we recruited in Reinwick and various other kingdoms."

"This is all so fascinating."

"Does your father have any ships?"

"Alas, no. At one time, he considered building some, but the cost was prohibitive, and he became worried such an undertaking would only worsen relations with the empire."

"If I might be so bold," said Charlaine, "how long has Halvaria been keeping ships here?"

"Ever since the Temple Knights of Saint Cunar announced their intention to leave, they've kept at least one warship in the bay."

"At least one?"

"Yes," said Rebecca. "There are sometimes more. Before the arrival of the *Conqueror*, there were three in port. Even now, there are likely others farther out to sea."

"I'll have to keep that in mind," said Danica. She looked at Charlaine. "A word, if I may?"

They moved aft, out of earshot of the princess.

"I'd like to send for more ships," said Danica.

"You don't need my permission."

"True, but I value your opinion."

"Very well. What are you thinking?"

"That I might leave *Valiant* here and send *Vanguard* back to Temple Bay to summon a couple more ships."

"Any ships in particular?"

"*Invincible* and *Indomitable*."

"I doubt the Halvarians will like that."

"Probably not, but I also want one of our larger ships nearby, perhaps *Fearless*."

"That was their flagship at Temple Bay."

"It was," said Danica, "but hear me out. I wouldn't bring it here, to Lidenbach. Instead, I'd keep it anchored at Vilnitz."

"A good idea, but I doubt its presence would go unnoticed."

"Perhaps that's a good thing. We need something to counter Halvaria's domination of the trade lanes hereabouts."

"I think it a sound idea," said Charlaine. "We could also start escorting merchants here once the *Vanguard* returns. You can claim it's merely to reduce piracy."

"It means we're increasing the chance of conflict at sea, but it'll demonstrate we're not willing to give up without a fight."

"I agree."

"Good," said Danica. "I'll take out *Valiant* tomorrow and rendezvous with *Vanguard*. Don't worry. I'll be back long before dark."

"There's something else you should know," said Charlaine. "Small groups of Halvarians have been crossing into Arnsfeld."

"And the king has done nothing?"

"It appears he's eager to avoid a diplomatic incident."

"So they wander around freely?"

"I don't possess the full details, but that appears to be the case."

"And where were these incursions? Not here, surely?"

"No, in a place called Braunfel. Her Highness's husband is the baron there."

"That might be worth visiting."

"My thoughts exactly," said Charlaine. "I hoped the *Valiant* would take us there. It's on the river."

"You mean the river that forms the border? That might be tempting fate. If the empire cuts off all traffic, it could leave us stranded."

"I understand it's a risk, but at the same time, the presence of one of our ships would send an obvious message to them."

"I like your thinking," said Danica. "When would you want to sail?"

"Not for a few weeks yet. There's still a lot of work to do here."

"Like what?"

"Waiting for the promised reinforcements to arrive and getting the old Cunar commandery up and running."

"How's that going?"

"The doors are intact, and we finished repairing the shutters, but all the furnishings need replacing. It's not as if we can go out and purchase fifty beds. Thankfully, we found carpenters willing to take on the task, but it takes time. I worry our reinforcements will arrive before we're ready for them."

"Anything I can do to help?"

"Not really," said Charlaine, "other than listen to me grumble."

"I have an idea," said Danica. "Perhaps it's time we found ourselves a wealthy patron?" Her eyes flicked to the princess. "Know anyone who might be suitable?" She led Charlaine back to the midships, where the princess was examining the mast.

"Your sails are different," noted Rebecca. "Your yardarms are fore and aft; I don't believe I've seen that in these parts."

"It's a triangular sail," explained Danica. "Perhaps you'd like to see it in action?"

"You mean now?"

"Of course, providing you have the time."

"That would be marvellous. Thank you."

Danica called out orders, and the crew sprang into action, weighing anchor and unfurling the sail. The *Valiant* began moving, turning west to clear the mouth of the bay before picking up speed, sending a fine spray off its bow.

"You might want to hold on to something," said Charlaine. "The sea gets choppy at times."

Rebecca grabbed the railing. "What an odd sensation. It's as if the ground is moving."

"You've never been aboard a ship before?"

"No, never. I suppose that sounds strange to you."

"Most knights never put out to sea, but I must admit, I've had my fair share of voyages."

"Did you grow up by the water?"

"No. I come from the heart of the Continent, a place called Hadenfeld."

"I'm afraid I'm not familiar with it."

"Nor would I expect you to be, for it lies a considerable distance from here."

"And have you family?"

"My parents live in Malburg, one of the larger cities there."

"You must miss them dearly."

"I do, but the order is my family now."

"Might I ask what inspired you to become a Temple Knight?"

"It's a long and complicated tale, and those who've taken vows don't typically discuss such things."

"I'm sorry," said Rebecca. "I meant no offence."

"And I've taken none. We often get asked why we joined, as if the average person cannot understand our devotion to the cause. The truth is most of us see it as a calling."

"Then I shall press you no further for details. Is it permissible to ask how long you've been a knight? I only enquire because you appear relatively young for a Knight Commander."

"You mean Temple Commander," said Charlaine. "And to answer your question, I am reasonably young for such an undertaking. The vast majority of commanders are, I believe, ten years my senior, if not more."

"And the admiral?"

"She'd be considered young as well, although there is no one to compare her to. She's the only admiral in the order."

"How did she manage that?"

"By distinguishing herself in service to Saint Agnes."

The *Valiant* dipped, then a large spray of water drenched them as the bow hit the bottom of the trough.

"Sorry," said Charlaine. "I should have warned you."

"Nonsense, it's invigorating! You were saying?"

"The admiral and I served together in Ilea."

"And how long were you Temple Knights before that?"

"It was her first posting, as it was mine. Truth be told, she's served a little longer than me."

"No offence," said Rebecca, "but you look older."

"I am, but I didn't join until I was twenty-four."

"And is that common?"

"Not from what I understand."

"Regardless of your age, I'm glad you're here. Saints know we need your guidance."

8

DEPARTURE

SUMMER 1102 SR

Danica stared aft. They'd set Princess Rebecca ashore, along with Charlaine, and were now sailing northeast to locate and rendezvous with the *Vanguard*. The weather was clear, the wind strong, and the *Valiant* was making good speed.

"Missing the place already?" asked Vivian.

"Lidenbach? No, but I am curious about that." She nodded to where a distant sail stood above the horizon.

"Another merchant?"

"Possibly, though if it is, it's a small one."

"What else could it be? Unless you're suggesting we're being followed?"

"Let's find out, shall we? Have the ship turn to port."

"That will take us farther out to sea."

"Precisely. A place where no reasonable merchant would sail."

Vivian gave the order, and the ship turned north, its sail straining as the wind filled it. The *Valiant* picked up speed, slicing through the water with ease.

Danica kept a close watch on the interloper. "It appears our friend is changing course."

"Could they be trying to contact us?"

"I suppose it's possible. Keep on this heading for a little while, and if it keeps following, we'll turn around."

"Aye, Admiral."

If there was one thing Danica had learned well, it was that ship encounters are a prolonged process. Those ashore always thought it was a sudden clash of melee, but the truth was, it could take half a day or more of positioning before anything could even be contemplated.

She turned towards the crow's nest at the top of the *Valiant's* mast. "Can you make out any details?"

"A single-master," came the reply, "but a small one."

"How small?"

"Similar in size to that small merchant we met on the way to Arnsfeld."

"You mean the *Cygnet?*"

"Aye, that's the one, but this one's rigged with a triangular sail rather than a square one."

"Can you make out how many are aboard?"

"Difficult to tell at this range, but it couldn't hold over ten. It also looks high in the water, so I doubt they're carrying much in the way of cargo."

"Have the knights don their armour, Captain," ordered Danica.

"You think they'll fight?" said Vivian.

"I doubt it, but it doesn't hurt to be prepared." The sky was cloudless, the wind strong—the perfect weather for sailing. "Stand by to bring *Valiant* about."

The hands rushed to take up their positions on the ropes. Bringing the ship about involved much more than rotating the rudder, for the sail flapped uncontrollably as they turned into the wind, requiring men to adjust the ropes.

Valiant was a nimble ship, easily handling the turn, and its crew experienced enough to compensate for the change in the wind without constant reminders. They passed the point where the ship was bow-on to the wind, then as the nose pointed south, the sail filled once more.

"Any change?" the admiral called out.

"They're turning," came the reply from the lookout.

Vivian appeared at Danica's side. "It seems they're not here to contact us."

"Indeed."

"Then why are they here?"

"Perhaps they believe we'll lead them to *Vanguard.*"

"How would that help them?"

"If the empire plans on moving into Arnsfeld, they need to secure the coast. The last thing they want is our ships interfering with that."

"I'm afraid I'm still not following," said Vivian.

"If war comes, one of their first priorities will be to sweep us from the sea, and they can't do that if they don't know where we are."

"That, I understand, but finding *Vanguard* now won't help them weeks down the road."

"True, but it would give them some idea of where she's patrolling. I suspect that should they find her, more Halvarian ships would make their presence felt along that part of the coast."

"And you believe the kingdoms hereabouts would permit that?"

"Who would dare oppose them?" said Danica. "We're the only ones with any experienced warships in the area."

"But Burgemont must possess some ships, surely?"

"It does, but not enough to threaten the empire's dominance. In any case, they'll avoid conflict for fear of being dragged into war."

"So war is inevitable?"

"I'm afraid it's not a matter of , but when. I only hope more Temple Knights arrive in Arnsfeld before the fighting begins."

"Are you sure that's wise?" said Vivian. "If we fight here, it'll drag the entire Church into the conflict."

"And if we don't, our entire existence becomes meaningless. Are we to simply abandon lands to the empire until there are no Petty Kingdoms left?"

"Do we have the ships to take them on?"

"That's a difficult question to answer, especially when we have no idea of their fleet size." Danica paused a moment before continuing. "You raise an interesting point. Perhaps we should find out for ourselves once we've contacted *Vanguard*."

"What are you suggesting?"

"Simply that we sail within sight of their ports."

"They won't like that."

"Nor would I expect them to, but *Valiant* is a fast ship. I'm sure we could outrun anything they might send after us."

Vivian looked south to where their shadow kept its distance. "And what do you propose we do about our new friend?"

"Resume our course for the coast of Burgemont."

"But won't they change course to follow us?"

"I'm counting on it."

"Might I ask your intentions?" said Vivian.

"I thought we might stay close to shore."

"How close?"

"Close enough that the shoals could pose a problem for that ship over there."

"It's likely got a shallower draft than us."

"Then we'll need to be doubly careful. You're the captain here, Vivian; if you doubt the crew's ability to do that, best you say it now."

"We can do it, Admiral. I'm just not sure that will help us lose them."

"It will if we keep at it until dark."

"In these waters? That's asking a lot. Mind you, I'm not complaining, merely expressing concern."

"A concern that is noted. As captain, this ship is your responsibility. If you feel the crew's safety is endangered, it's your prerogative to sail farther out to sea."

"We'll try it your way for now," said Vivian, "but we'll re-evaluate once darkness falls. I don't want to run *Valiant* aground."

Their original intention had been to rendezvous with the *Vanguard*, then return by nightfall, but with a possible spy following them, their plans needed to change.

The *Valiant* sailed close to shore, so much so that some feared they might run aground. They passed by several villages, near enough they could make out individuals watching their progress.

Whoever sailed the ship following them was doing a good job, for they kept their distance throughout the day. As the light faded, the *Valiant* furled its sail and dropped anchor. Now it became a waiting game.

Danica paced, eager to be free of their tail, but it was close to midnight before they finally made their move. First, they doused all lights, making the ship invisible. Then the *Valiant's* seasoned hands weighed anchor and unfurled the sail, making a sharp turn away from the shore. Ordinarily, it would've been a simple matter, but the darkness and the desire to run silently complicated matters.

Sailing in the unknown was nerve-wracking, for the clouds had moved in, blocking the moonlight. A silent prayer to Saint Agnes was all Danica could muster, and then word passed that they'd cleared the shallow water. They kept the ship on a course taking it far out to sea, ensuring it would be out of sight by daylight.

Morning found them in open water, the coast of Burgemont nothing more than a slight smear on the horizon.

With no signs that the vessel had shadowed them, Danica ordered the *Valiant* to make sail for its rendezvous. There was no way to calculate the exact position of *Vanguard*, but Danica had laid out its patrol route in excruciating detail before they arrived in Arnsfeld. Soon after entering the area, they caught sight of the ship and, by mid-morning, rowed across to pass on orders to its captain, Sister Nadia.

Now safely back on *Valiant*, they set about returning to Lidenbach, following the coastline and keeping watch for any signs of trouble.

The winds, erratic as they often were, shifted around, making westward travel more difficult. They needed to continually tack, sailing in a zig-zag motion against the wind to make progress.

A call from the lookout alerted her to trouble towards the shore, where a small vessel had run aground, its mast damaged and hanging over the side. They anchored the *Valiant*, then went out in the ship's boat to investigate.

As they drew closer, Vivian could make out the ship's name. "The *Pelican*," she said. "Does that name mean anything to you, Admiral?"

"No, but it looks a lot like that one that was following us."

They continued until the water was only waist deep, then two of the rowers went overboard to steady the boat. Danica waded over to examine the wreck. "No sign of any bodies."

"My guess is they abandoned ship," said Vivian. "Any sign of damage?"

"The hull's split; I'm guessing they bottomed out." She climbed aboard the water-logged vessel, which was much like the *Cygnet*, its hull old and grey with age. The mast had snapped off, leaving jagged splinters, its sail ripped and torn. "No sign of cargo, there's nothing here worth salvaging." Danica's gaze drifted to the shore. "That beach isn't too distant."

"Perhaps there's evidence they made it ashore?"

"It's worth a look."

"And the wreckage?"

"Leave it. It's of no use to us."

They climbed into the boat and rowed to the beach but found little. Between the surf and the wind, there were no signs of footprints, or survivors, for that matter. The return to *Valiant* was quiet, and it wasn't until they were back aboard that Danica spoke. "What did you make of that wreck?"

"Not much," said Vivian. "They likely ran aground, trying to follow us in the dark."

"Agreed, but what of the *Pelican* itself?"

"I'm not sure I understand what you're asking?"

"It's a small ship, not well-suited to these waters."

"Neither was the *Cygnet*, if you recall. In fact, the two ships are very similar."

"Precisely. I'm of the opinion that ship is not Halvarian."

"But who else would try to follow us?"

"Let me clarify," said Danica. "It's likely a ship local to Lidenbach that the Halvarians hired. That, I think, is closer to the truth."

"What makes you say that?"

"Halvaria does everything on a grand scale. Their warships are large, and their cogs, like the *Leviathan*, are built to carry heavy loads."

"Your point?"

"Their ships are not ideal for shadowing us."

"So they hired the *Pelican*?"

"That would be my guess, and why not? The people hereabouts are on hard times; a few coins would go a long way."

"Yes, but how could the Halvarians trust the owner of a small vessel to report the truth?"

"I think they carried someone with them for precisely that reason."

"So, a spy hired them?"

"It's certainly feasible, and if I'm right, the *Pelican's* owners will probably never be seen again."

"Why?"

"The spy, whoever they are, won't want their identity getting out."

"So he or she simply kills off the crew?"

"Quite possibly. Of course, I could be wrong, but if that's true, why follow us in the first place? Who, other than the empire, would want to know where we're sailing?"

"Other pirates?"

"I've a hard time believing pirates would be that organized. Out of all the ones we've tracked down, how many would be willing to do something like this?"

"None," said Vivian. "Assuming Halvaria hired them, what do we do now?"

"Find the one responsible. If we can identify them, it'll be much easier to neutralize their efforts."

"Are you suggesting we kill them?"

"No," said Danica, "of course not, but we can expose their treachery and prevent them from repeating this sort of thing."

"I assume we start back in Lidenbach?"

"Yes. We'll report the wreck of the *Pelican* first, without mentioning what it was doing. Once we know who operated it, we can look into their known associates."

"You make it sound similar to a gang."

"Well," said Danica, "it is if you think about it. The Halvarians are like a large gang who control an entire country, and now they want to move into our territory."

"Not while I'm alive," said Vivian.

"Nor I, but we must be careful not to raise suspicions amongst the Halvarians. I suggest we start by talking to fishermen hereabouts. They'll know all the local gossip, and I've yet to see one who refuses the offer of coins in exchange for information."

"We're not making much headway against this wind, and there's no chance of making Lidenbach by nightfall. I suggest we anchor here for the night."

"Very well," said Danica. "But post guards, to be safe."

"And the shoreline?"

"Keep an eye out in case any survivors show themselves ashore."

"Do I send more knights to search?"

"No. If they don't want to be found, they'll be long gone by now."

They sailed into the harbour just before noon, dropping anchor in the middle of the bay and preparing the ship's boat to take them ashore. They were halfway to the docks before Danica noticed the presence of a new vessel. Beside *Conqueror*, hidden from *Valiant's* view by the great ship's mass, was one of the smaller Halvarian warships akin to the provincial vessels the order had captured.

"That's new," said Danica, looking up as they passed by its stern. "*Vindicator*. Not exactly the most pleasant of names."

The boat came to rest against the dock, and she climbed out. "You can return to the ship. I shall be some time."

She headed along the dock, her destination the commandery, but after taking only a few steps, she came face to face with six Royal Troops blocking her way.

"Can I help you?" she asked.

"Are you Temple Captain Danica, Captain of the *Valiant*?"

"I'm not the captain—that would be Sister Vivian."

"Yet you command it, do you not?"

"I suppose you could say that. Why?"

"You are to be brought before the king."

"Am I under arrest?"

"That largely depends on your actions. At the moment, His Majesty merely wishes a word with you, but should you refuse his summons, we are empowered to take you into custody."

"Then I am happy to oblige the king with my presence. Lead on, and I shall follow."

Two guards took the lead while two more fell in behind. The last pair stood on either side, boxing her in and making any escape attempt difficult.

Once they reached the Royal Castle, they were granted immediate access. All eyes were on her as they marched her into the great hall where the king sat on his throne, watching the procession as it made its way towards him.

"Admiral Danica," he said, "or would that be Admiral Meer?"

"Either will do," she replied, "although it is common amongst the sisters of the order to use only first names with such titles."

"You dare to lecture your king?"

"I seek not to lecture, Majesty, merely to inform, and in any case, you're not my king." She straightened herself. "I am a Temple Knight of Saint Agnes—as such, I do not serve kings."

"Do not tempt my anger, Admiral."

A flush coloured her cheeks as she tried to calm herself.

"Have you any idea why you're here?" continued the king.

"I'm guessing it has something to do with the Halvarian warship *Vindicator.*"

The king looked at one of his aides. "What's this, now? Another ship to trouble the peace?"

The gentleman whispered something in his ear.

"Ah," said the king. "I should have known." He waved the fellow away, returning his attention to Danica.

"It has come to my attention that your ship, the *Valiant*, has outstayed its welcome."

"In what way, Majesty?"

"I've received complaints about the conduct of your crew towards my subjects."

She knew he lied, for none had left the ship except Vivian and herself. Did this have something to do with his daughter?

"I apologize if there's been a misunderstanding," she said. "It was not our intent to put anyone ill at ease."

The king appeared satisfied with the response, but then Lord Corbin made a grand appearance. "Your Majesty," he said, his voice loud and strong. "I see you have brought this renegade to account for her actions."

"I have done nothing," said Danica.

"Nothing? You attacked the empire's ships without provocation, and now you deny it?"

"What ships am I accused of attacking?"

A sly smirk spread across Corbin's face. "I have a list," he said, holding out his hand while a servant brought him a scroll. "With Your Majesty's permission, I shall elucidate."

"By all means," said the king.

"This so-called pirate hunter and her fleet are responsible for our loss of the warships *Warrior*, *Invincible*, *Terror*, and *Devastator*, not to mention the provincial ships *Ravager* and *Annihilator*. I demand reparations in the emperor's name."

"Well?" said the king. "What have you to say for yourself?"

"My pardon, Your Majesty," said Danica, "but I wish to clarify a minor detail. Those ships were not lost—they were captured, all except for the *Warrior*, which we sank."

"You see?" said Corbin. "She even admits her crimes!"

"We committed no crimes! We fought in defence of Reinwick, an action sanctioned by the duke himself. I might also point out that your ships carried warriors intending to invade the duchy."

"That," said Corbin, "is nothing but an outrageous lie."

"You do not need to take my word for it, Majesty. Write a letter to Lord Wilfhelm Brondecker, Duke of Reinwick. He can confirm my version of events."

"She knows full well it will take months to get there. This thief seeks only to delay her punishment."

"Lord Corbin makes a valid point," said the king. "How do I know you're not just wasting my time?"

"I would, in answer, respond with a question of my own. If Halvaria's ships did not plan to invade, then why was such a large fleet in Reinwick's waters in the first place? Perhaps Lord Corbin would care to explain that?"

All colour fled from Corbin's face. "It is not my place to question the actions of my superiors."

"So, you admit it was an invasion?"

"I admit nothing of the kind. This discussion concerns your presence in port, not the loss of Halvarian ships."

"Yet you attempt to make it so. You accused me of misdeeds, not the other way around."

"I've heard enough," said the king. "It is clear to me there is bad blood between Halvaria and the Temple Knights of Saint Agnes. To ensure this conflict does not escalate, the *Valiant* will confine its activities to the eastern docks while the empire will continue to use those to the south. Are we understood?"

Lord Corbin immediately responded. "A brilliant solution, Majesty. My congratulations. I will inform my people with all haste."

"As will I," added Danica.

9

TAKING CHARGE
SUMMER 1102 SR

Charlaine finished her writing and waited while the ink dried. Her duty as a commander was to regularly report to the grand mistress of the order, yet she couldn't help but feel all her efforts so far were nothing more than stop-gap methods. Perhaps the coming season would allow her to make better progress.

Marlena opened the door. "Someone to see you, Commander."

"Oh? I didn't know we were expecting anyone?"

"We weren't."

"And who is this mysterious visitor?"

"Temple Captain Miranda."

"I knew a Miranda in Ilea. Could it be the same person?"

"You'd know better than I. Shall I show her in?"

"Of course."

The captain who stepped through the doorway had a shock of red hair, along with a patch covering her left eye.

Charlaine stood. "Miranda," she exclaimed. "It is you!"

The captain remained calm. "You were expecting someone else?"

"I don't know what I expected, but this is a pleasant surprise."

"I bring reinforcements—a full company, to be exact."

"I was wondering when they might arrive."

"I understand there are more coming, but the grand mistress was eager to get you help as soon as possible."

"And where did your knights come from?"

"All over the place. Unfortunately, almost a third are recent recruits. The rest we picked up piecemeal as we marched through the Petty Kingdoms."

"I assume you came from the Antonine?"

"They summoned me there from Ilea, then rushed me through training only to send me directly here." Miranda paused a moment, looking over the room. "If I may say so, you've done well for yourself."

"Ignore the furnishings—they're left over from my predecessor. You remember Sister Nina?"

"I could hardly forget her," replied Miranda.

"She's a Temple Commander now."

"A commander? Surely not." She paused, taking a moment to realize the implications. "Actually, that explains a lot."

"And by that, you mean?"

"The grand mistress told me I was hand-picked for this assignment. Said she wanted people you could trust."

"Does that mean I can expect others from Ilea to join me?"

"I couldn't say. All I know was that I was to bring the first company to reinforce you here."

"How is Captain Giselle?"

"She is well and sends her regards."

"She knew you were coming here?"

"Yes. My orders to report to the Antonine indicated as much. Once I met with the grand mistress, she told me the situation here was dire but gave few details.

"Where is your company?" asked Charlaine.

"I left them outside the city, in the countryside to the east. Should I bring them here?"

"No. I have other plans for them. What do you know of the Cunars?"

"I was told they pulled back from the Halvarian border. Is that what this is all about?"

"In a word, yes. Their withdrawal left behind a lot of simmering resentment towards the Church, particularly Temple Knights. It also, rather conveniently, left behind a commandery, which is where your company comes in."

"Where is this place?"

"I'll have someone take you there once we're done here. I should warn you, though; our brother order didn't leave it in very good shape."

"Meaning?"

"We're a little short of furniture at the moment, but at least the building is secure. We've also restored the stables, thank the Saints, and restocked the kitchen, but I'm afraid some of the sisters will be sleeping on the floor while we struggle to get enough beds."

"They marched cross-country for weeks on end. I'm sure they'll find it preferable to being outdoors in the rain."

"Once the place is operational, I'll transfer my office there."

"Might I ask why?"

"It has a commanding view of the harbour. Which reminds me, you remember Danica?"

"Of course."

"She's ranked a Temple Captain now but is also Admiral of the Fleet."

"And she's here?"

"She is, aboard her flagship, the *Valiant*. We'll coordinate things with her occasionally, so you'll see her around."

"What of our duties here in Lidenbach? I assume we'll be conducting patrols?"

"You will, but Captain Bernelle will deal with the city. I want your knights to take responsibility for the countryside."

"I would like a few weeks to get the company into order first. They've had precious little time to operate as a cohesive unit."

"I can give you two weeks. Any training after that will need to be done in your spare time."

"Fair enough," said Miranda. "Anything else I should be made aware of?"

"Yes. The Halvarians maintain a presence here."

"As in warriors or diplomats?"

"Both, though their soldiers have remained aboard ship so far. An envoy, by the name of Lord Corbin, is making his presence felt at court, and he's pressuring the king to ban our ships from the harbour. As I said earlier, there's also some resentment from the populace due to the Cunars' abandonment."

"And how, might I ask, do we counter that?"

"By doing exactly what we did in Ilea: visiting people and showing we have their best interests at heart. I've already increased patrols within the streets of Lidenbach. I'm hoping it will prove more effective in the country."

"You can count on me, Commander."

"I'm glad to hear you say that. I'd introduce you to Captain Bernelle, but I think getting your company into their new home first is better. Marlena?"

Her aide poked her head in. "Yes, Commander?"

"I'd like you to show Temple Captain Miranda to the Cunar commandery. When you're finished, I'll have a note for you to take to the admiral."

"For the grand mistress?" said Marlena.

"Eventually. She can forward it through Reinwick the next time she sends dispatches."

"You don't send them by courier?" asked Miranda.

"We have our own, more secure, lines of communication."

"Are you suggesting we can't trust the normal methods?"

Charlaine considered her new captain. Could she trust her with what she knew of the order and its problems? "I don't know how much you are aware of," she finally said, "but there've been some problems of late in the Antonine."

"The grand mistress hinted at such things but never came out and spoke about the details."

Charlaine glanced at Marlena. "Close the door and join us, will you? I don't want anyone overhearing."

She waited until Marlena sat down beside the captain. "What I'm about to tell you is known by only a few, you understand?"

"Of course," replied Miranda. "I shall keep it in the strictest confidence."

"When Danica and I left Ilea, we reported to the Antonine, much as you did. While there, however, we discovered a corruption infesting the halls of the Church."

"Corruption?"

"Yes. People out to serve themselves rather than the ideals of the order."

"How prevalent was this corruption?"

"That's difficult to say. It extended to at least one Temple Commander, but there are likely more out there. There was evidence the Cunars were also under the influence of an outside force."

"An outside force? You mean the Halvarians?"

"That was our assumption, though we couldn't prove it."

"Is that why they abandoned Arnsfeld?"

"I believe so," replied Charlaine. "Their departure left a power vacuum, which had the overall effect of heightening the empire's influence. We now find ourselves at a dangerous crossroads, for there is a very real chance war will soon be upon us."

"And if they invade, do we fight?"

"That has yet to be decided."

"But you'd need permission from the grand mistress for that, surely?"

"Normally, I would," said Charlaine, "but she is weeks away, even for a fast courier, and decisions may need to be made quickly if we are to avoid disaster."

"So, you will fight without permission if needed?"

"I will."

"Then I'm with you," said Miranda. "Who else knows of this?"

"Marlena, Danica, and likely her captains as well."

"And the first company's captain?"

"Captain Bernelle? I've yet to inform her of any of this."

"Why the delay?"

"We are in a precarious position, not only in terms of Halvaria but within the hierarchy of our own order. There are also powerful forces at work outside of the Church. Are you familiar with the name Stormwind?"

"They're court mages, aren't they?"

"They are," said Charlaine. "Back in Reinwick, we learned they were working with Halvaria. One of their mages tried interfering with our attempts to dislodge the empire from Reinwick waters."

"Could it be only one individual?"

"I thought that at first, but I saw fit to warn a friend about their influence. Sometime later, he discovered another Stormwind trying to foment rebellion in his home kingdom. It's a bit more complicated than that, but you know what I mean."

"Where was this?"

"Hadenfeld."

"Why does that sound familiar?" asked Miranda.

"It was my home before I joined the order."

"So, how do we decide whom to trust?"

"I have a select group of people, including the grand mistress."

"You realize she can be replaced."

"I'm well aware, which is why we must extend our influence while we still can."

"And if they do replace her?"

"That would largely depend on what her successor did."

"Are you suggesting it could be the end of the order?"

"I don't want to make any predictions, but it's possible."

"That makes our success even more imperative."

"It does," said Charlaine. "I trust I can count on your support?"

"Of course, Commander."

"Glad to hear it. We'll talk more about this once you've had a chance to settle in. Now, you'd best be going if you want to install your people in your new home before the sun sets." She reached out her hand. "Welcome to Lidenbach, Captain."

Miranda shook her hand. "It is my honour, Commander."

"If you come this way," said Marlena, "I'll show you to your new home."

Charlaine waited until they left before going over to the window, staring out at the Royal Castle dominating the city. She held no doubt that the Halvarians were pushing the king to expel her Temple Knights. The question was, how far were they willing to go to achieve their objectives?

· · ·

As the days rolled by, Charlaine was pleased the folk of Lidenbach were finally coming to appreciate the order's regular patrols. Violence on the streets appeared to be waning, and the approach of Temple Knights no longer brought out jeers and grumbling. Her strategy of winning over the town was beginning to bear fruit.

Captain Miranda's group settled into their new home, training as a company in one of the commons. This, in turn, brought folk to watch, and soon, others set up stalls, selling goods as the Temple Knights went through their paces. No doubt, news of this would eventually trickle up to the king, but the vendors were happy for now.

Charlaine rode through the city streets on a chilly morning, a reminder summer was almost at an end. She'd only gone three blocks when a voice called out her name. She turned to see Ashan, the Fire Mage, riding towards her.

"Good morning, Commander. I trust all is well?"

"As well as can be expected," replied Charlaine. "But I sense this isn't a chance encounter."

He grinned. "I confess it is not."

"Then perhaps you'd best get to the heart of the matter?"

"Very well. First, let me say I am here in an unofficial capacity."

"Are you suggesting the king knows nothing of this?"

"That is precisely what I mean. I suppose you might say I'm here to offer you a friendly warning."

"About what?"

"It's Lord Corbin," said Ashan. "He's pressuring the king to refuse safe harbour to the *Valiant*."

"He's done that since it arrived."

"True, but I can't help but feel he has a more sympathetic ear of late. He's also suggesting Halvarian troops be allowed in the capital to help keep the streets safe."

"That is our duty," said Charlaine.

"I'm merely reporting what I know," he replied, "not claiming responsibility. If you have any complaints, you should take it up with the king or, better yet, Lord Corbin himself."

"I doubt that would do much good. In any case, the streets are safer now than they've been in months."

"That is not the message Corbin is presenting to His Majesty."

"What are you suggesting?"

"Merely that the king is concerned there might be an impending uprising."

"I'm curious why you brought this to me when the envoy and I don't exactly see eye to eye."

"I'm trying to watch out for your interests. Think of me as a friendly face at court if you like. I don't want the situation to escalate."

"What would you have me do?"

"Well," replied Ashan, "you might start by relocating some of your knights to the countryside. That would, at the very least, show you're willing to accept a diplomatic solution."

"You should inform His Majesty that if he wants us gone from Lidenbach, all he need do is order us to leave. After all, it's his kingdom. In the meantime, my Temple Knights will continue to patrol the city streets."

"The king won't order you out—he hasn't the stomach for it. However, I can't guarantee he won't change his mind in the future. He appears to be more amenable to Lord Corbin's ideas every day. It would not surprise me to see Halvarian warriors on the streets by Midwinter."

"That would be a grave mistake," said Charlaine.

"I agree, yet he won't listen to me anymore."

"Perhaps I should visit the king and try explaining things?"

"That, I fear, would play directly into Lord Corbin's hands. Better to lie low for a while, and give it time for all this to blow over."

"Are you suggesting I ignore the orders of my superiors?"

"What is more important in the long run? Following orders or ensuring the region's stability?"

"My orders are to do all I can to keep the realm safe."

"Then heed my warning," said Ashan.

"What is the princess's view of all of this?"

"Why does it matter? She can never rule."

"Yes, but if I'm not mistaken, her husband will eventually succeed to the Throne."

"I suppose that's true, but I'm afraid he's back in Braunfel, far too distant to have any say on matters here."

"Does he take no interest in matters at court?"

Ashan shrugged. "All I can tell you is that I've yet to see him there."

"Then it appears that will need to change."

His knitted brow revealed his concern. "What are you suggesting?"

"It might be time for me to visit an influential benefactor. Good day to you, Master Ashan, and thank you for bringing this to my attention." She spurred on her horse, easily outdistancing him.

. . .

By noon, Charlaine was on the docks, watching a familiar ship enter the harbour.

"I thought I'd find you here," came a voice from behind her.

"Highness, what are you doing here? I sent word that I would visit you."

"Looking for you. I went to the commandery to see what you wanted, and they told me you were here." She followed Charlaine's gaze. "What are we looking at?"

"The *Barlowe*—a merchant out of Andover."

"And that is?"

"A kingdom south of Reinwick."

"And why, might I ask, is that of interest?"

"The captain is a friend of mine," said Charlaine. "And aboard that vessel is my horse, Stormcloud."

"An interesting name, that. Is she grey?"

"Yes. She's a Calabrian."

"I've heard of those. They say they're fast."

"I can't speak for the entire breed, but Stormcloud is certainly fleet of foot."

"How does a Temple Knight acquire such a mount? I was under the impression they were expensive?"

"They are, but she was a gift. In fact, I had to have permission from my superiors to accept her."

"A fascinating tale, I'm sure, but we seem to be avoiding the fact that you wanted to see me. Might I enquire what that was about?"

"Sorry," said Charlaine. "I shall try to be more direct. Some time ago, we talked about visiting your husband's holdings."

"And now you've decided it's time to follow through on it?"

"Yes, providing that would be acceptable to you, of course."

"How many of you would be going?"

"Myself, my aide, and the *Valiant's* crew."

"You still mean to sail?"

"It would be quicker and give us a splendid introduction to the coastline."

Rebecca smiled. "And it would also remove your ship from Lord Corbin's notice for a while, is that it?"

"The thought had crossed my mind. I also wanted your husband's opinion on several matters."

"You mean the Throne, don't you? Don't look so surprised. I knew it would come to this, eventually."

"Come to what?"

"By virtue of his marriage to me, my husband is next in line for the

Crown. I'm no fool. I know my father is falling under the Halvarian's influence."

"I'm not plotting to overthrow him, if that's what you're implying."

"I know," said Rebecca.

"Then what is it you imagine I'm up to?"

"You're making contingency plans, should things turn out for the worse."

"At the very least, we should look at getting you and your husband out of the kingdom."

"I'm flattered you would consider us that important, but I can't abandon Arnsfeld—it's my home."

"If the empire attacks, you may have no choice."

"We'll cross that bridge when we come to it."

"And does your husband believe the same?"

"He does. Unfortunately, if Halvaria attacks, they're likely to invade our lands first."

"At least we have some time," said Charlaine.

"Why would you say that?"

"Summer is almost over, and the Halvarians will require considerable time to conquer the entire realm. If they intend to invade, it'll likely come in the spring or early next summer, which gives me time to visit Braunfel and assess their probable attack route first-hand."

"A distressing thought but a practical one. Very well. I would be pleased to have you and the *Valiant* visit us. Perhaps you'd care to bring your horse with you?"

"A splendid idea," said Charlaine.

The princess chuckled.

"You find something amusing, Highness?"

"I was wondering what the Halvarians would make of a Temple ship visiting Braunfel."

10

THE JOURNEY
SUMMER 1102 SR

Stormcloud shifted as the ship hit a wave, sending a fine spray of mist drifting across the deck. Charlaine placed her hand on her horse's nose, attempting to calm her.

"She's nervous," said the princess.

"That's to be expected, considering the sea isn't her natural environment."

"But she sailed all the way to Lidenbach, didn't she?"

"She did, but in the *Barlowe's* hold. Here on the *Valiant*, she's out in the open on deck." Charlaine looked at the trees lining the shore. "That's quite a forest."

"Yes, the Brinwald. They say all manner of creatures live there."

Charlaine chuckled.

"You don't take me seriously?"

"My pardon, Highness, but the same thing is said for pretty much every forest in the Petty Kingdoms."

"That doesn't mean it's not true. Besides, it gives the place an air of mystery."

"It is a very thick forest," said Charlaine. "I can't see more than ten paces into it."

"The Brinwald borders Braunfel on the north. My husband goes hunting there sometimes."

"What does he hunt?"

"Deer, mostly, but occasionally boar. He says the place is like a maze."

"That being the case, it's an unlikely spot for the Halvarians to attack. Is the whole border like that?"

"It is, except for a clear stretch west of our lands."

"How much of a stretch are we talking about?"

"I'm not sure, maybe ten or fifteen miles? Why? What are you thinking?"

"Sorry. I'm assessing the terrain as a possible invasion route. Tell me, what lies to the south of Braunfel?"

"On the border? More heavy woods until you get to Kronberg, and then you have a marsh to deal with."

"And does that extend to the southern border of Arnsfeld?"

"No, but it runs for some twenty miles or so. I believe beyond that is more heavy forest."

"That makes Braunfel of strategic import."

"So my husband is fond of telling me."

"Speaking of your husband, what can we expect upon our arrival? Will he welcome us?"

"We get so few visitors these days. I'm sure he'll be most pleasant."

"And what does he make of your father's rule?"

"He is in no hurry to become king, if that's what you're asking."

"Does he keep up to date on the kingdom's politics?"

"Ordinarily, yes," said Rebecca, "but he's been too busy this year to leave Braunfel. It's these Halvarian incursions that are causing the problem. Handrik thinks they're up to something."

"And what do you think?"

"I would tend to agree. They never entered our territory before the Cunars left."

"Wait a moment," said Charlaine. "You mentioned them before. Just how many Temple Knights were stationed there?"

"I'm not sure. How many fit into a commandery?"

"A company of fifty could easily fit, but the last time you mentioned them, you indicated they were a detachment; I thought there were only ten or so."

"I assumed you already knew all about them. You're both fighting orders."

"Unfortunately, no. Temple Knights don't generally share information of that nature between orders, and theirs, in particular, has been very secretive of late."

"Weren't they always thus?"

"I suppose they were," said Charlaine, "but something feels different about all of this."

"You suspect treachery?"

"I won't speak ill of a fellow order, but it wouldn't surprise me if Halvaria sought to take advantage of their absence."

"Do you believe their withdrawal will lead to war?"

"Halvaria has a history of expansion using any means at their disposal."

"But they're huge, aren't they? Couldn't they just cross the border in overwhelming numbers?"

"They'd like you to think that," said Charlaine, "but the truth is, a small, determined garrison at a strategic position could hold them off for weeks."

"Are you suggesting a siege is in our future?"

"Most likely. Assuming, of course, you have a keep."

"We do, though it's not as grand as the Royal Castle in Lidenbach. As to whether it could withstand a siege, that would be my husband's area of expertise. He'd be delighted to discuss it in great detail."

Danica approached as the two of them chatted.

"Problem?" asked Charlaine.

"I'm not sure. The lookout reports a ship at the mouth of the Stillwater."

"Let me guess—it's Halvarian."

"It is. A provincial, by the look of it."

"Provincial?" said Rebecca.

"Yes," replied Charlaine. "Provincial ships are largely crewed by men from the conquered regions. As such, they are relatively lightly armed and of poorer quality."

"As opposed to?"

"Their elite, or imperial ships, as we like to call them. The fighting complement wears heavier armour and has better training, but they seldom venture ashore."

"And their armies?"

"They are a mix of both provincial and imperial troops. At least that's what we've heard."

"Heard from whom?" asked Rebecca.

"We've taken a few Halvarian prisoners over the years, mostly provincials."

"What did you do with them?"

"We set some free; of those, almost a third elected to join our cause. Of course, there were also the fanatics, and there was little we could do to sway their opinions. Most of those remain prisoners to this day."

"What do you want us to do with this ship?" asked Danica.

"What would you recommend?"

"We can't fight them. We're not at war, and they're not engaged in piracy. That leaves us only two options: ignore them or acknowledge their existence."

"That's an excellent idea," said Charlaine. "Perhaps we can wrangle an invitation to go aboard their ship. It might be handy to get an idea of what they're doing here."

"Very well. I'll have us brought alongside."

The *Dominator* proved to be similar in design to the smaller ships captured at Temple Bay. Of course, smaller was a relative term, for it was still longer than the *Valiant* by half, with a stern castle from which archers could ply their trade, although there were only two on duty.

The *Valiant* slowed, reducing sail as it floated into position some fifty yards from the Halvarian vessel.

"Greetings!" called out Danica. "We are the Temple Ship *Valiant*, out of Korvoran."

A man with an ill-trimmed beard appeared at the railing. "We are the Halvarian Warship *Dominator*, Captain Douglas commanding."

"May we come aboard to pay our respects?"

"You want to do what?"

"Pay our respects. Come now, Captain. We are not at war, are we?"

"No, we are not."

"Then it behooves us to act in a civilized manner, don't you think?"

"I suppose it does. Very well, you may come aboard."

"Prepare the boat," ordered Danica. The crew leaped into action, and before long, she, Charlaine, and Princess Rebecca sat in the ship's boat on their way to the Halvarian warship.

A sailor threw a rope ladder over the side to assist in boarding, and all three were soon on the deck.

"Captain Douglas," said Danica, "I am pleased to present to you, Her Highness, Princess Rebecca of Arnsfeld, and Temple Commander Charlaine deShandria."

The man bowed. "Good day, Highness, Commander. I had no idea we would be in such august company. May I offer you ladies something to drink?" He snapped his fingers, and a servant brought forth a tray. When they hesitated, he continued, "I promise you there is no attempt here to poison you. As you said earlier, Admiral Meer, we are not at war."

"I never told you my name."

"True, but the *Valiant* is well-known to us, as is the admiral behind the Temple Fleet. Though, admittedly, I expected someone older."

"She gets that a lot," said Charlaine as she glanced around. "This is a fine ship you have here, Captain. Have you commanded her for long?"

"Long enough to dread this assignment."

"Which is?"

"Merely to report on the comings and goings on the Stillwater."

"You not going to try to stop us from going upriver?"

"Now, why would I do that? Are we not all happy mariners sharing a love for the sea?"

Rebecca took hold of a cup and tasted its contents. "My congratulations," she said. "This is a fine vintage."

"I'm glad you like it. I brought it from home."

"Which is?" asked Danica.

"Geishafen."

"I'm not familiar with it."

"It's a fishing village on the empire's northern coast."

"You were a fisherman?"

"My parents were. I always aspired to greater things." He opened his mouth to say more, but the door to the aft cabin was flung open, and a man in black came onto the deck.

"What is this?" the fellow demanded.

Captain Douglas stiffened. "We have guests, Your Grace. May I present Her Highness, Princess Rebecca of Arnsfeld?"

"And you are?" she replied.

"Lord Aramar." A frown creased the corner of his lips. "And who are these two Temple Knights?"

"Temple Commander Charlaine deShandria and Admiral Danica Meer, Your Grace."

Lord Aramar moved closer. "Your names are familiar to me, but I hardly think that warrants an invitation to come aboard this ship. See them off, Captain, or I'll ensure this is the last ship you ever command." He wandered aft, not even deigning to wait for a response.

The captain bowed stiffly, even though his superior was no longer watching. "Of course, Your Grace." He turned to face his guests. "My apologies, Your Highness, but it appears the time for pleasantries is at an end."

"I trust there will be no impediment to our journey upriver?" asked Danica.

"Not today, no."

"Then I bid you a good day, Captain. May the wind be ever at your back."

"I would wish you the same, Admiral, but I fear my superior would disagree with such sentiment."

"I understand completely."

They made their way over the side of the ship and were soon heading back to the *Valiant*.

"What did you make of that?" asked Danica.

"We've seen that type of person before," said Charlaine.

"I'm not sure I understand," said the princess.

"Lord Aramar is someone of great import, enough that he expects the captain to follow his orders."

"You mean a noble?"

"Yes, or whatever passes for one in Halvaria. Possibly a mage, for we know they employ them on some of their ships."

"Or," added Danica, "he could be the equivalent of a governor, a member of their government charged with overseeing operations at sea."

"Either way, he bears remembering."

"And the ship?" asked Rebecca. "Is it a threat to us?"

"Not at present, but if things go awry, we could find ourselves facing off against the *Dominator* at sea."

"Let's hope it doesn't come to that just yet," said Danica. "I don't much fancy the idea of fighting her on our return. There's very little room to manoeuvre at the mouth of the river."

Before long, they were back aboard *Valiant*, and the crew busied themselves, getting ready to sail upriver.

Charlaine watched the *Dominator* as the Temple ship got underway. Her eyes met those of Captain Douglas, and they both nodded, an acknowledgement that, eventually, they would be forced into battle.

The Stillwater was aptly named for this far north, for the river was wide with a slow current. The riverbanks were hidden by trees whose roots stretched out into the water, their thick underbrush obscuring any further observation.

Charlaine stared at them, not due to an interest in nature but a curiosity about how easy or difficult it would be to traverse the terrain with an army. The more she stared, the more convinced she became that such a route would prove disastrous to those attempting it.

Danica joined her. "Am I interrupting?"

"Not at all. Why? Something on your mind?"

"According to the princess, Braunfel is only around twenty miles upriver. We'll be there well before nightfall at the rate we're sailing."

"And what will we find once we arrive?"

"A dock to tie up on, if that's what you're worried about. Apparently, riverboats sometimes stop by with goods."

Charlaine looked towards the bow. "How deep would you say the water is here?"

"Deep enough for easy passage. Even one of those Halvarian ships could navigate this, although I have no idea how far south they could get."

"I was thinking more from the point of view of someone ashore."

"You mean could footmen cross here? They could build rafts, but it's far too deep for a horse to wade across."

"What if they brought warships upriver to carry their men across?"

"I doubt they'd do that," said Danica. "There's no room to manoeuvre here. One little mistake, and they'd be colliding with each other. Mind you, it might not be as bad farther upstream, but I can think of better ways for them to use their fleet."

"What would you do, assuming you were them?"

"The first thing I'd do is blockade Lidenbach, preventing the king from using ships to send help. Of course, I'd also send patrols to seek out any Temple ships and destroy them before they could interfere."

"Anything else?"

"That depends on how many vessels we're talking about. We have no idea how large their fleet is, but if you remember, they managed seven ships back in Reinwick. Presumably, they'd have more at their disposal here so close to home."

"So, your best guess would be?"

"Twenty, maybe even thirty?"

"Not what I was hoping to hear," said Charlaine. "How many of those you believe would be provincial?"

"Based on what we've learned so far, about two-thirds. Any way you look at it, we're vastly outnumbered, even if we brought up the rest of the fleet. Of course, the longer we wait, the closer we get to completing the construction of more ships, but I could say the same for the enemy."

"How many do you have in the works?"

"*Valour* is to be completed by early next year. Beyond that, there are three more warships like the *Furious*, but we've been copying the Halvarian designs plank by plank, which is a time-consuming process. What we should be doing is designing our own."

"Do we have the expertise for that?"

"We will. Every ship we launch builds on our knowledge, and we have some gifted shipbuilders. The *Vanguard* is proof of that. I just don't know if we're ready to design larger vessels on our own yet."

A movement in the water caught Charlaine's attention. "What was that?"

Danica leaned over the railing, but the only thing visible was a series of waves. "Whatever it was, it dove. What did it look like?"

"I don't know—the water was muddy, so I only saw a dark shape beneath the surface."

"How big?"

"Bigger than a horse."

"I suppose it could've been a porpoise," offered Danica, "but if that were the case, it would break the surface to breathe."

"Could it be a small whale?"

"In a river? I doubt it."

The princess approached. "What are you two looking at?"

"You tell us," said Danica. "Charlaine saw something large beneath the water. Is there anything in these waters like that?"

Rebecca hesitated before answering, "It was probably just an old log."

"Swimming against the current?" said Charlaine. Stormcloud reared up, fear in her eyes. "Something's got her spooked." She moved closer, attempting to soothe her horse.

The *Valiant* shifted, and then a shudder ran across the deck a moment later.

"We've hit something," said Danica, "or something struck us."

"Over here," called out Vivian.

Danica and Rebecca ran to the starboard side just in time to see a crest break the water's surface.

"A river serpent," said the princess.

"Quiet, everyone," called out Danica.

The crest paralleled the *Valiant* for a moment before sinking once more. Everyone's nerves were on edge as the ship kept moving, born along by the wind, but another scrape came along the portside, and then they slowed.

"Crossbows," said Danica, her voice calm. "Load and prepare to loose on my command."

The Temple Knights armed themselves with crossbows, drawing back the loaded bolts. Once ready, they stood amidships, awaiting their admiral's command.

Portside, forward of the mast, a dragon-like head with a long snout and rows of razor-sharp teeth rose out of the water, biting down on the *Valiant's* railing, shattering wood and sending splinters everywhere.

"Loose!" ordered Danica.

Six bolts flew forth, with one sticking into what appeared to be an ear, hanging like some macabre piece of jewellery. The only other one to hit struck the creature in the mouth, sinking into the serpent's fleshy tongue.

It let out a bellow before pulling back and submerging under the water while the knights dutifully reloaded and waited. Time seemed to halt as everyone stood there. Charlaine's heart pounded, and Stormcloud was close to utter panic. She talked to the horse in Calabrian, trying to calm her down.

Danica moved aft, staring at their wake. "What do you see?" she asked the man at the tiller.

The fellow looked behind them. "Ripples," he replied.

"I think it's gone." She turned to the others. "Who hit that thing in the mouth?"

"I did," said Sister Zivka.

"Good work. And to think you used to be one of our worst archers!" She noticed Charlaine stroking her mount. "How's Stormcloud?"

"Nervous, but she's calming. How much farther to the dock, do you think?"

"Some distance yet," said Rebecca, "but once we arrive, it's only a short walk from there to the keep."

"I shouldn't like to come across one of those again," said Danica. "I shudder to think what it could do to men trying to cross the river."

"That could work to our advantage," said Charlaine.

"How? It's not as if we can control it." Danica turned to Rebecca. "You knew what it was. Why didn't you warn us?"

"I've heard of it attacking small boats, but never something as large as the *Valiant*!"

"How many of those things are there?"

"Only one, so far as I know. Admittedly, until now, I'd never seen it myself, but the villagers talk of it from time to time."

"You should have said something."

"I honestly thought it would ignore us. And even if I had told you there was a river serpent in these waters, would you have believed me?"

"She makes a good point," said Charlaine. "And we haven't seen a sea-unicorn as you have."

"It wasn't a unicorn," said Danica. "It was more like a porpoise or maybe a small whale with a horn on it."

"A horn longer than a spear, according to your account."

"Let's get back to the matter at hand, shall we? Have any other ships come across that thing?"

"I've never heard of it attacking anything larger than a rowboat. It appears to be getting more brazen."

"What are you thinking?" asked Charlaine.

"That we must be extra careful returning to the sea," said Danica. "The last thing I want to do is run across that again." Danica looked at the railing. "We'll have to repair that. I don't suppose there's a carpenter in that town of yours, Princess?"

11

BRAUNFEL

SUMMER 1102 SR

The dock consisted of little more than a wooden walkway extending into the water. The *Valiant* eased up, tying off on its port side against the beams before dropping its boarding ramp to facilitate the unloading of Stormcloud.

"I'm still not sure why you chose to bring her," said Danica. "It's not as if she enjoyed the trip."

"True," said Charlaine, "but I'll be riding back to Lidenbach."

"You're not coming with us?"

"No. I need to assess the land in these parts. If the empire is determined to invade, the most direct route will be from here to the capital. I'd prefer to see the terrain now rather than worry about it later."

"You mean to pick out a place of battle," said Danica.

"Likely several. Somewhere that we can use their numbers against them. You and I both know that when they come, it'll be a large army."

"And what of the keep?"

Charlaine looked at the distant structure sitting atop a small rise to the northeast, giving it a commanding view of the town. "That depends on how defensible it is."

"It looks pretty solid from here."

"No doubt, but we must also consider the quantity and quality of Lord Handrik's men."

"They won't run," said the princess as she moved up beside them. "Sorry, I couldn't help but overhear. My husband's men won't abandon the town; their families are here."

"Tell me," said Charlaine, "and be honest. Is that keep large enough to house the entire population of Braunfel?"

"No. Nor store enough food for them if it came to a siege."

"As I thought. What of the land to the east?"

"Flat, for the most part, ideal for farming."

"I'm assuming there's a road leading to Lidenbach?"

"There is, and it runs beside the keep's walls."

"Good," said Charlaine. "That makes it harder for someone to use, should a siege develop."

"You speak as if they've already invaded."

"In a sense, they have. Look." She pointed towards the far end of the dock, where a pair of men watched them unloading her horse. "Recognize those surcoats?"

"A dragon coiled around a tree," said Danica.

"Halvarians," said Rebecca. "They're acting like we're already part of their empire."

"Surely your husband could force them to leave?"

"And go against the king's wishes?"

"What do you think?"

"Before I spoke to you, I didn't usually concern myself with politics; that was more my husband's responsibility."

"And the baron?"

"His oath constrains him to uphold my father's commands. You, on the other hand, are not bound in service to him."

Charlaine chuckled. "So, you're proposing we Temple Knights urge these people to leave?"

The princess smiled shyly. "I could never suggest such a thing, not officially, at least."

"What about you, Danica?"

"Those men wear the dark green and white of imperials rather than provincials."

"That makes sense. They couldn't trust their second-tier warriors not to desert."

"True, but it also means they're less likely to be easily intimidated."

"We'll have to see about that. In any case, we must be off to pay our respects to the baron."

"Hopefully," said Rebecca, "he won't be too upset with our unexpected arrival."

"I thought you said he'd be pleased to see us?"

"I did, but your arrival here will still be something of a surprise."

"A good one, I hope?"

"That largely depends on what has transpired since I left for the capital."

Vivian led Stormcloud over to them, passing the reins to Charlaine. "She's skittish," the sister warned.

"The same could be said for everyone here." Charlaine took the reins, leading her mount across the boarding plank, all the while humming.

"What's that tune?" asked the princess.

Danica smiled. "It's a Calabrian lullaby."

"And that soothes the horse?"

"See for yourself."

They watched as Stormcloud crossed the plank onto the dock, her horseshoes clattering against the wood. The two Halvarians watched closely, moving aside as Charlaine passed by them.

"Gentlemen," she said, nodding at them.

Danica shook her head. "She's always so polite."

"And you're not?" replied Rebecca.

The admiral grinned. "I'm not in the habit of meeting Halvarians on the street. Anytime I've seen them, they were aboard an enemy vessel, trying to kill me."

"Is that why you and Charlaine are both wearing your armour?"

"One should never take chances when in the presence of your enemies."

"You surprise me. You make it sound like they are your sworn enemies."

"In a sense, they are," said Danica, "but I'll keep things civil for your sake. Let's hope these two do the same."

They walked past the Halvarians, ignoring them, while Charlaine was already up the street, walking Stormcloud back and forth to let her acclimatize to being on land once again.

Their presence drew considerable attention from the townsfolk, many of whom stopped what they were doing to take in the sight of the Temple Knights.

"You mentioned there used to be a Cunar detachment here," said Charlaine. "Where does it lie?"

"To the east, on the outskirts of the town."

"We shall have to visit it. Did they slight it by chance?"

"Slight it?"

"Yes, intentionally damage it when they left."

"Not that I know of. They locked it up, but their captain seemed to be under the impression their absence would only be temporary."

"And was this before or after they abandoned the capital?"

"Before, by several weeks at least. Why? Is that important?"

"I want to be clear about the proper sequence of events."

They passed by a larger building with a slate roof.

"The Skrill," said Danica. "What a strange name for a tavern."

"It's the local name for the water serpent," explained Rebecca. "Legend has it that it's the physical embodiment of Akosia, and during the full moon, she takes on her Human form and wanders the land in search of the unfaithful."

"Fascinating."

"I suppose that means you and your fellow sisters should take care; there's a full moon in two days."

"I'm not worried," said Danica. "We might be followers of Saint Agnes, but a Sacred Mother of Akosia blessed the *Valiant*."

"You surprise me. The Cunars would have thought that blasphemous."

"Just one of the many differences between our orders."

"Yes," added Charlaine. "We like to live in harmony with our charges, not suppress their beliefs."

"Do your superiors know you do that?"

"Of course. Does that surprise you?"

"I suppose it shouldn't," said Rebecca, "but I've been around the Cunars for so long, their beliefs just naturally started rubbing off on me."

"You should consider yourself lucky. Normally, they don't associate with women unless they're at court."

"I just happened to be present whenever they visited."

They began climbing the hill towards the keep. The onlookers soon lost interest and returned to their own affairs.

"What do you think of the keep?" asked Rebecca.

"I've seen one very similar back in Verfeld," replied Charlaine. "Square keeps like this are the most common type in the Petty Kingdoms. It has the advantage of offering a decent amount of protection while not being overly expensive. Of course, it's all relative; a keep of any kind is still costly to build."

The door atop the high set of stairs opened, and a guard exited the building.

"Highness," he called out as he descended. "We didn't expect you back until the autumn."

"It is autumn," said the princess, "or it will be shortly. Is Lord Handrik at home?"

"He was in the courtyard, Highness, but I believe he's gone into the great hall for a meal."

"Courtyard?" said Charlaine. "Now, that's unexpected. I thought this keep a simple square."

"It's built around a central courtyard, much like your commanderies, though on a smaller scale."

"Shall I take the horse?" offered the guard.

"Yes," said Charlaine. "Thank you."

She handed over Stormcloud's reins.

"Come," said Rebecca. "Let's go and meet my husband, shall we?"

She rushed up the steps, leaving the Temple Knights behind.

"Ah," said Danica. "The passion of youth. I remember it well."

"You make it sound like you're ancient," said Charlaine. "She's the same age as you or close enough to it. Come on, let's show this woman we still have some life left in us."

They took the stairs two at a time, quickly catching up.

"This is the entrance," said Rebecca. "There's a portcullis above that can be dropped if attacked, along with a couple of murder holes."

They walked through a cobblestone corridor that led into a courtyard, around which was the bulk of the keep itself.

"You can't enter the keep directly from the front door," explained Rebecca. "You must go through here first, creating a trap for would-be attackers, concentrating them in one place and making them easy prey for archers. At least that's how Handrik explained it to me."

"And how many archers are there?"

"You know, I'm not entirely sure."

They halted before an elaborately carved wooden door at the far end of the courtyard.

"Beyond this lies the great hall," said the princess, pushing open the door to reveal a room taking up most of the keep's eastern end. A long table stretched down the length of the room, culminating at a well-padded chair upon which sat a dark-haired man, sporting a well-trimmed beard and moustache, picking away at a plate of food. Upon hearing them enter, he looked up, a smile creasing his features.

"Ah," he said, "you're back, and it looks like you brought company!"

"I have indeed, my lord. Allow me to introduce Temple Commander Charlaine deShandria, and Temple Captain Danica Meer, Admiral of the Northern Fleet. Ladies, this is my husband, Lord Handrik Sommer, Baron of Braunfel."

"Pleased to meet you, my lord," said Charlaine. "I hope our arrival is not an inconvenience to you?"

"Not at all. I presume you came by boat?"

"Yes, aboard the Temple Ship *Valiant*. How did you know?"

"The walls of this keep offer a superb view of the river, and my soldiers are good at keeping me apprised of anything of note. Won't you join me?" He swept his hand, indicating the other seats.

"Most assuredly."

Rebecca took a seat on her husband's right, while Charlaine sat opposite, with Danica at her side.

"I'm surprised to see you here," said the baron. "I didn't think the Church held any interest in us of late."

"I invited them," said Rebecca.

"Yes," said Charlaine. "We're interested in what the Halvarians are up to. We thought it worth investigating in person."

"Did you bring knights with you?"

"Only six, and they'll need to remain on board the *Valiant*."

"Could you perhaps convince the Cunars to return? Saints know we could certainly use them."

"I'm afraid that's very unlikely, all things considered. I understand you used to entertain them here in the keep."

"I did. Captain Marcellus was a wonderful fellow. He dined with me at least once a week. Say, you don't know him, do you? I would so much like to find out how he's fared since leaving."

"I can't say I've had the pleasure."

"A pity. You would've liked him, I'm sure."

"What if I were to take over the commandery?"

"You're more than welcome to it," said the baron, "but I hardly think six sister knights will worry the Halvarians. Now, if they were Cunars, that might be another matter."

"Would it surprise you to know we've fought the Halvarians before?"

"Have you?" He set down the chicken leg he'd been about to bite into. "You must tell me more."

"Both Captain Danica and I have had numerous skirmishes with them, along with two fleet engagements and a land battle."

"And the outcome of these conflicts?"

"We were victorious in each instance," said Danica. "Temple Commander Charlaine is one of our most distinguished leaders and possibly the most experienced."

"She's being modest," said Charlaine. "She's downplaying the fleet's role, but she has a point. We know the Halvarians and what they're capable of."

"I hate to admit it, especially in the presence of my wife, but perhaps we might be better off avoiding war and capitulating. Does it really matter who sits on the throne so long as our lands prosper?"

"I've seen for myself the effects of a Halvarian occupation. They will move in, seizing anything of value and place their own people in this keep. And as for your townsfolk, they'll force many of them into service in their provincial companies, then immediately march them off to war."

"A dire prospect, but our losses could be even worse if we choose to fight them. What hope have we against such a colossus?"

"That does not mean we meekly surrender!" said Rebecca.

"You must forgive my wife's outburst," said the baron, "but she is naïve, and does not understand the ways of the world."

"You underestimate her potential," said Charlaine. "She's made an excellent point. Surrendering to the empire will do nothing to guarantee your safety, only serve to hasten the Halvarian's campaign to conquer the Petty Kingdoms."

"Which ones?"

"All of them, eventually."

"My garrison consists of less than one hundred men, many past their prime."

"Even the mightiest of armies have their weaknesses, and this keep is one of them."

"Preposterous."

"Is it? The only place to cross the river is here, at Braunfel, and to get to the capital, they must march right past this very structure. Any delay your men could cause would gain valuable time for the king to organize a defence."

"We are a small kingdom, Commander, with few troops. I doubt His Majesty could scrape together anywhere near enough men to stop Halvaria."

"I know they outnumber us, but if everyone thought as you, the entire Continent would be under their thumb."

"We must do our part," urged Rebecca.

"Even if it means our ruin?" replied Handrik.

"Even then."

He pushed away his plate. "Very well. I shall take measures to hamper any invasion to the best of my abilities, but in return, I want your assurance you will keep the princess safe."

"If war should come, I will remain with you," insisted Rebecca.

"No, you won't," said the baron. "I can't give this my full concentration if I'm worried about your safety. You're the king's daughter, and your place is in the capital."

"I might remind you we're not at war," said Charlaine. "And there's still a very real possibility we could avert it altogether."

"I'm listening. How would we proceed?"

"The first thing I'd like to do is examine the Cunar commandery."

"I'm afraid it's locked, and I don't have the key."

"Surely there's a locksmith in town? Or at least someone who could force the door?"

"There is, but shouldn't you seek keys through your formal chain of command?"

"We haven't the time," said Charlaine. "A request of that nature would have to go all the way to the Antonine, which would take months. Right now, it stands empty. It only seems right that it be used for its intended purpose."

"Are you suggesting you have enough knights to fill it?"

"I will."

"And where would these knights come from?"

"From my order, though I cannot predict when they might arrive."

"And until then?"

"I shall send a half company from Lidenbach to prepare it for use."

The baron nodded. "A clever tactic, but a dangerous one. The king will surely not look kindly upon your interference."

"Then let's not tell him of it. Naturally, he'll learn in due course, but by then, I hope he's seen the threat the Halvarians pose."

"I would not pin all my hopes on that if I were you," said Rebecca.

"There is little choice," said Charlaine. "If we do not act decisively, we lose what little chance there is of stopping them. Naturally, the lord of these lands must invite us to send a garrison."

"You have it," said Lord Handrik, rubbing his hands together. "Now, what else can I do to put a burr under their saddle?"

"What can you tell me of your garrison here?"

"I maintain one company of footmen and one of archers, but admittedly both are under strength."

"I suggest you change that, if possible, and the sooner, the better."

"When do you estimate the empire will make its move?"

"Next spring, at the earliest, possibly even later."

"Their fleet can give us a better idea," offered Danica.

"What makes you say that?" replied the baron.

"Any attack in Arnsfeld could easily be held up here in Braunfel. They'll likely land a large force farther up the coast to get around that. They might even assault the capital directly if they can get enough ships together, but if I were them, I'd land on the coast. It's easier to assemble the army there before they fight than to fight their way ashore in Lidenbach."

"And how will we know when they're ready?"

"I'll have ships watching their ports," said Danica. "If a large fleet sails, we'll be aware of it long before it threatens the capital."

"It's good that someone is looking out for us. What else can we do here to prepare?"

"Do you have a militia?"

"No."

"Then you might want to take some steps to create one. I suggest you gather all eligible men once a month and instruct them in the use of the spear or bow. They won't stand against Halvarian regulars but could at least harass their supply lines once they cross the river."

"I shall issue orders at once to that effect."

"Good. I'd also like your blessing to deal with the Halvarians in town."

"Deal with them, how?"

She smiled. "I'll ask them to leave in a most professional and polite manner."

"And if they don't?"

"Then my Temple Knights will be more persuasive."

12

CONFRONTATION
SUMMER 1102 SR

That night, at the princess's insistence, they stayed at the keep, but years of conditioning as Temple Knights led both Charlaine and Danica to rise early.

With no duties to attend to, they strolled through the town, taking in its sights. Many local shopkeepers were just opening their places of business, but two knights wandering around in their plate armour was enough to pique their interest.

Charlaine had intended to make their way to the *Valiant*, for she believed any Halvarians in town would be watching the Temple ship. However, the townsfolk's interest delayed their trip to the docks considerably, and it was mid-morning by the time the dock came into view. Sure enough, the same two men who'd watched them disembark had returned. Charlaine walked right up to them, her approach noted by the older of the pair.

"Sister Charlaine, isn't it?" he asked.

"Yes. And you are?"

He bowed his head slightly. "Captain Nargrun, and this is my aide, Hadmar. Is there something I can do for you?"

"Indeed, there is," said Charlaine. "I would very much like to know why you're here in Braunfel. In case you're wondering, the Halvarian border is over there." She pointed across the river.

"So it is," he replied, "but we are here seeking some deserters. I'm sure you understand how important it is to keep discipline in one's army?"

"Temple Knights do not abandon their posts."

He smiled politely, but somehow it looked smug. "Yet isn't that exactly what the Cunars did?"

"I'm not here to debate the actions of a fellow order."

"Oh? Then why are you here?"

"To inform you that you have until nightfall to return to your side of the river."

"Or what?"

"My knights will physically remove you."

"You wouldn't dare!"

"You appear to be under the misconception that I work for King Stefan," said Charlaine. "Let me set the record straight. I am a Temple Knight. As such, I owe allegiance only to my superiors."

"Of that, I am keenly aware," said Nargrun. "But you must also weigh your decisions carefully or risk being banished from the kingdom. Now, be on your way before I make an official protest to His Majesty."

"I've given you fair warning, but perhaps you didn't understand. The presence of you two, or any other Halvarians, for that matter, is no longer tolerated here in Braunfel. If you're not gone by the time the sun sets, I shall order my knights to arrest the pair of you."

"You're bluffing. It's all a lie to frighten us off."

"Temple Knights don't lie."

He stared back a moment, his eyes flicking from Charlaine to Danica. "Very well," he said. "We'll leave, but sooner or later, you'll go back to Lidenbach, we'll simply return."

"You're welcome to try," said Charlaine, "but you'll need to do so quickly. Upon my return to the capital, I shall send a permanent garrison here."

His face betrayed his shock.

"Shall we ferry you across the river now?" offered Danica.

"It will be a cold day in the Underworld before we accept the charity of a Temple Knight. We have our own boat."

"Then I suggest you get aboard it with all haste."

"Commander Charlaine gave us till nightfall."

"She did, but the river is my domain, and if I find your boat on this side of the river after midday, I shall be forced to impound it."

"You wouldn't dare!"

Danica looked at her companion. "He seems to like that expression."

"I was going to give you the rest of the day," said Charlaine, "but the admiral has made an excellent point. Now, shall you go down to your boat peacefully, or do we take you there by force?"

"We're going," he grumbled, taking one last look at the *Valiant* before spitting on the ground, the sneer on his face revealing his revulsion. They then walked down the dock to where they'd tied up their small skiff.

"Keep an eye out for the skrill," called out Danica.

Charlaine chuckled. "Was that entirely necessary?"

"No," she replied, "but it was immensely satisfying."

That afternoon, they visited the Cunar commandery, along with the baron and a locksmith. It took only a moment to break the lock before they entered and began their inspection.

"You know," said the baron, "in all the time they were here, this is the first I've set foot in the place."

"The layout of commanderies is always the same," explained Charlaine. "The captain's office will be on the top floor, facing west."

They made their way down the hallway. "You'll note each section has its own door," she continued. "In the event of a breach, they would all be closed, making it easier to defend the place."

"And has a commandery ever been attacked?"

"Not that I'm aware, at least not since we adopted this particular design."

"They weren't always like this?"

"No," said Charlaine. "Not at all. After the disaster of Herani, all the orders underwent a reorganization."

"When was this?"

"In the mid-seven-forties. This design followed shortly thereafter."

"And they're the same everywhere?"

"They're supposed to be, but there are smaller regions, like our outpost in Ilea, where a building this size would be too expensive to justify."

"Why is that?"

"They designed the commanderies to house an entire company, but several locations maintain smaller garrisons. In such cases, they tend to use available buildings in the region."

"And are your companies the same size as the Cunars?"

"Yes, fifty Temple Knights, though the number is seldom exact. A company is considered at full strength if it numbers between forty and fifty-five."

"And if it has more?"

"Then the command is split up into more manageable components. It's rare for that to happen, though."

"Why is that?"

"Simple," said Danica. "There aren't enough women willing to take up arms. However, our brothers, the Cunars, encounter no trouble recruiting knights."

"Well," said the baron, "there is a strong tradition of knighthood in the Petty Kingdom. I've heard they only take trained knights. Is that true?"

"It is," said Charlaine. "The same cannot be said of our order."

"I can well imagine. Outside of your order, I know of no other female knights. That, it seems, is the sole prerogative of men, and I understand why. It takes years of training to become proficient in the sword, and with all due respect, women aren't equipped to do so."

"You do realize you're talking to two women?"

"Of course," said the baron. "But, come now, I meant no offence."

"We train our sister knights to a very high level of proficiency," insisted Charlaine.

"Yes, but compare that to an average knight? How can you possibly hope to compete?"

"If we're talking about individual strength, I would agree with you," said Charlaine, "but all Temple Knights are trained in close-order tactics, something the knights of the Petty Kingdoms dismiss as unnecessary."

"How curious," said the baron. "I never would have thought such training necessary. Is it effective?"

"It proved its worth in Reinwick."

"Fascinating as that is, perhaps we should turn our attention to affairs here, in Braunfel. I assume the commandery will remain empty for the time being?"

"No," said Danica. "I shall leave six sister knights to patrol the streets until we can send replacements."

The baron raised his eyebrows. "But won't that strip the *Valiant* of Temple Knights?"

"It will, but it's only temporary, and there are other ships we can call on. Until then, I suggest your own men patrol the streets. If the Halvarians return, you'll need to keep us informed."

"I will. I promise you. In the meantime, I'll send a few men down to help stock this place. You'll need food and eventually hay for the horses; anything else you can think of?"

"That will be fine, thank you."

"Don't mention it. It's the least I can do."

"Actually," said Danica, "you might consider posting men to watch the river. If the Halvarians intend to return, that's how they'll get here."

"Consider it done."

They finally reached the stairs and made their way to the upper floor.

"This place is huge," said the baron. "The design is deceiving."

"You must remember, the centre of the commandery is a large, open courtyard. As for the rest, take out the stables, the dining hall, and the kitchen, and there's barely enough room for all the knights."

"Is there a smithy?"

"No. We rely on the town for such things."

"Why is that?"

Charlaine chuckled. "If you think women knights are scarce, try to find a female smith willing to join the order."

"Yes, I suppose I never thought of that."

Danica's sudden burst of laughter startled the baron.

"You find that humorous?" he asked.

"My pardon, but you're actually in the presence of one."

"You're a smith?"

"Me? No, I was referring to Temple Commander Charlaine."

"Are you serious?"

"Oh yes, and not just an apprentice—she's a master smith!"

"Remarkable."

"And irrelevant," said Charlaine. "We're here to assess the commandery, not boast of our past. Such things are beneath us."

"Sorry," said Danica. "I suppose I got carried away in the moment. Forgive me."

"Of course. In any case, it's not like I could bear a grudge against you for long."

"Are you two related?" asked the baron. "Sisters, perhaps?"

"Only through our vows. We do consider each other family, however."

"And is that true of all Temple Knights?"

"I can't speak of other orders, but it's often true of our own. Temple Captain Danica and I have served together for seven years and have come to rely on each other's opinions without reservation."

"Fascinating. The Cunars were always so secretive about their order, but it appears you have no qualms speaking of such things."

"Saint Agnes believed in being open and honest with people."

"Some might see that as a weakness."

"True, but appearances can be deceptive. In truth, it's our greatest strength." She noted their progress. "Ah, here's the captain's office."

Danica opened the door, revealing a sparsely decorated room. True to form, a window was behind the desk, though the shutters were closed, allowing only thin streams of light into the room.

"Do you know why this office always faces west?" asked Charlaine.

"I'm afraid I don't," said the baron.

"It's symbolic. It's meant to face the Holy City of Herani."

"But that's to the south, isn't it?"

"It is, but calculating its exact position relative to every commandery would be too difficult. Besides, it's hundreds of miles away, far too distant to be seen. No, it's merely a way of reminding us of our duty."

"Your duty to recapture the place?"

"Precisely."

"And when is that to happen?"

"Likely not in our lifetime," said Charlaine, "but the Church hierarchy still has their mind set on it."

"You don't agree with it?"

"I do, but I feel as though there are more immediate problems to deal with."

"Like Halvaria?"

"Precisely." She threw open the shutters to look over the town. "The view from here is magnificent. I can see the top of *Valiant's* mast."

Danica, who had been examining the room, came to stand beside her. "No sign of any old records, which indicates their withdrawal wasn't hurried."

"Good. That means everything else is likely in its place."

"Well," said the baron, "much as I enjoyed this little tour, I must get back to the keep. I promised you some guards to help with this place, and then I should set some archers to watch the river. I'll leave you to it, shall I?"

"Very well," said Charlaine. "And thank you, my lord. Your help is much appreciated."

The baron's footsteps echoed down the hall as he made his way out.

"Well?" said Danica. "What are you thinking?"

"That my time here is coming to an end. I need to return to Lidenbach."

"So soon? But we only just got here."

"I should like you to remain for another day or two."

"And then?"

"I have orders for you to take to the capital."

"You're still intent on riding back?"

"I am. As I mentioned earlier, I want to get an eye for the terrain in these parts, and the best way to do that is to take the same route as the Halvarians would."

"Be careful. I wouldn't put it past them to try to waylay you on the road."

"I'll make sure to take care."

"Perhaps you should take the orders back yourself."

"Nonsense. The *Valiant* can sail back to Lidenbach long before I get there."

"I thought I might stick around here to keep an eye on things."

"Are you sure?"

"Absolutely. Don't worry. I'll bring her back once your detachment of knights arrives."

"It'll take me three or four days to reach the capital and then just as many days for them to return. Are you positive you want to wait that long?"

"I think it wise, don't you? If nothing else, the presence of the *Valiant* shows the Halvarians our commitment to keeping them at bay."

"You're the admiral. Just try not to start a war."

Danica laughed. "Now you're making my job more difficult." She turned her attention to the desk. "At least it isn't made of shadowbark like your desk back in Lidenbach."

"Yes, that reminds me, I need to see if I can't sell that off. Saints know the coins would be useful."

"Speaking of the capital, when were you thinking of heading out?"

"First thing tomorrow. I, at least, owe the princess another visit."

"My understanding is the road runs along the edge of the Brinwald."

"I'm sure it'll be safe enough. The road's been in place for years. That would hardly be the case if it were under constant threat."

"Are you sure I can't convince you to take a sister knight with you?"

"And how would they keep up—by running? I doubt even the fittest of them could match Stormcloud's pace."

"I'd feel much better if I knew you had someone to watch your back."

"If it makes you any happier, I'll say a prayer to Saint Agnes before I leave."

"That's not much of a promise; you do that every day."

"All right. What if I promise to wear my armour?"

"I could live with that."

"Good," said Charlaine. "Now, let's return to the keep, shall we? There's still a dinner to prepare for."

Princess Rebecca leaned back, her meal concluded. "I'm curious, Commander. How many knights do you expect to station in Arnsfeld?"

"That's difficult to say," said Charlaine. "Ideally, I'd like several hundred, but I doubt the order can afford to spare that many."

"How many do you have now?"

"There are two companies in Lidenbach, but I've been informed more are coming. In addition, as regional commander, I'm also in charge of the garrisons in Burgemont, Angvil, and Rudor."

"And how many are there?"

"According to my records, one company in each. I know that doesn't sound like a lot, but with enough warning, I can assemble them here in Arnsfeld in time to repel any expected attack from Halvaria."

"I doubt that would be enough," said the baron. "We know Halvaria can field a large army. Even with all those Temple Knights, they'd badly outnumber you."

"Surely my father would help?" said Rebecca.

"I'm not so sure. I fear Lord Corbin's influence is strong."

"What of the other barons?" asked Danica. "Could they send help?"

"Possibly," replied Handrik, "but Kronberg is likely the only place close enough to get here in time."

"How far is Kronberg?"

"Forty miles or so to the south. Of course, that's assuming the Halvarians don't attack them as well."

"I doubt that would be likely," said Charlaine. "The terrain in those parts is unfavourable. Nature has given this kingdom natural defences, except in Braunfel. There can be little doubt that when the attack comes, it will be here."

"And the question isn't where," added Danica, "but when. Charlaine thinks next spring, which would be a logical conclusion, but it could come much later, even two years from now."

"Why would they wait?"

"Only the empire could answer that. Suffice it to say, they'll attack when they're confident of victory."

"You believe we will fail?"

"My pardon, my lord. I meant to imply they will be assured of victory in their own minds. Naturally, we will do all within our power to dissuade them of that eventuality."

"And the strategy for that? You talked of holding the keep, but little else."

"My strategy," replied Charlaine, "would be to perform a fighting retreat while you hold on here."

"To what end?"

"The deeper we pull them into the countryside, the farther they'll have to extend their army. We Temple Knights, however, are more flexible in our deployments. Our supply lines will only get shorter as theirs increase."

"You'd still need to fight them eventually, though."

"We would, and that's one of the reasons I want to get to know the area between here and Lidenbach."

"That's interesting," said the baron. "About twenty miles up the road, there's an area where it cuts between two forests. I'm no expert in such things, but I imagine it would be an ideal place to fight."

"Why there?" asked Rebecca.

"If an army lined up there, the woods would secure both flanks, effectively neutralizing their expected numbers."

"I shall be sure to note it," said Charlaine.

"What can we expect from the Halvarians regarding their army?"

"They're organized into cohorts of six hundred men."

"And how many of these cohorts do they possess?"

"It's believed four, at least half of which are provincial troops."

"Four?" said the baron, doing the calculation in his head. "Are you suggesting they'd attack with twenty-four hundred men?"

"Assuming they only send one legion."

"Legion?"

"Yes. Their name for an army."

"There's more than one?"

"The empire's size alone suggests it."

"And who leads these armies of theirs?"

"We don't know. When we fought them in Reinwick, they had several mages, but whether or not they were in charge is anyone's guess. However, I believe we can make a few deductions."

"Such as?"

"An emperor leads them, but there is no record of him commanding any invasions, so we must assume he has subordinates to carry out his orders— let's call them generals. Now, a single person couldn't oversee an army of twenty-four hundred, so there are likely multiple commanders beneath those generals, although I'm only guessing at the titles here. I suspect one for each cohort, but there's no way to be absolutely certain. However, we do know their companies are larger than ours."

"How much larger?"

"A hundred men at full strength."

"Any way you put it, it still looks grim."

"True," said Charlaine, "but if there's one thing we learned fighting the empire, it's that they lack initiative, especially the provincial troops. Their methods are blunt and often rely on overwhelming numbers to achieve their objectives."

"Easy to do when you have such large armies at your disposal."

"They can be beaten, my lord. Our successes have proven that time and again, but I won't lie to you; if they do eventually invade, you should expect the fight of your life."

13

ON THE ROAD
SUMMER 1102 SR

Charlaine was on the road early the following day, leaving the town behind her by first light. The sky remained clear and the sun warm, but the night's chill persisted, reminding her that summer was almost over.

The road was easy to follow, which was helpful, for the land in these parts was flat, with little to serve as landmarks other than trees or the occasional stream. Off to the northwest stood the Brinwald, the thick cover of its canopy plunging the trunks into perpetual darkness.

To the southeast, she could just make out the edge of another forest, and it wasn't long before she came across the area Lord Handrik had spoken of, a relatively narrow pass between the two woods.

The small stream that cut through this would not stop an army but would undoubtedly inconvenience anyone off the road. She slowed as she drew closer, noting someone had built a small bridge here. Although it was little more than a few planks laid across a pair of stout wooden beams, it had evidently sat there for some time, for it was grey with age, worn down by countless wagons and horseshoes.

Up ahead, the road curved around an old structure, most likely the ruins of a farm, but she soon realized it was nothing of the sort. Someone had taken great pains to build a fence around a strange rock jutting from the ground.

As she followed the road around it, she noted it wasn't one rock, but three, arranged to form a doorway of sorts. She halted, not quite believing her eyes. Two vertical stones, with a third laid across the top—she'd seen this type of thing before, back in Verfeld.

The sight of it reminded her of Ludwig. He'd claimed the stones were

Therengian, but this part of the Continent was far from the area that ancient kingdom had once dominated. Could the history of that dead realm be wrong, or were these stones merely evidence of something far older?

She dismounted, leading Stormcloud closer for a better look. The fence was more decorative than functional, for it would do naught to keep animals at bay, being little more than long poles sitting in x-shaped uprights. The fence, if that's what it could even be called, was old, but there was evidence someone had taken care to repair it in places, the new sections not aged like the rest.

Off to her right, a stone struck the fence, and she turned to see a youth of eleven or twelve years old with long, unkempt hair, standing near the woods.

"Hello, there," she called out.

He froze.

"I mean you no harm," she continued. "My name is Sister Charlaine."

"Are you a Temple Knight?" The look of fear on his face was easy to spot.

"I am."

"But you're a woman."

"Yes. I serve the Temple Knights of Saint Agnes. Who are you?"

"Luca," the lad replied.

"Do you live around here?"

He nodded. "At my grandmother's house, over there." He pointed at the trees to the south.

"What is this place?"

The lad tentatively approached, gaining courage. "An ancient shrine dedicated to the old Gods." He suddenly paled as if he'd said something he wasn't supposed to. "Not that anybody uses it anymore."

"The fence would indicate otherwise," said Charlaine. "Does your grandmother tend this place?"

"She does. She says it's important to remember our past."

"She sounds like a wise woman."

"Do you want to meet her?"

"I'd like that very much. Will you take me to her?"

"You promise you won't hurt her?"

"Why would I?"

"Because that's what Temple Knights do."

"Who told you that?" asked Charlaine.

"I've seen it myself."

"These Temple Knights didn't happen to wear grey surcoats, did they?"

He nodded.

"Those were Temple Knights of Saint Cunar. They won't trouble you anymore."

"How do you know that?"

"They left," said Charlaine. "My order has come to take their place and protect the people of this land."

"And will you destroy the shrines like they did?"

"We live in harmony with the ancient religion, not in opposition to it."

He stared at her a moment before finally nodding. "Follow me, and I'll take you to my grandmother." He set off at a brisk pace, not bothering to check if she followed.

Charlaine followed in his wake, leading Stormcloud on foot. They soon found themselves amongst the trees to the south, heading down a narrow pathway. After a few dozen paces, a small hut came into view, and off to one side, an old woman looked up from where she tended to a garden.

"What have we here?" she called out.

"Greetings. My name is Charlaine deShandria, a Temple Knight of Saint Agnes."

"So I see from your surcoat. What is your business here?"

"I was curious about the standing stones to the north."

"Why? So you can destroy them?"

"I assure you that is not my intention."

The old woman moved closer. "You are no ordinary Temple Knight."

"You're very observant. I'm a Temple Commander, in charge of the entire region."

"And what is your business here?"

"As I said, I'm very interested in those stones. I've seen something similar hundreds of miles from here, in the land where I was born."

"Then you have travelled here from afar?"

"Yes. A place called Hadenfeld. Have you heard of it?"

"I have not," the woman replied. She glanced at her house and then back to Charlaine. "Where are my manners? My name is Orlina Day. I hope Luca introduced himself?"

"He did," said Charlaine.

"Come inside, and I'll brew us something to drink unless you're in a hurry?"

"Not at all. I'll see to my horse, shall I?"

Orlina placed her hand on Stormcloud's forehead and spoke softly to the beast. "Leave her here. She'll be fine."

Charlaine wanted to say otherwise, but something in the old woman's eyes convinced her all was well. She let go of the lead and watched the horse wander over and start nibbling on the grass.

"I must admit," said Orlina, "it's been some time since we've had visitors. I hope you don't mind the mess." She wandered over to the hut and opened the door, revealing a surprisingly well-kept interior.

Charlaine followed her in. The place looked like it was falling apart from the outside, yet the inside was quite the opposite. A long line of shelves crammed with dried plants and clay pots occupied one wall.

"You're an herbalist," said Charlaine. She picked up a golden sickle. "And a successful one, if this is any indication. I am curious why it's made of gold; it would make for a very soft blade."

Orlina made her way to a nearby table and grabbed a kettle, shaking it to ensure it contained enough water. "That," she said, "is for special occasions."

"Such as?"

The old woman crushed some leaves, adding them to the kettle. "Have you ever heard of Tauril?"

"Yes, the Goddess of the Woods. They say the Elves worship her."

Orlina chuckled. "Not only the Elves." She moved to hang the kettle over the fire.

"You're a Sacred Mother."

"I'm surprised you're familiar with the term."

"Back in Reinwick, Elsbeth Fel, Sacred Mother of Akosia, blessed our ships."

"I find that surprising, considering your devotion to the Church."

"My order respects the beliefs of others."

"That's more than I can say of your brothers, the Temple Knights of Saint Cunar."

"Yes, I gathered that from talking to Luca. I assume you had trouble with them in the past?"

"I have indeed. Their patrols would often come to desecrate the stone arch."

"That's why the fence looks mended. Though I'm surprised they didn't pull the stones over."

"Not even a Temple Knight would dare such a thing."

"That would hardly stop them."

"The standing stones contain the power of the earth within them."

"Are you suggesting they're magical?"

Orlina nodded. "They are Tauril's gift."

Charlaine's gaze swept over the room. "This place," she said, "you've disguised it to look old and worn from the outside."

"Yes."

"You're an Earth Mage."

"I haven't heard that term in years," said Orlina. "We prefer the term Tauril's Chosen, but yes, you are essentially correct."

"When you say those stones are Tauril's gift, what does that mean exactly?"

"They make my magic stronger when I am nearby."

"You mean within the fence?"

Orlina smiled. "I see you have a gift for understanding. You are no mere Temple Knight."

"As I said, I'm a Temple Commander."

"It is more than that. You have a gift when it comes to people. Perhaps your Saint works through you?"

"Saint Agnes guides us with her wisdom, as set down in the Book of Agnes. It was she who said, 'Fear not the ancient ways.'"

"I shall not debate the teachings of the Saints, but I am surprised to learn she valued our beliefs."

"Those, like yourself, who worship the old Gods, still have the same beliefs and desires as those who worship the Saints. We are not so different, you and I."

Orlina took a seat, inviting Charlaine to do likewise. Outside, they heard Luca running around, followed by the occasional snort from Stormcloud.

"You are here to plan a great battle."

"How did you know?"

"I have seen the ground stained with blood."

"You have visions?"

The old woman nodded. "On rare occasions, when I am praying by the stones, I enter the world of dreams. In this state, I see things that will come to pass."

"Such as?"

"The death of Luca's mother, for one."

"You mean your daughter?"

"Luca is not my grandson; he's an orphan, abandoned by bandits after they attacked a wagon many years ago. His mother, whoever she was, is buried just beyond the circle's perimeter."

"Have you tried to discover if he has any other family?"

Orlina nodded. "I've gone into Braunfel from time to time and even as far afield as Lidenbach, but I've discovered nothing of his kin. I can only conclude they were foreigners."

"And when you saw the ground stained with blood, did you see who'd been fighting?"

"No. You must understand these visions are sometimes difficult to decipher. They are shown to me as images as if someone painted the scene."

"I've witnessed magic first-hand, so I know how powerful it can be. Still, I cannot say I believe it portends disaster."

"I never said it did," said Orlina, "although I suppose a loss in battle would be considered such for the one who is defeated. Your coming here, at this moment in time, is fortuitous. Could your Saint have guided you here for a purpose?"

"And what purpose would that be? To bring war to your home?"

"War will come whether I see it or not, but I hope you'll consider me a friend. That, in and of itself, is a gift worth having, is it not?"

Charlaine smiled. "It is."

"I sense you're skilled at judging people's character. What does your heart tell you about me?"

Charlaine sat there silently, staring at the older woman. "That I can trust you."

"Then all is as it should be."

"I don't suppose you know when this battle will occur?"

"I'm afraid my visions don't work like that."

"That's a pity," said Charlaine. "I need to plan for an invasion that I have no idea when it's going to happen."

"But you know it's coming, which, in itself, gives you an advantage."

"I would greatly appreciate any words of advice you can offer."

Orlina wrapped a rag around the kettle's handle, then made her way back to the table and began pouring. "You'll know when the time is right."

"How can you be so sure?"

"Let's just say I'm a good judge of character, much like yourself. In any case, when that time does finally come, you know where to find me. Now, are you ready for some of this?" She handed a cup to Charlaine, who sniffed it.

"What is it?"

"It's a mint infusion, though I added some honey to give it a sweet taste. You may prefer to let it cool a tad before you drink."

"I've never met an Earth Mage, though I hear they can move through walls."

"Where did you hear that?"

"From a friend of mine," said Charlaine. "He wrote to me telling how an Earth Mage softened the walls of a keep to gain entry."

"This friend of yours must be well-connected. Most of us tend to keep to ourselves."

"You possess a gift. Why not share it with others?"

"Tauril granted us this power for the betterment of all, but the greed of men knows no bounds. Were I to tell others of my magic, there would soon be no end of visitors wishing to employ my services."

"And that would be a bad thing?"

"Such folk seek to destroy rather than nurture."

"Yet you offered to help me if battle comes."

"I did," said Orlina. "This is my home. I'll protect it any way I can, but there's more to it."

"I'm listening."

"Those who come from the west seek to undo the balance of nature. They destroy all that stands in their way and hold no respect for the ways of our ancestors. They are, if you like, a blight on the face of the Continent."

"You'll get no argument from me," said Charlaine. "But they are presumed to have the largest army ever assembled."

"And that is where I come in."

"You are but one person, and even a powerful mage has little effect on the battlefield."

"Perhaps, but I have a big advantage."

"Which is?"

"Time," said Orlina. "Look around as you leave, Commander, for when you return, it shall look very different."

"How so?"

The old woman chuckled. "You shall see. In the meantime, I suggest you gather allies, for you will need them."

"I will bear that in mind."

"I hate to interrupt you, but if you intend to make the next roadside inn before dark, you should be on your way."

"My apologies," said Charlaine. She tried to hand over the cup, but Orlina was having none of it.

"Take it with you," the old woman insisted. She moved to the door and opened it to look outside.

Stormwind, sensing her presence, trotted over and then stood patiently. Charlaine stepped outside, then climbed into the saddle, no small feat with a cup in hand.

"Thank you," she said. "I shall not forget your words."

"Go with the grace of Tauril," said Orlina, "and may your Saint watch over you."

Charlaine turned around, making her way down the path, slowing only to wave to Luca. Soon, she was within sight of the road, ready to continue to Lidenbach, but before turning east, she rode down the length of the stream, trying to get a feel for the terrain. Orlina indicated it would change by the time she returned, and she wondered exactly how.

Would the banks sprout trees? Would the stream flood? Logic told her such things were impossible, yet she knew magic existed. Back in Ilea, she'd witnessed the healing power of a Life Mage when the Elf, Lord Gwalinor, used his magic to heal her hip. That memory inevitably led her to think of Teresa, who'd been taken to the island of the Elves to be healed. Would she one day return?

She chided herself. War was coming, and this was no time to be reminiscing. She finished her exploration of the area and rode east towards Lidenbach.

Charlaine entered the capital two days later, and by mid-afternoon, was back at her desk in the commandery. Marlena was quick to welcome her, presenting her with several letters, both official and otherwise. She opened the one from the grand mistress first, perusing its contents several times before setting it down.

"Trouble?" said Marlena.

"No, good news for once. There's another company on its way."

"Any idea when it'll arrive?"

Charlaine scanned through the letter once more. "Unless I'm reading it wrong, it should be here already." She handed it over. "Here, you tell me if I've missed something."

Marlena read the entire thing. "You're right. They should be here by now. Perhaps they ran into some trouble?"

"Trouble? What kind of trouble would delay an entire company of Temple Knights?"

"I'd suggest sending out patrols, but we don't know what direction they're coming from."

"There are three roads out of Lidenbach," said Charlaine, "and I just travelled the road to Braunfel. That leaves the Dubrow road, along with the one to Nausig."

"How would you like to proceed?"

"Have Captain Bernelle head south, to Dubrow, with twenty knights. I want Captain Miranda heading east to Nausig. Hopefully, between the two of them, we'll get some word of what's happened."

"How far do you want them to go?"

"No farther than the next town. If we don't hear anything by then, we must regroup and devise a better plan. Do we have any ships in port?"

"*Valiant* hasn't returned yet," said Marlena, "but I can get word out to *Vanguard* if you like. We know her location, and it would only take a few coins in a local fisherman's hands to send a message."

"Very well, draw the necessary coins from the treasury, and have the *Vanguard* sail up the coast as far as Vilnitz to see if there's anything on the wind."

"On the wind?"

"Yes. Have them talk to any ships they encounter; find out if anyone has heard anything."

"So, we're to trust rumours now?"

"I'll try anything if it finds our missing company."

"You believe this is more than a simple delay, don't you?"

"I do," said Charlaine. "It can't be a coincidence that we're missing a company when we need one the most."

"Anything else?"

"I intended to send half of Miranda's company to Braunfel, but we'd better hold off on that until we discover what's happened to these reinforcements."

Marlena stood. "I'll send word to the captains immediately."

Charlaine stared at the remaining letters as the door closed. For the most part, they were regular reports from the companies under her command, but one with a finer grade of parchment bearing a familiar seal caught her attention. She smiled as she saw the Barony of Verfeld's coat of arms adorning it.

"Well, well, my friend," she said as she opened it. "What have you been up to of late?"

14

REINFORCEMENTS

AUTUMN 1102 SR

"We found them," said Marlena.

Charlaine looked up from where she pored over the ledgers. "I assume you mean our reinforcements?"

"I do. Captain Bernelle's knights ran across them on the Dubrow road."

"Have we any information on what delayed them?"

"Not yet, but Sister Enna reports they looked like they'd been in a fight."

"A fight, you say. With whom?"

"No idea. Captain Bernelle sent her back as soon as she spotted them. I imagine the rest aren't far behind."

"Any idea who commands?"

"No," said Marlena. "Shall I find out?"

"We'll know once they get here. Inform me as soon as they're within sight of the commandery, and I'll greet them in person."

"Wouldn't it be more fitting to meet her up here?"

"It might, but I want to assess their condition. If they were in a skirmish, I need to see first-hand how they handled it."

"You mean to question them all?"

"Eventually," said Charlaine, "but you can tell a lot about an encounter by how badly damaged their armour is."

Sister Johanna appeared at the door.

"Yes?" said Charlaine.

"Captain Bernelle is in sight, Commander."

"Is she alone?"

"No. She's in the company of another individual, a captain, if her sash is any indication."

Charlaine looked at Marlena. "It appears things are moving a little faster than I anticipated." She rose, as did her aide. "We'll meet them in the courtyard."

Johanna nodded and disappeared down the hallway.

"Tell me," said Charlaine. "Have you ever wanted to be a Temple Captain?"

"Perhaps one day," replied Marlena, "but I'm content to act as your aide for now. Why do you ask?"

"I'm wondering if I need to replace a captain."

"You've plenty of candidates amongst the fleet, if you are so inclined."

"They're of more value aboard ship, especially now they have so much experience."

"There's likely a reasonable explanation why the company was delayed. You should at least give the new captain the benefit of the doubt."

"Are you doubting my concerns?"

"You told me to be honest with you at all times."

"Yes, I did, and I meant every word of it. Very well. I shall try to keep an open mind. Now, let's head downstairs, shall we? We've got a captain to meet."

They entered the courtyard to find the two captains dismounting. Charlaine was about to welcome them when the newcomer turned, revealing a familiar face. "Florence?"

"You know each other?" asked Captain Bernelle.

"Sister Florence and I served together in Ilea."

"Good day, Commander," said her newest captain. "I understand you've done well for yourself."

"I must admit this is a bit of a surprise."

"Did Miranda not mention we were at the Antonine together?"

"She did not," replied Charlaine, "although admittedly, I never pressed her for details. I heard your company ran into a delay?"

"That's putting it mildly," said Florence. "While riding through Angvil, we found our way blocked."

"By whom?"

"As it turns out, Temple Knights from the Order of Saint Cunar."

"What did they want?" asked Charlaine.

"They warned us to turn back, claimed the Church hadn't authorized our expedition."

"I'm curious how they knew you were coming."

"I'm afraid I can't speak to that. However, one thing was certain—they expected us to back down."

"What did you do?"

"I ordered the company to close up, and then we advanced towards them, using our horses to force them apart when they failed to clear the road."

"I'm guessing that led to a fight."

"It did, although I must confess, I can't tell you who took the first swing."

"How many of these Cunars were present?"

"Half a company. I got the impression the rest were watching another road."

"Were there any casualties?" asked Charlaine.

"Only a few minor injuries, mostly bruises and dented armour, that sort of thing. Once it was clear they wouldn't back down, I withdrew the company."

"I'm curious why? You should have outnumbered them two to one."

"We did, but they are the senior order and, by tradition, had the right of the road."

"Yet you're here now. How did you get past them?"

"I used a ruse," replied Captain Florence. "We set up a camp that night, leaving the fires burning while we rode cross-country, bypassing that section of the road. Unfortunately, navigation in the dark is quite difficult, and we became lost, hence the delay."

"And where is the company now?"

"In the fields to the east of the city, along with Captain Bernelle's knights."

"I wasn't sure where you wanted them," added Bernelle. "Both commanderies are full at the moment."

"They are," admitted Charlaine. "But your arrival comes at a fortuitous time, although I'm afraid you have more travel ahead of you."

Florence straightened. "Travel?"

"Yes. I was going to send a half company to Braunfel, but now that you're here, you can take their place."

"And once we get there?"

"There's an old Cunar commandery that you'll be taking over. Don't worry. Danica and I had a good look at it, and it's in fine shape. You'll also need to coordinate your efforts with Lord Handrik, the baron."

"Did you say Danica?"

"Yes," said Charlaine. "Haven't you heard? She's the Admiral of the Northern Fleet."

"Does that make her a commander like you?"

"She's ranked a Temple Captain while ashore."

"And while at sea?" asked Florence.

"She outranks us all."

"And when are we to begin this trip?"

"We'll rest your command for a day or two first. It'll give us a chance to re-provision you."

"Might I ask a question?" said Florence.

"By all means."

"My orders to report here were vague."

"In what way?"

"I was told to put my company at your disposal, but nothing else of what was going on."

"That's not a question," said Charlaine.

"True. I suppose what I'd like to know is what precisely the situation is here in Arnsfeld?"

"To put it simply, the Temple Knights of Saint Cunar abandoned their commanderies, pulling back into the interior of the Petty Kingdoms."

"Why would they do that?"

"That's a good question," replied Charlaine. "They claim it gives them more time to muster their forces should an invasion come."

"And you don't believe that?"

"Let's just say I've seen evidence to the contrary."

"What, exactly?"

"The Cunars have turned their backs on the other orders of late."

"Didn't you say they abandoned Arnsfeld?"

"I did, but I talk of Reinwick, my previous assignment. As you know, we work closely with the Temple Knights of Saint Mathew, which hasn't changed, but in the year before coming here, I found the Cunars growing more insular. They even stopped sending their captain to the duke's court."

"Do we know why?"

"I have some theories," said Charlaine, "but I'll keep them to myself for the time being. In the meantime, let's get some food into you first, and then you can write down a full account of your… troubles. After that, you should return to your company."

"Yes, Commander."

Captain Bernelle led Florence into the commandery.

"You're worried," said Marlena. "Care to explain why?"

"I have my doubts about our new captain."

"Because she avoided a fight?"

"No, it's more than that. When we served together in Ilea, Florence was prone to throwing around her seniority. Needless to say, it caused a few issues. She was also close to someone who tried to discredit our captain. In the end, I forgave her for that, but I never saw her as someone with leadership potential."

"You fear she might work against us?"

"I shall try not to let the past dictate my actions, but at the same time, I'll need to keep a close eye on her."

"Yet you're still sending her to Braunfel? I should think that would make it hard to watch over her."

"I suppose it would, but I must work with what I have."

"What if you sent Captain Miranda instead?"

"No. I'd prefer her here in Lidenbach. Her knights have become friendly with the folk in the surrounding countryside, and I don't want to jeopardize that."

"Something else is bothering you."

Charlaine smiled. "You know me too well. I'm concerned about this encounter with the Cunars. I knew they opposed us coming here but to actively seek to block us to the extent that they would be willing to spill blood makes it so much worse. I fear if war does come, we may find them refusing to take on the empire or, worse, joining them."

Marlena's mouth fell open. "Surely not! Do you realize what you're suggesting?"

"I don't make the claim lightly, but it still bears considering."

"That's close to blasphemy. If I were you, I'd keep that to myself."

"Don't worry. I intend on doing just that."

Two days later, Charlaine saw Captain Florence off as she led her command down the Braunfel road. Once they disappeared from view, she and Marlena began making their way back to the commandery.

"Let's return by way of the harbour," said Charlaine. "I'm hoping the *Valiant* will soon be back amongst us."

"Have you heard any news?"

"Nothing specific, but a few fishermen reported ships flying our flag in the area."

"That would probably be *Vanguard*."

"In two different places on the same morning? I doubt even the *Valiant* is that fast."

"They're sister ships. Wouldn't that make them capable of the same speed?"

Charlaine chuckled. "It would, but you missed the point I was trying to make."

"Oh, I understood it, but fishermen aren't always the most reliable of witnesses."

"Why would you suggest that?"

"On account of some of them being rather partial to drink."

"Don't let Danica hear you say that."

"Still," continued Marlena, "what's more likely? That the *Valiant* is back, or someone saw the *Vanguard* and misidentified her?"

"We'll find out soon enough." They were getting closer, for the smell of the sea hung in the air. Eventually, they emerged onto the dock only to see two ships flying the order's standard.

"Well, well," said Charlaine. "It appears we have two vessels in port."

"Yes, although I can't tell them apart from this distance."

"And to think you didn't believe those fishermen!"

"Don't blame me; they are sister ships."

"In more ways than one." Charlaine laughed at her comment.

"I'm not sure I follow?"

"They're identical, but at the same time, they belong to the order and carry sister knights."

"Ah, I see. That's very clever, but I wouldn't suggest taking up the calling of a bard quite yet."

"Don't talk to me of bards," said Charlaine. "I had my fill of them back in Reinwick."

They continued down the dock until they came across one of *Valiant's* boats tying off to a post.

"Sister Zivka," called out Charlaine. "What's *Vanguard* doing here?"

"Storm damage," replied the knight. "I came ashore to arrange for some repairs."

"Nothing serious, I hope?"

"She took a battering off the coast of Burgemont and was driven onto some rocks. Not enough damage to sink her, but she's leaking."

"And *Valiant?*"

"We were on our way back here when they saw us limping into port. The admiral decided it best to stick close and render what assistance we could."

"Have you an estimated time for repairs?"

"Not yet, but I'll let you know when we have a better idea."

A crowd had gathered, drawn, no doubt, by the presence of the two well-known pirate hunters. Charlaine spotted a familiar face pushing his way through the traffic, but upon spotting Charlaine, he altered course.

"This is all your doing," said Lord Corbin. "His Majesty won't like this at all."

"Come now," she replied. "Surely you wouldn't deny a damaged ship the ability to obtain repairs?"

"Those ships are nothing more than brigands, preying on the empire's shipping."

"The empire's shipping? You mean like those warships you sent into Reinwick waters?"

"I shall not stand here and listen to such lies."

"Lies? How do you explain their presence?"

"They were simply over-exuberant captains, trying to make a name for themselves."

"So, you admit your navy lacks discipline?"

Corbin's cheeks flamed. "Do not twist my words." He gazed out at the bay. "When will these so-called repairs be complete?"

"That largely depends on how readily available supplies are. Of course, if you're concerned, your people could assist in repairing the damage?"

"I shall authorize no such thing!"

"Then I'm afraid that ship will remain here for the time being."

"I will bring this to the king's attention."

"I would insist on it," said Charlaine. "In fact, I might just see His Majesty myself."

Corbin stared back a moment. "I know what you're up to."

"Then perhaps you'd care to enlighten me."

"You already doubled your garrison here in Lidenbach, and now there are reports that even more knights have arrived. Such news has greatly distressed the king. If I were you, I'd tread very carefully."

"You appear to take great delight in threatening me, Lord Corbin. Perhaps it's time you took a more diplomatic approach. You are, are you not, an envoy of the emperor?"

"What nonsense is this? Of course I'm an envoy for the emperor. Who else would I represent?"

"Then, in your duties as a diplomat, you might try to act in a more statesmanlike manner."

"This, coming from a common smith?"

Charlaine smiled at his unconscious admission of interest. "I see you learned all about me. I shall endeavour to take that as a compliment."

Corbin leaned closer, lowering his voice. "I would watch my step if I were you."

"Oh yes? Why is that?"

"Your time here is limited, Commander. Make of it what you will, for when the storm finally breaks, you will be swept aside, like so much flotsam."

"I have weathered my fair share of storms, my lord, and I assure you those of my order are more than capable of surviving intact. As for your threats, let me say this: I was there when we defeated your fleet on the Shimmering Sea and when we destroyed your little expedition in the Five Sisters. It is you who should be worried, for when a Temple ship attacks, it expects no mercy."

Corbin stared at her, looking as if he wanted to say more, but then something took hold of him, causing him to back up a pace. "Good day to you," he snapped before wheeling about and stomping off.

"Do we really expect no mercy?" asked Marlena.

"Of course not," replied Charlaine. "I wanted him to know we're not intimidated."

"And his threats concerning the king?"

"You mean his implication that he'll tell His Majesty? I'm afraid he'd do that regardless of anything I said."

"So, we just wait until we're summoned to court?"

"I doubt it'll come to that, but if it does, I'll go alone."

"Surely you jest?" said Marlena.

"There's no sense in dragging you into this."

"Isn't it a little late for that?"

Zivka interrupted their conversation. "I'll be in the city for a bit. Do you want to row over to the *Valiant*?"

"I would, but I have my horse to look after."

"I'll take her back," said Marlena.

"I suppose that settles the matter," said Charlaine. "Very well, I'll accept the offer of your boat, Zivka." She dismounted, passed the reins to her aide, and was soon sitting in the stern of the *Valiant's* boat, heading into the harbour.

Danica appeared at the railing. "What are you doing here?"

"I came to see you."

"Then you best come aboard. There's much to discuss."

Charlaine climbed aboard, taking Danica's hand. "You've repaired the damage from the water serpent."

"We had that fixed before we left Braunfel." Her gaze drifted to the *Vanguard*. "Unfortunately, I can't say the same for our sister ship."

"I hear they got caught in a storm."

"Quite a violent one, some sixty miles up the coast. We were fortunate we didn't lose her."

"How badly damaged is she?"

"Mainly the mast and rigging, including the spare sail, but the hull sprang a leak. Nothing we couldn't handle, but I'd like a more comprehensive inspection before she puts out to sea again. How are things at court?"

"I wouldn't know. I haven't been there yet."

"You should have been back here some time ago."

"And so I was," said Charlaine, "but one of our companies was delayed getting here. That reminds me, I sent them on to Braunfel. They're under the command of Temple Captain Florence."

"Florence? Not the same Florence we served with in Ilea?"

"The same."

"And the grand mistress sent her?"

"She did," replied Charlaine.

"I know you made peace with her, but I can't imagine her as a captain."

"People do change."

"I'm sure they do," said Danica, "and I'd be more accepting of her if we weren't up to our neck in Halvarians."

"Meaning?"

"I suppose I see Florence as having a temper. Something like that could easily cause trouble, especially so close to the border."

"That's what I thought, too, but then I realized we need someone exactly like that if we're to stop the empire from taking advantage of the king's indecision."

"You want her to create an incident?"

"I doubt she'll cross the border, if that's what you're worried about." Charlaine chewed her lip thoughtfully. "You know, it's strange to be having this discussion with you."

"Why is that?"

"Because I just had a similar one with Marlena, except I took your point of view."

"So, now that you've seen both sides of the argument, does it change your mind?"

"No. I believe it does precisely the opposite. It makes me all the more determined to see Florence safely ensconced in Braunfel. In any case, even if I had changed my mind, it's too late to call her back now."

"Am I going there anytime soon?"

"Not until the spring," said Charlaine. "If the river should ice up, it would leave you stranded there."

"We've a little bit of time before we need to worry about that."

"True, but I got another earful from Lord Corbin right before I came out here."

"Let me guess—he objects to our presence here?"

"Naturally."

"Will that see us kicked out of port?"

"Not with a damaged ship," said Charlaine. "Though I can't make any guarantees for *Valiant*. Which reminds me: did you order any other ships to Vilnitz?"

"I did. Nadia reports the *Fearless* arrived first, followed by the *Invincible* and *Indomitable*, all with a full complement of Temple Knights. They're tied up at the dock as we speak."

"And that didn't present any problems?"

"Not at all. In fact, the king seems pleased with them being there. It appears Arnsfeld isn't the only kingdom feeling threatened by Halvaria."

"It's good to know we have five ships at our disposal."

"Yes, and almost a full company of Temple Knights."

"And provisioning?"

"The King of Burgemont has taken it upon himself to feed them all over the next few months. Apparently, he sees it as a small cost compared to the threat of the empire."

"I'd feel better if I had some idea of how many ships Halvaria has in the region."

"I had thought to do some scouting of my own," said Danica, "but the damage to *Valiant* proved ill-timed, and the last thing I want to do is enter their waters with only a single ship."

"There is time," said Charlaine. "Though exactly how much is still unknown."

15

SUMMONS

AUTUMN 1102 SR

"I should've expected this," said Charlaine, tossing the note aside. "I've been summoned to appear before the king. No doubt this is Lord Corbin's doing."

"Let me guess," said Danica. "He's complaining about us being in port."

"It doesn't say, but that's likely the case. Tell me, is that Halvarian warship still there?"

"You mean the *Conqueror*? Unfortunately, it is, along with the *Vindicator* and that cog of theirs."

"Speaking of which, have we any idea what it's doing here?"

"They're unloading," said Danica, "but they only work in the dead of night."

"I thought they'd have emptied the thing by now."

"So would I. Though, if it helps, they're floating a little higher in the water of late. Perhaps that means they'll be leaving soon?"

"Let's hope they take their warships with them."

"When does the king demand your presence?" asked Danica.

"This afternoon."

"Shall I accompany you?"

"I don't believe that would be wise," said Charlaine. "Let me take the brunt of it while you concentrate on getting *Vanguard* fitted out."

"You shouldn't go alone."

"Why not?" asked Charlaine. "I still carry the power of the Church behind me. I'm certain that's enough to convince him to treat me with at least a modicum of respect."

"I'm not so sure. You said Captain Florence ran into a group of Cunars coming here. If we're at the point where the orders have turned on each other, how can we trust the Church to support us?"

"You make a good point, but you must consider this from all angles. The only people who know about that encounter are our own knights."

"Not quite true," said Danica. "The Cunars who were present would certainly be aware of it."

"Yes, but are they likely to tell anyone else of it?"

"Their superiors, definitely, but not anyone outside the Church. Then again, we know there's corruption within their order. What if they're actively working with Halvaria? We could end up having to face them on the battlefield. I don't fancy the idea of taking on other Temple Knights."

"Nor do I," said Charlaine, "but maybe we're reading too much into this summons. The king might be planning a Midwinter Feast."

"Then wouldn't he simply send an invitation?"

"You could have at least let me enjoy the thought for a moment before crushing all hope."

"Sorry, but we must be realistic."

"Yes, I suppose we must. It's been some time since our arrival, and things are only getting worse as the days go by. The truth is, I don't know if I can salvage this situation."

"That doesn't sound like you," said Danica. "I'm not a Temple Commander, but you can confide in me. I promise you."

Charlaine smiled. "Thank you, and I am glad you're here. I couldn't imagine dealing with this on my own."

"So how can I help?"

"Let's talk about the fleet. Any further word on the *Vanguard's* repairs?"

"The repairs to the mast are complete, but we're finding it difficult to find sailcloth."

"Why's that?"

"Someone has bought up all the supplies in the last few days. I don't suppose you'd like to hazard a guess as to who might have done such a thing?"

"I suppose it shouldn't surprise me," said Charlaine. "Is there anywhere else we could find what we need?"

"The *Vanguard* uses the same rig as *Valiant*, and luckily we have a spare for just such an emergency. The problem is that it now leaves us with none. Should we run across a bad storm on our own, we'd be stranded."

"What of Vilnitz?"

"They'd likely have some," said Danica, "but I don't fancy sailing these waters without a spare sail between us."

"Could you send word overland for what you need?"

"We could, but that would mean further delay."

"Still," said Charlaine, "I believe that's the better plan, don't you? In the meantime, I suggest you leave *Valiant* with both sails, just to be safe."

"So you're suggesting *Vanguard* wait it out here?"

"Precisely, but the final decision is yours. If you choose to send word to Vilnitz, I'll supply a suitable escort."

"We could sail there in *Valiant*, wait for the sails and then return."

"I'd prefer you didn't," said Charlaine. "That would leave us without a usable ship, and we need your eyes out at sea."

"Very well, I'll stay here. I might suggest in future, however, that we store extra sailcloth here for just such emergencies, providing you have the space, of course."

"An excellent idea. Then again, maybe the Cunar commandery would be better suited since it's closer to the bay. In any event, I'll discuss it with my captains and let you know their thoughts."

"In that case, I better get out to *Vanguard* and inform them of what's happening. As for you, I suggest you change; you want to look your best for your audience with the king!"

Charlaine arrived at the Royal Castle mid-afternoon to be met by a silent servant, who escorted her to a door guarded by two warriors. The servant knocked, announcing her arrival, then left without any further word.

The door opened, revealing a young man, likely not quite twenty, wearing an immaculate set of ornate plate armour, save for a helmet. A smile curled the corners of his lips as his eyes met hers. "It is the Temple Commander, Majesty," he announced.

Charlaine entered, making sure to bow. "Greetings, Your Majesty," she began. "I understand you wanted to see me?"

King Stefan sat at a table with a plate of picked-over meat before him while grease dripped from his fingertips. He held out his right hand, and a servant rushed over to wipe it with a damp cloth.

"Come," he said, waving her closer. "Ah yes, where are my manners." He used his left hand to pick up a drumstick, pointing at the well-armoured man. "This is Sir Hugo, Knight of the Silver Spur."

"Pleased to meet you," said Charlaine.

"And you, Mistress Charlaine."

"A simple 'Commander' is—"

"Now," interrupted the king, "let us get down to business, shall we?" He used his clean hand to lift a parchment. "Would you care to guess what this is?"

Charlaine felt trapped, for it would make things worse if she brought up the wrong subject. She elected to feign ignorance instead. "It appears to be a letter, although I have no idea what it concerns?"

"And if I said it was from Lord Corbin, would that give you an inkling?"

"His Lordship is better placed to tell you the contents of his own letter, Your Majesty."

The king knit his brow in consternation, yet he held his temper in check while calmly setting the letter back down. "Tell me, Commander, is it true you maintain not one but two Temple ships in the harbour?"

"You already know the answer to that, Majesty, else you wouldn't ask."

"So you do not deny it, then?"

"Of course not, for to do so would be to lie, and as we all know, Temple Knights do not lie."

"I understand your ship, the *Valiant*, brought you here to Lidenbach, but now that you've settled in, can you not send it back to whence it came?"

"That is not my decision to make."

"You are the regional commander, are you not?"

"I am," replied Charlaine.

"And, if I'm not mistaken, the woman in charge of your fleet is a mere Temple Captain, yes?"

"She is, but she also holds the appointment of admiral and outranks me when it comes to naval matters."

"But you have influence over her, surely?"

"I do," replied Charlaine, "but I've yet to see a compelling reason to send it on its way."

"What if I were to order you to do so?"

"With all due respect, Your Majesty, I serve the Church, not you. Your commands hold no sway over me. You are welcome to suggest such a move, but then I must report that to my superiors. Are you sure you wish to cross the Church at this time?"

The king tore the cloth from the servant's grasp, wiping his other hand. "Is that a threat?"

"No, Majesty. Only a question."

"I might be inclined to overlook the presence of a single Church ship, but two?"

"It's not a Church ship," said Charlaine.

"I beg your pardon?"

"The *Valiant* does not belong to the Church, nor does the *Vanguard*."

"But your knights protect it, do they not?"

"They do, but that's because they belong to the Temple Knights of Saint Agnes."

"Thus making them Church ships. You can't escape that logic, Commander!"

"I seek only to clarify," replied Charlaine. "They fall under the exclusive control of my order, and only the grand mistress can countermand the admiral's orders."

"Come now. We are talking of two ships, not a fleet. Surely you wish to remain in my good graces?"

"Of course, Your Majesty, just as I imagine you would want to remain on the good side of my order, especially considering they are the only allies you possess at the moment."

"Don't talk to me of allies," spat out the king.

Charlaine had hit a nerve but struggled to make sense of it.

Stefan sat back in his chair. "Ah, I see I've caught you by surprise. I assume you've heard nothing of recent diplomatic failures?"

"Failures?"

"I've been pleading for months with my neighbours, but none of them are willing to assist me in the defence of my realm."

"Then I would think you grateful for our assistance, Majesty."

"Your very presence here has caused me no end of trouble."

"How so?" asked Charlaine.

"Every step you take drives us closer to war with Halvaria, a war we cannot hope to win."

"What are you suggesting? That you surrender your land to them? Such an action would doom not only your subjects but those of your neighbours."

"Don't complain to me about my neighbours' woes; they've brought them on themselves. Had they sent me warriors when I asked for them, I wouldn't be in this predicament."

"And what predicament is that, Majesty?"

"The Halvarian Empire has formally requested I ban your ships from the port of Lidenbach."

"Why?"

"You know why! Because you've made a career out of attacking their ships."

"If we have, it's only in the name of self-preservation. Our ships patrol the sea to keep pirates and marauders at bay, Your Majesty, nothing more."

"Ah, but that's not quite true, is it, now?" The king smiled in delight. "By your own admission, you attacked a fleet of Halvarian ships in the Five Sisters a few years back. Don't try to deny it!"

"Perhaps you might ask yourself why they were there in the first place. The truth is, we were there to roust out a camp of bandits. Yes, they belonged to the empire but were in those waters without the duke's permission."

She paused a moment to gather her thoughts. "You've known the full story for some time, Your Majesty. Why is it only being brought up now?"

"I am under pressure."

"To do what, might I ask?"

"Lord Corbin suggested I allow the fighting complement of the *Conqueror* and the *Vindicator* ashore to patrol the streets and maintain order."

"What gave you the impression there's a need?" said Charlaine. "My knights regularly patrol the streets of Lidenbach. Admittedly, there's still some crime, but the number of incidents has dropped precipitously."

"He has also graciously offered for their fleet to safeguard the merchant ships which frequent our port."

"I urge you to refuse the offer, Majesty. It will only make you beholden to them."

"What other choice have I? You are new to the area, so I will forgive your ignorance, but the Halvarian Empire is like a sleeping giant. We are better to let it lie rather than risk disturbing it and incurring its wrath."

"I know my history," said Charlaine. "The empire will not stop until it has engulfed all the civilized lands."

"Come now. That is merely the ramblings of old women."

"What of the people of Calabria or the Holy City of Herani? Did they believe the same?"

"What would you know of such things?"

"I've been to Alantra and witnessed what they do to the lands they conquer."

"Is it really that bad? Some would argue they merely exchange one set of rulers for another."

"In Calabria, they seized property, forced men to serve in their legions, and killed any who spoke against their rule. Is this the fate you want to deliver to your people?"

Stefan's shoulders slumped in defeat. "What else can I do? Any attempt to face them down merely strengthens their resolve to invade us. No army has ever stood against the might of Halvaria."

"I would argue the point," said Charlaine. "We beat them at sea twice. I see no reason why we can't duplicate that feat ashore."

Stefan shook his head. "You have no idea what they're capable of."

"Then why don't you educate me?"

"There are endless legions waiting to descend on us. Some would say their success is inevitable."

"They said the same thing about the Old Kingdom, yet that was defeated."

"That was a different time when the Petty Kingdoms could band together for the greater good."

"And they can do so again."

"No. The old alliance is dead, driven apart by petty jealousies and ancient prejudices. No one will come to our aid, Commander. We shall be wiped out."

"Better that," offered Sir Hugo, "than be forced to our knees without a fight!"

"I admire your spirit," said the king, "but I have no wish to throw away lives when there is no hope of success. Better to accept their rule and join their cause."

"You'd support their war upon the Petty Kingdoms?" asked a stunned Charlaine.

"When have the Petty Kingdoms ever helped me? Did they send me aid in my hour of need? No! I say to the Underworld with them. At least this way, we shall end up on the winning side."

"You are mistaken, Majesty. If you surrender to the empire, they will remove you from the Throne and take you away in chains. That's always assuming that they don't kill you outright."

"Why would they do that? Particularly after I handed them my Crown?"

"A deposed king becomes a rallying point for insurrection," replied Charlaine. "You believe your abdication will save your people, but it's far more likely to lead to further deaths as people take up arms in your name."

"Then I shall order them to stand down."

"By then, it'll be too late. Once you surrender your Throne, the Halvarians will flood the country with legions, taking what they want, putting their own people in charge, then forcing your subjects into camps."

"Camps?" said King Stefan.

"Aye. I've seen them for myself in Calabria. I can't explain how they work, but those taken there change."

"Change, how?"

"All hope is driven from them, replaced by a fanaticism bordering on madness."

"Some would claim the same of the Temple Knights."

"The difference," said Charlaine, "is that Temple Knights join of their own free will."

"Please," said Sir Hugo, "listen to the commander, Majesty. She knows what she's talking about."

The king looked down, contemplating his plate of food, the silence stretching out until Charlaine wondered if he'd fallen asleep.

Stefan finally raised his face, a look of pleading in his eyes. "What would you have me do, Commander?"

"I suggest you start by denying Lord Corbin's request to patrol the streets."

"And when he objects?"

"Remind him that you are the king here, and he remains only at your pleasure."

"He won't like that."

"No doubt," said Charlaine, "but what else can he do?"

"He could declare war!"

"He is an envoy. I doubt he has the power to do such a thing. Likely, he will try to cajole you, attempt to belittle you, or perhaps he'll try taking a more diplomatic approach."

"Which would be?"

"I imagine he'd begin by casting aspersions on the Temple Knights, telling you they are only here to safeguard their own interests."

"And would he be right in that assessment?"

"He would, but he doesn't know our true interests."

"Perhaps you might enlighten me?" said the king.

"We protect people, particularly women, which is our primary purpose and most sacred vow. So no, I will not apologize for defending those who depend on us for protection."

"And what of the ships in the harbour?"

"*Valiant* will soon be back out at sea," said Charlaine, "but *Vanguard* must remain until we can carry out repairs. If Lord Corbin objects, you might point out that there are now two Halvarian ships of war in harbour, whereas we have only one that is serviceable, and a smaller one at that."

The king nodded. "Very well. I shall consider your... proposal. Now leave me, the both of you."

Sir Hugo escorted her from the building, waiting until they were on the streets of Lidenbach before speaking. "His Majesty means well."

"He has a funny way of showing it," said Charlaine. "He was on the cusp of surrendering his Crown."

"Your words brought him back from the brink, but I fear there is still much to navigate. Lord Corbin will not like the stiffening of Stefan's resolve."

"Then we must do what we can to help him make a stand."

"What are you suggesting?"

Charlaine halted, turning to look directly at the knight. "How many knights in your order?"

"The Knights of the Silver Spur? A hundred, I think. Why?"

"And where would I find them?"

"They're scattered throughout the kingdom," said Hugo. "Many serving the barons directly."

"Aren't they sworn to the king?"

"They are, at least in theory, but most were knights in service to the barons before being elevated to the Silver Spurs. The king believed forming a royal order would ensure their loyalty."

"And did it?" asked Charlaine.

"I'm not sure what you're trying to get at?"

"Then let me be blunt. If the king succumbs to pressure from the empire, will the knights lay down their arms or fight?"

Sir Hugo stood straighter, pulling back his shoulders. "They'll fight. Of that, I have no doubt."

"Have you much influence amongst your order?"

"I do."

"Then might I suggest you take steps to gather them."

"Here, in Lidenbach?"

"No. That would draw the king's attention. Better, I think, to station them close by. I believe Kronberg is only a short march from Braunfel, and Dubrow could reinforce the capital on short notice, could it not?"

"It could, along with Nausig. But to do that, I'll need to explain the strategy to the barons."

"And do you think they would allow such a move?"

"There's only one way to find out. I'll ride for Dubrow tomorrow morning, but I warn you, it will take some time to complete this task."

"Then take what time you must," said Charlaine. "It is too late in the year for the empire to invade now. However, spring may be an entirely different matter."

16

THE SAPPHIRE
WINTER 1102 SR

As autumn finally faded, the first snow of winter fell, and with it, a serenity came over the land as if the blanket of white had somehow calmed the hearts of men. Even as the cold settled in and the rivers froze, the fleet continued to patrol the icy waters of the Great Northern Sea.

With only two days until midwinter, the *Valiant* sailed up the coast, looking for any signs of piracy. Danica stood at the bow as she was prone to, the fine mist forming icicles in her hair. The frigid wind reddened her cheeks and made her eyes water, yet she felt alive!

"Admiral?"

She turned, her reverie broken by Vivian. "Yes?"

"The lookout reports something in the water."

"Where?"

"There. To the north."

Danica moved to the railing to get a better view. "A shipwreck, perhaps?"

"That would seem to be the case," replied Vivian. "Though what they're doing sailing in this weather is beyond me."

"I might remind you we're out in the cold. How is it so surprising that others might do the same?"

"The Northern Sea is an unforgiving mistress. Few merchant captains would risk their ship sailing this time of year."

"I imagine the profit is greater for those who do."

"They would put profit over the lives of their crew?"

"Don't we?" said Danica. "We don't prize profit, of course, but we take a risk by sailing in these frigid temperatures."

"Says the woman with ice in her hair."

"You forget, I grew up on the shores of this great sea." Danica was about to say more, but something in the water grabbed her attention. "Get a hook over here," she called out.

Zivka was soon beside her, a boat hook in hand.

"There," said Danica, pointing.

The knight bent over the railing to snag a dark shape floating in the water. "It looks like cloth of some sort."

"The remains of a sail?" asked Vivian.

"That's no sail," said Danica. "That's a flag."

"Not one I'm familiar with. You?"

Zivka lifted the cloth, depositing it on the *Valiant's* deck. There was no denying its nationality or what it signified.

"It's Calabrian," said Danica. "Only one ship in these parts dares fly that flag." She scanned the area. "Take in the sail. Unless I miss my guess, the *Sapphire* went down somewhere around here. Send the ship's boat to look for any bodies."

"You mean survivors, don't you?" replied Vivian.

"That water's too cold. Even floating on a piece of wreckage, a person wouldn't last long."

"Then why look for bodies?"

"We could at least give them a decent burial. We might also get a better idea of what happened to their ship."

"We don't have much light left."

"Then we search in the dark," shouted Danica. She saw the look of shock on Vivian's face. "Sorry. I didn't mean to snap at you, but something strange is happening here."

"Ships get wrecked at sea all the time."

"They do, but this involved fire." The admiral stepped closer to the flag, pointing at one edge. "See here? It's partially burned."

"So, someone started a fire?"

"And then did what, cut loose the flag? If the ship had burned down to the waterline, wouldn't the flag still be connected to the rigging?"

"Rope burns," replied Vivian.

"It does, but the islets for the flag are intact."

"I'm not sure what you're suggesting."

"Someone took this flag down. I'm guessing the fire came later."

Zivka was back at the railing, pointing at the water. "More wreckage, Admiral."

Danica returned to the side of the ship. Casks floated by, as well as broken bits of timber and damaged planks. There was no mistaking the *Sapphire's* fate. "Those planks are partially burned."

"You were right," said Vivian.

With its sail lowered, the *Valiant* slowed, allowing the crew to ready the ship's boat. While the salvage crew went through what remained of the *Sapphire*, Danica headed to her cabin to record their position. Darkness had descended by the time they returned, their hands numb from scouring through the wreckage, looking for clues. They had to be helped aboard lest they slip and sink into the inky depths.

Footsteps interrupted Danica as she worked in her cabin, then came the familiar knock.

"Come," said the admiral.

Vivian entered the cramped confines of the room. "We found two bodies."

"And the ship?"

"Lots of burned timbers, as you surmised, but the bulk of the *Sapphire* is nowhere to be seen. I suspect she, along with most of her crew, are at the bottom of the sea. A fire at sea is a terrible thing."

"It is," said Danica. "Let's look at those bodies, shall we?"

"They're not in good shape. One is missing its limbs, while the other's lost its head. No doubt the creatures in this part of the sea have been feasting on them."

Danica threw on a cloak, grabbed a lantern, and then walked out on deck. Her Temple Knights had gone below to warm up, leaving the sailors to look after the bodies. Someone had laid blankets over what was left of the *Sapphire's* crew, giving them a bit of dignity with which they might make their way to the Afterlife.

The sailor Brendan sat nearby, cutting linen with a knife. He'd been a crew member long before the *Valiant* entered the order's service and was its most experienced hand. He looked up at the admiral. "I thought I'd prepare their shrouds. One shouldn't feel the icy embrace of Akosia without looking their finest."

"Of course," said Danica. She knelt, lifting the blanket to peer at the first body, then did the same for the second.

"Problem, Admiral?" said Vivian.

"Sea creatures didn't do that damage—axes did."

"Are you certain?"

"See for yourself." Danica waited as her captain examined the bodies. "You'll notice the cuts are large, as if something hacked off the limbs, and what type of sea creature would eat arms and legs while leaving the torso alone? And a head? I know of no such fish, do you?"

"Do you think pirates are responsible for this?"

"Not pirates, Halvarians."

"Why would the empire do such a thing?"

"Captain Carvahlen flaunted the flag of a country now under Halvarian rule. I don't imagine that sat well."

"Yes," said Vivian, "but why destroy the ship? Surely it would have been better to capture it?"

"They weren't interested in plunder; they're after something bigger."

"That being?"

"I suspect they intend to put a stranglehold on Lidenbach. Without sea trade, its coffers will dwindle. And if ships keep going missing, fewer captains will visit these waters."

Vivian clenched her jaw. "How do we stop that? We don't have enough ships."

"I've been giving that much thought of late, and I believe I have a solution, though it's an unusual one."

"That being?"

"We form the traders into groups of ships and accompany them as they sail."

"Can we afford to do that?"

"*Valiant* and *Vanguard* are the best suited to such a role, yet that would leave Lidenbach unprotected."

"Couldn't you bring a ship from Vilnitz?"

"I could," said Danica, "but I'll need to consult with Commander Charlaine. The presence of another warship in the bay, particularly an ex-Halvarian one, might cause problems."

"When would you seek to start this plan of yours?"

"As soon as possible. Merchant vessels are scarce enough in these waters; we must act before they disappear entirely."

"And what of those responsible for the destruction of *Sapphire*?"

"If it is the Halvarians, then tracking down one ship will do little to curb their campaign of terror."

"But if we found them, surely that would constitute enough proof that they're the guilty ones?"

"And then what?" said Danica. "Are you suggesting the empire will roll over on its back and apologize? We're in a campaign for the survival of the Petty Kingdoms here, Vivian. A single ship makes little difference in the long run."

"I disagree. One ship, in the right place at the right time, can make all the difference. The *Valiant* is proof of that."

. . .

Charlaine looked out over the bay. She'd finally transferred her office to the old Cunar building, though they now referred to it as the north commandery. Reports sat on her desk, awaiting her attention, but instead, she watched *Valiant* as it dropped anchor. Marlena entered the room, depositing a collection of papers on the desk.

"What have you there?" asked Charlaine.

"More dispatches from the surrounding areas. Routine, for the most part, but you might want to pay particular attention to the correspondence from Temple Captain Florence."

"Come now, you're my aide. As such, you've read them all. Can't you summarize?"

"She reports an increase in the number of incidents of late, likely due to the river freezing over, making it easier for the Halvarians to cross."

"I thought we had people watching?"

"We do," said Marlena, "but she suspects they're crossing under cover of darkness. She's sending out nightly patrols, but it's had little effect."

"Are they causing trouble in town?"

"Not so far. In fact, quite the opposite. They're quite friendly once caught."

"And why wouldn't they be?" said Charlaine. "All we do is send them back across the border. It's not as if there's any real punishment waiting for them. Are they spending much time in Braunfel?"

"No, and that's the strange part. Those they rounded up were out in the countryside."

"They're getting to know the lay of the land, which could mean they plan on a spring invasion."

"That reminds me," said Marlena, digging through the pile. "There's a letter from Sir Hugo somewhere in here."

"Has he news on the Knights of the Silver Spur?"

"He does. The barons agreed to gather the order, at least in principle."

"Meaning?"

"There is still some discussion about where they might best be concentrated. The general feeling is that they should gather in one place, but each baron feels their own lands best suited to such an assembly."

"I thought we'd settled all that," said Charlaine. "Don't they realize the fate of the kingdom rests on their shoulders?"

"It can't be helped," replied Marlena. "And without their support, we have little chance of stopping the empire. At the risk of sounding like a merchant, it's the price we must pay to stay in business."

"Perhaps it's time I took more direct action."

"What are you suggesting? That you visit the barons yourself? I fear that might only undermine Sir Hugo's efforts."

Charlaine looked out the window. "Yes, I suppose it would, yet I can't help but feel we're stagnating here."

"How can you say that?" asked Marlena. "Since your arrival, the streets of Lidenbach are safer, and even Lord Corbin has fallen silent."

"Yes, he has, but that only makes me feel worse. I sense he's up to something. Tell me, am I right to fear that, or am I just imagining things?"

"The history of Halvaria is one of deceit and deception. I would trust your feelings in this."

"Meaning my fear or that I'm imagining things?"

"I wouldn't call it fear. Rather, I'd refer to it as cautious mistrust."

Charlaine laughed. "You're becoming quite the diplomat. Are you sure you wouldn't prefer to represent us at court?"

"I'll leave that in your capable hands. Now, best get to work, Commander. Those letters won't answer themselves."

Marlena left the room, leaving Charlaine to the stack of papers. She'd been putting it off all morning, but the time had come to work her way through them.

Engrossed in writing a letter, Charlaine didn't bother to look up when someone entered her office. "Just set it down over there," she said.

"Would that be my arse you're referring to?"

"Danica? What are you doing here? Is something wrong?"

"Can't I just come to visit my friend?"

"Of course, but then Marlena would have announced you. That you entered straight away indicates something important has happened."

"It just so happens that it has. We found the wreckage of the *Sapphire*."

"Do I know that ship?"

"I think I mentioned it once or twice. She was a Calabrian under Captain Guillermo Carvahlen."

"I'm sorry to hear of its loss."

"Not lost so much as destroyed," said Danica. "It appears someone set fire to it."

"And the crew?"

"Lost and presumed dead. We recovered two bodies, but they were butchered."

"Pirates?"

"Pirates like to capture ships and sell their cargo. No, this attack was more personal. I suspect it was the result of the Halvarians."

"What makes you say that?"

"The two bodies showed signs of axe wounds, and we know how much the Halvarian provincials favour that weapon."

"Have you any definite proof?"

"Nothing that would hold up at court, if that's what you mean. Even if we did, who's likely to take on the empire?"

"Was this an isolated attack?" asked Charlaine. "Or do you think it was part of something bigger?"

"I'm inclined to believe they're trying to intercept any ships bound for Lidenbach."

"What about that other ship you found some months ago? The *Pelican*, wasn't it? Could the two be connected?"

"I don't see how," said Danica. "We discovered the *Pelican's* owner went missing, but no word on who hired his ship. In any event, neither he nor his crew has been seen since."

"Have there been any more attempts to follow you?"

"No, nor the *Vanguard*, for that matter."

"I'm no expert in the ways of merchants," said Charlaine, "but I assume few ships are at sea in the wintertime."

"That's true, but come the thaw, they'll be racing up and down the coast, trying to beat each other to market. If there's a warship out there preying on innocent merchants,it'll play havoc with trade."

Charlaine stared at her closest friend. "I know that look; you have a solution."

"I do, but it could prove troublesome."

"Then tell me what it is, and I'll judge if it's worth doing."

"I thought we'd organize an escort for merchants sailing up the coast."

"We haven't enough ships, have we?"

"We would if we convinced them all to sail together."

"And you'd escort them in *Valiant*? I hardly think one ship is sufficient."

"I figured we'd use both *Valiant* and *Vanguard*. Of course, the downside is we'd be at sea most of the time, leaving no ships here. Naturally, there's a way around that, which brings us to the matter of politics."

"Let me guess," said Charlaine. "You're going to suggest we bring one of our warships here to Lidenbach."

"I was. How do you feel about that?"

"Perhaps the more important question is how the king will react. He's finally started developing a backbone; the last thing I want is for Lord Corbin to exert pressure again."

"So, no warship, then?"

"I didn't say that," said Charlaine. "But we'll need to approach this a little more diplomatically."

"And just how do we do that?"

"I shall seek an audience with the king and hope to convince him that having more Temple ships here is in his best interest."

"And if you can't?"

"Then we're no worse off than we are now. In the meantime, I suggest you broach the subject of escorting ships with whatever merchant captains remain in Lidenbach. You can draw on our commanderies for extra knights if you need them."

"I will most certainly take you up on that offer. I have a question, though."

"Which is?"

"What if we come across a Halvarian ship attacking a trader?"

"Tell me this," said Charlaine. "If we were back in Reinwick, what would you do?"

Danica smiled. "We'd attack it as if it were a pirate."

"Then you have your answer."

"Even if it could lead to war?"

"What other choice do we have? Should we sit back and watch them destroy every ship they come across? And who would Halvaria declare war on? The Church? We're not a kingdom. Besides, we've been expecting this for months now."

Danica visibly relaxed. "I suppose I've been overthinking things."

"Just out of curiosity, which ship would you bring?"

"*Fearless.*"

"That was the former flagship of the Halvarian fleet!"

"It was, but what other choice have we? The smaller provincial ships won't be seen as a threat. At least, this way, we'll have something to rival the *Conqueror.*"

"And will you remain with the *Valiant?*"

"No. Vivian is more than capable of escorting merchants. I'll transfer my flag to *Fearless* once it arrives, assuming the king approves of its presence."

"Very well. Make whatever arrangements you deem necessary, but let's not arrange for *Fearless* to arrive until spring. That will give me some time to smooth things over with the king."

"It looks like I'm going to be busy in the coming weeks."

"Not too busy, I hope," said Charlaine. "It's Midwinter Eve. Surely you won't abandon us right before the big feast tomorrow?"

"You know, with everything going on around here, I'd completely lost track of time."

"We'll be serving our first meal at noon, so send half your crew. The others can take part in the evening festivities, along with yourself."

Danica licked her lips. "My mouth is watering just thinking about it. It'll make a pleasant change from sea rations."

"Come now, I've seen what you eat aboard *Valiant*. That's nothing to complain about."

"True, but at least here, I don't need to worry about my food rolling off the plate when we hit a wave."

"You haven't seen our plates."

Danica stared back, unsure whether to take the statement seriously. It wasn't until Charlaine broke into a grin that she realized it was meant in jest.

"Don't you have work to do?" asked the admiral.

"I've been busy replying to correspondence all afternoon. It seems like that's all I do these days."

"You need to get out more. You should come out to sea. You're always welcome aboard *Valiant*."

"I'd love to, I really would, but there's far too much work to be done here."

"You have an aide, you know. Couldn't you delegate some tasks to her?"

"I do that already," replied Charlaine, "but when push comes to shove, it's still my responsibility."

"Then I shall leave you to your letters, but I'll see you tomorrow night for dinner." Danica opened the door, almost bumping into Marlena. "What have you got there?" she asked.

"More letters for the commander."

"More?" said Charlaine with a sigh. "At this rate, Midwinter will be long done by the time I'm finished."

17

MIDWINTER

WINTER 1102 SR

C harlaine stared down at her plate. The meal had been delicious, the camaraderie delightful, yet all present knew the new year would likely bring war. This knowledge dampened their spirits, despite the celebratory nature of the Midwinter Feast.

"Well," said Danica. "It's been close to half a year since your arrival. How do you think you've done?"

"That's difficult to say," replied Charlaine. "I had a lot of trouble with Lord Corbin in the early days, but that seems to have subsided."

"And to what do you attribute that?"

"The increased presence of our patrols helped win over some of the townsfolk, although it's a bit early to call that a victory. Those in the countryside also seem friendlier, but we have a lot of work left to do to win over the merchants."

"I'm sure they'll come around once spring gets here and we start escorting their ships."

"I hope so," said Charlaine. "I also need to thank you for keeping ships here. I think it helps people realize we want to help them rather than take advantage of their suffering."

"Vivian is a fine captain."

"Yes, and you are an even finer admiral. You've handled your responsibilities with great success."

"You make it sound like I'm ready to be reassigned!"

Charlaine chuckled. "You don't get off that easily. I still need you to coordinate your plan to create a flotilla of merchant ships. Have you approached anyone about it yet?"

"Since yesterday? Even I can't move that fast. Don't worry. I'll get started on it first thing tomorrow. What about you?"

"Me?"

"Yes," said Danica. "What's your next step?"

"I've been so busy I haven't had time to think. I suppose I'd like to return to Braunfel before the spring thaw."

"To what end?"

"I've read all of Florence's reports, but the written word can often leave out important details."

"You think she's omitting something?"

"Not intentionally," said Charlaine, "but sometimes you can overlook things in the heat of the moment."

"You make it sound like we're already at war."

"In a sense, we are—a war of nerves. Sometimes I feel as though we're one misstep away from a complete disaster."

"That doesn't sound like you."

"Being a commander is a far cry from a captaincy. I must juggle multiple commands in the best interest of not only Arnsfeld but its neighbours as well. On top of that, I have to take care not to upset the fragile peace we're currently enjoying."

"A peace in which the Halvarians are preying on ships."

"Yes, which compounds the matter. Were it up to me, I'd order all my companies to concentrate here, in Lidenbach."

"Then why don't you?" asked Danica.

"There isn't enough space to house them all."

"What if you sent them to nearby cities?"

"Once again, we have the problem of where they would stay. It will be different once summer gets here, but it could be too late by then." Charlaine lowered her voice. "Frankly, it may already be too late."

"Whatever do you mean by that?"

"On paper, I command three hundred Temple Knights, which are spread over four kingdoms. A sizable contingent, to be sure, but that pales in comparison to a full Halvarian legion."

"But you'd have the Knights of the Silver Spur's assistance, wouldn't you?"

"Assuming the barons agree to my plan, yes. Don't get me wrong, knights are great on the battlefield, but the footmen bear the brunt of the action. We're also deficient in archers."

"How many Temple Knights did the Cunars have before they left?"

"Only two hundred," said Charlaine, "but they control the Holy Army, and the threat of their intervention served as the biggest deterrent—now they're gone."

Marlena had overseen the noon feast for those currently on duty and, as such, was not expected to attend the evening service. Her arrival now could only mean one thing—something that required Charlaine's attention.

Sure enough, she went straight to the head table. "Sorry to interrupt the festivities, Commander, but you've received an urgent summons to court."

"How urgent?" asked Charlaine.

Her aide handed over a note demanding the immediate presence of the regional commander of the Temple Knights of Saint Agnes. Perhaps even more surprising, though, was that Charlaine's name was absent from the summons.

"When did this arrive?"

"Just now," replied Marlena. "The messenger is waiting for a reply."

"Please convey I shall be there directly." Charlaine got up and turned to Danica. "It appears my meal is done."

Her admiral also stood.

"What do you think you're doing?" Charlaine asked.

"I'm coming with you. I meant what I said earlier—you are not alone."

"I hardly consider this the time for solidarity."

"I respectfully disagree, and as you're so fond of reminding me, I command the fleet and, thus, do not fall under your command."

"Very well," said Charlaine. "We shall go together, though a change of attire is in order. I don't know about you, but I've been sweating up a storm."

"That's only because you gave a speech. It's surprising when you think of it."

"What is?"

"That you get so nervous addressing others. You've led Temple Knights into battle numerous times and shown no fear, yet you're so anxious here, addressing your own command."

"I can't help it. I suppose, deep down, I'm worried about saying something wrong."

"All the more reason for me to accompany you to court. Now, let's get going, shall we? We don't want to keep the king waiting."

If the Temple Knights' arrival surprised the king's servants, they gave no indication of it. They guided the two visitors to the great hall, where the lords and ladies of Arnsfeld sat around a sumptuous table. Charlaine recognized Sir Hugo amongst the attendees but kept her eyes on King Stefan.

She bowed. "Your Majesty."

The king looked up from his plate. "Ah, Commander Charlaine. It's about time you showed up. Who have you brought with you?"

"My apologies for my tardiness, sire, but I was overseeing the order's Midwinter Feast. Allow me to introduce Temple Captain Danica Meer, Admiral of the Fleet."

The scraping of a chair caught Charlaine's attention, and she turned to spot Lord Corbin rising from his seat.

"Ah, we meet again. The so-called Admiral Meer."

"That would be Admiral Danica," said Charlaine. "We don't typically use our last names when referring to our positions."

"And yet you introduced her as such, did you not?"

"Only for the sake of completeness. His Highness is, of course, the king and therefore deserving of such."

Stefan's laughter forestalled any comment the envoy was about to make. "Hah. She has you there, Corbin. It seems the Temple Knights count wit amongst their weaponry. Rather a surprising turn of events, if I do say so myself."

"Perhaps," came the voice of Rebecca, "you might explain to the commander why you summoned her, Father?"

The king hid his scowl by wiping his face with a napkin. "It seems your order has overstepped its bounds, Commander."

"In what way?" asked Charlaine.

"Your Temple Knights crossed into Halvaria at Braunfel and assaulted the empire's warriors."

"Who makes this accusation?"

"I do," said Lord Corbin. "I received word of it this very day."

Danica leaned forward, whispering in Charlaine's ear, "The *Dominator* arrived only this morning."

"That's the ship we saw at the mouth of the river, wasn't it?"

"The very same."

"Are we boring you?" asked Corbin, garnering everyone's attention. "Perhaps you'd like to share what you two are chattering on about?"

"Admiral Danica informed me of the arrival of yet another Halvarian warship. That makes three, if I'm not mistaken."

Corbin smiled knowingly. "It does indeed, with more on the way."

"Come now," said the king. "We have yet to conclude our discussion on the previous subject." He turned back to Charlaine. "Now, where was I? Oh yes, the complaint concerning your knights. Apparently, they were a little overzealous in the pursuit of their duties. What have you to say for yourself?"

"I cannot comment on something I've not yet heard the particulars of. I assure you, however, I place great importance on learning the true nature of these accusations."

"And how do you intend to do that?"

"I'll set out for Braunfel first thing tomorrow."

"You'll need to ride," said Lord Corbin. "The river is frozen solid at this time of year."

"A fact that I am well aware of, thank you."

"We are set to return home tomorrow," added Princess Rebecca. "We would be grateful for the company."

"And I would be pleased to supply it," replied Charlaine, then turned back to the Halvarian envoy. "Might I have the details, my lord?"

"I'm sorry, I didn't quite hear you." Corbin's smile indicated he was enjoying this.

Charlaine swallowed her pride and prepared to rephrase her statement, but Danica beat her to it.

"Commander Charlaine humbly asks for the details of the alleged attack, my lord." She moved to stand beside his chair. "I assume you saw fit to bring a copy of this complaint in writing?"

"I did." He held out his hand and waited as a guard skittered forward with a scroll. Corbin examined it before holding it out for Danica, forcing her to come and get it. She plucked it from his grip, surprising the fellow with her speed.

"Thank you, Your Grace. I'm sure she'll find this most illuminating." Danica returned to her commander's side but kept the scroll.

Charlaine locked eyes with the king. "Is there anything else I can do for you, Your Majesty?"

"I don't suppose you'd consider giving us a blessing for this meal?"

Charlaine stared back, not quite believing her ears. The blessing customarily happened before the meal was served, not after they'd devoured it. She considered reminding the king of this but realized it would do little to improve the situation she found herself in.

"Very well," she said instead, moving to stand beside the king.

Charlaine bowed her head. "Let us pray." She paused to gather her thoughts. "Blessed Saint Agnes, we call upon you today to bless this meal. Watch over us as we serve in your name, give us the strength to triumph over our enemies, and keep us safe that we might serve you in all your glory." It was a brief prayer she'd used with some modifications before battle, but it suited the occasion. "Saints be with us," she said, completing her blessing.

"Saints be with us all," came the reply, though only from a few souls.

"Excellent." The king looked pleased with the results. "I must thank you, Commander. It's not every day we receive a blessing from a high-ranking member of the Church."

"High-ranking?" said Lord Corbin. "She is but a Temple Knight, sire, and thus has no standing outside her own order."

"The envoy is mistaken," said Danica. "Temple rank is recognized all over the Petty Kingdoms by kings and dukes alike."

"What nonsense is this?"

Charlaine smiled. "I wouldn't expect you to understand, my lord, for I don't believe your empire has any orders of knighthood. Of course, you're free to correct me if I'm wrong."

"What has that got to do with anything?"

"Membership in an order of knights is considered a great honour across the Continent. The king's own Silver Spurs are a fine example of that. Or would you care to disagree?"

"So they are," replied Corbin, "but I might remind all present that the Silver Spurs are a fraternal order, as are all orders outside the Church."

"And that is our loss," piped up Sir Hugo. "Commander Charlaine here has more than proven her military prowess, as have her sister knights. The admiral, too."

"Admiral?" said Corbin. "Don't make me laugh. An admiral commands a fleet, not a ragtag collection of run-down ships."

"Those ships have brought piracy to its knees," replied Charlaine. "Piracy which, I might add, was being aided and abetted by the empire."

"What is this?" demanded the king.

"It's true," added Danica. "Just this last summer, when we captured a notorious pirate ship called the *Sprite*, we discovered a large amount of Halvarian coins aboard her."

"That proves nothing," insisted Corbin, "only that he preyed on our ships as well as yours."

"But your ships are always escorted, or are you saying your vessels are easily overcome?"

"You're twisting my words!"

"Not at all, my lord. I'm merely reporting the facts."

"Facts? Where is the proof? Are we to simply take your word for it?"

Sir Hugo stood. "You are impugning the word of a Temple Knight, my lord. Such a thing cannot go unpunished."

"Are you, a mere knight, challenging me, Sir Hugo? If so, I should warn you I am an accomplished swordsman."

The king rose, ending all discussion. "That is quite enough, all of you. Sit down, Sir Hugo, and let cooler heads prevail. Now, Lord Corbin, you must forgive my knight. No doubt, he was overcome with emotion at the thought of a fellow knight being maligned and didn't consider the consequences."

"I should be glad to, providing he apologizes for his words."

Everyone stared at Sir Hugo. The knight stood, then bowed to the king. "My apologies if I have offended you, sire. My intent was not to disrespect this court or suggest a duel as the only way to settle matters."

"You call that an apology?" said Corbin. "If I were king, I would see this man beheaded for his impudence."

"Then it is a good thing you do not rule here," said Stefan. "Your ways are not ours, my lord, and I would remind you that you are the visitor here. You would do well to remember that."

"And what of the insult these Temple Knights have inflicted on the good people of Halvaria?"

"Commander Charlaine has agreed to look into the matter, and I have full confidence in her sincerity."

"That is not enough!" shouted Corbin.

"Perhaps not, but it's all you're likely to see for the foreseeable future. Once the investigation is complete, we can take further action, but until then, I must insist you keep your opinions to yourself."

Corbin stood, then bowed towards the king. "I shall not remain to suffer this indignation. Good evening, Your Majesty. I trust that when we meet again, you will have reconsidered your attitude regarding investigating this slight against the Halvarian Empire." He strode from the room, leaving many stunned at his behaviour.

King Stefan started chuckling, then let out huge guffaws, with everyone joining in until he suddenly broke into a coughing fit. He raised a kerchief to his mouth, then pulled back the blood-stained cloth.

Servants rushed forward, lending what help they could. The coughing subsided, leaving Stefan pale and exhausted. As he stood, so did his guests, who remained deathly quiet as two knights escorted the unsteady king from the room.

"Please," said the princess, "everybody sit. I'm sure His Majesty would want you to finish the feast." She looked at her husband. "My lord, would you do the honour of hosting in the king's absence?"

Lord Handrik moved to the head of the table even as servants removed the king's plate. Rebecca, for her part, followed after her father.

Charlaine moved to intercept her. "What can we do to help?" she asked.

"My father has been ill for some time. Unfortunately, the ministrations of the Royal Physician have done little to help. If you truly wish to be of assistance, you can pray for his health to improve." She rushed from the room.

Danica appeared at her friend's side. "I had no idea he was so sick."

"Nor I," replied Charlaine. "I'm no expert, but this bodes ill."

"Perhaps he'll recover?"

"That would certainly be my preference. I only wish we had a Life Mage here, then we'd be able to help him."

"And if he dies?"

"I hate to say it," said Charlaine, "but his death would likely trigger the Halvarian invasion."

"But Lord Handrik is named as his successor? Surely that accounts for something?"

"It does, but a king's death always results in a period of uncertainty, which can be exploited to great effect in the right hands. We must be ever vigilant, or else we might find our nightmares coming to the fore before we get our people into place."

18

TROUBLE

WINTER 1102 SR

The following day found Charlaine and Danica readying their horses in the early morning chill. They eschewed their armour in favour of warm clothing, for the winter winds had picked up of late. They reckoned it to be a three-day trip accompanying the princess's carriage, but with snow blanketing the ground, it could take considerably longer.

Charlaine was just placing her foot in the stirrup when Marlena burst into the courtyard. "Commander?"

"Something wrong?"

"We've received an urgent plea for help."

"From whom?"

"Brother Gatan. There's a riot at the Mathewite mission."

"Where are their Temple Knights?"

"He doesn't mention them."

"Then order the morning patrol to assemble." She turned to Danica as her aide ran back inside. "I'm afraid I shall be delayed. You go rendezvous with the princess, and get her on her way. I'll catch up with you later."

"Are you sure?" asked Danica. "I can always wait."

"It would be best for her to make the safety of an inn by nightfall. I don't know how long this will take."

"Very well. I'll see you later this evening." Danica pulled herself into the saddle. "Good luck and be careful."

"I will," replied Charlaine.

The knights ran into the stables to prepare their mounts. Charlaine considered donning her armour but knew time was of the essence. She waited until some of the sisters had emerged from the building.

"You six, come with me. The rest assemble under Captain Miranda, and meet us at the mission." She led her knights out into the streets of Lidenbach.

The Brothers of Saint Mathew ran a mission that helped those most in need. As such, they served meals to the poor and assisted those suffering from various ailments or injuries. It was always a busy place, particularly in winter when the cold weather brought its own hardships.

Charlaine could hear voices calling for violence when they were still three blocks away. She led her knights around a corner, coming upon a huge crowd of people pushing in on the mission's doors, their faces filled with desperation as those in the back tried to force their way forward.

Charlaine brought her knights to a halt, then trotted ahead of them. "Stand aside!" she shouted.

The townsfolk closest to her backed up while the rest, caught up in the heat of the moment, beat upon the mission doors.

"Advance," ordered Charlaine.

She eased Stormcloud forward, and soon more people took notice. She noted a few at the back who ran off, and then the yelling subsided, replaced by looks of fear and uncertainty.

The Temple Knights of Saint Agnes pushed the crowd away from the door, then turned, now guarding the mission. Charlaine dismounted, stepping forward to address the townsfolk. These were ordinary people; what could have turned them so violent?

"Why are you here?" she called out, trying to keep her tone friendly.

"We're here for food," replied an old woman, "but there's none left!"

"Not true," came a reply as Brother Gatan exited the building. "There is plenty of food inside for everyone, but we can only sit a small number at one time. You must be patient."

The woman looked around, searching the crowd behind her.

"Looking for someone?" asked Charlaine.

"That young fellow with the black hair. He said you were hoarding food and refused to give it to us! Others backed up his story."

"What others?"

"The tall fellow with the well-trimmed beard," called out a man's voice.

"And where is this man?"

The townsfolk looked around as if their curiosity might make him appear.

"You've been lied to," said Charlaine.

"Easy for you to say," came the reply. "I don't see you suffering for lack of food."

Charlaine pointed at the old woman. "You. Come with me." She searched the crowd. "You, too." She directed this at the man who'd spoken up. "We'll take you inside so you can see for yourselves and report back to your neighbours."

Her knights shifted their mounts, creating an opening through which Charlaine led the two witnesses. Brother Gatan opened the door for them.

"Go straight through," he said. "The storeroom is just behind the kitchen."

They went inside, past the tables crowded with people eating a modest meal. The kitchens were even more congested as lay brothers, along with a few volunteers, scrambled around, preparing food.

Brother Gatan caught up to Charlaine, leading her and the two witnesses into the storeroom. "As you can see, there is plenty here, but the size of our kitchen and dining area limits us. We've appealed to the Church for a larger space, but I'm afraid the funds are unavailable for such an undertaking."

"I don't understand," said the old woman. "We were told you were out of food. Who would say such a thing?"

"Who indeed?" replied Brother Gatan. "Someone was obviously trying to make a scene, though to what end I cannot say."

"We must remain vigilant," added Charlaine. "Perhaps we should station some of our Temple Knights here, just in case."

"That would be much appreciated. Thank you."

Charlaine led the pair back outside. The crowd, now consisting of only twenty or so, was lined up and waiting patiently. Their comrades rejoined them, telling of all they'd seen.

"My thanks, Commander," said Gatan. "Things were turning quite ugly, and I feared blood might be shed."

"We are happy to help, but what of your Brother Knights?"

"Your commandery was closer, and we lack the numbers to deal with this."

"Then I shall leave these six sisters under your capable hands for the moment. Captain Miranda will, no doubt, be arriving shortly with further reinforcements."

"And what of you? I hope this situation hasn't ruined your plans?"

"No, merely delayed them a little. I shall return to my office, write a report, and then set out for Braunfel."

"It'll be a hard ride to reach an inn by nightfall."

"True, but I have a sturdy horse, and the weather is clear. Fear not, Brother. I shall be fine."

"I'll make sure of that," called out Danica.

"What are you doing here?" asked Charlaine. "I thought I told you to accompany the princess?"

"She has guards aplenty, and I really have little in common with Her Highness. Better, I think, to travel in the company of someone I'm familiar with."

"You didn't need to do that."

"You're right, I didn't, yet I chose to anyway. That's what friends are for."

Charlaine smiled. "I thank you for the company, but I'm afraid I've work to do before we set out."

"I can wait. It's not as if *Valiant* is going anywhere. Actually, disregard that. *Valiant* IS going somewhere, just not with me."

"Oh?"

"Vivian is taking her out on patrol. After that attack on the *Sapphire*, we need to increase our presence in these waters."

"And you're not accompanying her?"

"She's a fine captain," replied Danica, "and I can't always be looking over her shoulders. It's time she learned to stand on her own two feet." She cast her gaze around. "I assume you've settled everything here?"

"For the time being. I've posted guards, just to be sure. These are well-meaning folk, but someone's been agitating them."

"Let me guess, Halvarians?"

"Maybe, but it could also be a criminal element, trying to take advantage of an opportunity."

"How is attacking a mission an opportunity?"

"I haven't a clue, but hopefully, we'll learn more in the fullness of time. Now, come along. I must write my report before we get on the road."

One thing led to another, and it was well past noon by the time they got on the road to Braunfel. Once they cleared the farmland surrounding the capital, the countryside opened up, and a frigid breeze blew across the road.

Charlaine shivered as the wind ripped through her cloak. "Don't you ever get cold?"

Danica broke into a grin. "You forget. I grew up on the coast, so I'm used to this."

"Yes, but that was years ago, not to mention hundreds of miles from here."

"True, but this region isn't so different from Andover in terms of weather. I've also spent a lot of time on the *Valiant* these last few years. There's nothing like the brisk chill of the Great Northern Sea to get you used to cold weather."

"Good for you," said Charlaine, "but I'm of Calabrian descent. My ancestors saw fit to adapt to a warmer clime."

"Stop your griping. It could be worse."

"How?"

"You could be dressed for battle. Nothing chills you so fast as wearing plate armour in the cold."

"I hadn't considered that. When did you become the wise one?"

"When I started taking up with you!"

"Well, I'm glad you did."

"As am I," said Danica, looking around the countryside. "It's pretty flat here."

"There's a roadside tavern a mile or so down the road. It might be a good idea to stop there and see how far behind the princess we are."

"We can grab a bite to eat as well."

It didn't take long to spot the tavern in question: a modest affair, boasting a walled-in courtyard, helpful in fending off the winds blowing in from the sea.

Their approach must have been noticed, for two stable hands waited for them as they entered. The Temple Knights dismounted, handed off their reins, and stepped inside to the warmth of a roaring fire.

"This is nice," said Danica as she removed her cloak.

A serving girl came towards them, recognizing their scarlet cassocks. "Sisters," she said. "Welcome to the Barking Hound. Can I fetch you something to drink?"

"Yes," replied Charlaine, "and some food if you could. We have a good distance to travel and need sustenance to ward off the cold."

"There's a hunter's stew on the fire, if that will suffice?"

"That would be wonderful, thank you."

They took a seat, waiting for food, as she placed two mugs of ale before them. An older couple sat near the fire while a group of four men, farm labourers by the look of them, filled another table.

"Did you come from the capital?" asked the older woman.

"We did," replied Charlaine. "Why do you ask?"

"You're the second lot from there today. I heard that a carriage stopped here earlier. I don't know who it was, but they must be important to warrant guards."

"Those are the people we're trying to catch up to. Were they here before noon?"

"Aye, that's what we heard," the woman's husband replied. "But you'd best be on your way if you hope to catch them by nightfall. They've got quite a lead on you."

"I'm not worried," said Charlaine. "There's an inn half a day's ride from here where they will likely settle in till morning. It'll mean a late night for us, but we should make it by midnight."

"If you don't mind me asking, where are you off to?"

"Braunfel," offered Danica. "We're inspecting the local commandery there."

"Inspecting, you say? You must be very important to be given such a task."

"My friend here is the regional commander of the order."

"Then we are blessed indeed by your presence."

The serving girl returned, depositing a bowl of watery stew for each of them. Two of the labourers got up and left, leaving their companions chatting over an ale.

"Tell me," said the serving girl, "is it true what they say?"

"Is what true?" asked Charlaine.

"That war is coming. The people hereabouts are concerned that, come spring, an enemy army will march up the road to Lidenbach."

"It's certainly possible, but we shall do all we can to prevent that eventuality."

"The Saints be with you."

"And with you," said Charlaine.

Having eaten their fill, they returned to the road, their horses in fine spirits. The sky remained clear, and the troublesome wind from earlier had subsided. They'd gone no more than a mile when Danica reached back to grab her waterskin and noticed two men following them.

"It appears," she said, "that we have company."

Charlaine took a quick peek. "It could just be someone going in the same direction."

"Odd that we didn't see them earlier?"

"I suppose it is. In any case, they're not gaining on us. As long as they're willing to keep their distance, I'm fine with it."

"And if they're not?"

"Then we'll turn about and confront them," replied Charlaine.

"Good enough for me."

Half a mile later, as they came around a bend, they noticed two more riders in front of them. Unlike regular travellers, these weren't headed towards the knights. Instead, the men sat astride the road, blocking the way.

Charlaine slowed, prompting her companion to do likewise. The two men kept their eyes locked on the knights.

"Make way," called out Charlaine. "We are Temple Knights of Saint Agnes, and you are blocking the king's road."

Without a word, one of the pair loaded a crossbow.

"Not exactly a friendly response," said Danica.

Charlaine looked knowingly at her friend. "Are you thinking what I am?"

"That these fellows mean us harm?"

"Precisely!"

They urged their horses into a charge, drawing their swords as they closed the distance. The crossbowman sent a bolt sailing through the air, but it flew wide into the underbrush on the side of the road.

Charlaine reached over Stormcloud's head and sliced down, the blade digging into the crossbow, cutting its string and then sending the weapon flying out of her opponent's grasp.

Danica swung out, but her opponent skillfully deflected the blow. The horses pressed in closer until they were almost stirrup to stirrup, and then she thrust the tip of her sword into his armpit. The fellow grunted before he slumped forward, forcing the blade in even farther. His weight tore the weapon from her grasp as he fell from the saddle. He hit the ground to lie still, a pool of red forming on the white blanket of snow.

Charlaine struck while her opponent clumsily drew his sword, digging into his shoulder blade and scraping along the bone. He let out an agonized howl as he struggled to maintain control of his horse but then fell forward in the saddle, his mount racing away from the fight.

A sudden surge of pain pierced Charlaine's left bicep, and she looked down to see a crossbow bolt protruding from her arm. In all the excitement, she'd forgotten about the men behind her. She shouted a warning to Danica before turning Stormcloud around, but the last two attackers, having witnessed the skirmish, were already galloping off.

"You're wounded," said Danica. "Let me have a look."

Gritting her teeth, Charlaine dismounted. She felt light-headed and then unceremoniously sat on the snow.

Danica leaned over her, probing the wound. "You're lucky. The tip went clean through. Hold on. This is going to hurt." She grasped the bolt with two hands and broke off the tip. Charlaine let out a scream.

"That's the easy part," said Danica. "Now, I must pull out the shaft. Brace yourself." She received a nod in reply. "I'll pull it out on three. One—Two—" She pulled with all her might, using her foot to brace against Charlaine's arm. The bolt came out far easier than expected, sending Danica tumbling into the snow. She was back on her feet moments later, tearing a strip off her cloak and tying it around the wound.

"What happened to three?" asked Charlaine.

"I thought it better to surprise you so you wouldn't flinch."

"Well, you succeeded."

"We need to get you back to Lidenbach."

"And lose all that travel time? I don't think so."

"Then let us at least return to that tavern. That wound needs tending to."

"I'll be fine until we reach Braunfel."

"Braunfel? Are you mad? Somebody just tried to kill you!"

"All the more reason to continue? Someone wanted to stop me from getting there, and I need to know why."

"I don't think this has anything to do with Braunfel; I think it was an attempt to kill you. The riot at the mission was meant to delay you until their people were on the road?"

"And by 'people', you mean Halvarians?"

"Who else? Of course, those men could be local thugs, but I don't think there can be any doubt their orders came from Lord Corbin. We should at least go back and grab some knights for additional protection."

"No," said Charlaine. "We must get to the bottom of Corbin's claim against our order, and the only way to do that is to talk to Florence. We'll continue."

"I don't agree with your reasoning," said Danica, "but you're the commander."

She helped Charlaine to her feet, then they mounted up and were soon on their way again.

Darkness descended, and with it came a snowfall that obliterated all signs of the road. Charlaine and Danica tried to continue on, but they were clearly lost. Rather than wander around aimlessly, they decided to wait out the storm under cover of some trees. They built a fire and then settled in, even getting in some sleep before the night was done.

The storm abated early the following morning, allowing them to navigate their way back to the road. By midday, the Brinwald could be seen to the west, and then the standing stones came into view.

Charlaine halted at the sight of them.

"What's wrong?" said Danica.

"The land hereabouts—it's changed."

"Well, it is winter after all."

"No, I don't mean the snow. There's something else." She trotted Stormcloud closer. The stream was still visible, but the eastern bank now sat higher as if the ground had blistered up. "Orlina Day must have done it."

"Who?"

"Orlina Day, the Sacred Mother of Tauril. Didn't I mention her?"

"You most certainly did not," said Danica. "Are you suggesting she created these hills?"

"Yes. She's an Earth Mage."

"What was this area like the last time you saw it?"

"That stream was little more than an inconvenience. Now, it's like a collection of defensive positions. She has certainly been busy."

Danica took in their surroundings. "I assume this is where you intend to make your stand if Halvaria invades?"

"Yes, but it all hinges on finding enough men to hold the line."

"Do you think the king will be able to send aid?"

"I would like to believe so, but there's the danger the empire might also strike from the sea."

"Let me worry about their navy. You concentrate on stopping them here." Danica looked around. "This woman, Orlina Day, doesn't happen to be an herbalist, does she?"

"How did you know?"

"I've heard it's common with practitioners of Earth Magic, though I've never met one in person. Do you think she could help with your wound?"

"My arm will be right as rain in a few days. Now, let's ride on, shall we? I want to get to the commandery before Florence sends out her next patrol."

19

PRISONERS

WINTER 1102 SR

The two guards outside the commandery welcomed them as they rode into the courtyard, only to find a detachment preparing to head out on patrol.

Captain Florence was already mounted, but her superior's arrival surprised her. "Commander? We didn't expect you."

"Nor did I have time to warn you of our coming. Events in the capital have moved quickly, and we've come to get a first-hand look."

"Of what, might I ask?"

"The Halvarian envoy claims a patrol of Temple Knights crossed over into their territory and assaulted some of their warriors."

"I assure you we've done no such thing."

"I believe you, yet such an accusation still requires a thorough investigation on my part. I will need to discuss the matter with you at some length, but I don't wish to interrupt your patrol."

"Perhaps you'd like to accompany us?" asked Florence. "Then you can see for yourself what we're up against."

"I would, but I still have to take statements from your knights."

"I can do that while you're out riding," offered Danica. "It will give you an idea of what the empire has been up to of late."

"It appears I am to accompany you," said Charlaine.

Florence turned and examined the twelve knights waiting behind her, then urged her mount forward, leading them out of the courtyard.

Though no one spoke to them as they rode through town, it was clear that the folk in these parts appreciated their presence. More than one person waved as they passed, while young children occasionally followed them down the street, only to be hustled back by their parents.

They headed towards the docks, then turned south, following the river's eastern bank. The wind picked up, causing the snow to form into little whirlwinds on the frozen water.

"We generally follow the road until we reach the thick forest, then continue eastward around the farms. After that, we'll turn north once more and return to the commandery."

"And have things been quiet of late?" asked Charlaine.

"We still find stray Halvarians from time to time, if that's what you're asking, but we escort them back to the river."

"Have any of these encounters led to bloodshed?"

"Not at all. Although we have two in the infirmary, one fell from her horse, and the other received a kick to the chest. Had she not been wearing armour, she'd likely be dead. It took the armourer the best part of a day to work out the dent."

"And the baron's men? Have they had any trouble?"

"None that I'm aware of. Then again, it's midwinter, and most folks hereabouts were more concerned with preparing for the feast. I expect we'll start seeing more activity from across the river now that it's over." She paused as a thought sank in. "Do the Halvarians even celebrate the Midwinter Feast?"

"I have no idea," said Charlaine. "Nor am I particularly eager to find out."

Captain Florence slowed, scanning the area. "This is new."

She was looking at where a sizable number of people must have crossed the river sometime this morning, for there was no denying the tracks they'd left in last night's snowfall.

"I assume you haven't seen this before?"

"Individual tracks, yes, but this many, no. I'd say at least fifteen. Hmm. It appears this patrol won't be routine after all. Shall I dispatch some knights to escort you back to the commandery?"

"Why would you do that?" asked Charlaine.

"I noticed you are favouring your arm, and you have no armour."

"I assure you my arm is only a minor inconvenience. As for my lack of armour, I'm more than willing to stay back and let your knights take care of any fighting, assuming it even comes to that."

"Very well, Commander." Florence turned to address her knights. "Keep your wits about you. This group is sizable and might prove troublesome. If anyone spots anything of interest, be sure to speak up. The last thing we want is to ride into an ambush. Understood?" Her command nodded back. "Good. Now, let's track these villains down."

The trail was easy to follow, and before long, they cut east.

"Why here, I wonder?" said Florence. "It was not a large enough group to be part of an army."

"I suspect they're scouting out the region," offered Charlaine. "When war does come, they'll likely try to bypass the keep."

"They'll have a hard time of it. The terrain in these parts isn't exactly easy to navigate. In any case, if they wish to march to Lidenbach, the road's their only option."

"True, but they could leave a small force to bottle up the keep's garrison while they send the rest to the capital. The problem with that, though, would be getting their supply wagons past the keep."

"I agree," said Florence. "The countryside is fine for horses and such, but once the spring rains come, I'm told it'll turn into a quagmire. I suppose they could always wait until the summer?"

"That's certainly a possibility. The empire has an incredible amount of patience when it comes to launching its attacks, but once they decide to start a campaign, they're known for coming in overwhelming numbers."

"And if they do, what's our strategy? Do we hold on to the commandery or retreat up the road to Lidenbach?"

"A fighting retreat. The plan is to make a stand to the northeast of here, but you'll need to buy us some time to get the reinforcements in place. I know that's not what you wanted to hear, but I'm afraid it's the best we can hope for. Even then, they'll vastly outnumber us."

"Just how many men does the king have?"

"I'm still working on that. I'll let you know once I have the final numbers."

A crossbow bolt sailed out of the woods off to one side.

"Bows on the right," called out a knight.

"For Saint's sake," said Florence. "They're in the trees. They must have created this trail, then doubled back out of sight."

"Dismount," ordered Charlaine. "We'll never get the horses in amongst the underbrush."

More bolts sailed forth, one bouncing off a knight's helmet. The sisters were soon afoot, with two taking the horses and leading them out of danger. The rest drew swords, making their way south, towards the enemy.

The attack did little against the Temple Knights' armour, but that didn't stop the raiders from keeping up a constant stream of volleys.

Charlaine almost followed them into the woods but then remembered that she was unarmoured. Instead, she held her ground, watching as Florence led her knights in amongst the trees. The sound of swordplay soon reached her ears, then a pair of knights emerged to wave the horses forward.

Florence appeared shortly after, pushing an injured man before her. "Six dead and five wounded, none of them ours. The rest fled."

"You did well," said Charlaine.

"With your permission, I'll dispatch six knights to harry them back to the river."

"It's your command, Captain."

Charlaine watched as Florence gave the orders. It was strange to be present yet not a part of the action. She wondered if all commanders felt this way but then remembered she wouldn't be inactive for long. The empire would cross the borders soon, and then she would be called upon to use all her wits to stem the invasion. Would she be up to the task?

With knights sent off in pursuit, and the prisoners bound, the remainder of the group turned around, heading back to the commandery.

"I'm surprised they attacked," said Florence. "Had they simply waited, we would have passed them by, and then they could have made their way back without fighting."

"I think that ambush was to test your resolve. Likely, they were expecting you to break."

"Temple Knights do not break."

"There's a first time for everything," said Charlaine. "The empire doesn't know our capabilities like it does the Cunars."

"I assume that means we passed the test?"

"I would think so."

"It's too bad some of them got away."

"It actually works to our advantage," said Charlaine. "After that skirmish, they'll have a healthy respect for us, and I expect it will alter their plan of attack."

"How so?"

"They'll need to dispatch warriors to tie us down and prevent us from causing problems. A direct attack on the commandery would seem the most likely method of doing this, which makes it all the more important that when the time comes, you make it out into the open, where you can do the most damage."

"You really think this will all come to war?"

"I'd prefer to be prepared for a war that doesn't happen than unprepared for one that does."

"Spoken like a true warrior," said Florence. Her gaze fell on the prisoners. "What do we do with these?"

"Take them to Lord Handrik. He can keep them in the dungeon for the time being. Who knows? We could be lucky, and one of them might reveal their attack plan."

They rode north, back towards Braunfel. By the time they reached the keep, the rest of the patrol had rejoined them, having chased the interlopers as far as the river.

Apprised of their arrival, Lord Handrik greeted them in person. "What have we here?" he asked.

"Halvarians," said Charlaine. "They and their comrades attempted to ambush us while we were on patrol."

"Is this the beginning of an invasion?"

"No, though it would seem their scouting of the area has become more aggressive. We hoped that we could prevail upon you to keep them locked up."

"Certainly," said the baron. "Who knows, a little persuasion might even loosen their tongues. It would be helpful to know what forces lie across the border, don't you think?"

"Most certainly," said Charlaine, "although I don't condone torture."

"You and I do not see eye to eye on this, but I shall respect your wishes in this case." He waved forward a group of soldiers to take the prisoners into custody. "Will you stay while we look into matters?"

"No. I have business to attend to at the commandery. If you have any news, you can reach me there."

"Very well. I shall let you know if we discover anything of interest."

Charlaine turned around, guiding Stormcloud back down to the town. Florence followed, her knights now in single file.

"I don't like this escalation," she said. "I may need to increase the size of my patrols."

"You must do what you think is best," replied Charlaine. "You're the captain here; it's entirely your decision."

"What would you do if you were in my place?"

"Is that your way of asking what to do?"

"I'm merely seeking your advice. That doesn't necessarily mean I'll take it."

"Very well. I'd increase the size of patrols to eighteen or possibly even twenty knights. You might also consider increasing their frequency. Had you earlier warning of that intrusion, you could have prevented them from setting an ambush."

"Wise words," said Florence. "I'll keep them in mind." She kept looking at Charlaine as they rode on a bit farther, then looked away. "Do you mind if I ask you a question?"

"Not at all. What do you want to know?"

"What was your first command like?"

"I was sent to Reinwick to replace someone who had died."

"And were you accepted?"

"There was some animosity when I first arrived. The senior knight there thought she was going to be named captain."

"And what was your replacement like when you left?"

"I was permitted to appoint my own successor."

"That's rather unusual, isn't it?"

"I'm led to believe it is," said Charlaine.

"The grand mistress must think highly of your abilities."

"It's more about sharing the same vision for the order."

"Which is?"

Charlaine smiled. "That's a complicated story best left for another day."

"Then I shan't press you for details. I am curious, though, how Danica is still serving with you. I didn't think the order did that sort of thing?"

"What sort of thing is that?"

"Allowed you to use your influence to keep her at your side."

"Is that what you think happened? Nothing could be further from the truth. The fact of the matter is she travelled to Reinwick to purchase ships for the order."

"Why would we want ships in the first place?"

"Do you know nothing of our history?" asked Charlaine. "The Temple Knights of Saint Agnes originally commanded the Holy Fleet in the south."

"I thought the Cunars had that honour?"

"They do now, but that's a relatively recent development."

"So, Danica works directly for the Church now?"

"No. She's subservient to the order, the same as us."

"But she's the admiral, isn't she?"

"Yes," said Charlaine, "and the fleet belongs to the Temple Knights of Saint Agnes, not the Church."

"I'm not sure I understand the distinction."

"It's all about possession. The northern fleet is in our hands, preventing any other order from taking command of our ships."

"Are we expecting trouble with the other orders?"

"You tell me. We didn't abandon Arnsfeld, and you saw for yourself how far the Cunars were willing to go to block your way."

"You don't suppose they'll actively interfere with our defence here, do you?"

"I can't say with any certainty they'll remain neutral should the war prove long, but in the short term, at least there's little they can do. They've not only pulled out of Arnsfeld but from Burgemont, Angvil, and Rudor as well. If they hope to return here, they've got a lot of marching to do to make that happen."

"Couldn't they come by ship?"

"They could if they had any," said Charlaine, "but if they had a fleet in the north, Danica would have heard of it by now."

The sight of the commandery put an end to their discussion. Charlaine entered the courtyard and dismounted, only to see a familiar face approaching.

"Something wrong?" she called out.

"Not at all," replied Danica, "but I was wondering when you'd return."

"We ran into a spot of trouble, a small raiding party."

"How small?"

"Twenty or so, though they didn't line up to make counting easy. In any case, we chased most of them off but managed to capture a few prisoners. They're with the baron's people at the moment. How did you make out here?"

"I've finished talking to the sisters. Well, all except for those who accompanied the patrol."

"And?"

"They all swear none of them crossed the border. It appears the accusations were a complete fabrication. Do you want me to interview the rest?"

"Yes, just to be complete. In the meantime, I'm going to find a place to lie down for a while. It's been a busy day."

"How's the arm?" asked Danica.

"Still throbbing, if you must know."

"You should have someone look at it."

"I will. I'll get the Brothers of Saint Mathew to look at it when we return to Lidenbach."

"And in the meantime, you'll just be in constant agony?"

"I suppose that's one way to interpret things."

The sound of the door opening woke Charlaine. A solitary figure bearing a candlestick entered, but it took a moment for her eyes to focus on the face.

"Danica? Has something happened?"

"That depends on how you define 'something'. A messenger arrived from Lord Handrik."

Charlaine sat up, forgetting her wound until she put weight on the arm, leading her to wince.

Danica shook her head. "You're a wonderful friend, and I love you dearly, but you've got to be the worst patient I've ever met."

"Are you just going to mock me or help me get dressed?"

"All right, sleepyhead. Where did you put your cassock?"

Ordinarily, it would have been a simple matter to throw on her clothes, but her injury made lifting her left arm difficult, which greatly complicated her getting dressed. With Danica's help, they got Charlaine looking presentable, then went to the captain's office, where an older man, a seasoned warrior, judging by the condition of his chain shirt, stood waiting.

"Good day, Commander," he began. "I'm Sergeant Grier Burke. The baron sent me."

"Please," said Charlaine. "Sit and tell us why you're here."

The man remained standing. "You know those prisoners you found? It seems luck was with us, for you killed their captain."

"How is that to our advantage?"

"These men are provincial troops. Without the presence of their officer, they've been more than willing to cooperate."

"So, it didn't take long to get a confession out of them?"

"To be honest, they're likely still babbling on. Once they realized we weren't going to kill them, they began telling us everything they could think of."

"Which is?"

"We are now aware that an Imperial legion sits across the river, ready to invade. None of them know the exact date, but they believe it won't be for some time yet. Even better, each has signed a written confession. His Lordship wants to send them to Lidenbach to His Majesty, the king."

"Any idea of when they'll leave?"

"Sooner rather than later, I think. Perhaps even as early as tomorrow morning."

"I'd suggest sending along some guards. If word gets out that we have prisoners, there may be an attempt to rescue them. Particularly if they believe they'll reveal their plans."

"Don't worry," said the sergeant. "His Lordship has things well in hand. That reminds me, he's wondering what your plans are."

"Much as I'd like to stay and visit, I have things to do. This incursion tells me the enemy is moving into the next stage of their campaign."

"Which is?"

"Testing our defences. In the next few weeks, you might find some of your men coming under attack, although I doubt any of it would involve large numbers."

"Then we shall be sure to show them how we deal with bandits and thieves."

"I'd like to be there when the prisoners are presented to the king."

"I shall be sure to pass that on to Lord Handrik. Now, unless you have further questions, I must be off. Those prisoners won't ready themselves for transport."

"Of course," said Charlaine. "And thank you again for bringing this to our attention."

They waited while two knights escorted him down the hallway.

"Finally," said Danica. "The break we've been waiting for."

"I'm not so sure I'd call it a break," replied Charlaine, "and I doubt even a signed confession would rattle Lord Corbin. The more important result is that we now have a much better idea of how many men will be invading."

"A legion. That's more than two thousand, perhaps even three."

"Twenty-four hundred would be a more accurate assumption, providing it's at full strength."

"And how many will we have to withstand them?"

"Not enough. Not nearly enough."

20

TRAGEDY

WINTER 1102 SR

Morning came far too early for Charlaine's liking. She struggled out of bed and headed down to the dining hall to find the place packed.

"You're finally awake," called out Danica. "Come. I've saved you a seat."

Charlaine slumped down beside her. "You look exhausted."

"I didn't sleep well last night."

"I can't say I blame you," replied Danica. "Not after Sergeant Burke woke us. Your head must be swirling with possibilities. After all, it's not every day we get to wring a confession out of the Halvarians. I don't imagine Lord Corbin will be too pleased."

Charlaine grunted.

"Are you sure you're up to travelling? You don't look well."

"I'll be fine," she snapped back. "And before you ask, I promise to seek out the healers at the Mathewite mission upon our return to Lidenbach."

"You can be awfully stubborn at times."

"I'm told it's my most redeeming quality."

Danica ignored the comment. "We'd best get some food in you if we want to be on the road before noon."

"Is it that late?"

"It's well past sunrise, if that's what you mean."

"You should have woken me," said Charlaine.

"If you want someone to wake you up, you should have brought along Marlena. She is your aide after all."

"And have her pester me about my arm as well? No, thank you." Charlaine rose. "Come on, let's get the horses ready."

"You don't want to eat?"

"I'm not particularly hungry this morning."

"Fine, then wait a moment while I finish yours," Danica used her spoon to shovel the porridge into her mouth. "That was delicious. I wish the ship's cook could make a meal like that."

"It's porridge," said Charlaine. "How difficult can that be?"

"All I know is the fellow makes it taste… well, I'm not sure what it tastes like, but it's certainly nothing like this."

"Let's get going, shall we? You can tell me all about your woes on the road."

They made their way through the commandery, finally emerging into the courtyard where a Temple Knight stood waiting, holding the leads to their mounts.

"What's this?" asked Charlaine.

"I thought it best to have the horses readied while we ate," replied Danica, "though perhaps I should say while I ate."

Charlaine climbed into the saddle, then noticed Danica watching her. "Are you going to mount up or merely amuse yourself by staring at me?"

"Can't I do both?" Danica put her foot into the stirrup, pulling herself up. "There. All set and ready to go. Yourself?"

Charlaine remained silent, urging Stormcloud forward. They trotted out the gate and were soon amongst the streets of Braunfel.

"I wonder how long it will be before we're back here," mused Danica.

"Spring, at least," replied Charlaine, "but there's a good chance it'll be at the head of an army, providing I can scrape one together. On the other hand, you'll be far too busy trying to destroy their fleet. Any idea how you'll accomplish that?"

"My first step will be to locate where they've concentrated their ships. I've gotten hold of a few charts of the Halvarian coast, enough to make an educated guess as to where they might mass."

"How did you manage that?"

"The fishermen hereabouts regularly travel up and down the coast, following the catch."

"And they keep maps?"

Danica laughed. "No, but I've had them relay what they know to my mapmaker, which gave us a good idea of what to expect. Once the warmer weather arrives, I'll send *Valiant* and *Vanguard* out to patrol the coast."

"I thought you were going to use them to escort merchants?"

"I decided to use *Invincible* and *Indomitable* instead."

"Why the change of heart?"

"If the empire attacks shipping, it'll be with their larger warships."

"Why would you say that?"

"I'm afraid we're victims of our own success," said Danica. "*Valiant*, in particular, is known as a very manoeuvrable ship that can sail circles around a fleet. Unfortunately, it only carries a small detachment of knights in times of peace, and it's far too small to carry more troops on an extended voyage."

"And what of *Fearless?*"

"We'll leave that at Lidenbach, at least until war breaks out. When the invasion finally starts, its first objective will be destroying any Halvarian ships in port."

"A tall order," said Charlaine. "Have you a tactic in mind for doing that?"

"I thought I might use fire, but that could prove a double-edged sword. We also don't want to set the entire harbour aflame, just the Halvarians."

"So, what's the alternative?"

Danica smiled. "Now, now. I can't give away all my secrets."

The road brought them out of the town through the surrounding farmland. At this time of year, there was nothing to see but open fields of snow and the occasional farmhouse or barn. The land looked peaceful as if the entire realm rested before a colossal confrontation.

"Over there." Danica pointed. "Do you see it?"

Charlaine spotted a patch of red-stained snow and felt a moment of panic as if a fist had grabbed her heart. "There's been a fight here. We'd best investigate."

They trotted over to a scene of carnage, where bodies of men and horses lay scattered around the area.

"This was no fight," said Charlaine. "It was a slaughter."

"Bandits?"

"No. Bandits would've taken the horses, and there's no evidence of anyone plundering the bodies. What kind of thief would give up a chance of free coins?"

They dismounted, tying their horses off to a nearby tree. Charlaine wandered around the scene of the massacre while Danica knelt to examine one of the bodies.

"This was recent," said Danica. "This one's warm, which indicates whoever did this is likely still close. I don't suggest we remain in the area."

She'd expected a reply, yet none was forthcoming. She looked up to see Charlaine standing over a body, then she fell to her knees. At first, Danica took this as a desire to pray, but when her closest friend toppled over backwards, she ran to her.

"Charlaine!" she called out as she knelt, feeling for a pulse. Charlaine was pale, her breathing shallow and her eyes closed.

"Hold still. I'll be back in a moment." Danica ran and fetched the horses, then struggled to haul Charlaine to her feet. It took some doing to get her into the saddle, but finally, Danica led them to the road. She paused here, trying to decide which way to go. Her sense of duty told her to take Charlaine to the comfort of the commandery in Braunfel, but the home of Orlina Day was closer.

She struggled with the choice until common sense took hold. The commandery housed no skilled healers, whereas the Earth Mage knew about herbs. Danica turned the horses eastward, but it was nerve-wracking, for she was constantly stopping to steady Charlaine in the saddle.

They'd crossed the stream when young Luca appeared, walking along the top of one of the new hills, poking the ground with a stick. Upon sighting the Temple Knights, he shouted and waved.

"We need help," called out Danica. "My companion is wounded!"

The lad took off to the south, though whether he sought help or was running away was impossible for her to tell. Danica struggled up the hill, her mind consumed by the possibility that she was too late.

Charlaine fell from the saddle just as they reached the top, the snow cushioning her landing. Danica was quickly by her side, cradling her head. "Charlaine? Can you hear me?"

Tears filled her eyes as she lifted her face skyward, praying to Saint Agnes. She wasn't sure how long she sat there, then a reassuring hand pressed on her shoulder.

"What has happened?" came an old woman's voice.

"She was injured by a crossbow bolt a few days ago," said Danica, looking up. "We removed it, but I fear the wound has become corrupted."

"Then we must get her to my home where I can cleanse it."

"I shall carry her."

"You would be wiser to sling her across her horse. Come. I will help you."

With Luca's assistance, they lifted the unconscious Charlaine and placed her across the back of Stormcloud, securing her as best they could.

"It's fortunate that I happened to be nearby," said Orlina as she placed her hand on the horse's shoulder, gently nudging it forward. "I'm not usually out this time of day, but I was working on the defensive mounds when Luca found me."

"Defensive mounds?"

"Yes, the hills this side of the stream. My magic only allows me to manipulate a certain amount of the ground each day. Over the last few months, I've wrought much change, don't you think?"

"I can't say," said Danica. "I never saw the area before you began your work."

"They're huge," added Luca. "Why, they're taller than me now!"

They entered the trees, and before long, her house came into view. "I shall need your help to get her inside," the old woman said.

Together, they pulled Charlaine down, with Danica taking one side, Orlina the other, and between them, they half walked, half dragged their patient inside. They set her down on the bed and paused to catch their breath.

"I'm not as young as I used to be," Orlina said. "Take off her cloak and bare her arm so I can see the wound." She turned to the young lad. "Fetch me the warriors moss, Luca."

Danica sat Charlaine up and removed her cloak, exposing a blood-soaked shirt sleeve. The unpleasant smell of corruption wafted up as Danica cut away the material.

Orlina hovered over her. "That looks nasty."

"Will she die?"

"Not if it is within my power to prevent it."

"And the arm?"

"With a bit of luck, I can save it, but I'm afraid she won't be able to travel for a few days."

"I must get word to the baron and let him know his men were attacked."

"Then take the road back to Braunfel. Once you reach the fields, you can find a farmer who can carry your message to Lord Handrik."

"Perhaps I should stay here instead? Charlaine needs me."

"There is nothing further you can do here," said Orlina. "Leave me to my work."

"Very well, but I'll return before dark."

"Luca will keep an eye out for you."

Danica wiped away tears. "She must survive. She's destined for greatness."

"One could say the same of you."

"Me?"

"Oh yes. You are, I assume, Temple Captain Danica?"

"I am. How did you know?"

"Let's just say a little bird told me."

"Now you're being cryptic."

"Am I? I suppose it's only natural, considering my vocation. In any event, I've been expecting you for some time."

"I'm an admiral. Why in the name of the Saints would you expect me?"

"Well, the two of you, to be more precise. You carry the weight of the kingdom on your shoulders, no easy burden."

"We are but two knights."

"Ah," said Orlina. "You are much more than that. Tauril guided you here for a reason."

"We were merely on our way back to Lidenbach. It was the road that brought us here."

"Yet you spoke of an attack on the baron's men. I assume you were delayed in your journey?"

"Yes. How did you know?"

"It was not your fate to die in that ambush."

"Are you suggesting Tauril delayed us?"

Orlina smiled. "That is precisely what I'm suggesting, though if it makes you more comfortable, you may attribute it to your Saint."

"The Saints don't interfere in our lives."

"If you truly believed that, then you wouldn't have taken Holy Vows."

"I shan't debate theology with you," said Danica. "Let us instead be grateful you can save her. You can save her, can't you?"

"I shall certainly try. You, however, must be on your way if you want to be back here before dark."

Charlaine stood alone in the mist as the battle raged all around her. In her heart, she knew the fate of the Petty Kingdoms hung in the balance. Despite the stakes, she felt a sense of calm, as if she were safely wrapped in a pair of loving arms. Was this the Afterlife? Was she being embraced by Saint Agnes? She went over all she'd experienced in the last few months with a dispassionate mind. An invasion was imminent, the Continent in danger, yet part of her wanted to remain in this endless embrace, safe and content.

What was the reckoning of her life? Had she done all she could to make the Continent safer, or had it all been for naught? She felt immense sadness when her thoughts turned to Danica, not for her death but for the friendship left behind.

A voice beckoned from the mist, saying her name. Was this Saint Agnes calling on her one last time? She took a step, her eyes struggling to look through the fog to where a figure floated there, indistinct, yet at the same time, easy to see. She felt pulled towards it, urged on by an inner sense of devotion. She somehow knew she was about to gaze upon the face of Saint Agnes and feel the blessing of her presence.

Charlaine took another step, but then something shook her, and the mist faded. Darkness descended, lasting only a moment before a face hovered over her as she opened her eyes.

"Charlaine?" said Danica. "Can you hear me?"

"I'm here," she croaked. The room slowly came into focus behind her friend. "Where am I?"

"The house of Orlina Day."

"What happened? How did I get here?"

"Your wound almost got the better of you. You collapsed on the Braunfel road."

"There was a battle," stated Charlaine.

"Yes, an ambush. The baron's men were killed."

"The confessions?"

"Gone, I'm afraid."

"And the prisoners?"

"Slain, to a man."

"Then we've failed," said Charlaine.

"Not yet, we haven't. There'll be a fight come spring, and if the Halvarians take Arnsfeld, we'll make sure they pay a heavy price for it."

"How long have I been out?"

An old woman's voice drifted towards them. "Two days." Orlina Day appeared over her. "You're lucky your friend brought you to me. Another day, and it would've been too late."

Charlaine tried to get up, but the movement sent a spasm of pain up her arm.

"Sit," said Danica. "You need to rest."

"What of my wound?"

Orlina smiled. "I packed the wound with warriors moss and gave you an infusion of Kingsleaf. I also took the liberty of dosing you with numbleaf for the pain."

"Then I'm afraid it's worn off."

"It's working fine. Were it not, you would be writhing in agony. You're lucky I didn't have to take the arm off."

"When can I leave?"

"You've only just awoken," the old woman replied. "You need to rest at least another day, perhaps two. We'll need to get some food into you if you expect to remain in the saddle for any length of time."

"You had me worried," said Danica. "I thought you were going to die."

"I can't," replied Charlaine. "At least not yet. My work here is not done."

"This war may not end in our favour."

"I'm not talking about just this war, but the Continent as a whole."

Orlina leaned closer, staring into her eyes. "You had a vision."

"I did."

"Tell me what you saw."

"And endless battlefield," said Charlaine. "And I saw her."

"Saw who?"

"Saint Agnes."

"Nonsense," said Danica. "Saint Agnes was a mortal, not a goddess."

"Yet I saw her in the mist."

"You were delirious. Your mind was playing tricks on you."

Charlaine smiled. "You should have more faith."

Danica stared back, seeing her friend's look of utter certainty. "You truly believe you saw her?"

"I didn't see her features, only a shape in the mist, but I knew it was her."

"Did she speak to you?"

"I thought she was calling me, but perhaps it was you."

"I'm hardly Saint Agnes."

"But you serve the cause." Charlaine reached up, taking Danica's hand in a firm grip. "I'm so glad to see you."

"And I, you." She wiped away a tear. "From now on, you only travel with your armour, agreed?"

"You'll get no argument from me."

Danica turned back to Orlina. "Will there be any long-term damage?"

"She'll likely feel pain sometimes, but I doubt it will prove too much of a burden. She'll be able to use a shield again, if that's your question."

"And a forge?"

"If she were so inclined, although I cannot speak to her stamina. She may find it better to work in short bursts."

"It matters little," said Charlaine. "I'm not one to use a forge these days."

"Nonsense," insisted Danica. "It's about time you got back to it if only to keep you away from the stress of command."

"Oh? Are you an expert in such things now? Last time I checked, you were the one who was constantly worrying about the fleet."

"And where do you think I got that from?"

"It appears you two have much to talk about," replied Orlina. "As for me, I have work to do. Herbs don't gather themselves."

"It's the middle of winter," said Danica. "Surely you have to wait for spring?"

"Not at all. Winterberries are quite common this time of year."

"And what are they used for?"

Orlina chuckled. "They help reduce joint pain in older folk such as myself."

"So they would help Charlaine?"

"No. Her wound is in the bicep and is mostly muscle damage. Numbleaf helps with the pain, but there is likely some bone damage as well. I assume you will travel to the capital once she can ride?"

"Yes," said Danica. "Of course."

"Then I'll place this in your care." She handed over a small pouch. "If the pain should prove a distraction, have her chew a single leaf. It should have a minty flavour; otherwise, it's gone bad. You can also brew it into tea but don't overdo it. Constant use builds up a tolerance, and then it will become less effective."

"I'll ensure she uses the correct dosage."

"I shall have Luca make you some tea."

"More medicine?"

Orlina chuckled. "No, unless you count overcoming thirst to be medicinal in nature. I offer it merely as a beverage."

"Thank you," said Danica. "That would be most appreciated."

The old woman threw on a cloak before she stepped outside, allowing a cold gust of wind to whip through the house.

"What now?" asked Danica.

"Apparently," said Charlaine, "I rest another day or two."

"And then?"

"Then we shall have to see what awaits us in the capital. Hopefully, nothing has come apart in our absence."

21

FLAGSHIP

WINTER 1102 SR

The trip to Lidenbach proved quiet, and by week's end, Charlaine once again stood at her office window, staring at the ships anchored in the bay. The Imperial Warship *Conqueror* sat in port, evidence that Lord Corbin remained at court. She considered that a good sign, for it was doubtful he would be here if war were about to break out.

Beside the Halvarian flagship lay the slightly smaller *Vindicator*, although she couldn't guess for what purpose. Notably absent was the *Leviathan*, which must have sailed out during her absence.

As she watched, *Valiant* raised a blue flag displaying three white waves, indicating the admiral was aboard. Danica had arranged to rendezvous with the *Fearless*, reminding Charlaine she needed to meet with the king.

She mulled over the situation. *Fearless* was the same size as *Conqueror*, although they'd stripped its upper hull of its ornamentation and painted it scarlet, befitting the colours of Saint Agnes. What, she wondered, would Lord Corbin make of that?

Even from this range, she could see men on the deck of *Vindicator* scrambling around, raising the sails. Before long, the Halvarian vessel began moving forward and then turned towards the bay's entrance. It appeared the warship was putting out to sea.

Marlena opened the door. "You have a visitor," she announced. "Sir Hugo."

Charlaine turned from the window. "Show him in."

"Are you sure you're up to it? You're supposed to be resting."

"And I shall, I promise you, but if Sir Hugo has come all this way, we can't simply dismiss him out of hand."

"Then you should at least use your chair." Marlena waited until Charlaine sat down at her desk.

"There, is that better?"

"Much," replied her aide. "I'll show Sir Hugo in now."

Charlaine chuckled. It was odd to have Marlena ordering her around like a nursemaid, but she recognized it as a sign of affection.

Sir Hugo stepped into the room. "I hope I'm not interrupting?"

"Not at all," said Charlaine. "What can I do for you this fine day?"

He grinned. "It's more about what I can do for you."

"You have news?"

"I do indeed. The barons have finally come to an agreement regarding the Order of the Silver Spur. They are to gather in Dubrow come spring."

"Might I enquire as to their numbers?"

"The order has one hundred knights, give or take a few, but they have additional men that we refer to as auxiliaries at their disposal. These number one hundred and fifty, two-thirds of them footmen, the last third armed with crossbows."

"Two hundred and fifty men in total, an impressive number. And the auxiliaries will be marching to Dubrow as well?"

"Yes, although admittedly, not until the spring rains subside. Hopefully, that won't be too late."

"If the rains are as bad as everyone says, they're likely to slow the empire as well. We'll have the time. What we really need is more soldiers."

"Have you talked to the king?"

"Not since I returned from Braunfel, but I need to."

"Perhaps you might allow me to talk to him on your behalf? I can raise the spectre of war without the complaints of Lord Corbin. Other than men, is there anything else you wish to discuss with him?"

"Yes, there is. I want to bring *Fearless* into Lidenbach."

"I assume that's a ship of war?"

"She is," said Charlaine. "One of our biggest, but there's more to this than simply her size."

"Care to explain?"

"It used to be a Halvarian ship—an Imperial Flagship."

"Meaning?"

"You've seen the *Conqueror*?"

"I have," said Sir Hugo.

"The *Fearless* is the same design."

"So, let me make sure I understand you. You want me to convince the king to allow you to bring a captured Halvarian warship into the bay?"

"That sums it up nicely," replied Charlaine. "Of course, if you don't feel up to it, I could present that to him myself."

"Oh no," he said. "I insist on doing it if only to see the look on his face when I propose it."

"It won't get you into trouble, will it?"

Hugo grinned. "Nothing I can't handle, I assure you. Besides, it wouldn't be the first time I felt the king's wrath."

"Truly?"

"Oh yes. Truth is, I'm known for speaking freely. Fear not. His Majesty is a just and honourable man. He won't hang me for it."

"In that case, I accept your gracious offer."

"Have we any idea when the *Fearless* is set to arrive?"

"That's entirely up to the admiral, but I suspect we'll see it sometime before spring."

"Any other surprises you'd like to share?"

"None at the moment," said Charlaine. "Unless you know of any warriors for hire?"

"I wish I did, but I'm afraid mercenaries are rare in these parts of late."

"It makes sense. From what I know of mercenaries, they prefer an easy fight, and the empire promises to be anything but."

"I'm surprised to hear you say that," said Sir Hugo. "I wouldn't have expected you to associate with the likes of sell-swords."

Charlaine chuckled. "I don't, normally, but a good friend wrote to me of his exploits amongst such a group."

"I don't suppose they're available for hire?"

"I doubt it, and in any case, they're back in Erlingen, a long way from here."

"Well," said Sir Hugo. "I shall trouble you no more."

"And the king?"

"I'll seek an audience this very afternoon, though perhaps tomorrow might be more reasonable. In any case, I will send word if I'm successful in either endeavour."

"Thank you," said Charlaine. "It's most appreciated."

Danica looked out over the grey expanse of the Great Northern Sea. The dark sky threatened rain, but with a bit of luck, it would blow over by late afternoon. Off in the distance, a whale surfaced, which was a good omen amongst fishermen.

The lookout called out, indicating they'd sighted a ship to the east. The *Valiant* continued while all hands on deck stared ahead as the unknown vessel approached until the distinctive red flag bearing the three waves of Saint Agnes became visible.

When she realized it was the *Fearless*, Danica relaxed, and both ships slowed, finally coming to rest less than a thousand paces apart. She ordered the ship's boat lowered into the water, then made her way across to her new flagship.

A golden-haired knight peered over the side of the ship. "Greetings, Admiral."

"Good to see you, Anya," said Danica. "All is well?"

"Indeed." She waited until the admiral came aboard before continuing the conversation. "The captains in Vilnitz send their regards. They can't wait to get into it with the Halvarians."

"I might remind you we're not at war, at least not yet anyway."

"Sorry. You're right, of course. It's just that everyone is in such high spirits."

"They'll need that when push comes to shove."

"Have we any idea how many enemy ships are in the area?"

"Not yet."

Anya smiled. "I assume you have a plan?"

"I do, and it involves sailing into Halvarian waters, which is why I sent for *Fearless*. She might not have all the gold leaf anymore, but with a dash of paint, I imagine we could fool them from a distance."

"A ruse? So we just sail into one of the empire's ports?"

"Not quite. I intend to sail close enough to count ships, not actually to force a fight."

"We'll be flying a Halvarian flag? Isn't that dishonest?"

"We won't pretend to belong to the empire, if that's what you mean, but we could lower our flag. Call it a ruse of war, if you like."

Anya shook her head. "I don't know where you get your ideas from, but I'm glad you're on our side."

"I'll take that as a compliment."

"As you should. Have you any orders pertaining to our present situation?"

"I'd like you to continue patrolling the coast towards Vilnitz for now. I doubt we'll run into much this time of year, but you never know. In the meantime, I'll retire to the admiral's quarters." Danica dug into her satchel, producing a small blue pennant. "Hoist this to the mainmast to signify I'm aboard."

"This is new."

"It is the first of several changes I intend to bring to this fleet."

"Might I ask why we would want to advertise your presence?"

"Sea battles are chaotic affairs. We need to be able to identify where the commands are coming from."

"Commands? But we're at sea; how do you expect to issue orders—by yelling?"

"No, with flags. I'm still working out the details, but I know the Southern Fleet uses something similar. Think of it in simple terms. A red flag means engage the closest enemy, while green indicates we should mass in one location, that sort of thing."

"And how would the other captains know all this?"

Danica laughed. "Don't worry. Instructions will be forthcoming."

"The *Valiant* is turning about, Admiral."

"As should we. You may resume your patrol route, Captain. Let me know if you come across anything of interest."

The *Fearless* continued, finally anchoring as darkness fell. The coast of Burgemont lay off to the east, although this part held very little in the way of civilization. In fact, they could see only one light from their current position, likely a farm or fisherman's hut.

Danica looked down at her notes. The *Fearless* typically held a complement of twelve Temple Knights, but she'd doubled that due to the current crisis. She hoped that would prove sufficient, yet there was no way of knowing until battle was joined.

The ship had originally mounted two ballistae, but they'd replaced the one at the forecastle with a Dwarven Arbalest. They'd also placed weapon chests at strategic places on deck to allow the crew to arm themselves in the event of boarding, but the Temple Knights made up the true power of the *Fearless*.

Danica took pride in their improvements to the ship since its capture. Removing the gold leaf and replacing a sizable figurehead had lightened it considerably, leaving a much more manoeuvrable vessel. She hoped the changes would prove decisive in the coming war, but it was merely speculation on her part.

She closed her journal. Staring at its leather-bound cover, she wondered if future generations would look back on her notes or if would they be forever lost to history.

Above her came the sound of boots as the watch paced the deck. It was getting too late for her to still be awake. She put down the journal and climbed into bed, falling into a fitful sleep.

.   .   .

A knock on her door woke her. "What is it?" she snapped.

"Enemy ship in sight," came Anya's voice.

Danica staggered out of bed, throwing on a cloak. "What nonsense is this? We're not at war." She opened the door, immediately noting the concern on the captain's face.

"We've spotted a ship in distress," explained Anya. "It's under attack by a pirate. I've ordered the Temple Knights into armour, and we're altering course to intercept."

"I'll be up directly."

"Do you need help donning your armour?"

"I think I can manage, thank you."

"You should consider getting an admiral's aide," said Anya. "Saints know you've got more than enough to do to keep one busy."

"Ha-ha. I have little enough time for myself. How, then, am I to find more in which to train an aide?"

"I'm sure I could find a volunteer, Admiral."

"I'll consider it, but you'd best get back to the business at hand."

It took longer than Danica cared to admit to don her armour, and by the time she finally came out on deck, the larger vessel had grappled the smaller one, an open-topped ship built in the ancient style, and was in the process of hauling it closer. Warriors stood at the railing of the pirate, ready to board at the first opportunity.

"I know that smaller ship," said Danica. "It's the *Cygnet*. And that so-called pirate ship is Halvarian."

Anya leaned forward, staring at the scene before her. "There's a name on the bow," she said. "*Vindicator*. Have we heard of it?"

"She sailed out of Lidenbach just before *Valiant*, but I never expected to find her here, on the coast of Burgemont."

"Your orders, Admiral?"

"You have permission to engage the enemy, Captain."

Anya stood to attention. "Aye, Admiral."

At Anya's command, the Temple Knights retrieved their crossbows and loaded bolts before moving to the side railing, ready to launch a volley once they were within range.

Danica watched the battle unfold. Like most naval engagements, the conflict would be drawn out as the ships tried to gain the advantage of the wind. At the approach of the *Fearless*, the Halvarians had cut the lines securing *Cygnet*, allowing the *Vindicator* to move freely. Sure enough, its sails billowed out as sailors ran to man its forward ballista.

The *Vindicator* could've easily turned to port and outrun the Temple ship, but seeking glory, the Halvarian captain closed the range.

"Stand by," shouted Danica. "Let them get within range before we turn to starboard, then let loose with a volley." She spotted the *Cygnet* attempting to turn into the wind, desperate to put distance between her and her attackers, but with her sail now ripped, she could only drift, a victim of the currents.

Vindicator, meanwhile, remained on an intercept course with *Fearless*. Unlike its Temple counterpart, the Halvarian ship only had an aft castle, its forward deck flush with the midships.

Anya, knowing her business, ordered the Temple Knights to the forecastle. They lined up, crossbows ready, careful not to block the view of the deck-mounted arbalest.

A familiar sense of calm settled over Danica. The pieces were in motion, and there was little to do now but wait. Closer and closer the two ships came until she could make out individual faces on the *Vindicator's* deck. The Halvarian warriors stood ready, weapons drawn, boarding planks set to lower at a moment's notice.

The first ballista bolt sailed across the gap, missing the port side of the *Fearless* and plunging into the sea. The crew reloaded it as the archers let loose.

Anya waited, saving their first volley for maximum effect. An arrow struck one of the Temple Knights, bouncing off a vambrace, and then more followed with similar results.

The wind behind *Fearless* made boarding a tricky proposition. The *Vindicator* had two choices: turn into the wind and come alongside, or cut in front of the Temple ship and board through its bow, a difficult tactic, considering the raised forecastle.

Anya took the choice from them when, at the last moment, she veered the *Fearless* to starboard, crossing the bow of the *Vindicator*. The arbalest released its grappling bolt as the Temple Knights let loose with their first volley.

Packed into their ship's bow in preparation for boarding, the enemy warriors took horrendous casualties, with at least six going down from the crossbows. The arbalest bolt brought down another three as it sailed across the deck, digging into the far railing. The knights on the windlass sprang into action, reeling in the enemy vessel as others reloaded the arbalest.

Danica knew the tactic well. They would pull the enemy alongside *Fearless*, and then the melee would begin. She moved to the railing, drawing her sword in preparation.

The *Fearless* lurched as the line went taut, and then the Halvarian warship slewed to port, attempting to break free of the grapple. Men rushed along the deck, using axes to cut the line, but another bolt from the arbalest scattered them. Then the aft ballista of the *Fearless* let loose, sending a bolt sailing across to smash into *Vindicator's* hull.

The enemy vessel loomed large, its bowsprit tangling with the rigging of the *Fearless*. The bow struck the side of the Temple ship, almost knocking Danica from her feet, but she recovered just as the enemy warriors readied their boarding ramps, little more than long planks of wood with spikes at the end intended to sink into an enemy deck. She held back until the first one fell, then stood over it, waiting for the attackers to gather enough courage to advance.

The enemy warrior was halfway across before Danica stepped forward and swung low, smashing her sword into a fellow's leg and knocking him from the ramp. He cried out in surprise as he fell, splashing into the water, where his chainmail shirt dragged him down into the icy depths.

She backed up and parried another foe, then returned the attack only for him to block her this time. A step back placed her on the deck of *Fearless* once more, and then, as her opponent neared the end of the plank, she rushed forward, shoulder-blocking him, trusting in her armour to keep her safe. He fell backwards, with her atop him, then a wild scramble ensued, both desperate for a handhold to stop the sea from claiming them.

Danica grabbed the railing of the *Fearless*, but her opponent wasn't so lucky. He'd crashed into the man behind him, causing that fellow to stumble forward onto him, and they both rolled off the plank into the sea.

With the two ships grappled together, the Temple Knights rushed from the forecastle and pushed across the boarding ramp onto the *Vindicator*.

Danica let them go, keeping her eyes on the Halvarian ship as the vessel swung into the side of *Fearless*. Anticipating this, the enemy captain had sent a group of warriors aft to ready another boarding ramp. A man in *Vindicator's* sterncastle gesticulated, then a bolt sank into his chest, and he fell to the deck.

"I hate mages," said Anya, the crossbow still in her hand.

A shudder ran through *Fearless* as the two ships bumped hulls again, but a second Halvarian assault never materialized, for the Temple Knights had boarded, pushing the defenders aft until such was the carnage that the empire's warriors lay down their arms.

"I'm going aboard the Halvarian vessel," said Anya. "Would you care to join me?"

"By all means, but watch your step. The plank is slick with blood."

Anya crossed first, as befitting a victorious captain. In her haste to follow, Danica failed to heed her own advice and slipped, falling to her knees. A hand steadied her shoulder, preventing her from toppling over the side.

"Careful," said Anya. "We can't afford to lose you."

Danica rose, making her way to the deck of the *Vindicator*, this time taking her time. "Have we prisoners?" she asked.

"Most of the fighting complement is dead or wounded, but the rest of the crew is largely intact."

"And the captain?"

"We'll get nothing out of him—he's dead. Someone's checking the mage, but few could survive a bolt to the chest."

Danica chuckled. "You were always good with bows."

"You know what they say, 'practice makes perfect.'"

A knight appeared before them, her armour soaked in blood. "The ship is ours, Captain."

"And the cost?" asked Anya.

"Three wounded, one seriously."

"Let's take a look, shall we?" The knight led them to where an injured sister lay on the deck, her breastplate punctured by a hammer. The blood flowing freely from the wound was in stark contrast to her colourless face.

"Is the ship safe?" she gasped out.

"It is," said Anya. "You may rest knowing you have done your duty to your Saint. Agnes awaits you."

A smile creased the knight's face, and then her eyes went blank as her head rolled to the side.

Anya stood, tears rolling down her cheeks. "Sister Samara's sacrifice will not be forgotten."

Danica took three fingers and made a wave pattern across her chest, the blessing of her Saint. "May Agnes watch over her."

The entire ship fell silent in a moment of respect.

Danica cleared her throat. "Who commands here?"

The prisoners all looked at one individual, an old man with a weather-beaten face. She moved to stand before him. "And you are?"

"Laldor Morningstone, sailing master."

"Your captain is dead. Will you surrender the ship?"

"I have little choice, for you've won it by force of arms. What do you mean to do with us?"

"We'll transport you to port, where the appropriate authorities will decide what to do with you."

"Can I ask that you take us to Lidenbach?"

"I would have thought Vilnitz closer," said Danica.

194 | TEMPLE COMMANDER

"Aye, it is, but at least in Arnsfeld, there is someone to speak on our behalf."

"You mean Lord Corbin?"

"I do."

Danica turned to Anya. "What do you think?"

"Don't look at me. You're the admiral."

"Very well. Lidenbach, it is, but let's see to *Cygnet* first, shall we?" She looked at the sailing master. "We'll place a contingent of knights aboard your vessel. Will your crew sail *Vindicator* into Lidenbach, or do I need to replace them?"

"That depends. Are they sailing to their executions?"

"Your captain is dead. I see no reason why he shouldn't shoulder the blame for your piracy, do you?" She didn't wait for an answer. "This ship, however, will remain in the order's hands, at least for the time being."

"Then we'll set sail for Arnsfeld on your command."

22

POLITICS
WINTER 1102 SR

The anchor dropped as the *Vindicator* slowed to a stop. Danica waited for *Fearless* to take up its station on the starboard side, then it, too, lowered its anchor.

Just to port, the *Cygnet* rowed past, heading for the docks. The ship had suffered no lasting damage other than a torn sail, but it would have been much worse had the Temple ship not stumbled across the scene.

She made a mental note to seek out the ship's owners, Sandro and Nadine Ripley, and see how they were doing. Laldor, the *Vindicator's* sailing master, approached, his steps unsure.

"Problem?" asked Danica.

"That depends on your point of view."

"I'm guessing some people wish to remain aboard."

"How did you know?"

"This isn't the first time we've captured a provincial ship like the *Vindicator.*"

"You have to understand our predicament," said Laldor. "Most of these men were forced into service. The conditions amongst the fleet are harsh, and the pay is poor. If it weren't for the presence of the warriors, some might consider desertion. Tell me, are the rumours true?"

"What rumours are those?"

"Some say you pay your mariners a fair wage and that they eat like kings."

"Like kings?" Danica tried to contain her laughter but failed. "No, but we try to feed them decent food. Those who crew the order's ships are all volunteers, so we provide them with enough to feed their families back home."

"Would you be willing to take some of us into service?"

"Yes," said Danica. "Though we'd split you up amongst the fleet until you've earned our trust. About a third of our present sailors were crewmen aboard ships like yours. I assume some want to return home?"

"Yes. They have families there, and the empire can be vengeful."

"And how many wish to enter our service?"

"None of the warriors, but out of a crew of twenty-four, ten are willing to serve your order."

"I'm curious as to why you mention this now. We've been sailing for the better part of two days."

Laldor rubbed the stubble on his chin. "It's difficult to bring up if I'm being honest. Tell the wrong person what you're considering, and the next thing you know, you'll have a fight on your hands."

"So, these ten men, can you vouch for them?"

"Aye, they're all skilled men of the sea. There are two or three others you might sway, were you so inclined, but they fear repercussions."

"I'm afraid I can't make any guarantees in that regard, but those who serve us will receive fair treatment."

A look of relief flooded his face. "Thank you. You won't regret it."

"And what of you?" asked Danica. "Do you count yourself amongst those willing to serve?"

"Aye, I do."

"How well do you know the northern coast of Halvaria?"

"I've sailed as far west as the Scattered Isles and east to the coast of Reinwick and know every inlet and river between the two."

"We found no charts in the captain's cabin."

"No doubt the captain threw them overboard when it looked like he'd lost the ship. Don't worry, though. Give me a quill, ink, and some parchment, and I'll draw you an approximation of the region. Of course, it won't be as accurate as the captain's charts, but it'll be more than enough to help you navigate those waters."

"You spoke of the Scattered Isles. What lies beyond them?"

"They say that farther west lies lands populated by all manner of creatures."

"Meaning?"

"Orcs, Elves, Dwarves, even dragons. Not the sort of place I'd care to sail, I can tell you. Of course, if it's accurate maps of the region you want, you could always ask the *Conqueror's* captain for them." He nodded across the bay to where the Halvarian flagship anchored.

"I somehow doubt he'd be willing to hand them over. Still, it's nice to know they exist. Did the *Vindicator* have such things?"

"No. They don't trust provincials like us with such things. Once upon a time, I had my own maps of the Scattered Isles, but that was before the empire came."

"You weren't born in Halvaria?"

"No. I was born in Cyrellia, one of the northern kingdoms, but Halvaria subjugated it more than thirty years ago. I had my own ship then, a small trader not too different from the *Cygnet*."

"What happened?"

"Our king was weak and allowed the empire's influence to spread, then a blight took most of the crops, and the people fell on hard times. Next thing you know, groups of armed men stormed the Palace."

"I'm guessing they were Halvarian?"

"Like as not," replied Laldor, "but at the time, we all thought it had been a popular uprising. Once the dust settled, we were part of the empire. Next thing I know, my ship's impounded, and they've forced me into the provincial fleet. I've been serving them ever since."

"Yet you hold no loyalty to them."

"I've risen as high as I can under their banner. The fact of the matter is they don't trust people like me, preferring instead to draw their captains from their own folk. Imperials, we call them, fanatics all." He was about to say more, but something drew his attention. "Here now," he said. "What's this?"

Danica followed his gaze to where a boat approached, full of Halvarian warriors, with a tall fellow wearing an ornate cloak standing in the middle.

"You there," he called up. "Are you the one in charge?"

"I am. Danica Meer, Admiral of the Fleet of Saint Agnes."

"On behalf of the empire, I thank you for returning our ship. My men and I will now assume command of her."

"You shall do no such thing. We seized this vessel in the act of piracy, and it is now the property of the Church."

"Do not trifle with me, Admiral. This ship is the property of the Halvarian Empire. You will hand over this vessel immediately."

"Or?"

The fellow's face turned crimson. "I demand you relinquish control of this ship!"

"You can demand all you like," said Danica. "This ship will remain in the hands of the Temple Knights. However, we have some of your countrymen who we're willing to release into your care, but your boat appears too full to take them. Perhaps you'd prefer to return when you have more space?"

"I shall not forget this insult!"

"I wouldn't expect you to. And please make sure you spell my name correctly when you report this to your superiors. That's Admiral Meer, spelled M—E—E—R."

The man snarled out an order, and the boat turned, making its way to the *Conqueror*.

Danica turned back to the deck of the *Vindicator*. "Sister Margo!"

"Yes, Admiral?"

"I'm going ashore. You're in charge until I return."

"And if the empire sends more men?"

"Then you shall refuse them permission to come aboard, at the end of a sword if necessary."

"Might I enquire how long you'll be gone?"

"I'm going to arrange for more knights to join you aboard *Vindicator*, but I have some things to see to after that. Expect my return by nightfall."

"Yes, Admiral."

"I need help," said Danica.

"So I noticed," replied Charlaine. "Do my eyes deceive me, or is that another Halvarian ship I see flying our flag?"

"We found her attacking the *Cygnet*. You remember her?"

"Of course. The Ripleys, wasn't it?"

"Yes. Thankfully, we came across the *Vindicator* before they could board."

"I assume you want additional knights to protect her while in port?"

"Yes, please."

"And will she be setting back out to sea?"

"Eventually, but we may have to make some repairs."

"She was damaged?"

"No," replied Danica, "but they've neglected her of late. If nothing else, we must repair the rigging and replace some sails. There are also some leaks that need looking at. Nothing too serious, but the sea has an unforgiving nature, and I don't want to take chances. I don't suppose you know where I can find a Sacred Mother of Akosia?"

"Why? Are you already thinking of renaming her?"

"Most certainly. I was thinking of *Illustrious*."

"I would say the fact that you captured it would suggest it's been anything but."

"True," said Danica, "but under the care of the order, it would have a chance to live up to its new name."

"The choice is yours. For my part, I'll make some enquiries and see if we can't find you a Sacred Mother."

"Perhaps Orlina Day might know of someone?"

"It certainly bears looking into. Have you spoken with the Ripleys?"

"Not since we came into port. Why?"

"It seems to me they might be just the sort of people to help spread the word about us escorting merchants."

"You're right," said Danica. "I should've thought of that, but I was so worried that the *Vindicator's* presence might cause problems that I came straight here. I suppose now that I've discharged my duties, I'm free to seek them out."

"Not quite yet, you're not," said Charlaine. "I'll need your help at court. I suspect Lord Corbin will make a big fuss over this whole affair, and I require you to give your side of the story."

"I should be happy to. When are you next to meet with the king?"

"I have an audience this very evening."

"Good. That will allow me sufficient time to get statements from the Ripleys. A handy thing to have when trying to counter the lies of the empire."

"I'll meet you at dusk, down by the docks. We can walk up to the castle from there."

"How about an escort?"

"The streets are safe enough for the present, though I might suggest wearing your armour."

"Why?" asked Danica. "You think someone will attack us?"

"No, but if we show up at court, ready for battle, it emphasizes how important this matter is to us."

The servant opened the door, admitting the two Temple Knights into the great hall. The room quieted as the other guests turned to watch Charlaine and Danica walk to the king. Stefan sat slumped down on his throne, leaning tiredly to one side, his weight resting on his left arm.

Charlaine bowed. "Greetings, Your Majesty."

"It seems to me," said the king, "that you only grace this court with your presence when a problem requires your personal attention."

"I freely admit it. To do otherwise would burden you unnecessarily."

"No doubt you have come to explain why your ships have taken it upon themselves to attack a Halvarian vessel?"

Charlaine nodded at Danica, who took a step forward. "The ship in question," she began, "the *Vindicator*, was engaged in the act of piracy. In my possession, I have sworn statements from the owners of the *Cygnet*, who corroborate this crime."

King Stefan waved her forward, an act that sat uncomfortably with his guards, for they moved to intercept. "Back," he snarled at his men. "I am certain the admiral wishes me no harm."

Danica stepped closer, handing him the scroll. The king unrolled the paper, scanning its contents while all in the room collectively held their breath. He then dropped it to his lap, staring at the Temple Knights until he finally nodded.

"It is as you say. The *Cygnet* was attacked with no provocation." He scanned the crowd, seeking a familiar face. "What say you, Lord Corbin?"

The Halvarian envoy pushed his way forward. "They lie, Majesty, as one would expect from such zealots. The *Vindicator* was on a peaceful mission patrolling the coast when it came across this so-called merchant engaging in smuggling."

"Your excuse has several holes in it," said the king. "You claim to be patrolling the coast, but that is the sovereign territory of Arnsfeld or Burgemont, if you like, depending on the exact position." He turned back to Danica. "Where was this alleged attack?"

"Off Cape Maralan, Majesty, in waters belonging to Burgemont."

"There, you see? I was correct. Tell me, Lord Corbin, by what right do you patrol our coasts? I certainly don't recall giving you permission to do so."

"The same could be said for the Church," replied the Halvarian. "And yet you ignore that fact."

"The Temple Knights of Saint Agnes, by virtue of their allegiance to the Church of the Saints, are acting in the best interest of all. On the other hand, your empire's interests don't necessarily align with those of the Petty Kingdoms. I'm sure I speak for the King of Burgemont when I say your ships have not been given the freedom to attack shipping at your leisure."

"In the name of the empire, I demand that you order these knights to return the *Vindicator*."

"You are labouring under the impression I have control over such things. The truth is they caught your ship in the act of piracy. As such, it is forfeit, its ownership transferred to the Temple Knights of Saint Agnes to do with as they please."

"And what of our people?"

"Admiral," said the king, "would you be willing to release the crew back into the custody of the Halvarians?"

"Yes, Majesty," replied Danica, "providing that is their wish."

"What is this, now?" said Corbin. "Of course it's their wish. Why wouldn't it be?"

"Despite your belief in the empire, not everyone under Halvarian rule wishes to remain so. I have been informed that some are interested in serving our fleet."

"And how do we know this is what they truly desire? These so-called Temple Knights could be using the men as pawns in a game of politics."

"Then I invite His Majesty to send a delegate aboard *Vindicator* and speak with these men."

Stefan sat up a bit straighter and chuckled. "It seems they have beaten you at your own game, Lord Corbin. I could send Sir Hugo to verify these claims."

"He would be most welcome," replied Danica.

"Then I see no reason for an inspection by one of my knights."

"I beg your pardon?" said Lord Corbin. "Will you not even pretend to carry out an inspection?"

"Why would I?" replied the king. "The fact they are willing to allow such a thing proves they have nothing to hide."

"And our ship?" said Corbin.

"As I have already stated, that is now the property of the Temple Knights of Saint Agnes. If you have a complaint, I suggest you speak to them directly. This is no longer of any interest to me." He waved them away with his hand. "Now, it's time we moved on to other things. Chamberlain, what is the Royal Treasury's current status?"

Charlaine and Danica backed up, ensuring they kept facing the king until they'd gone a suitable distance before turning, ready to exit the room, only for Lord Corbin to block their way.

"You might have won this round," he said, "but you shall bear the conse-quences."

"I don't believe in idle threats," said Charlaine. "If you mean to take revenge, then let us have done with these games and get to the point."

"You have sealed the fate of your precious fleet. From this day hence, the Empire of Halvaria will treat your ships as they deserve, as cutthroats and thieves, fit only to be swept from the sea."

"Are you declaring war against the order?"

"War? You are not a kingdom or even a duchy. I can't declare war against the likes of you. No, consider it a holy quest to wipe you from exis-tence. That should suit your religious mindset."

"I regret we could not settle our differences," replied Charlaine. "How-ever, if there is to be open warfare between us, then I must advise you that any Halvarian ship found outside a safe harbour will be considered an enemy vessel and be dealt with appropriately."

Lord Corbin smiled. "It's always good to know where one stands, don't you think?" His gaze fell on Danica. "I particularly look forward to hearing of your demise." He turned around, striding from the room.

"That's not good," said Danica. "I shouldn't have attacked *Vindicator*."

"And what else could you have done, allowed them to take the *Cygnet*? Don't fret over your choice to engage. It was the right thing to do."

"Even at the cost of open war?"

"We've been at war with Halvaria since we took out their fleet at Temple Bay. All this does is free up your choices."

"How so?"

"Simple," said Charlaine. "You've always had to take care around the empire's ships, not knowing if they were hostile or not. Now the issue is decided for you. If you see them, they're a fair target."

"I would have preferred to know more about their fleet before fighting broke out."

"And I would prefer if they withdrew to their border, but we don't always get what we wish."

"That's hardly reassuring," replied Danica.

"Tell me, what ships have we under construction back at Temple Bay?"

"The *Valour* should be ready to launch any day now."

"Anything else?"

"I've had people working on building larger vessels, but I doubt we'd see any of them before spring. Now that we've moved on to open warfare, I suppose I'll have to double up our patrols. I imagine the empire will begin a systematic effort to hunt us down and destroy us. I'd hate to guess what would happen if they captured one of our ships. We don't want a repeat of Alantra."

"I might remind you we won that battle."

"We did," said Danica, "but it cost us dearly. If you recall, they tied Temple Knights to their masts as a warning. How do you deal with brutality like that?"

"The same way we did at Alantra—by not sinking to their level."

"And you still think we can beat them?"

"Have faith," said Charlaine. "It's no coincidence we're both here in Arnsfeld when the empire is ready to make its move. Call it fate, if you like, or a calling, but we're right where we're meant to be when we're needed most. The Saints move in mysterious ways."

"You're the one who keeps telling me the Saints don't control us, merely offer us advice."

"And that's still the case. Look, we control our actions; there's no doubt about that, but you must admit our faith carries us forward. If that's not some sort of divine inspiration, I don't know what is."

"You're right. Sorry. I'm a little overwhelmed that we're now at war. I suppose I need to get word to the fleet. The last thing we want is someone stumbling into a lopsided battle."

"You'll need to recruit a crew for the *Vindicator*, or whatever you call it. Are you sure you want to name it *Illustrious*?"

"It would suit, wouldn't it? Besides, who am I to upset my own naming convention."

Charlaine burst out in laughter. "Very well. It's your ship after all. Anything else you'd care to discuss?"

"Not particularly. Why? Are you in a hurry to abandon me?"

"Not at all, but we recently received a donation of wine from a local merchant. I thought we might sample some of it to ensure it's suitable for Temple Knights."

"You should have mentioned that earlier."

"And spoil the surprise?"

23

FLOTILLA

SPRING 1103 SR

The cold winds of winter stopped blowing, ushering in the warmer days of spring, and thoughts turned to shipping once more.

The *Cygnet*, having stayed in Lidenbach during the remainder of the winter, now stood ready to sail. Leery of Halvarian marauders, the Ripleys, along with a few other captains, agreed to travel under the escort of Temple ships. Thus, *Fearless* and the newly renamed and refitted *Illustrious* readied themselves to get underway.

Danica paced the deck, scanning her new responsibilities. Six ships had agreed to this arrangement, most of them smaller vessels like the *Cygnet*. The largest, a cog named the *Antoine*, wallowed in even the lightest waves. If there was to be any trouble at sea, this one was the most likely cause, forcing the admiral to consider the possibility of leaving her behind. It would mean a faster sail to Vilnitz, but she knew, in her heart, she couldn't refuse the pleas of *Antoine's* captain, for to do so might condemn the vessel to a Halvarian attack.

The sterncastle on the *Fearless* gave her an excellent view of her new command. Off to the right, the *Illustrious* unfurled her sails. Once underway, the merchants would follow its lead, with her own ship behind.

"Clear weather," sang out Sandro Ripley as he raced past. The *Cygnet* might be small and manoeuvrable in the calmer waters of the harbour, but out at sea, it would be a different matter, for the waves would pick up, and a vessel of her nature could easily get swamped.

Danica waved back, feeling a sense of accomplishment. It hadn't been easy convincing these people to accept their help, and many fretted they would lose the advantage of getting to market first by arriving at the same time, but the benefit was protection from the ravages of the empire. These waters had become dangerous of late, and none doubted their fate if they encountered a Halvarian ship while sailing alone.

Anya interrupted her thoughts. "We're ready to set sail on your command, Admiral."

"You may get us underway, Captain. I shall leave it to you to worry about the details."

The captain turned, bellowing out the orders. The crew sprang into action, climbing up both masts, ready to deploy the sails.

As Danica felt the ship move, she instinctively sought out the *Illustrious*. Even from this range, she spotted Zivka aboard her new command, reminding her of her old crew from the *Valiant*. Grazynia now captained the *Vigilant*; Nadia, the *Vanguard*; while Vivian, the *Valiant*, the very same vessel that had taken them all to sea for the first time. Of the rest, Anya was on the *Fearless* with her, while Laurel had been named to the *Invincible*. Zivka, the last of that group, now captained *Illustrious*. Even apart, they all shared an unbreakable bond from sailing together on the order's very first vessel.

There were other captains, and more would be needed as the fleet expanded, but there was something special about the Valiant Six, as they had come to be called.

"Admiral?"

She turned to see a Temple Knight waiting. At first, she thought her to be Sister Samara, then remembered that brave soul had gone to the Afterlife. Danica struggled to place the face. "Sister Grace, isn't it?"

The woman smiled, pleased at being recognized. "Yes, Admiral. I'm to inform you the *Antoine* is already lagging behind."

"I expected as much. She's a very poor sailer, and the owner has little experience with her."

"Owner? You mean the captain, surely?"

"The ship's previous captain swore off sailing after the attack on the *Cygnet*. Master Alpen tried to find another to take his place, but was forced to take command himself in the end."

"Surely the crew would know better?"

"I'm told he lost half of them when their captain abandoned the ship. I offered him some of ours to help train the new crew, but he refused, and there's only so much we can do."

They weren't even out of the bay yet and were already having issues. Was this to be the pattern for the entire trip? She noted the knight still waited. "Was there something else?"

"No, Admiral. Only, Captain Anya told me to stand by and assist you if needed."

"Assist me?"

"Yes. To act as your aide."

"But I don't need one," said Danica.

"Nevertheless, the captain was very explicit in her instructions."

"Well, I haven't anything for you to do at this particular moment," she snapped, then felt guilty. "Sorry. I shouldn't have directed that at you." Danica looked over the tiny flotilla. "Tell me, Sister Grace, what do you think of all this?"

"All what?"

"This entire voyage. Are we wasting our time?"

"We are ensuring the safety of these people," said Grace. "I hardly believe anyone would call that a waste."

"Let me put it another way, then, shall I? Will our presence be enough to keep the Halvarians at bay?"

"Most assuredly, Admiral. I doubt any captain would care to close with the *Fearless*."

"You know," said Danica, "I'd prefer you give me an honest opinion rather than telling me something you think I want to hear."

"I'm afraid I have little experience in ship battles."

"But you were there when we captured the *Vindicator*, were you not?"

"I was, but that was my first battle."

"Where did you come from?"

"The commandery at Vilnitz."

"No, I meant originally. Are you from the northern coast?"

"I was born in Talyria but left to become a Temple Knight."

"And has it been all you expected?"

Grace's wry grin spoke volumes. "I doubt I could ever have foreseen serving on a ship, if that's what you mean."

"Life often takes us in strange directions. Had they not sent me to Ilea, I wouldn't have found my calling."

"Your calling? But isn't that what drives us to join the order in the first place?"

"We each have our own path to tread. I believed becoming a Temple Knight would solve all my problems, but we can't escape our past as we carry it with us. The secret is learning to deal with it and move forward."

"And how did you do that, if you don't mind me asking?"

"I had the good fortune to serve with Temple Commander Charlaine. It's the bonds of friendship that make us stronger, Grace. Remember that."

"I shall, Admiral."

The *Antoine* was finally picking up speed. The *Fearless* followed in its wake, still under reduced sail, while the rest of the flotilla had cleared the bay and turned eastward, following the coast, the *Illustrious* leading the way.

Danica waved over Captain Anya. "Let's move the ship up a little, shall we? I don't want us caught between the coast and our own ships. If we should run across any Halvarians, we'll need an open sea to manoeuvre in."

"Aye, Admiral."

With the sails fully unfurled, the *Fearless* picked up speed. A slight course correction avoided any chance of colliding with *Antoine*, and then they started moving up along the port side of the line of merchants. The *Cygnet* led them, followed by the cog, *Liddy*, named after the Arnsfeld capital. Behind that came the *Icewind* and *Moonfish*, both small ships similar to that of the Ripleys'.

Now that it was underway, the *Antoine* was making nice progress, quickly catching up, and Danica finally began to relax. They were in safe waters, at least for the moment, giving her hope that the trip might prove uneventful.

With the wind at their backs, they made good progress, and by mid-afternoon, they turned north. This leg of the journey would bring them farther out to sea, but it wouldn't be long before the coast of Burgemont was off their starboard bow.

The farther they got from shore, the rougher the water became, slowing the three smaller vessels' progress. Both *Fearless* and *Illustrious* prepared to move in closer, ready to lend a hand should it prove necessary, but as they started changing course, a yell from the lookout alerted them of ships visible to port. Danica leaned on the railing, struggling to make out the details.

"Three ships," called out the watch, "and they're bow on to us."

"They're closing," said Anya. "Prepare to engage!"

The Temple Knights disappeared below decks to don their armour while the crew grabbed weapons and began loading the ballista and arbalest. Both ship-mounted weapons were bolt throwers, but being made of Dwarven steel, the arbalest discharged its load at a much higher velocity, making it deadly in battle. The downside was the expense, for it took weeks to create such a weapon, and they were in short supply.

The distant ships continued advancing until Danica could make out the distinctive forecastle on one of the intruders, marking it as an Imperial design, much like the *Fearless*. However, the other two had flush foredecks, the telltale sign they were provincial vessels, or at least that was the assumption. The truth was, there was no way of telling for certain until they were close enough to see their fighting complement.

Anya had the situation well in hand, and the *Fearless* turned to port, heading directly for the trio of Halvarians. The *Illustrious*, noting the course change, moved in amongst the flotilla's ships, ready to counter any move to attack one of their charges.

The battle, if that's what it was to be, unfolded slowly. The enemy ships advanced in formation, the larger Imperial vessel in the middle, the other two slightly behind and off to either side.

The *Fearless*, having turned into the wind to close the range, slowed considerably while the fleet, following Danica's pre-arranged orders, moved starboard to keep the enemy at a distance. *Illustrious* coordinated all this by flying a red flag, indicating they should follow the Temple ship's lead. *Fearless*, now between the Halvarians and the flotilla, turned to starboard, zigzagging to make headway against the wind.

As the enemy closed, it looked more and more like this would end in a boarding action. The Temple Knights returned to the deck in their full plate armour while Sister Grace carried Danica's chest and back plates.

"If you don't plan on donning your armour, you could at least put these on."

Danica nodded, removing her cloak so her new aide could strap on her armour. It wasn't easy to do, for the admiral's attention kept moving from one side of the ship to the other to keep an eye on both the enemy and the flotilla.

The other sisters took up their stations on the forecastle, loading the arbalest. Danica, now partially armoured, ran up to join them.

"Don't release until we're close," she ordered. "And when you do let fly, aim for the hull."

"The hull?" said Sister Margo. "What good will that do?"

"We'll be bow to bow. I want you to hit as close to the waterline as possible."

"That's not easy to do on a moving ship."

"I have faith in you."

Margo grinned as she swivelled the arbalest, ready to loose once they were within range. Danica clenched her fists so hard, her fingernails dug into her palms. To relieve the stress, she shook her hands, trying to concentrate on the enemy fleet.

Sister Margo interrupted her focus. "Which ship do I target?"

"That one." Danica pointed at the centre vessel where enemy archers were crammed into the forecastle, ready to release a volley. "But let them get closer."

The other knights readied crossbows as the trio of warships kept advancing until they could make out faces on the Halvarian decks. A yell drifted across the water, and then a cloud of arrows flew forth, clattering to the deck and bouncing off armour. Danica felt an arrowhead graze her leg but didn't let it distract her.

"Loose!" she called out, and Margo released the arbalest's bolt. It looked like it might miss its target, but then the enemy flagship crested a wave, exposing its lower hull. The projectile punctured a fist-sized hole in the wood before the ship's bow fell into the trough, obscuring all sight of the damage.

"Hard to starboard!" shouted Anya.

The *Fearless's* crew held on as the rudder came hard over. Danica struggled to remain standing, steadying herself against the railing as the ship lurched, picking up speed as the wind filled her sails.

The Halvarian flagship turned to port, attempting to avoid a collision, but in doing so, it moved too close to its ally, and the two hulls smashed together, sending a terrible grinding noise over the water.

The Temple Knights released another volley, taking down two archers on the enemy flagship, but nothing came in reply. Danica watched triumphantly as the Halvarian ships tangled bowsprits, slowing to a crawl. The last of the three furled its sails, trying to slow down, giving up any idea of pursuit.

"Shall we turn to engage?" asked Anya.

"No," said Danica. "Our job is to protect the flotilla. Keep on our current heading and close with the rest of our fleet."

"Will they pursue?"

"I doubt it. Thanks to Sister Margo, they have a hull to repair."

The captain looked down. "You're bleeding, Admiral."

"Am I?" Danica was reminded of her wound and glanced down to see blood soaking her leggings.

"I'd best have a look at that," said Sister Grace. "Let's get you to your cabin where I can wrap it."

Danica stared out at the enemy fleet, but the distance between them was increasing. There was always the possibility the Halvarians might leave the flagship behind and pursue with their two provincial ships, but she thought it unlikely. There was a pecking order of sorts within the empire, and the person in charge would undoubtedly be aboard the stricken vessel. By the time repairs could be completed, they would have a tough time trying to catch up to the flotilla.

"Admiral?"

She turned to see Sister Grace looking at her expectantly.

"Your leg?" pressed her aide.

"Yes, of course." Danica took a step, then her leg gave out.

"A little help here," called out Grace.

With the assistance of two other Temple Knights, they carried Danica to her cabin, laying her down on the bed while Grace cut away the legging, exposing the wound.

"You're lucky. It doesn't appear as if it did any permanent damage." The knight applied pressure, then turned to the others. "You can leave us now." She waited until they'd left. "You should've donned your armour like the rest of us. This could easily have been the end of you."

"I took a wound to my leg, not my chest."

"And had it nicked a vein, you might have bled to death, not to mention the possibility of corruption to the wound. Do you even understand how much filth there is in seawater?"

"I thought you were from Talyria. Isn't that in the middle of the Continent?"

"It is."

"Then how do you know so much about the sea?"

"I pay attention to the crew," replied Grace. "Most of them have been sailing for years." She finished wrapping the leg. "There. That should see to it, although I recommend you rest it for a day or two."

"I'd love to, but I have a fleet to attend to." As Danica sat up, she began laughing.

"You find something humorous?"

"I had a very similar conversation a few months back, but I wasn't the wounded one—Commander Charlaine was."

"And did she heed your advice?"

"Eventually, but she kept putting off resting until she collapsed."

Grace gave her a stern look. "We shall have none of that aboard this vessel, Admiral."

"Oh? Did I miss something? Do you outrank me now?"

"Only when it comes to your health. I am, after all, your aide, which means I bear the responsibility of keeping you in fighting shape. I can't do that if you disregard all instructions regarding your wound."

"Very well. I accept your advice, but I will need to go up on deck eventually."

"Then I shall see that a chair is made available."

"You expect me to command a fleet from a seated position?" asked Danica.

"Only while your wound is healing. Now, do we have a deal?" Grace held out her hand.

Danica stared back. "What's this?"

"We need to shake to confirm the deal." Grace noted the puzzled look. "My father was a merchant; it's how he conducted business. Sorry, is it not acceptable within the Temple Knights to shake hands?"

"It is, but I'm used to it being a way of greeting, not confirming an agreement." Danica reached out, shaking Grace's hand with a firm grip. "It's a deal. Is that the right expression?"

"Most assuredly."

A knock at the door announced a visitor, then Anya poked her head in, taking in the bandaged leg. "I trust all is well?"

"It is," said Danica. "Sister Grace has done an excellent job of dressing my wound. I am, however, confined to a chair for the time being. Have you news?"

"I have. *Fearless* has rejoined the flotilla, and the coast of Burgemont is in sight.

"And the Halvarian ships?"

"Still within sight but falling rapidly to the rear. I expect we'll have lost them by nightfall."

"We must remain vigilant. I wouldn't put it past them to try again, and they may not be the only ships in the region. Did anyone identify the ones that attacked us?"

"I haven't had time to find out yet, but I'll make it a priority." Anya paused, unsure of how to proceed.

"Something on your mind?" asked Danica.

"I suggest we anchor off the coast for the night. The last thing we want is one of the ships getting lost in the dark."

"Very well, but let's post extra sentries. The empire may try a nighttime attack."

"That would be as dangerous to them as us, wouldn't it?"

"It would," said Danica, "but we've pricked them. They may come seeking revenge."

"I'll pass the message along to the rest of the fleet."

"Oh, and Captain?"

"Yes, Admiral?"

"Good job today. Give my compliments to the crew, particularly Sister Margo. Her bolt likely saved the flotilla. I shall be sure to mention her contribution in my battle report."

"Battle report? But that was only a skirmish."

"True," said Danica, "yet there are still lessons to be learned. That's why I compose these after-action reports."

"I thought you did it to inform our superiors at the Antonine?"

"And to a certain extent, you'd be correct, but the true value of such things is to allow us to discover what tactics work against our enemies, and pass those lessons on to others."

24

ACCUSATIONS
SPRING 1103 SR

Charlaine stepped into the great hall with Marlena by her side, dressed in their finest armour and bedecked in long ceremonial surcoats hanging to the floor, a far cry from the more serviceable type, cut just below the waist.

Marlena struggled in hers, almost tripping as she passed by the servants at the entrance. "I'm not sure I'll ever get used to this. Remind me again why we're being so formal?"

"It's the king's birthday," replied Charlaine, "and we want to make a good impression. Things have been quiet for the last month, and I'd like it to stay that way."

Sir Hugo waved at them from across the room.

"It appears we're being beckoned," said Marlena.

The king's birthday was a grand celebration, with people coming from far and wide to bid the monarch the happiest of days on such a joyous occasion. They threaded their way through the crowd to join the knight on the other side.

"You made it," said Sir Hugo. "Though I never thought to see you in armour."

"We are Temple Knights," replied Charlaine, "and this constitutes our formal attire. I'm surprised you aren't armoured yourself."

"The Knights of the Silver Spur feel such attire is suitable only for the battlefield."

"You may correct me if I'm wrong, but weren't you wearing armour the first time we met?"

"Yes, I suppose I was, wasn't I?" He chuckled. "Well, there goes that excuse." He leaned in closer, lowering his voice. "The truth is, it's much more comfortable in courtly attire. I would think such things second nature to a Temple Commander?"

"Our order has very strict rules regarding dress."

"And yet you wear no helmet?"

"One can hardly carry out a conversation while wearing it," said Charlaine. "But you may rest assured the servants can retrieve them at a moment's notice."

Sir Hugo's gaze flicked to the entrance, and then he nodded at the fellow entering the great hall. "It looks like Lord Corbin has returned to court, and he doesn't appear to be in a good mood."

"No doubt he shall lodge a complaint," offered Marlena. "He does that a lot these days."

Charlaine locked eyes with those of the Halvarian envoy for only an instant, yet the hatred within them was hard to miss.

"Why does he dislike you so?" asked Sir Hugo.

"Haven't you heard? We're at war, at least as far as the open sea goes."

"We're at war? Why didn't anyone see fit to inform me?"

"Our order's at war, not Arnsfeld. Your kingdom is safe now, although I can't guarantee that will hold true in the coming months."

They watched Lord Corbin approach King Stefan, bow, take another step forward and then speak to him in hushed tones.

"That doesn't bode well," said Sir Hugo.

"Good day," came the voice of Ashan. "I hope I'm not interrupting?"

"Not at all," replied Charlaine. "We were discussing the arrival of the Halvarian envoy. I don't suppose you've heard why he's here, have you?"

"I'm afraid not," replied the mage, "but knowing Lord Corbin, it can't be good."

The king beckoned.

"Now he's done it," said Sir Hugo. "Which one of us is in trouble, do you think?"

"I couldn't hazard a guess," replied Ashan. "Perhaps all of us?"

"And why would you be in trouble? Been setting too many fires, have you?"

"No, but I am known to have a"—he paused for the briefest moment— "fiery temper from time to time."

Marlena groaned. "That must be the worst thing I've ever heard you say, my lord."

"Thank you. I'll take that as a compliment."

"Come," said Sir Hugo. "It's not wise to make the king wait."

The quartet proceeded towards Stefan, bowing deeply upon their arrival.

"I am glad to see you all made it today," said the king, "but I'm afraid Lord Corbin has brought some disturbing news."

All eyes swivelled towards the envoy. "Once again, Temple Knights crossed into Halvarian territory and inflicted grievous wounds on its people."

"Come now," said Charlaine. "We've heard the accusations before. You make baseless claims with no evidence to support them."

Corbin smiled. "Ah, but that's where you're wrong. This time we have a body."

"A body?" replied the king. "What's this, now? Commander, I thought you said none of your Temple Knights crossed the border?"

"I assure you they haven't," replied Charlaine.

"Yet His Lordship claims to possess a body? How do you explain that?"

"Where is this body?"

"I received word it's on its way," said Corbin. "We used magic to preserve it."

"Magic?" asked Marlena.

"Preservation is a Life Magic spell," said Ashan. "I assume your truthseekers are capable of such?"

"They are, indeed," replied Lord Corbin. "I see you are familiar with our culture."

"Perhaps you'd care to explain to the rest of us," said Sir Hugo. "What's a truthseeker?"

"An instrument of justice," replied the envoy. "Truthseekers travel the empire acting as judge and jury, using their magic to get to the truth of matters, hence their name."

"They can use magic to tell when a person is lying?"

"Yes. They read the colour of a person's aura and determine when they're telling the truth."

"And who corroborates this?" asked Charlaine.

"Corroborates? Why in the name of the emperor would we need to validate the findings of a truthseeker? By their very nature, they are dedicated to weeding out lies."

"A power that, in the wrong hands, could easily be misused."

"Have you so little faith in magic?"

"It's not magic I distrust, but those who claim to use it to detect lies."

"Be that as it may," replied Corbin, "we are not here to discuss the merits of Halvarian society. We are discussing the body of a Temple Knight recovered in territory belonging to the empire."

"And when, might I ask, is this body to arrive?"

"Within the week. The Imperial Warship *Glorious* will bring it, along with other evidence."

"What other evidence?"

"Written statements."

"More manufactured lies?" said Charlaine.

Lord Corbin clenched his teeth, then took a breath, keeping his voice calm. "You will doubtless deny the accusations, as you previously did. That is only natural, but I assure you the presence of a body is not something you can easily dismiss." He turned to the king. "Your Majesty, I put it to you that the final verdict is yours alone to render."

King Stefan looked surprised. "And if I find this evidence of yours convincing, what would you have me do?"

"Banish the Temple Knights from your realm, or, at the very least, deny their fleet sanctuary in your port."

"This so-called intrusion is a land matter," said Sir Hugo. "It has nothing to do with the Temple Fleet."

"While that's true, I can hardly demand you expel all knights of her order; that would be too impractical. On the other hand, their so-called fleet could easily find shelter elsewhere."

"You make a compelling argument," said Stefan, "but I shall not render a verdict until you present the evidence for my people to inspect."

Lord Corbin bowed. "Of course, Your Majesty. I would have it no other way."

"Your Majesty," said Charlaine, "might I ask a question?"

"By all means."

"You were willing to hear Lord Corbin's opinion on what should transpire, should you decide his story has merit. Might I ask what would happen if this is found to be a lie?"

"I hardly think that bears consideration just yet, don't you?"

"On the contrary, sire. The envoy continues to make claims that impugn the honour of my order without any proof. Where does it end?"

"Come now," said Corbin. "As I already stated, we have a body. What more proof is required?"

"And you claim to possess written statements as well. Tell me, Lord, how many of your countrymen can read and write?"

"I beg your pardon?"

"The question is simple. Have you a literate population that can read and write, or are they uneducated in such things, as most farmers tend to be these days?"

"Our truthseekers took the statements; they were not written down by some peasants."

"And who might these witnesses be?"

Corbin growled with irritation. "How should I know? They'll be here when *Glorious* arrives. I'm sure once that happens, I'll be able to answer all your questions. In the meantime, you shall just have to be patient."

Charlaine turned to King Stefan. "Should we prove these accusations false, sire, I ask that you banish all Halvarian ships from the harbour."

"You can't be serious?" said Corbin.

"There is an old proverb attributed to Saint Agnes," replied Charlaine. "Turnabout is fair play."

The king broke into a wide grin. "She's got you there, my lord. Very well, if there is to be a threat of banishment, let it be balanced equally between you. Whomsoever is found to be lying shall have their ships banished from our harbour. Now leave me. I have guests to attend to."

Charlaine wrote copious notes to the grand mistress, detailing all that had occurred these last few days. Doubtless, Danica would add her own accounts once she returned from Vilnitz.

Marlena entered and deposited a tray with food and drink on the desk before wandering to the window to enjoy the view. "It looks like we have a new arrival."

"That's nothing unusual," said Charlaine.

"This one's flying Halvaria's flag."

"Perhaps it's the *Glorious*, come to play its part in this farce." When her aide didn't reply, Charlaine looked up, which only served to pique her interest even more. She walked over to the window, following Marlena's gaze to where a vessel larger than *Conqueror* stood in the harbour.

"Three masts," said Marlena. "That's the biggest ship I've ever seen."

"Likely the largest in these waters. I'm surprised they let us see it."

"It must be the *Glorious*, bringing the body to King Stefan. I expect we'll receive a summons in the not-too-distant future."

"Tell me," said Charlaine, "if you were the Halvarian Emperor, how would you go about all of this?"

"You mean this whole narrative about a raid? Assuming it wasn't against my moral code, I suppose I'd have someone killed and blame it on the body."

"Yes, but surely it would be easy enough to provide proof we haven't lost any knights?"

"You said they were making this entire thing up. Couldn't they claim we were inventing our own proof to deny it?"

"You make a good point," said Charlaine. "The problem we face is credibility. What we need is a neutral third party both sides trust to render an unbiased opinion."

"Is there such a person?"

"That depends entirely on who the Halvarians would trust."

"Lord Corbin put the matter into the king's hands."

"Yes, but he wouldn't do that if he didn't believe the verdict clear."

"So, you suspect he's up to something? Murder, perhaps? Or blackmail?"

"I doubt blackmail would work, but other types of threats might."

"Such as?"

"Invasion? Stefan is terrified the empire is planning to launch an all-out war. Peace could be the prize they're dangling before him."

"You don't truly believe the empire will stop there?"

"I expect they'll promise anything to achieve their objective," replied Charlaine.

"That being the case, how do we react?"

"I've already sent orders to Temple Captain Florence to return to Lidenbach to give an account of her actions these last few weeks."

"But if she broke the rules, wouldn't she cover them up?"

"Whose side are you on?"

"Sorry," said Marlena, "but you know that's exactly what Lord Corbin would say."

"That's why I told her to bring her record book."

"And that will help, how?"

"We know the exact number of Temple Knights we sent to Braunfel. If that body belongs to one of us, there should be a corresponding note recording her loss."

"Couldn't she just cover that up?"

"She could," replied Charlaine, "but our order tracks everything. A thorough examination of the records would likely uncover if we were one knight short."

"I'm afraid I'm still not understanding."

"Temple Knights like us have a very strict diet. Were they a person short, their kitchen records would reveal a surplus, not to mention the duty roster would be missing a name."

"That sounds like a lot of digging through their records."

"Precisely, which is why you'll need plenty of sleep before Captain Florence arrives."

"Are you saying that's my job?"

Charlaine smiled instead of answering.

"That's not fair," said Marlena.

"No one ever claimed the life of a Temple Knight was fair."

"But why me? There must be plenty of other sisters who can read?"

"That's true, but I need someone I can trust."

Marlena sighed. "Well, if you put it that way."

"It's your own fault, when you look at it."

"How's that?"

"You're the one who made yourself indispensable. In any case, it won't be for a few days yet. I've only just sent for Captain Florence. Now, we'd best dress in our finest. Unless I'm mistaken, we're soon to receive a Royal Summons."

"Don't we have to wait until they deliver the body?"

"I imagine Lord Corbin will look after that as soon as possible. He's far too eager to see us pushed out of the port."

"The only ship we have in the harbour is the *Vanguard*," said Marlena.

"Still, if the king rules in favour of the Halvarians, she'll have to put to sea."

"Shall I send a warning to Captain Nadia?"

"Under the circumstances, that would be advisable."

They dressed quickly, then headed to the docks to witness the body brought ashore in what appeared to be a coffin. The Halvarians placed it into a wagon, draping it in the flag of the Temple Knights of Saint Agnes before marching it to the Royal Castle, with Lord Corbin himself leading an honour guard. Charlaine thought it a bit theatrical, especially considering the animosity the envoy felt for them, but the spectacle impressed the people of Lidenbach. The townsfolk lined the streets, lowering their heads to acknowledge the brave knight's sacrifice.

As Charlaine wondered who actually lay in the coffin, she had to admit there was a possibility Florence had overstepped her orders and crossed the river. If true, that one reckless disregard of duty might cost them the entire campaign, for without the fleet, the enemy could sail into the capital while their legions kept everyone else busy on the western border.

Florence had grown accustomed to throwing around her seniority in Ilea. Of course, that didn't necessarily mean she was the type to disobey orders, but at this point, even the fact she was considering such a possibility told Charlaine Florence had yet to gain her trust.

Charlaine and Marlena fell in behind the procession, following in silence. Eventually, they reached the castle, and the doors were thrown wide open to allow the group to proceed into the courtyard. The king's men awaited them, ready to guide the body to a small chapel, where it would be examined.

The king stood on a balcony high above them, his gaze glued to the flag. The Halvarians halted, then six men clad in chainmail lifted the box, removing it from the wagon. They moved slowly and with great reverence, placing the fallen Temple Knight before the king's men. They, in turn, lifted the coffin and carried it from the courtyard.

The entire procession, save for Lord Corbin, turned around, heading back to the docks. Charlaine moved aside as they marched past.

"Strange to see them treating the body with such reverence," said Marlena.

"It isn't reverence—it's theatre. This is all to impress the king and convince him it's real."

"Do you think it worked?"

Charlaine looked up at the balcony. "Hard to say from this distance, but it's a distinct possibility. Now, come. We don't want to leave the body out of our sight for long."

"You really believe Lord Corbin would try something?"

"No, but that body is purported to be a Temple Knight, and no self-respecting member of our order would leave it unguarded if there were even the slightest chance that was true."

It wasn't until late afternoon that King Stefan arrived.

"Have we a name?" demanded the king.

"No, Majesty," replied his short, bald-headed companion. "The Halvarians are not the type to make such demands of those they slay."

"Well, let's open this coffin, then, shall we?"

Charlaine removed the funeral flag from atop the coffin with great reverence, then folded it carefully and handed it to Marlena. Two of the king's guards then pried open the top of the coffin, revealing the body of a woman draped in white linen.

Stefan turned to Charlaine. "What do you think, Commander? Can you shed any light on the identity of this individual?"

"I regret I cannot." She moved closer. "I don't recall ever seeing this woman before; though, in truth, I can't remember every Temple Knight under my command."

The king turned once more to his bald companion. "Come now, Asmirius. Work your magic, and tell us what you can of this woman."

"As I have told you many times, Majesty, it's not magic, merely my powers of observation." He moved closer, squinting as he examined her face, then lifted one of her arms. "Remarkable. I have never witnessed a body preserved by magic before. It's almost as if she only died in the last few hours. There is no corruption at all!"

"Fascinating, no doubt, but we are here to determine the body's identity, not gush over the application of magic!"

"Yes, of course. Your pardon, Majesty. Whoever this is, was a seasoned warrior, in my opinion."

"And what leads you to that conclusion?"

"There are several old scars, no doubt the work of weapons, and the muscle definition would suggest someone who practiced regularly, as I believe the Temple Knights do."

"What do you say to that, Commander?"

"Temple Knights are not the only female warriors on the Continent."

"Oh?" said the king. "I wasn't aware there were others. Who, pray tell, would you be referring to?"

"Mercenary companies are known to count women amongst their ranks, and the armies of the Old Kingdom were composed of men and women in almost equal numbers."

"Do not talk to me of the Old Kingdom," said Stefan. "To even broach the subject is to invite calamity." He diverted his attention to Asmirius. "Anything else you can tell us? Her age, for example?"

"I would put her in her late twenties or early thirties."

"Why is that?"

"Her skin has a weathered look, but her hair has not yet begun to grey. You'll note the wrinkles under her eyes, which tends to occur naturally in the late twenties."

"An interesting observation," noted Charlaine. "And one that substantiates my claim she was not a Temple Knight."

"Perhaps you'd care to enlighten us as to how?" asked Asmirius.

"The company I sent to Braunfel consists almost entirely of recent recruits. As such, their average age is only twenty."

"And yet, you yourself are older, are you not?"

"I am, but I joined the order later than most."

"I was taken to understand the average age of a Temple Knight is much older."

"And it would be anywhere else on the Continent, but my superiors had to go on a recruiting drive to fill the commanderies of Arnsfeld on such short notice."

The king cleared his throat. "So, you're telling me you can neither confirm nor deny this is a Temple Knight?"

"Not at this time. I sent word to Temple Captain Florence but am yet to receive a reply. It would be difficult to hide if she is missing a member of her command."

"This entire affair is proving to be troublesome. These are difficult times, Commander, and my kingdom is on the brink of invasion. I can afford no missteps, or else I might plunge my realm into war. In the interests of peace, I'm afraid I must insist all Temple ships be banned from Lidenbach Bay. I expect any in port to leave by sundown tomorrow. Naturally, I would not wish them to depart without provisions, so I will provide the necessary assistance to ensure they carry sufficient stores aboard to reach Vilnitz."

"I must protest, Majesty. There is still no absolute proof this woman is a Temple Knight!"

"Nevertheless, my decision is final." The king's face softened. "I know the stakes here, Commander, but if we are to meet the enemy with any chance of success, we must bide our time."

"Until when, might I ask?"

"Until I can finish equipping an army with which to fight back!" Stefan's red face revealed his frustration. "I fear I've said too much. You are to speak of this to no one."

"Understood, Majesty," replied Charlaine. "Are you certain I cannot change your mind regarding our ships?"

"For the time being, no, but I shall reconsider once summer arrives, unless the invasion is upon us before then, in which case they may do as they please." He took a deep breath, letting it out slowly. "I'm well aware of what you've been doing with my knights," he added.

Charlaine opened her mouth to speak, but he held up a hand, forestalling her. "I will not get in the way of that, for you have done quite well without my interference. Do you consider me a weak king?"

She was too stunned to reply.

"I know some think me so," he continued, "but your words last fall convinced me not to surrender my Crown. I have since given orders that each baron raise additional troops for the kingdom's defence, but we cannot hurry such things, not when they must forge armour and weapons. When the time comes, they shall mass in Dubrow. If I cannot command them, I expect you to see to their disposition."

"Me?" said Charlaine. "Surely your general is a better choice?"

"I have reason to suspect my general's loyalty."

"Then why not replace him?"

"Why indeed? Arnsfeld is not blessed with an overabundance of experienced field commanders, while you have fought the empire not once but twice, and both times you've come out on the winning side. I would see you repeat that with my army."

"You honour me, Majesty."

"There. I feel better already for getting this off my chest. I shall inform those concerned about my decision to place you in command, should it prove necessary. However, the empire must not move before summer, or else we'll have little to face them with. Do you understand?"

"I do," said Charlaine, "and I promise you, I will do all I can to protect this realm."

Charlaine watched from her office as the *Vanguard* made its way into the open sea the next day. It would rendezvous with Danica's flotilla and pass on the news. No doubt *Fearless* and *Illustrious* would be returning soon with a convoy of merchants, but she doubted the two warships would have any trouble remaining at sea while the traders unloaded their cargo.

"Will we see her again?" asked Marlena.

"You startled me. Where did you come from?"

"I thought you might like an early dinner. You haven't eaten much of late."

"I'm worried."

"About?"

"A great many things. The *Vanguard* sails out to a sea full of Halvarian ships dedicated to hunting us down and destroying us. And to add to our worries, I'm to take command of the king's army, should he prove unable."

"You've commanded in battle before."

"Yes, but there's a tremendous difference between leading a small contingent versus an entire army. Then, just to make things worse, we must somehow convince the Halvarians to wait until summer before making their move. Any ideas how we might achieve that?"

"What if we sent more knights to the border?"

"Where would we house them?"

"They could camp as an army does."

Charlaine smiled. "You may be onto something there. The Temple Knights of Saint Cunar often hold field exercises; we could do the same." She moved to her table and readied a quill. "Send word to Captains Bernelle and Miranda. I want them here tomorrow evening to discuss our new strategy. I'd also like you to invite Brother Gatan."

"Brother Gatan? But he's one of only six Temple Knights of Saint Mathew. Surely you don't expect them to participate?"

"There are more ways to contribute than simply fighting. Now, off you go. I've got plans to make."

25

VANGUARD

SPRING 1103 SR

"The admiral is here to see you, Commander."

"The admiral? I had no idea she'd even returned. You'd best show her in."

Marlena opened the door, admitting Danica.

"I'm a little surprised to see you," said Charlaine. "I thought you'd still be returning from Vilnitz."

"So did I, but our merchant friends were eager to make the return trip. Apparently, the scarcity of shipping has led to some rather nice profits."

"And the return trip was uneventful?"

"More so than the trip out, where we ran across a trio of warships."

"I assume you handled them?"

"We put a hole in the hull of their flagship, which dampened their ardour. I must admit, though, it was a little awkward having to take a ship's boat into the harbour."

Charlaine smiled at the news. "At least you got *Vanguard's* message. I'd hate to think what their reaction would have been had you sailed into the bay."

"*Vanguard's* message?"

"Yes. I assume that's how you knew not to enter the port?"

"We never saw *Vanguard*," said Danica.

"Then how did you know the Temple ships were unwelcome?"

"We got word from a local fisherman. Where was *Vanguard* headed?"

"Vilnitz. The king ordered her to leave port."

"And why would he do that?"

"There've been some developments in your absence."

"Let me guess," said Danica. "Lord Corbin?"

"Yes. Once again, he claimed Temple Knights assaulted his people, but this time he presented the king with a body."

"And is it one of ours?"

"I won't know for a certainty until Florence arrives to account for her actions on the border."

"And when is that to be?"

"Any day now, I'd warrant. I sent word right away, but it's a long ride, and if things are getting serious in Braunfel, she might need to delay her departure."

"What does your gut tell you about this body?"

"That it's not one of ours," replied Charlaine, "but I'm afraid the damage is done. For the foreseeable future, the king has banned all our ships from the harbour. That doesn't apply to the merchants, so you'll still be able to organize these trips of yours; it'll just make things a tad more complicated. As far as *Vanguard* is concerned, I'm sure she's halfway to Vilnitz by now."

"I don't think so," said Danica. "I hate to say it, but I've got a bad feeling about this."

"Couldn't she have passed you in the night?"

"No. My standing orders are for ships to anchor off the coast at night. Had she done that, we would have seen her."

"Maybe she headed farther out to sea. Perhaps to help a ship in distress?"

"I'd be inclined to agree if it weren't for that trio of ships the empire has sailing out there. If they ran across *Vanguard*, they might have engaged in battle."

"Surely Nadia could outsail them?"

"Ordinarily, I'd agree," said Danica, "but the winds out at sea can be fickle."

"Should we organize a search?"

"No, it's too dangerous. Let's hope she cut across the open sea and missed us. I'll look into it once we return to Vilnitz."

"And if she's missing?"

"Then I'll send out *Invincible* and *Indomitable* to search. There's only so much sea between here and Vilnitz; *Vanguard* has to be somewhere. In the meantime, what can I do to help here?"

"I'm having a meeting with my captains," replied Charlaine. "I'd like you there if at all possible."

"Just tell me when."

"This evening. I'm hoping Florence will arrive by then, but if not, we'll go ahead without her."

"I sense something big is coming."

"There is, but I'll explain all that tonight. I don't want to repeat myself. Why don't you get yourself cleaned up? You smell like the sea."

"And this is a bad thing?"

"Let's just say it's an acquired taste," said Charlaine.

"Very well. This evening, it is."

Charlaine had assembled her leaders in the dining hall, the easier to accommodate their numbers. Marlena and Danica were present, along with Captains Bernelle and Miranda. Thankfully, Florence arrived in time for the meeting, though still covered with the dust and dirt of her journey. Brother Gatan rounded out the group, his brown surcoat standing in stark contrast to the scarlet attire of the sister knights.

"I had no idea we were all to be present," said Florence. "I thought I was the only one summoned?"

"That was originally the plan," replied Charlaine, "but events have been moving quickly of late, forcing me to make some changes. Before we get into that, I'd like to ask you a simple question."

"By all means."

"Have you lost any members of your company?"

"My entire company is present and accounted for. Why? Are there rumours to the contrary?"

"Have you, at any time, sent anyone across the river?"

"No, of course not," said Florence. "That would be tantamount to a declaration of war. What's this all about?"

"A few days ago, the Halvarian envoy presented the body of a supposed Temple Knight to the King of Arnsfeld. As a result, His Majesty banned all Temple ships from his port."

"I assure you, it's no knight of mine. In fact, I resent the implication."

"I believe you," said Charlaine, "but it's a question that had to be asked. In any event, there's more."

"Go on."

"Before I delve into the details, I must have everyone's word that this conversation shall not be repeated to anyone outside this room."

They all nodded, prompting Charlaine to continue. "King Stefan revealed he is raising an army, but it won't be ready until the beginning of summer. In the meantime, he's charged us with delaying invasion as long as we can."

"And how do we do that?" asked Miranda.

"I intend to send most of our knights from Lidenbach to Braunfel for some field experience."

"And by experience, you mean we're to be a deterrent?"

"Precisely. Unfortunately, that means we'll no longer be able to keep up our patrols around the city and the surrounding countryside. That's where Brother Gatan comes in."

"Me?" said the Mathewite. "But my order has only six men here. What can we possibly do?"

"I was hoping you might be able to pull knights from other cities to help patrol the streets. Of course, it wouldn't be permanent, and I would make rooms here at the commandery available during their stay."

"I know several in Dubrow and Nausig who could be spared. Given enough time, I could likely get a few more from Burgemont, and our regional commander is based out of Vilnitz. How many would we need?"

"No more than twenty," said Charlaine. "The idea would be to send out small patrols to give the appearance that all is well."

"I shall send word this very night."

"Thank you. It's much appreciated. Now, as for the rest of us, we must organize a march."

"How many sisters are we taking?" asked Miranda.

"All of them, save a few caretakers to watch over the commanderies in our absence."

"Two entire companies?" said Bernelle. "What about supplies?"

"We'll have to work together to sort out details, but consider this a dry run for the actual campaign."

"Dry run?" said Danica. "This could very well be the start of the war."

"Which makes it imperative we do things properly. Florence, you'll head back first thing in the morning. I want you to increase the frequency of your patrols, but more importantly, any Halvarian agents you find in Braunfel are to be locked up."

"But we haven't any place to put them!"

"I'll send a letter with you asking Lord Handrik to make his dungeons available to us. The empire has been scouting out the region for months. Our objective is to blind them to what we're doing until we're in place."

"And once you arrive with the other companies?"

"We'll make our presence known at all possible crossing locations. We can't keep this up forever, but we must do everything we can to delay their plans until the king's army is ready."

"I'm a little confused," said Florence. "King Stefan has been having trouble with Halvaria for some time. Why is he only raising an army now?"

"It all comes down to his treasury," said Charlaine. "An army is expensive to maintain. He reached out to his neighbours, asking for help, but they've all refused. I suspect they fear being dragged into a much larger conflict. In any case, he's had smiths working around the clock equipping his men."

"I've seen no evidence of this," said Bernelle.

"That's because he's doing everything outside the capital lest the Halvarians get wind of it. Of course, there's always the possibility they already know of his plans, in which case they might invade sooner rather than later, and that's where we come in. The weakest part of their invasion is the river. If we stop them there, they won't be able to concentrate their forces."

"It's a smart move," offered Danica. "You can only send so many across a ford at one time, and we would hold the riverbank. They could wear us down with enough time, but it would cost them dearly."

"I think it would be sufficient to delay them," said Charlaine, "but the spring rains have swollen the river right now. Once summer gets here, there will be more places to cross."

"And how long do we keep our companies down there?" asked Miranda. "Is this to be a permanent thing, or do we eventually return to Lidenbach?"

"I can't answer that at present. It will largely depend on the empire's reaction to our strategy."

"I'm not sure I understand?"

"If we start imprisoning their scouts, there's a chance they might send even greater numbers across to discover what's happening. Should that be the case, we'll have our hands full, but they may also back off and reconsider their short-term strategy. Should that happen, I'll consider sending some knights back here to Lidenbach."

"What of the fleet?" asked Danica. "Anything we can do? Should I send ships upriver to help repel the invasion?"

"No," said Charlaine. "I fear the river would leave too little room to manoeuvre. They are better employed hunting down the enemy invasion fleet."

"Invasion fleet? Why would they land troops when they can cross the river in great numbers?"

"They know, as well as we, that there's only one path to the capital. By now, they've figured out where we've chosen to make our stand, but we'll need to commit every warrior we've got to the battle. If they were to land troops between Lidenbach and us, they could hit us from behind or even march on the capital. Your task will be to stop that, not by taking on the warships, but by concentrating on the ships carrying their warriors."

Danica nodded. "The most opportune time to strike is when their ship's boats are getting ready to land men."

"I'll leave the matter entirely in your hands, but whatever you do, don't let them get ashore."

"And if the enemy should force a crossing?" asked Miranda.

"Then we'll conduct a fighting withdrawal."

"To where?"

"I'll show you once we march."

"That sounds awfully mysterious. Care to give us a hint?"

"As I mentioned, there's only one route for an army to reach the capital. Some time ago, I picked a spot to make a stand."

"There's more," added Danica. "In our absence, the ground has been modified."

"Modified?" said Bernelle. "You mean with earthworks?"

"That's one way of describing it. Let's just say that if we finally make a stand there, the terrain will be to our advantage."

"Yes," agreed Charlaine. "And I want to ensure the empire remains ignorant of the changes. It will serve us well if it comes as a surprise to them."

A knock on the door interrupted the proceedings.

"Come," said Charlaine.

One of the order's knights entered bearing a note which she handed to Temple Captain Miranda, who read it in silence.

"It seems," she said at last, "that some wreckage has washed up east of Lidenbach."

"How is that of our concern?" asked Bernelle.

"Two bodies were floating in the water, both wearing cassocks of our order."

"The *Vanguard*," said Danica. "It must have been attacked. How far to this wreckage?"

"We could be there by dawn."

"Then let us waste no further time," said Charlaine. "To horse, ladies, and let us discover what calamity has befallen our comrades."

"What of me?" asked Brother Gatan.

"Your company would certainly be welcome, should you wish to join us."

Marlena stood. "I'll alert the watch to prepare the horses. How many knights do you want to accompany us?"

"A dozen should do," replied Charlaine. "We can always send for more should it prove necessary."

"I'll meet you on the road," said Danica. "That will give me time to send word to *Fearless* and *Invincible* to proceed up the coast."

"And here I thought this would be an uneventful trip," said Florence.

．　．　．

By the time they arrived at the wreckage site, a small crowd had gathered and were picking debris out of the water.

"Who are all these people?" asked Florence.

"Local farmers, for the most part," replied Miranda. "I recognize most of them from our patrols."

Charlaine noted a small cluster gathered around something. It didn't take long to realize that a body had garnered their interest, for a few of them were using their fingers to trace the sign of Agnes across their chests. She dismounted, handing the reins to Marlena. The crowd parted as they approached, revealing the object of their fascination.

"Sister Ava," said Danica. "She was aboard the *Vanguard*. Where is the other body?"

"Over there," came a man's voice. An elderly fellow stepped forward with his hat clasped in his hands. "I'll take you to it, but I warn you, it's not a pretty sight."

He took them farther down the beach to where a pair of feet jutted out from behind a large rock. The body lay there—all, save for the head.

Charlaine fell to her knees. "By the Saints, this is barbaric!"

"I've seen this before," said Danica. "The bodies we retrieved from *Sapphire* were mutilated in the same manner. If you care to examine it closer, you'll note the telltale signs of an axe. These are not civilized men we're dealing with—they're animals."

"Then we shall treat them as such." Charlaine rose, making the wave of Saint Agnes across her chest. "This cannot go unanswered."

"There is little choice at present. They outnumber us by a significant degree, and were I to send ships out to hunt them down, it would leave the merchants exposed. This wouldn't have happened if King Stefan hadn't insisted on *Vanguard* leaving port."

"The king did what he needed to delay the invasion. I sincerely doubt he intended us any harm."

"And yet the ship is lost with all hands," said Danica. "This is a major blow to us."

"Do we not have replacements?"

"Several are under construction, but it will be a miracle if any sail before summer arrives."

"Is there nothing we can do?"

"Not at present. I'll send word back to Temple Bay, and hopefully, they can speed up the construction process."

"They would still need crews, not to mention a fighting complement." Charlaine looked out to sea, her mind racing. "Why did the Cunars abandon this realm?"

"You already know the answer to that."

"Do I? Can we honestly say the entire order is corrupt? Has it truly gotten that bad?"

"Whether it's all of them or not, we can no longer count on them to protect the Continent."

Charlaine turned to her closest friend, tears in her eyes. "This is an immense burden, Danica. I don't know if I'm equal to the task."

Danica moved closer and wiped away the tears. "We'll come through this. I promise you. The empire will get what's coming to them, and those responsible for this atrocity will pay with their lives."

"You're right, of course. Here I am blathering on about my own problems when war threatens us all."

"It's perfectly acceptable to shed tears," said Danica. "It's our compassion that makes us who we are."

"I doubt Lord Corbin would agree, but you make a good point." Charlaine straightened herself, forcing a smile. "We should let the others know of our discovery here. If we are to battle those who would commit such acts, then it's only proper that each and every one of our Temple Knights knows what's at stake."

They returned to the horses to find Marlena waiting alone.

"Where are the others?" asked Charlaine.

"They're searching the shoreline for bodies. Captain Miranda sent a rider back to gather more knights." Marlena paused a moment. "I assume this is what remains of the *Vanguard*?"

Danica nodded. "There won't be any survivors. The empire is very efficient when it comes to such things."

"Wasn't the ship lost at sea?"

"There've been no storms of late, and damage to the body over there indicates the use of weapons. There can be no doubt as to the *Vanguard's* fate."

"And Captain Nadia?"

"Hopefully, she died fighting."

"Hopefully?" replied Marlena.

"Yes," said Charlaine. "If they captured her, she'd suffer. At Alantra, they tied several sister knights to the masts as they sailed into battle."

"That's horrible!"

"They don't see us as people. To them, we are an obstacle they must push aside and discard, much like a stone wedged in one's boot."

"Even a stone can cause damage."

Charlaine smiled. "Yes. I suppose it can, can't it? And if enough stones pile up, they become a wall. Thank you, Marlena. You've given me hope."

"I have? I mean… you're welcome, although I don't know how I did that."

"You reminded me that even the smallest of things has its purpose. They may outnumber us and rule the seas, but we have the one thing they lack."

"Which is?"

"Our faith, not only in our Saint but in the people of this great kingdom. Saint Agnes said it best, 'Everyone is important, from the mightiest king to the lowest commoner.' Of course, that's a modern translation, but the sentiment remains."

"Will that be enough?" asked Marlena.

"It was enough to unite the Saints."

"Yes, but the Saints weren't facing an invasion by a massive empire."

"You forget your history," said Charlaine. "When the Orc tribes beset the Holy City of Herani, the Saints set out to secure a lasting peace."

"That was through negotiation, not violence. Words won't sway the empire from their goal."

"Then we must bloody their nose and send them running for home. No quarter will be given on the side of the empire, or any expected. The death toll will be high on both sides, but it's the price we must pay to ensure the safety of all the Petty Kingdoms, at least for the near future."

"So, we're only buying time?"

"The Halvarians have dedicated themselves to conquering the entire Continent. We can't sway them from that, but we can make them cautious about advancing their agenda in our lifetime."

26

THE BORDER

SPRING 1103 SR

I t took almost a week to finalize arrangements before the Temple Knights could finally ride out of their commanderies on their journey to Braunfel. Two companies, numbering over one hundred Temple Knights, rode in columns, followed by wagons bearing supplies.

Their progress was slow compared to that of a single rider, yet they managed twenty miles on their first day. At this pace, they would only need another two days to reach their destination.

That evening, as they rested by the roadside, Charlaine made it a point to wander the camp, stopping to chat with those under her command. By and large, they were in good spirits, and why not? The threat posed by the empire was distant, and the knights were confident in their abilities. Everyone in the order was sure of victory, but she worried that might change once they encountered the overwhelming numbers Halvaria would bring to bear.

She'd fought them at Alantra and the Five Sisters, yet neither of those engagements had set her against the full might of the empire's armies. Could a mere three companies of Temple Knights stand against an entire legion?

"Commander?"

She turned to see Marlena. "Is something wrong?"

"No," replied her aide, holding out a wooden bowl and spoon, "but it's getting late, and you've yet to eat."

"There are other things on my mind this night."

"You still need sustenance."

Charlaine smiled. "So I do." She took the bowl, giving it a sniff. "Vegetable stew?"

"There's meat in there as well, although admittedly, not much. I thought it best to use up any supplies that might spoil."

"An excellent idea. I wish I'd thought of it myself." She regarded her aide for a moment. Marlena had served her for nigh on six years, proving herself invaluable, but the thought struck Charlaine that the position limited her aide's options for advancement.

"Something wrong?" asked Marlena.

"Why would you think that?"

"You're staring at me like I've forgotten something."

Charlaine smiled. "No. I was just thinking it's time we found you a command of your own."

"No. I'm quite happy to serve as your aide, Commander."

"You no longer wish to command?"

"I gave up my life as a noble to join the order. Had I desired power, I would have remained back in Abelard and married a wealthy and influential member of the aristocracy. I chose, instead, to join the Temple Knights and help keep people safe. I desire only to serve where I can best make a lasting contribution, and it's become clear being your aide fulfills that role."

"You flatter me," said Charlaine. "I am but a humble Temple Knight."

"Humble you might be, but you are more than just a Temple Knight. You've led the order through one crisis after another, and now Saint Agnes has seen fit to place you here, where you are needed more than ever."

"Then perhaps she has finally made a mistake."

"Do not doubt your abilities, Commander. You've already done so much to prepare this kingdom for the coming invasion."

"Yes, but is it enough? The threat to Arnsfeld is far greater than what we faced back in Reinwick." Charlaine glanced around the camp. "What gives me the right to demand so much sacrifice?"

"Sacrifice?" said Marlena. "This order's sole existence is to thwart the Halvarian Empire." Charlaine opened her mouth to speak, but her aide cut her off. "I know what you're about to say, and I haven't forgotten we were founded to protect places of worship, but all that changed when the Cunars abandoned their duty. Whether you like it or not, we are, at this moment, the only thing standing between the Petty Kingdoms and enslavement by the empire. I wish it were otherwise, but we must face the truth. Yes, many of us may perish in the coming months, but we all took an oath to uphold our duty, regardless of the outcome. Do not doubt yourself, Commander. It only serves to weaken your resolve."

"You're right," replied Charlaine. "I have begun to doubt myself of late, which only serves to strengthen our enemies. I must put aside such thoughts and concentrate on the here and now. Thank you, my friend."

"Glad to be of service. Now, are you going to eat that food, or should I find someone to pin your arms in place while we feed you like a small child?"

"When did you become so bossy?"

"When Danica made me swear to watch out for you."

"And when was this?"

"Years ago," said Marlena. "And I take my promises seriously. Besides, if I let you have your way all the time, I'd have to answer to the admiral."

The day began far too early for Charlaine's taste. She was used to rising at sunrise, but the ominous clouds moving in from the west felt like a bad omen.

Her captains soon had her command on the move, but halfway through the morning, the rain started, turning the roads into a swampy mess, slowing their progress when the wagons got bogged down in the mud.

The effort had taken its toll on her knights by mid-afternoon, Charlaine decided to camp. The weather soon turned into a veritable monsoon, limiting visibility to a few yards, the blowing wind playing havoc with the covered wagons. With little in the way of shelter, all they could do was endure.

The rain continued as darkness fell. All efforts to light fires proved unsuccessful, and it was well into the night before the wind died down, but it wasn't until daybreak that the clouds finally broke, the sun shining through.

Charlaine considered resting for a day to dry out, but the threat of invasion was dire. She allowed a brief rest to light fires, but by mid-morning, they continued on.

Late in the afternoon, a series of stones came into view. It took Charlaine some time to realize they were at the stream where she'd chosen to make her stand.

Orlina Day had done an incredible job of continuing to shape the land. The hills upon which she intended to mount her defence were taller now, with massive stones pushing up from the ground here and there, breaking up any hope of an organized attack.

Charlaine halted their advance, allowing her command a quick break while she and Marlena examined the terrain.

"This is remarkable," said her aide. "I've never seen its like."

"You should have been here a few months ago when it was all flat with a tiny stream running through it."

"And all this was done with magic?"

"It was. Orlina is an accomplished Earth Mage, but even she needed time to prepare the area. Tell me, what do you make of it?"

"As I said, it's remarkable."

"That's not what I meant. How would you use this terrain to your advantage?"

Marlena surveyed the area. "With the stream in front of them, the hills form a good defensive position. What I don't see is a place where we can use our Temple Knights to their best advantage."

"A keen observation," said Charlaine, "but there's every chance we'll need to fight on foot."

"That means giving up our mobility."

"True, but I doubt we'd get the opportunity to use it, outnumbered as we're bound to be. They say a legion numbers twenty-four hundred souls. A charge of only one hundred and fifty Temple Knights against such odds would be suicidal."

"But the king would send men, surely?"

"That's the intention, but he can't muster those numbers until summer arrives."

"I know that, though I must admit to some confusion as to why?"

"They need to plant the crops," explained Charlaine. "There's no sense in holding off an invasion if the entire kingdom starves as a result."

"Then we'll have to keep the Halvarians too occupied to carry out their plans. Any ideas on that subject?"

"Plenty, but we must make it to the border first."

"Then why are we halting here?"

"Simple," said Charlaine. "The captains need to familiarize themselves with the terrain. If we are to make a stand here, I want to ensure everyone knows the plan. To that end, the captains and the senior knights we have should assemble there." She pointed at one of the hills. "We'll ride over the terrain and discuss tactics before moving on to Braunfel. It'll mean a late arrival, but it's worth it in the long run."

"Very well," replied Marlena. "I'll spread the word." She rode off, leaving her commander to ponder the area.

There was no doubt Orlina Day had done a fantastic job of preparing the terrain, yet all would be for nought if Charlaine couldn't assemble enough warriors to hold it. Her gaze drifted northward to the Brinwald, a dense forest that would prevent any attempts to outflank them, but the trees were sparser to the south of the road. Was this the weak link?

As she pondered the situation, she noted a solitary figure approaching.

"Good day," called out Orlina. The old woman came to a halt, spreading her arms wide. "Well? What do you think?"

"You've done an impressive job."

"Yet you appear to have some concerns."

"There are many," replied Charlaine, "but I can do little about them at this time."

"Then you should put voice to them. A burden shared is easier to bear."

"Are you reading the Saints now?"

Orlina chuckled. "Those words are attributed to Tauril, not the Saints."

"I shall not debate the phrase's origin, but my order has similar teachings."

"Then follow your religion and bear your soul."

Charlaine glanced towards her command, but they were well out of earshot. "I worry I may not have the knights needed to hold this ground."

"And what of the king? Will he not send men?"

"Only if we can delay the enemy long enough for the army to muster."

Orlina nodded in understanding. "A fair enough concern, but one over which you possess little control. What else ails you?"

"My southern flank. The trees there have little in the way of underbrush. I worry the enemy could get behind us through there."

"Fear not, for I've taken steps to ensure that doesn't happen."

"Might I ask what those steps could include?"

The old woman smiled. "I'd rather not reveal that at this precise moment. Better, I think, that you should trust what I say is true."

"You are a woman of mystery, Orlina. Very well, I shall take it on faith that you can guard our flank."

"I endeavour to do even more, but I cannot make promises right now. Some things are still very much in motion."

"I look forward to hearing more details."

"And I will be glad to provide them once I make some arrangements. Unfortunately, such things still require you to delay the inevitable."

"Then I shall do all I can to ensure you have the time you need."

"Good. Now, if you'll excuse me, there are things I must attend to." Without another word, Orlina walked back into the woods.

At the sound of a horse approaching, Charlaine turned to see Marlena riding towards her.

"They're assembled," called out her aide.

"Then I shall join them directly." Charlaine smiled.

"Was that the Earth Mage?"

"It was."

"And had she any news?"

"Yes, though, it was a little… cryptic."

"Meaning?"

"She promised help but was reticent about revealing what that might consist of."

"Her magic, surely?"

"Earthworks are one thing, but engaging in battle is dangerous for a mage."

"But what else could she be hinting at?"

"That remains to be seen," said Charlaine. "However, if there's one thing I've learned over the years, it's to place my faith in my friends."

"Friends? You talk as if you know her well."

"I've always found it easy to take the measure of a person."

"That didn't help you uncover the duplicity of Larissa Stormwind."

"True," said Charlaine, "but I didn't spend much time in her company. Orlina, on the other hand, helped me in my time of need. I can't explain how, but I just know she's trustworthy."

"It's Saint Agnes—she's watching over you."

"I'm only one individual, unimportant in the grand scheme of things."

"Unimportant?" Marlena laughed. "You're the order's best chance of stopping the empire."

"That's a lot of weight to place upon one person's shoulders. And in any case, it's not me who will stop them, but the combined might of all who resist the coming invasion."

"Yes, under your guidance. You are the key, Commander, the architect of victory. Where is the self-assured Charlaine I knew in Reinwick?"

"She is bent with the weight of responsibility. There's a big difference between leading a company versus an entire army. In Reinwick, the consequences of defeat were nothing like what we have here."

"It would have meant war," said Marlena.

"Yes, but here, it could well result in the subjugation of an entire realm. The stakes have never been higher."

"What can I do to help?"

"Little, I'm afraid. It's not so much the idea of battle that terrifies me as them launching an early attack. Without the time to gather our allies, there is no hope of holding them back."

"Then we must do all we can to convince them to delay their plans. Have you any particular ideas on how we might accomplish that?"

"A few," said Charlaine, "but it would involve some rather unorthodox tactics."

"Such as?"

"Crossing into Halvarian territory."

"Surely that would provoke a response?"

"Not if it's done by a few individuals. Lord Corbin essentially declared war on our order, so a military action is surely warranted. If we can do enough damage, we might give them pause to consider their coming campaign."

"What kind of damage are we talking about?" asked Marlena.

"Their weakness will be their supply lines. If we burn as many wagons as possible, we'll hamper their ability to feed their army."

"I'm in," said Marlena. "How do we proceed?"

"The first thing we do is seek out volunteers."

"I doubt that will be a problem. There's not a woman here who would refuse the opportunity to take the fight to the enemy."

"This won't be a field of honour," said Charlaine. "If they catch anyone, it'll be the death sentence. I should also remind you that the empire is not known for its humane treatment of captured foes, particularly Temple Knights."

"A good point. How many people would you want in this little expedition of yours?"

"No more than eight or ten, I should think. We'll need to move quickly and stay hidden until we find the enemy's camp. Of course, there's also the possibility they might have dispersed their army to make such a tactic more difficult."

"This is the empire we're talking about," said Marlena. "I don't imagine they consider us much of a threat, and they certainly don't anticipate anything like what you're proposing."

"I pray you're correct, but before we can organize any kind of raid, we need more information about what lies on the other bank of the Stillwater."

"Florence handed prisoners over to the baron. Could they prove useful?"

"That's exactly what I was thinking."

Marlena's knowing smile caught Charlaine's interest. "You find something amusing?"

"Only that it took the prospect of fighting to bring you back to your old self. Now, are you ready to address the sisters?"

"Yes, I suppose I am."

They rode over to the gathered assembly. Captains Bernelle and Miranda were present, along with twenty-five Temple Knights who represented the senior members of each company.

Charlaine halted Stormwind, then looked over the group. "I first saw this area some months ago when there was little to offer in terms of terrain, save for forests on each flank. As you can see, that has changed through the efforts of a woman named Orlina Day. Her magic made this place what it is today, but it will be our duty to make our stand here. To that end, I shall lead you over the terrain such that you might get better acquainted with it."

"Is that truly necessary?" asked Captain Bernelle. "You'll be here to lead us, won't you?"

"The fortunes of battle are fickle," replied Charlaine, "and I would ensure each member of our order knows what is expected of them, empowering them to carry out their duty if any of us fall."

"And what of Braunfel?" asked Miranda. "Are we to simply abandon our fellow sisters to their fate?"

"You mistake my meaning," said Charlaine. "This battle will not occur in the spring. Our job here in Braunfel is to use whatever means necessary to delay the enemy's campaign."

"And how do we do that?"

"That, I shall explain in due course, but for the moment, I want each of you to explore this area. Your life, and that of your fellow knights, may depend on your knowledge of it."

Marlena had arranged for the companies to set up camp as the group toured the area, for it would be dark by the time they finished. Charlaine returned to find a hot meal waiting, a rare treat while on the move. She removed her armour and settled down to eat, taking a seat by the fire.

"It's been a busy day," she said. "And tomorrow will likely be even more so."

"It's good to see you back to your old self," replied her aide.

"Everyone has doubts from time to time. Thankfully, you're here to remind me all is not lost."

"Did you ever have doubts when you were younger?"

"Of course, especially when I forged my first sword. My father told me it would turn out fine, but I wasn't convinced. You see, I'd sunk hours into the thing and feared it would break before I finished."

"And did it? Break, I mean?"

"No. My father's faith in me was rewarded."

"It must be nice to have such a supportive father. Does he still live?"

"Yes, though I imagine he doesn't work the forge as often as he used to. My understanding is he's moved on to more important responsibilities within the guild."

"And your mother?"

"Still alive, the last I heard. I received a letter from them right before we left Reinwick, but if there's been any further correspondence, it has yet to catch up with me."

"But if he's with the guild, couldn't he use their couriers?"

"Doubtless, he could," said Charlaine, "but I chose not to burden him with our troubles. As far as he knows, the only way to reach me is through the Church."

"He won't remain safe if the Continent falls into war."

"True, but he's already lost so much to the empire. He deserves to live out his life in peace insofar as he's able."

"And once this is all over, do you think you will visit your parents?"

"I can't foresee a situation that would permit it. It's not as if I could take a few months off and go home. How about you? Ever dream of returning to Abelard?"

"No," said Marlena. "There's nothing there for me anymore."

"But you have brothers, don't you?"

"Yes, two of them, but I can't say we were ever close." She looked around. "This is my home now."

27

THE RAID

SPRING 1103 SR

Temple Captain Florence had arrived the day before the two companies, and set up the practice field to accommodate them.

Charlaine met with all three of her captains that evening, the better to acquaint them with her intentions. She spoke not of infiltrating Halvaria but of increasing the size and frequency of their patrols. The Temple Knights were to become more aggressive, taking a hard line against any intrusions.

"And how long is this to continue?" asked Florence.

"Until further notice," replied Charlaine. "The intention is to blind their army. Any sign of intrusion is to be dealt with swiftly."

"Are you suggesting we attack them?"

"Have they not ambushed us on occasion?"

"Aye, they have," replied Florence. "And their attempts cost us three wounded knights over the last month."

"Does this mean we are to refuse their surrender?" asked Miranda.

"No," said Charlaine. "Those who throw down their arms will be taken into custody, but no one makes it back across the river. Am I clear?"

"Wouldn't they have a complete map of the area by now?"

"Doubtless they do, but I'd prefer they not have an accurate account of our numbers."

"I have an idea on that," offered Marlena.

Everyone turned to look at the aide.

"I wasn't aware we considered you a captain," said Florence.

"That's enough of that," said Charlaine. "I welcome any ideas put forward. What was it you wanted to suggest, Marlena."

"Simply that them having no idea of our numbers works to our advantage."

"How's that?"

"What if we gave them the impression there were more of us?"

"And how do you suggest we do that?" asked Florence. "Make puppets?"

"She makes a good point," offered Miranda, "though she should have waited her turn to speak."

Marlena continued, ignoring the remark. "We pick an area where our knights would be visible from the other side of the river."

"And?"

"We send our knights riding past, then double back and ride by a second time, making the column look longer."

Charlaine nodded. "I like the idea. Is there any area nearby that might suit our purposes?"

"Several," said Florence, "but what makes you believe the Halvarians would fall for that?"

"The empire is unlikely to send their best captains to watch the river; they'd use low-ranking warriors, most likely provincials."

"And?"

Charlaine chuckled to herself. "Let's just say our experience in Reinwick indicates such men have little tactical capacity."

"Are you suggesting they're simple-minded?"

"Not originally, no, but something about their conditioning tends to eliminate their initiative."

"Yes," agreed Marlena. "Likely to prevent them from rising up against those in charge."

"So, you're saying this could work?" asked Florence.

"I believe so," replied Charlaine. "In any event, even if it doesn't, what harm has it caused?"

"I think we can go further," added Bernelle. "Our companies each carry a standard. What if we made up some new ones for fictitious companies? We can then use them occasionally, just to keep things interesting."

"I like the idea," said Charlaine. "Coordinate your efforts with Marlena. I don't want to see any duplication of effort."

"Anything else?" asked Florence. "What about engaging the enemy? If we come across a major incursion, do we fight?"

"Most definitely, assuming you have favourable circumstances. If there is any contact with the enemy, even minor, send a rider back to the commandery. We'll dispatch more knights to reinforce if necessary."

"That could lead to an all-out war."

"Let's be clear on this," said Charlaine. "War is coming regardless of our actions here. Our job is to delay that eventuality as long as possible. Any resistance on our part forces them to re-evaluate their plans which buys us time. From this point onward, we must consider the border a wall, and those who cross it will be subject to severe punishment." She paused, noting the grim looks of her captains. The situation here was not something the order had ever faced before, and most of her knights were untested in battle.

"I know this is not an easy task," she continued, "but if the people of Arnsfeld have any chance of surviving the impending invasion, we must be willing to put our own lives at risk. Now, does everyone understand what's expected of them?"

They all nodded.

"Good. From this moment forward, Miranda's company will take two patrols out every morning. Bernelle, you'll go with the next two in the afternoons, with Florence leading hers later in the day. In addition to regular patrols, we'll place pickets along the river with orders to report any activity on the part of the empire."

"How large are our patrols to be?" asked Florence.

"Twenty-four Temple Knights, more if circumstances require it."

"Is that sustainable?"

"Why wouldn't it be?" asked Marlena.

"Knights fall ill occasionally or get injured. There's also the matter of horses which might go lame. With a company of only fifty, it leaves us few spares."

"If that should prove too burdensome, we'll lend knights from other companies. If that means a few knights have more than one patrol a day, then so be it. I know it's not ideal, but I'm hoping we won't have to maintain it for long. This new schedule will take effect in the morning, so I want Miranda's knights relieved from picket duty to be fresh for first thing tomorrow. Now, unless you have questions, you're all dismissed."

They filed out, leaving only Charlaine and Marlena.

"You didn't mention scouting across the river."

"No, I didn't," said Charlaine. "It occurred to me we haven't the numbers for it."

"So, we just ignore the buildup of the empire's army?"

"Not entirely, but of necessity, other things are taking priority at the moment. Get some rest. Tomorrow's going to be a busy day."

A Temple commandery is an imposing structure, easily defended against attack from without and within, but a secret escape tunnel, known only to a handful of senior officers, was a means by which they could send for help in the event of a prolonged siege. Charlaine now proceeded through this very tunnel, a lantern held before her, illuminating her path.

As she reached the end, she spotted a ladder rising to the ceiling. She doused the lantern, climbed up and then pushed open the hatch, revealing the ruins of an old building long since abandoned. Once she'd climbed out, she closed the hatch and knelt to relight the lantern.

"I wondered when you'd show up."

Charlaine almost jumped out of her skin. "Marlena! What are you doing here?"

"Waiting for you."

"How did you know I'd be here?"

"Come now. We've worked together for years. Do you truly believe I don't know what you're up to?"

"Who says I'm up to anything?" asked Charlaine.

"I know you; you're going to cross the river and spy on the Halvarians."

"And why would I do that?"

"Because you don't want to risk the lives of others. Don't worry. I'm not here to stop you."

"Then why are you here?"

"I've decided to go with you," said Marlena. "You need someone to watch your back if you're going into the empire's territory."

"I don't suppose I can talk you out of it?"

"Not unless you back out yourself."

"Very well," said Charlaine. "We'd best get on our way while it's still dark."

"I am curious about one thing, though. How do you intend to cross the river?"

"I might have arranged a rowboat."

"How did you manage that without my knowing?"

"Even you use the garderobe occasionally, and dispatching a sister knight to carry a message is easy enough when I'm surrounded by them."

"And who, exactly, supplied the boat?"

"The baron, but don't worry, he won't be accompanying us. His presence would most definitely lead to all-out war."

Charlaine used her flint and steel to relight the lantern, then held it aloft, bathing Marlena in its light. "Follow me, and I'll show you the way."

They cut through abandoned farmland, then entered the town of Braunfel. Cloaked to hide their armour, they garnered little attention from those few individuals who still roamed the street at this late hour. They proceeded along in silence, eventually making their way to the dock where a small boat waited with a pair of oars lying across its seats.

"Your presence is fortuitous," said Charlaine. "You can direct us while I row."

"You're a commander. Shouldn't I do the rowing?"

"This is my plan, remember? Besides, I'm the one who built up her muscles working a forge."

"You haven't worked a forge in months."

"Yet, as you said yourself, I'm the commander, so my decision stands. Now, get to the back and keep your eyes on the riverbank. You'll need to find a good place for us to come ashore."

They climbed aboard, pushing off from the dock. Charlaine then took up the oars and began rowing them across, the current pushing them slightly downriver.

"Bear left," said Marlena. "I see a nice, secluded spot."

"Your left or mine?"

"Port side, to use one of the admiral's affectations."

The boat altered course, and then something scraped along the bottom of the hull. Charlaine immediately thought of the water serpent that had troubled them on their first visit to Braunfel, but it turned out to be nothing more than a shallow patch in the river.

Charlaine stopped rowing as the western bank grew closer, letting their momentum carry them until a bump announced they'd reached the far shore. They dragged the boat out of the water, gathering branches to cover it.

"Make a note of the area," said Charlaine. "I'd like to be able to find this thing for the return trip."

Marlena looked around. "We're between two large oak trees, and I can see the keep's lights off to the east. Do you think we'll be back by daybreak?"

"I certainly hope so, but that largely depends on what we find."

"And where do we look?"

"Florence has been collecting information from the prisoners. By all accounts, a stream runs from their camp into the Stillwater. With any luck, all we need do is find it, then follow it westward. We'll have to remain quiet, though. If we alert the guards, this entire trip will be for nought."

Navigating in the dark proved troublesome, made even more so by the necessity of doing it without the lantern, which they'd left in the boat, ready for the return trip.

Marlena found the stream through the tried and true method of stumbling into it. One moment she was walking amongst the brambles, the next, slipping down a sudden drop, ending with her in water.

They followed the stream as it wound away from the river, stopping several times to climb the bank and peek westward. On the third such attempt, they spotted large bonfires burning brightly in the night, illuminating an open space amongst a myriad of tents.

"For Saint's sake," said Marlena. "This place is huge!"

"It is," agreed Charlaine, "but we must get closer if we are to ascertain numbers."

"There's some high ground off to the south that might provide us a better view."

"Good idea."

They left the stream behind, climbing up a heavily wooded hill that made progress slow but provided them with a convenient cover from which to observe the enemy's encampment. Finally, they settled in amongst the foliage, peering down at the sprawling Halvarian army.

"Interesting," said Marlena. "The tents are all in perfectly straight rows."

"Our knights use a similar pattern."

"Yes, but these are evenly spaced as if every tent peg was measured precisely."

"I imagine that's part of their effort to enforce unanimity," said Charlaine. She pointed farther westward. "Look over there and tell me what you see."

"An open area inside their camp. What do you suppose it is, a practice ground?"

"No. If you look closely, it's marked out by stakes. I think they're awaiting the arrival of more men."

"So, the army isn't fully assembled yet?"

"That would be my guess."

"I'm surprised there aren't more sentries," said Marlena.

"Why would there be? They're in friendly territory, and the campaign has yet to commence. How many men do you estimate are down here?"

"It's hard to be precise, but easily a thousand, perhaps even two?"

"And how would you assess the makeup of their army?"

"I see some temporary enclosures for horses, yet they appear far larger than needed."

"Meaning?"

"That they're still awaiting more cavalry?"

"I agree with that assessment," said Charlaine. "And note how they've divided the camp into two distinct sections, separated by what looks like the command tents. My guess is those to the east represent the provincials, while the Imperial troops are to the west."

"If it's true, then it's the Imperials they're waiting on."

"That's good news for us. It means they won't be starting the campaign any time soon. Unfortunately, we have little information to guide us on what the Halvarian strategy might be."

"Isn't it obvious?" said Marlena. "They'll cross the river in strength and then roll up the road to Lidenbach."

"Yes, but what order will they march in?"

"Why does that matter? We beat them on Patience!"

"We did, but that was primarily a naval expedition. To defeat them on land, we need to know more about their army and how they'll use it. Do they depend on cavalry to scout? How many archers do they have, and how many miles a day can they manage at the march? It would be useful to know all this if we're to face them in battle."

"Then we should consider the best way to discover that information."

Charlaine laughed. "I'm already ahead of you. I thought we might try to find ourselves a prisoner."

"That will be difficult for just the two of us, won't it?"

"Not as difficult as you might think." Charlaine pointed to where the stream ran alongside the enemy camp. "Do you see what I see?"

"You mean the lantern that's well outside the perimeter? It's probably just someone relieving himself in the stream." Marlena paused as the notion sank in. "Ah. I see what you're suggesting, but I doubt the fellow will condescend to remain in place long enough for us to get to him."

"Likely not, but chances are where one man goes, others follow."

"The trick is finding someone important. I doubt the average provincial knows anything of value."

"Then we'll get into position and wait," said Charlaine. "The Imperial troops are better equipped, so it shouldn't be too hard to tell them apart from their poorer cousins."

They made their way down the hill.

"Ugh," said Marlena, her voice revealing her disgust. "It just occurred to me we travelled along that stream. That means we've been walking in waste water for half the night."

"Too late to worry about it now. Try to focus on the task at hand. We haven't much time if we want to get back to the river before dawn."

They crept closer until the smell threatened to overwhelm them.

"This is near enough," whispered Charlaine. "Now, we wait."

.   .   .

Several men came to the stream in the dark, but the glow of their lanterns revealed their provincial uniforms. Charlaine's leg began to cramp, for she'd lain still amongst the bushes for so long, but then she spotted the perfect target. A well-dressed individual heading towards the stream, guided by a second man holding a lantern aloft, lighting the way.

Marlena was about to draw her sword, but Charlaine stilled her. "Daggers," she whispered. "They're quieter, and we want him alive."

"And his manservant?"

"We'll take them both, if we can, but the priority is the noble."

"Are we sure the Halvarians even have nobles?"

"Noble, officer, lord: it doesn't matter what we call him, but he's definitely a person of influence. Who better to provide information about their strength?"

The Temple Knights edged closer, working their way downwind. The stench invaded their nostrils, but their target faced upwind, making it easier to avoid detection. Charlaine moved up on the right, indicating Marlena should take the left. The only real danger of detection came from the lantern bearer, but he focused on holding the light over his master's head.

The first to reach the target, Marlena pressed her dagger against the servant's back, and as he turned in surprise, she put a finger to her lips.

Charlaine then moved out from the shadows, standing before the finely dressed individual as he squatted over the water.

"Hold the lamp still, will you?" the fellow said in irritation as he attempted to read a scroll.

Charlaine moved close enough to grab the note from the fellow's hands. He looked up in astonishment, which quickly changed to embarrassment as he realized how exposed his posterior was. His eyes flicked to his servant, and then a look of defeat crossed his face.

"If you plan on killing me," he said, "then please get on with it."

"Stand up," said Charlaine. "You're coming with us."

"Surely you jest? All I need do is call out, and the guards will surround you."

"By then, you'd be dead. Still, if you want to sacrifice your life in the service to your emperor, I'm more than happy to oblige."

The fellow's brow furled in indecision.

"Well?" pressed Charlaine. "What's it to be? Will you come willingly, or am I to slay you this night?"

"I shall come quietly," he replied, "provided you let me at least pull up my trousers. May I know the name of my abductors?"

"Eventually, perhaps, but for now, it's best you remain in ignorance. You are?"

"Narak Juran, Captain of the fifth company of the Emperor's Own."

"It's true," added his servant. "His Lordship is an important man. He commands the finest cavalry in all the empire!"

"Does he, indeed," said Charlaine. "How fortunate for us, then, that he needed to answer the call of nature while we were in the area." She glanced at the paper. It appeared to be a letter, although it was difficult to read by the relatively gloomy light of the lantern.

"Off you go," she continued. "We have much ground to cover by daylight."

"Douse that light," added Marlena, "then put your hands out in front of you."

Lord Juran stood straight, pulling up his trousers. He fumbled in the dark, cursing as he worked, and by the time he finished, his servant's hands were securely bound.

"Your turn," said Charlaine. She tied his hands together before prodding him to bear south. "No noise, or noble or not, I'll sink my dagger into your heart. Understand?"

"I shall give you no trouble," said Narak, "but I warn you, my absence will be noted."

"I'm sure it will, but we'll be gone before daybreak."

The trip back to the river took far too long, but eventually, the sound of water came to their ears. There'd been no sign of pursuit the whole night, but just then, a distant horn sounded behind them. They found the boat easily enough, and Charlaine indicated that Lord Juran should climb in, but he balked.

"You'll never get away with this," he said. "If I were you, I'd set me free."

"When I've come to know you so well?" She poked him with the dagger, just enough to make him wince. "Get the boat into the water. Quickly now, or I shall take more aggressive action."

The Halvarians pushed it into the water, then the lord climbed in, followed by Charlaine. The servant entered next, with Marlena bringing up the rear. Narak sat in the middle of the boat, eyeing the oars. "Surely you're not suggesting I row?"

"You seem fit enough to me."

He pulled on the oars, slowly at first but gaining speed as he became more accustomed to it. Voices erupted from the shore, and then a trio of riders appeared on the bank behind them.

"There they are!" one shouted. "Archers forward!"

The activity on the shore distracted Charlaine long enough for Lord Juran to jump over the side, the boat rocking violently as he did so. With only a dagger at hand, there was little she could do to stop him as he swam towards shore.

She grabbed the oars as arrows whistled past, one striking near her hand as she set the boat in motion. It would have been comical if their lives had not been at stake. In the end, the darkness saved them, for once they were mid-stream, the rain of arrows ceased.

"All that for nothing!" said Marlena.

"And what of me?" asked the servant.

28

INTERROGATION

SPRING 1103 SR

The prisoner, who went by the name of Lucius, took a drink of water, then looked around the room. "Thank you."

"You've rested and eaten," said Charlaine. "Perhaps you'd like to tell us about your master, Lord Juran. How long have you served him?"

"I've been in his household for ten years, the last five of which I was his manservant."

"And how did you come to serve him?"

"Through the luck of the draw, if I'm being honest. I inherited a cobbling business from my father, but my skill never quite reached his level. I soon found myself unable to pay my debts, and was left with no choice but to become an indentured servant so as not to be a drain on society. In any case, I joined the household of Lord Juran, who I'm sure you're aware is highly respected amongst the elite."

"Respected?" said Charlaine. "For what?"

"Why, for his military accomplishments. He served as a foot soldier during the campaign to subjugate Calabria."

Lucius took another sip of water before continuing. "I was lucky enough to come up for auction as Lord Juran's company marched through the town. One of his servants had met with an unfortunate accident, and he required a replacement. I was in reasonably good health at that time, so he purchased me."

"Purchased? Are you a servant or a slave?"

"Indentured servitude is common within the empire. It allows those of low station to make something of their lives. Those who chose to serve this way will often sign a contract varying in length depending on our debt load."

"And how long is your contract for?"

"Twenty years," said Lucius.

"You say you've been the captain's manservant for the last five years. How did that come about?"

"The one who'd been fulfilling the role passed away unexpectedly. He was old, but I don't think His Lordship truly understood how feeble the fellow was."

"I see," said Charlaine. "Now, what else can you tell me about this master of yours?"

"He's served for a good many years, working his way up to eventually command a company of the Emperor's Own, what you might call an elite guard. It's a position he's recently been appointed to, and, I might add, very prestigious."

"And what does this elite guard consist of?"

"Heavily armoured cavalry akin to your knights, though with more discipline."

"I am a Temple Knight," said Charlaine, "not the servant of a king."

"Ah, I see. Well, I cannot speak to a comparison between your order and the Emperor's Own, but I know they were created to counter the threat of knights from the Petty Kingdoms."

"Just how many of these companies are there?"

"I only know my master commands the fifth, though it has yet to arrive."

"And is this company the only elite unit assigned to this army?"

"I'm afraid I have no answer to that. However, the emperor himself has taken an interest in this campaign and, as a result, it's been delayed numerous times."

"Do you know why?"

"Not for certain," said Lucius, "but I suspect his Imperial Majesty is sending more elite warriors to claim the glory. We've gone to war in the past, but of late, the talk has become grander. Many, such as myself, feel it's only a matter of time before the great dream unfolds."

"The great dream?"

"Why, yes. The ultimate capitulation of the Petty Kingdoms. It is our destiny to conquer all."

"You are remarkably forthcoming with all of this?"

"I have nothing to fear by speaking the truth."

"So, this invasion is part of a grander scheme?"

"I'm afraid I'm not privy to all the details. Lord Juran was only a captain, although an important one, to be sure."

"And the legion sitting to the west," said Charlaine, "is it complete?"

"Not at the moment. The provincials are all there, but the Imperial companies are still gathering. As for the Emperor's Own, I don't know where they fit in. Captain Juran thought they would form companies within the legion, but some feel they will be attached as extras, bolstering the numbers."

"Very interesting," said Charlaine. "Have you any idea who commands this army?"

"Oh yes. The commander-general was in command of my master's company in Calabria, and has since risen to become a favourite of the emperor."

"And does this general have a name?"

"Yes, Commander-General Arak Thorn, the empire's greatest leader, save for the emperor himself."

"And on what do you base this claim?" asked Charlaine.

"On his career. There are few in Halvaria who don't know the storied history of the man."

"Perhaps you would care to enlighten me?"

A slight look of distaste crossed the fellow's face. "I would have thought you'd have taken pains to become familiar with the man you are to face in battle."

"Who says I'm to face him?"

"Come now. Everyone west of the river knows the King of Arnsfeld is a weak leader. You're the only person of consequence in the area. Who else would lead the defence of this pitiful realm?"

"The king's general?"

"Oh please," said Lucius. "Even I know what a complete fool the fellow is." He raised an eyebrow as he looked at Charlaine. "Honestly, I'm surprised they haven't already killed you."

"Are you suggesting they would murder me?"

"Of course. Any action is justified if it ensures victory. That's one of the emperor's favourite quotes, by the way."

"They've already tried and failed." Charlaine watched the smugness disappear from the man's face as uncertainty replaced it.

"That's not possible."

"Yet here I am, standing before you, alive and well."

"True, you are alive, but if the emperor wished you dead, you'd already be buried." His face brightened. "Ah, I see through your little ruse. You've lied about them trying to murder you."

"You may not be aware of this, but Temple Knights never lie."

Lucius shook his head. "No, no, no! This can't be. The God-Emperor is incapable of making mistakes!"

"His Imperial forces have been defeated at least twice."

"You lie! They are always triumphant."

"Have you not heard of their defeat at the Battle of Alantra?"

"Alantra? That's in Calabria, is it not?"

"It is," replied Charlaine. "And we destroyed the empire's fleet just east of there."

All colour fled from his face. "No, that cannot be. The emperor would never allow such a thing."

"I fought at Alantra, and that's exactly what happened."

"Perhaps the ships were mere provincials?"

"We took the flagship, and Imperial warriors were amongst the crew. There's also the Battle of Temple Bay. Surely you've heard of that?"

The blank look on his face said otherwise. "When was this?" he asked.

"Almost five years ago now. Our ships defeated a fleet of Halvarians, then engaged and defeated a small army which had landed in Reinwick's territory."

"I've heard nothing of this."

"Hardly surprising," she said. "I doubt those in charge wanted word getting around about their defeat."

"And where you present there as well?"

"I had the honour of commanding the assault that led to the empire's defeat. So, you see, I have plenty of experience fighting the emperor's warriors."

Charlaine watched a tear run down the prisoner's face, visibly upset at the news, yet at the same time, he clenched his jaw, a look of determination overcoming him.

"It matters not," he said. "It is all part of the emperor's plan."

"I beg your pardon?"

"It is not for me to question the God-Emperor's decisions or understand their complex intricacies. He will triumph in the end, and there's nothing you can do about that."

Charlaine stared back, trying to come to grips with the man's blind devotion. "Are you suggesting he threw away his fleet for some grander purpose?"

"Of course. Why else would he allow such a defeat?"

"Hundreds of men died at Alantra."

"What are their lives compared to the majesty of a god?"

"If that's true, then how do you know he's not willing to sacrifice your legion in the name of this greater plan?"

"I don't," said Lucius, "but I will play my part in his scheme to bring about the great dream."

"Even at the risk of your own life?"

"Are you not willing to sacrifice your life to achieve your order's wishes?"

She considered his words. Was her willingness to die in service to her faith any different from his? All her life, she'd believed in the teachings of Saint Agnes; could the same not be said of her prisoner? The most basic tenets of the Saints called for a willingness to accept other religions, yet many within the Church chose to ignore that. Was she doing the same now? True, it was difficult to swallow the notion that Halvaria's Emperor was a god, but what was a god, precisely? Could he simply be a man with magical abilities who'd risen to the heights of power? Or was he truly some divine being come to the world of the living to rule?

Charlaine shook her head. Accepting other religions was a far cry from believing Gods walked amongst the living. Even the worshippers of Akosia said the Gods did not intervene in the lives of Humans. Was she now to discard those beliefs? No. The Emperor of Halvaria must be a mortal man, of that she was certain. How, then, to deal with his vice-like grip over his subjects?

"We are done here," she said at last. "Unless you have anything else you'd like to add?"

"When the Imperial army finally crushes Arnsfeld," replied Lucius, "I shall remember my humane treatment at your hands. I doubt it will save your life; after all, you stood against the empire, but it should at least guarantee you a quick death."

"Guard!" called out Charlaine. A moment later, Sister Johanna appeared. "Yes, Commander?"

"Take the prisoner away, and let Sister Marlena know I'd like to speak with her."

The Temple Knight nodded, then grabbed Lucius by the arm. "Come along," she said. "It's time you were locked up."

Charlaine turned to the window, its western facing giving her a clear view of the rooftops of Braunfel. The town looked peaceful, but she knew it was only a matter of time before war would engulf them. The empire was not known for its humane treatment of defeated enemies, and she wondered how much of the town would survive the inevitable occupation. Even if she had enough knights, it was doubtful she could make a stand here. She'd planned to withdraw to a prepared position, but looking at the folk of Braunfel carrying on with their lives, she worried about the cost of that decision.

Marlena interrupted her thoughts. "You wanted to see me?"

Charlaine remained at the window. "I have a question for you, and I'd like an honest answer."

"Of course. What is it?"

"Do you believe in the existence of the Gods?"

"Yes. Even the Saints acknowledged that they exist."

"And do you believe them to be all-powerful?"

"The power of a god is given to them by its worshippers."

"That doesn't answer my question."

"I think the Gods are much like the Saints."

"The Saints were mortal."

"And so, I believe, were the Gods at one time. Over the centuries, however, their lives have become... well, myths, I suppose. We see the same thing happening within our own order."

"In what way?" asked Charlaine.

"Some amongst our number practice blind obedience to the words of the Saints."

"But the Saints are spiritual advisers. The idea of worshipping them as Gods is contrary to their teachings."

"There are very few Temple Knights who've read the *Book of Saint Agnes* from beginning to end. Mostly, they rely on others to interpret the words and meanings."

"Then perhaps it's time I put an end to that."

"Certainly," said Marlena, "though this isn't the most opportune moment to begin such an undertaking. Might I ask what brought this on?"

"It's the prisoner. He believes his emperor is a god."

"We saw the same thing with the prisoners back at Temple Bay."

"We did, but those were, by and large, provincial warriors, not clerks. As far as I can tell, our newest prisoner underwent no such conditioning."

"Does it truly matter?" asked Marlena. "We know the enemy to be fanatical at times; what matter the cause of it? Come to think of it, I suppose you could describe Temple Knights with the same words. What we see as a deep faith, others might view as zealotry."

"I was thinking the same thing, but it does present us with a problem. Fanatics seldom surrender. How do we defeat them? Especially when they outnumber us to such a degree?"

"They surrendered easily enough at Temple Bay. At least the provincials did."

"True, but this time we'll be facing more Imperials, and if Lucius's words are to be believed, the Emperor's Own will be present."

"Are you suggesting we withdraw?"

"Not yet," said Charlaine, "but we haven't much time to act. If we're to have any chance of halting this invasion, we must gather our forces now."

"What can I do to help?"

"I need to send word to our knights in Burgemont, Angvil, and Rudor to march to our aid as soon as they are able. They are to join us on the Lidenbach road, where we intend to make our stand. I only hope they can get here before it's too late."

"I'll have riders on the way within the hour. Anything else?"

"Yes. I need assurances from the king he'll march to support us. Unfortunately, I must do that in person, which means I have to leave."

"And what of here?"

"The enemy is still waiting on warriors, meaning they won't begin their offensive for at least a few weeks. That gives us some time to gather our forces, but we'll need to send word now if they hope to arrive in time."

"Understood," said Marlena, "but you won't be travelling to Lidenbach alone. We all know what happened the last time you went without an escort."

"I would argue, but I see that would be pointless. Very well. I'll accept an escort, but I warn you, it'll be a hard ride. I want to be back in Braunfel long before the enemy makes their move."

"I already have riders standing by."

"You do?" said Charlaine. "How did you know I'd need them?"

Marlena smiled. "It's the job of an accomplished aide to anticipate the needs of her superior."

Charlaine stared back for a moment before breaking into laughter. "You've had an escort waiting for some time, haven't you?"

"I can neither confirm nor deny that accusation."

"Very well. Please inform them we'll be leaving first thing tomorrow morning." Marlena turned to leave, but her commander wasn't finished. "And make sure they carry field rations for travel. We won't have time to cook."

"Yes, Commander."

They rode out in darkness, the early morning sun not rising until they were well clear of the outskirts of the town. Six knights formed the escort; seven, if you included Marlena, but Charlaine kept them going at a fast pace. The weather remained clear, and for once, the roads were dry, a sure sign summer was nearing.

They stopped only to water the horses but continued riding throughout the day, slowing their pace when needed to preserve their mounts' strength. The miles flew past, and only as the sun set did they finally come to a halt.

It had been a hard ride, but they'd covered half the distance to Lidenbach. Marlena organized a fire, and they all huddled around the flames, too exhausted to complain.

Charlaine dug through a sack and pulled out some buns, tossing them, one by one, to her companions. "We made good time today, but the journey's only half over, and we still have much work to do in the capital."

"Speaking of which," said Marlena, "what's the plan? Do we ride directly to the king?"

"No. We'll return to the commandery first, then stable the mounts and clean ourselves up. It wouldn't improve our chances to arrive at court covered in sweat and smelling like horses."

"Do you think the king will help?"

"I see no reason to expect otherwise. He knows this has been coming. The only question remaining is how long it'll take for his army to move."

"What do we know of his general?" asked Sister Johanna. "Is he accomplished?"

"It would appear not," said Charlaine. "His Majesty hinted there was an issue of trust, or rather lack of trust, between him and his general, but I don't know the details."

"Are you saying the general is a traitor?"

"I can't say for certain. In any case, the king intends to command the army himself."

"And if he fails to arrive in time?"

"Then he expects me to assume the burden of command."

Johanna grinned. "Then let us hope he doesn't show."

"Come now," said Charlaine. "The best chance of success is with King Stefan at the head of the army. Were I to take command, there could well be objections."

"From whom?"

"The barons would be my guess. The lords of Arnsfeld each command the troops from their own regions. I doubt they'd favour any plan removing that responsibility from their hands."

"And should you end up commanding the battle," asked Johanna, "have you an actual plan of how to position the army? Aside from lining the hills, I mean."

"I do," said Charlaine, "but only in the broadest of terms. I shan't be able to make detailed orders until I have a better idea of what we're working with. By that, I mean the breakdown of foot, horse, and bow."

"Do we know how many men the king has?" asked Marlena.

"No, but I'm hoping King Stefan can give me some estimate of actual numbers."

"Will that be enough?" asked Johanna.

"Only time will tell," replied Charlaine. "With a bit of luck, the Fire Mage, Ashan, will join the army. I'm hoping he'll offset the presence of enemy spellcasters."

"Don't forget Orlina Day," said Marlena. "She's already been a great help to us."

"She has, but I'm not sure what she can do on the day of battle. I'm afraid everything will likely come down to cold steel and the courage of our convictions."

29

THE GENERAL

SPRING 1103 SR

Charlaine bowed as the king entered the room.

"Ah, Commander," he said. "I wondered when you might put in an appearance. I hear you've been down in Braunfel?"

"I have, Your Majesty."

"What have you to report?"

"I fear the invasion will soon be upon us."

Stefan raised an eyebrow. "So soon? I thought we had till summer, though, it is, admittedly, almost here."

"So did I, sire, but their numbers grow daily."

"What kind of numbers?"

"It is as I feared," she replied. "An entire legion waits across from Braunfel."

"And you know this, how?"

"I took it upon myself to cross the border, Majesty. They are still awaiting more companies, including elite warriors, but I suspect the attack will begin in earnest, as soon as they arrive."

"It appears we have little time to act."

"Might I enquire as to your success in raising an army?"

The king winced. "They are massing at Dubrow even as we speak, but I'm afraid there's been a bit of a wrinkle."

"Could you be more specific?"

"My general, Lord Wallis, has increased his influence of late. As a result, a few of my barons are calling for him to lead the Royal Army."

"I thought you would command them yourself?"

"So did I," said Stefan, "but someone's spent a lot of coins to sway the opinions of my court. I have little choice other than to appoint him to command my forces. He is, after all, my general."

"You indicated some time ago you had reason not to trust him," said Charlaine. "I wonder if you might care to explain that sentiment?"

King Stefan walked over to a small table and poured himself a drink. He picked up the chalice, staring at it a moment before answering. "I suspect he's in the employ of the Halvarians."

"Might I ask why?"

"He's been spending a lot lately, far more than a man of his position should possess."

"You suspect they've bought him?"

"It makes sense, doesn't it? Think of the chaos that would ensue if he refused to march the army to your aid?"

"That being the case, why don't you arrest him?"

"Ah," said the king, "that brings us to the most disturbing thing of all. General Wallis has replaced the Royal Guards with his own men. I fear an attempt to arrest him now would only lead to a rebellion."

He downed his drink, then poured another. "It's my own fault. I should have seen it coming, but I was too distracted by Lord Corbin. Now I am paralyzed, unable to issue even the simplest orders without fear of repercussions."

"Something can be done, surely?"

"Had he not sunk his fangs into my barons, it would be a simple matter of ordering the army to march, but I fear doing so now would only lead to disaster."

"In what way?"

"Those still loyal would no doubt march, while those under the general's thumb would likely try to stop them. It could well lead to civil war."

"Thus, playing directly into the hands of the Halvarians," added Charlaine. "This couldn't have happened at a worse time."

"I suspect they planned to do precisely that. I'm afraid our enemies have outmanoeuvred us, Commander."

"There is still time, sire. Perhaps we can turn this to our advantage."

"I'm open to suggestions."

"Do we know which barons the general controls?"

"I've heard rumours, but nothing I can act on."

"But is this not treason?"

"There is no crime in socializing, and without proof they were plotting, my hands are tied. Now, if they were to take more direct action, that would be an entirely different matter." He paused for a moment before shaking his head. "No. Even then, I'd be hard-pressed to take action."

"Because you can't trust your own guards?"

"Precisely." He leaned closer, lowering his voice. "There is a very real chance I will be unable to join the army. Should that occur, I want you to have this." He pulled a scroll from his sleeve, waiting to allow her time to examine its contents. "It authorizes you, in my name, to assume command of the army."

"Will this be enough to overcome contrary orders from the general, should he choose to interfere?"

"That is a question I cannot answer. Ultimately, the choice to follow you or not, falls on the shoulders of each baron."

"Surely they would march to save the kingdom?"

"I would hope so," said the king, "but these are perilous times. Many might prefer to maintain their positions of influence under the empire's rule."

"That will never happen," said Charlaine. "The Halvarians don't retain local rulers; they are a threat to the future of the empire. Without the nobility, there is no way back to the old ways before subjugation. It's precisely the tactic they used in Calabria which has served them well for centuries."

Stefan took in a sharp breath. "Then we must do everything in our power to convince the barons before it's too late."

"Do you think we could convince Lord Wallis to stand against Halvaria?"

"I doubt it, though you're welcome to try."

"What can you tell me of him?"

"Wallis Falthorn has always been a proud man," said the king. "You might try appealing to his ego. The problem, of course, is he has a lot of wealth backing him, which gives him power. I assume your order doesn't use gold to persuade others?"

"No," said Charlaine. "It most certainly does not."

"A pity. I hoped you Temple Knights might have a reserve of funds hidden away somewhere." He chuckled. "Then again, even if you did, it would likely pale in comparison to what the empire could offer. No, I'm afraid we can't spend our way out of this."

"What of power?" she said. "Could we entice him with a position?"

"He's already a general," replied the king. "What else am I to offer him? I fear only the Crown would entice him now, and he likely believes it'll be his when the Halvarians are victorious."

"If," corrected Charlaine. "There is still much that could happen to prevent that eventuality."

"Come now. Do you honestly believe you can hold off the enemy with only a few hundred warriors?"

"I shall certainly do my best. Speaking of which, just how many men are we talking about?"

"Ah," said Stefan, "that's where things get complicated. My own guard consists of four companies, but they fall under the general's command. Due to the impending invasion, I've authorized each of my nine barons to raise a standing force of two hundred."

"Even so, that still gives you a potential army of eighteen hundred men."

"It does, though you must remember each baron will want to hold back some of those companies to safeguard their own lands. I should think a marching army of a thousand more realistic."

"Might I ask the breakdown of such an army in regard to foot, bow, and horse?"

"That is entirely in the hands of each baron. I expect the majority to be footmen, with some archers. As to horsemen, the expense alone would keep their numbers on the low side. Lord Wallis would have the exact tally, but I don't know how willing he'd be to share that information."

"What of the Knights of the Silver Spur? Do they fall within the general's domain?"

"No, they do not. And there, at least, I can give you an accurate accounting. The order maintains two full companies of knights, but it also has what they refer to as auxiliaries: three companies, to be exact, two of foot and one of crossbows. That means they could field some two hundred and fifty men, assuming they're at full strength."

"And is there a levy or militia that can fight?"

"There is, but I wouldn't put much faith in it. In Arnsfeld, the nobility is loathe to put weapons in the hands of low-born commoners, leaving most of them armed with little more than pitchforks. Still, if you just need men to absorb casualties, I suppose they'll serve."

His callous disregard for life shocked Charlaine. "I will not ask anyone to stand in battle without a reasonable chance of survival."

"It is the way of things. It has ever been so, and I fear, shall always remain so. It is the lot in life for men of low standing to bear the brunt of war."

"Under other circumstances, I'd love to stay here and debate the morality of that statement, Your Majesty, but if we are to have any hope of staving off this invasion, I must arrange an audience with Lord Wallis. With your permission, I shall seek him out."

"Of course. And I wish you well, although I fear it may be a fool's errand."

Charlaine bowed, then left the room, her anger nearly spilling over.

Marlena, waiting outside, quickly picked up on her commander's mood. "I assume things didn't go so well?"

"It seems the king's general has been up to no good."

"And by that, you mean?"

"He might be working for the Halvarians."

"Are you saying the army won't march?"

"Likely not in its entirety. It's bad enough that we must face superior numbers, but this makes things even worse. Just once, I'd like to meet a ruler who has a large, competent standing army."

"You mean other than the Halvarians?" asked Marlena.

"Do I really need to answer that?"

"No, of course not. Let's change the subject, shall we? I've sent word reiterating your demand for all the commanderies to ride for Arnsfeld. What else needs to be done?"

"Seek out Brother Gatan. Let's hope he can convince some of his brethren to join us."

"He only has six Temple Knights."

"You forget," said Charlaine, "he called on others to help keep the peace while we were away. With a bit of luck, he can call on a few more from the surrounding realms as we did. It would be an immense benefit if he mustered even a single company."

"Should we notify the Cunars?"

"No."

"They do form the bulk of the Holy Army."

"Yes, but they've pulled back into the heartland of the Continent. By the time word reached them, the war would be over. There's also the matter of trust. At this point, I'm not entirely sure which side they'd fight for."

"Very well," said Marlena. "I'll bear your request to the Temple of Saint Mathew with all speed."

"Good," replied Charlaine. "And while you're doing that, I'll see about having a chat with Lord Wallis."

The office of Lord Wallis Falthorn, General of Arnsfeld, was little more than a drawing room. Charlaine, used to the presence of books and, at the very least, a writing desk, was surprised to see nothing of the sort. Instead, the king's general lounged on a plump chair, his feet resting on an equally padded footstool.

"Ah," said her host. "I was wondering when you'd show up. Come, sit. There is much to talk about. Can I offer you something to drink?" A servant came out of nowhere, tray in hand.

"No, thank you."

"Suit yourself." The general took the proffered cup, setting it down beside his own with a flourish. "Can't have it go to waste now, can we?" He leaned back, crossing his arms. "I assume you want to see me about the army?"

"Indeed, my lord. I wondered if you could give me some idea of its composition?"

"Just as I suspected." He snapped his fingers, and a wall panel slid aside, admitting another servant bearing a tall but thin book. Lord Wallis took it, perusing its pages until finding what he wanted. "Ah, yes. Here it is. Each baron is now required to maintain a garrison of two hundred armed warriors. In the event of war, they must raise a levy of an additional two hundred from the local population."

"Is that all?"

"My dear, that alone would amount to a force of thirty-six hundred men, and we haven't even mentioned the contribution of the knights or the Royal Garrison of Lidenbach. As you can see, the Kingdom of Arnsfeld is more than capable of defending itself."

"I'm told each baron must also, from that number, subtract a suitable garrison to ensure the safety of their own holdings."

"I see you are familiar with our customs. I assume you've been to visit the king?"

"I have."

"And yet he sent you here to me."

"This was my idea," replied Charlaine. "How better to understand an army than to speak with the man in charge."

Wallis smiled, then turned to pick up his drink from the side table. "What else has His Majesty told you?"

"Very little. He knew numbers but could provide no solid details concerning the types of troops employed."

"And now you've come to seek answers here."

"Precisely."

"So, tell me, Commander. Why should I inform you of our strengths? You could be working for the enemy."

Charlaine struggled to maintain her composure. He was the one likely conspiring with the empire, yet he dared to challenge her loyalties.

"I could say the same for you," she finally replied, "but let's not make unfounded accusations. I feel it's more productive for us both to acknowledge the kingdom needs us, don't you?"

"Yes, of course. I am curious, however, why you need this information?"

"The empire is coming," replied Charlaine, "and like it or not, we must make a stand. It would go better for us if we devised a plan to incorporate my Temple Knights into the Royal Army of Arnsfeld."

"Agreed. Very well. Let us discuss particulars. Each baron currently has two trained companies of footmen, armed and armoured appropriately. Their two remaining companies vary by baron, but typically, at least one, if not both, are archers. A few have horsemen, although not of the same quality as knights."

"And how are they assembled?"

"That depends on need," replied Lord Wallis. "Under the current circumstances, they are expected to march to Lidenbach, although Dubrow is often a staging area for those coming up from the south."

"Just out of curiosity, how experienced in war are your barons?"

"What kind of question is that? The kingdom has been at peace for decades. One would hardly expect them to have seen battle. However, none of them lack for courage, if that's what you're trying to suggest."

"It was not my intent to offer insult," said Charlaine, "merely to ascertain capabilities. While relatively inexperienced, my command has several veteran warriors, including myself."

"You've seen battle?"

"Yes, against Halvaria. That's one of the reasons I was sent here."

Lord Wallis paled ever so slightly. "Might I enquire about the nature of this experience?"

"I fought at the Battle of Alantra," said Charlaine, "though I did not command the engagement."

"I've heard of it. I understand it was a decisive defeat for the empire."

"It was, primarily thanks to the Holy Fleet's intervention."

"Still, that was a naval battle. What we're facing here is a completely different animal."

"I wasn't quite finished," said Charlaine. "I also commanded at the Battle of Temple Bay, and that affair included landing an army to retake the island."

"You mean to imply you've defeated them twice?"

"I was present at both, yes, but that's a far cry from claiming to have defeated them by myself. My fellow knights enabled our ultimate victory."

"Just out of curiosity, how many warriors did you command?"

"Five companies."

Lord Wallis looked pleased. "A far cry from commanding the army of Arnsfeld. I suggest you'd be better employed looking after the disposition of your own knights instead of worrying about my army."

"You mean the king's army?"

"Yes, yes, of course. I meant the remark only in terms of the command structure." He took his feet off the stool and sat up. "Let's be perfectly frank, shall we? I'm the general here, which means that I, and I alone, bear the responsibility, nay the privilege, of commanding the army of Arnsfeld. Do I make myself clear?"

"As clear as ice," said Charlaine.

"Good. Now, is there anything further you want to accuse me of, or are we done?"

"There is one more point I'd like clarified, if you don't mind."

"Which is?"

"If something were to happen to you, who would assume command?"

"Is that a threat?"

"Temple Knights have no need of threats," said Charlaine, "but people suffer from things from time to time. Take indigestion, for example."

"I think it's time you left."

"Thank you for your time, my lord. You've been most helpful."

"I rather doubt that."

"Oh, on the contrary. It's always easier to act when a person knows where they stand, and you've cleared up any misconceptions I might have had regarding your loyalties."

"What are you implying? That I'm not loyal to Arnsfeld?"

"I find it interesting to note you used that particular turn of phrase. Most men in your position would claim loyalty to the king, or at the very least, the Crown."

"Now you're just twisting my words."

"I shall not argue semantics," said Charlaine. "Instead, let me tell you this. I will take to the battlefield, even give my life to protect this kingdom from the Halvarian Empire. I ask, nay, I urge the army of Arnsfeld to join me, but should you refuse, I will still sacrifice my knights to defeat the invader. Why? Because it's the right thing to do! Now, as for yourself, you can hide here, in the capital, and hope to better your circumstances when the invaders arrive, or do your duty and risk your life to protect your home. The choice is yours, General. What will you do?"

Lord Wallis stared back, his mouth agape.

"It is as I thought," said Charlaine. She turned and left.

30

PLANS

SPRING 1103 SR

"I've failed," said Charlaine as she stared out the window, watching the ships in the bay. "I came here to secure the Royal Army's assistance, and now I've thrown away any chance we had of their help."

"Don't be so certain," replied Marlena. "I'm sure some of the barons still wish to fight for their country."

"Fight or sacrifice? We're badly outnumbered, even with the prospect of help from the Royal Army. Without them, it's hopeless."

A familiar voice came from the door. "All is not lost."

Charlaine wheeled around. "Danica! Good to see you again, old friend."

"Old? That's the first time I've ever been called that." The admiral's laughter did nothing to ease the tension in the room. "Why the glum tone? Did somebody die?"

"Only our hopes of beating the empire."

"Care to explain?"

"It appears the man responsible for the king's army is under Halvaria's influence."

"That's terrible. Can nothing be done about it?"

"No. He's replaced most of the Palace guards with people loyal to him. The king fears any attempt to remove him from office could end in disaster."

"And so, instead, he'll let the empire subjugate his kingdom?"

"I haven't given up all hope, but this setback has the potential to be catastrophic. What brings you here? Have you news?"

Danica smiled. "I have indeed. You remember the *Sprite*?"

"You mean the pirate we captured back in Reinwick waters? Weren't you going to turn that over to the Mathewites?"

"I offered, but they thought it would be best kept in our service. We've employed it as a courier, ferrying fleet messages back and forth."

"And?"

"I'm pleased to report the launch of our two newest ships, *Fervent* and *Faithful*."

"That is good news. How long have they been at sea?"

"Long enough to make it to Vilnitz. We now have a fleet of eight ships in western waters."

"How goes the escorting of merchants?"

"On hold for the moment," said Danica. "Most of the trader captains are staying out of Arnsfeld waters until the coming war is over. That's not so good for trade, but at least it frees up our ships. On that note, I want to discuss something with you."

"I'll get drinks," offered Marlena. "I have a feeling this is going to take a while."

"It is," replied Danica, "and thank you."

"Sit," said Charlaine. "There's no need to be formal."

Danica took a chair. "These new ships are similar to *Fearless*, but since we built them ourselves, we made a few improvements."

"Such as?"

"Nothing that would be immediately noticeable to outsiders. We thickened the railings to provide more protection from archers and reinforced the deck where they'd mounted the arbalests."

"Anything else?"

"The hull is built of a sturdier wood: in this case, oak. It makes for a heavier ship, but they can take much more punishment. Of course, the downside is they're not nearly as fast as our lighter ships." Excited by the news, Danica continued on in a rush. "We also made some improvements below deck to make it harder for an enemy to capture."

"How did you accomplish that?"

"It was quite simple. We used our commanderies as an example."

"Let me guess," said Charlaine. "You placed doors at strategic points so you could contain any attack?"

"Exactly."

"And did you change the rigging to include triangular sails?"

"No," replied Danica. "I thought about it, and we may try that in the future, but for now, it's best to keep them as similar as possible to the fleet's other ships. It certainly makes training easier."

"Eight is an impressive number, but I fear the empire has more, including those three-masted behemoths like the *Glorious*."

"Shipbuilding is not the only thing we've been hard at work at."

"Oh?" said Charlaine. "You're not going to tell me you've gone on a recruiting drive, are you? Because that would be perfect."

"Not quite, but thanks to the efforts of Barbek, we have a new weapon in our arsenal."

"Which is?"

"Fire bolts."

"Are you suggesting you've found a Fire Mage?"

"No, and that's the best part. Barbek dug up a concoction that bursts into flames when exposed to air. He's placed the stuff in pots and attached them to arbalest bolts. We must take care in handling them, and there's not a lot, but initial tests prove encouraging. The only real downside is the cost, which is fairly high."

"How expensive are we talking about?"

"Enough that we can only afford one or two aboard each ship, so when it comes to battle, we'll use them sparingly."

"Do you mean to put them on both *Fervent* and *Faithful*?"

"No, every ship with an arbalest, including *Valiant* and *Valour*. Even as we speak, my flagship is transferring them. That reminds me, the king hasn't lifted the port restriction by chance, has he?"

"I'm afraid not."

"Never mind. Having to anchor off the coast is a little awkward, but we'll manage. While we're on the topic of the fleet, I want to run an idea past you."

Charlaine found herself drawn into Danica's excitement. "Go on."

"We both know war is coming, and soon, by the look of it. I've given it a lot of thought of late, and I suspect I know what the empire's strategy is, regarding their fleet."

"Go on."

"They'll send a large expedition to secure the capital while you face the enemy on the battlefield."

"What leads you to that conclusion?" asked Charlaine.

"It's simple. Any hope of defeating a land invasion requires the presence of the entire army of Arnsfeld. Why, we'd have to strip the capital of every man to have any chance of stopping an Imperial Legion, and an unguarded capital would be easy prey to a seaborne assault."

"You've given this considerable attention. I assume you have a countermove?"

"I do, as a matter of fact. I've divided my fleet into smaller squadrons. I intend to sail *Fearless* and *Illustrious* into Halvarian waters to find out what port the invasion will likely depart from."

"Two ships? Isn't that a little risky?"

"I'll take two additional ships as well. *Valiant* would extend our sighting range during the search, and we'd use *Sprite* to send word back to the rest of the fleet once we found our target."

"And if you do find them?"

"That largely depends on what we discover. At the very least, we could shadow their fleet until they decide to make landfall. With a bit of luck and good timing, we'd catch them with their boats in the water."

"It sounds like a solid plan, but Vilnitz might be too far. Are you sure the rest of the fleet could reach you in time?"

"You make a valid point," said Danica, "but one that's easily remedied. I'll have them maintain a position at Cape Maralan instead."

"Whatever you do," said Charlaine, "don't take too many chances. We need you… I need you."

"I hear you," replied Danica, her mood sobering, "and I promise you I'll be careful." She paused, basking in their friendship. "If I take care of the empire's fleet, can you hold off their army?"

"I shall certainly do my best, but a miracle or two would be nice."

"Have faith. It'll all work out for the best."

Charlaine couldn't help but be cheered. "I've missed your enthusiasm."

"And I, your eternal faith. We both have a part to play in all of this, but to be successful, we must be separated once more."

"So it would seem. You must go back to sea, and I south to Dubrow."

"Dubrow? What's there?"

"Theoretically, an army, or at least a portion of one. I arranged some time ago for the Knights of the Silver Spur to mass there. I'm hoping some of the barons brought their own men as well."

"Perhaps that's the miracle you've been waiting for?"

Charlaine laughed. "It's not a miracle. It's the result of a lot of hard work. I only hope all this effort wasn't wasted."

Marlena finally reappeared, a tray of drinks in hand.

"Sorry," said Danica. "I'm just leaving."

"I was only gone long enough to fetch this." She raised the tray slightly.

"Leave it here," said Charlaine. "We'll celebrate when we return. You and I are going on a trip."

"Back to Braunfel?"

"No. South, to find an army."

.   .   .

In terms of miles, Dubrow was the same distance from the capital as Braunfel, though in a more southeasterly direction. It was also a much more travelled road, bringing traffic from Rudor and Angvil.

The weather turned warmer, and clear skies accompanied the trip. Two days later, the city's rooftops came into view as the weary travellers topped a rise.

"There it is," said Charlaine. "The first city of Arnsfeld."

"First?"

"Well, the largest, certainly. I'm told it used to be the capital."

"How long ago was that?"

"I'm not sure, but a century at least."

"Odd that the roads all converge at Lidenbach?"

"I imagine that has more to do with trade routes," offered Charlaine. "After all, it's the only port." She halted Stormcloud and stared.

"Something wrong?"

A smile crept over Charlaine's features. "Fortune appears to be with us." She pointed to a field east of Dubrow where smoke drifted up from many fires, but even more impressive were the tents—scores of them. "The army has massed, after all, or at least a portion of it."

"Will it be enough?" asked Marlena.

"That has yet to be determined." Charlaine urged her horse onward. "Come on. Let's find out who's in charge."

They picked up speed, the horses galloping by the time they reached the edge of the camp. Their approach drew the guards' interest, but no one attempted to stop them. The tents were arranged around a rough rectangle, where twenty men marched with pitchforks on their shoulders.

Charlaine brought Stormcloud to a halt as she noted the approach of a familiar face. "Sir Hugo, it's good to see you. I feared you might not make it."

He looked up in surprise. "Really? You should pay more attention to the date. You wanted us here by summer. By my reckoning, that's only two days from now."

"How many men have you brought?"

"The exact count is one thousand twenty-seven, although admittedly, almost a third of that consists of the levy."

"Dare I ask how many barons answered the call?"

"Only three, I'm afraid, although more may join us in a few weeks. Would you like to meet them?"

"I would," replied Charlaine. She dismounted, passing the reins to one of Hugo's men.

"The barons of Dubrow, Kurtzenberg, and Agenhoff are all here, despite orders to the contrary."

"What orders?"

"Lord Wallis ordered all companies to report to assemble at Nausig."

"Nausig? That's to the east."

Hugo shrugged. "I know. It makes little sense, but who are we to argue with orders from the king's general."

"And yet you did by coming here."

"We didn't disobey orders so much as choose to be a little freer with our interpretation of them."

"I'm afraid you'll need to explain that one to me," said Charlaine.

"It's simple. To all intents and purposes, we are marching to Nausig. We just happened to be taking a different route."

"And now?"

"Well, I'm assuming you bring word of an invasion. We can't sit by and ignore that, can we?" He noted her stern expression. "How bad is it?"

"The enemy is waiting on the last of their companies before they launch their attack. When they finally cross the river, it'll be in large numbers."

"How large?"

"More than two thousand, I'm afraid."

"Have we time to get there and stop them?"

"I doubt it," said Charlaine, "but my strategy isn't to face them on the riverbanks."

"You mean to let them cross unopposed?"

"We'll put up some resistance, but ideally, we want to draw them farther east, up the Lidenbach road."

"A curious strategy, to be sure. Would you care to explain how you came up with this?"

"Most certainly," said Charlaine, "but such things are best discussed in the presence of the barons."

"Yes, of course. What was I thinking? Come, I'll take you to the grand master's tent. This time of day, they'll be discussing the state of the newest recruits."

He cut across the practice field as Marlena hurried to catch up. The grand master's tent was easy to spot, for the Knights of the Silver Spur's coat of arms decorated it. Two of those illustrious warriors stood guard but did not challenge the newcomers.

Sir Hugo led Charlaine and Marlena inside. "Your Grace," he said, "I have the honour of introducing Temple Commander Charlaine deShandria, and her aide, Sister Marlena." He turned to the new arrivals. "This is His Grace, Lord Kheymar Rudd."

"It is an honour," said the grand master. "Sir Hugo has told us much of your accomplishments. These stalwart fellows are Lord Randal Norwin, Baron of Kurtzenberg; Lord Austin Renholt, Baron of Agenhoff; and last, but certainly not least, our host, Lord Erskin Gerrit, Baron of Dubrow."

Charlaine looked at each in turn, meeting their gaze. "It is a pleasure to meet you, my lords."

"The commander was just about to tell me of her strategy," offered Sir Hugo.

"Oh?" said the grand master. "Perhaps you'd care to include us in the discussion?"

"Most certainly," replied Charlaine. "As you are undoubtedly aware, we've been expecting this for some time. We've known that when the enemy comes, it will do so in overwhelming numbers. How, then, do we attempt to even the odds? My first thought was to stop them at the river, but that has its own problems, and we cannot dismiss the possibility the empire might cross the river at another point."

"Then what do you propose?" asked Lord Erskin. "Hole up in Braunfel Keep?"

"The keep will play an important role, but it's not large enough to hold an entire army. Instead, it will serve to divert men from the main threat."

"Ah," said the grand master. "I see what you're hinting at. They'll have to tie up men to keep the place under siege. Very clever, Commander."

"The plan," continued Charlaine, "would be to draw them eastward, up the Lidenbach road and face them on a ground of our choosing."

"And what ground would that be? If memory serves, the terrain is rather nondescript in that part of the country."

"Defences have been prepared."

Lord Kheymar's eyes narrowed. "What type of defences?"

"Thanks to the assistance of a woman named Orlina Day, we now have earthworks."

"A woman, you say?"

"Yes, an Earth Mage whose use of magic made this entire plan possible. She has also promised additional aid, although I have no idea what that might consist of at this point."

"We can march," offered Lord Randal, "but we're still awaiting further reinforcements."

"I urge you to march sooner rather than later," said Charlaine. "Time is of the essence here."

"And if we're too early?"

"Then you'll have plenty of time to learn the terrain. However, too late, and we will miss our chance."

"I don't like this," said Lord Erskin. "It feels a little rushed. Surely another week or two wouldn't hurt?"

"And hand over the kingdom to the empire?" asked the grand master. "No, the commander has the right of it. Better to arrive early and rest the troops before battle."

"Yes, but how early? And what is the enemy up to?"

Everyone turned to Charlaine, awaiting her response.

"Sister Marlena and I crossed into Halvarian territory and saw their army with our own eyes. An Imperial Legion, at full strength, numbering some twenty-four hundred men. We also have reliable information that the emperor has sent some of his best warriors to aid in the invasion."

"What's this, now?" said Lord Randal. "The empire has knights?"

"Not knights exactly, but something called the Emperor's Own. They are, apparently, seasoned warriors."

"Fascinating," said the grand master. "I'd love to see how they fare against the Silver Spurs."

"This is not an affair of honour," said Lord Austin. "The very existence of the kingdom is at stake."

"Yes, of course." The grand master turned to Charlaine. "How many of your Temple Knights have you?"

"Three companies, all in Braunfel, but I've summoned more from the neighbouring realms."

"And how many more do you expect?"

"Four, provided they can get here in time."

"Impressive. That would give you more knights than me."

"They already have more than you," replied Lord Erskin. "You only have two companies."

"Not if you include the auxiliaries," added Sir Hugo.

"It's not a contest," said Charlaine. "We are all in this together."

"I should very much like to see this terrain," said Lord Randal.

The grand master chuckled. "And so you shall, once we march there. Well? What do you think, my lords? Are we in agreement?"

"I will march," said Lord Erskin.

"As will I," added Sir Austin.

Everyone turned to Lord Randal. "I suggest we march first thing tomorrow morning," he replied. "Providing the wagons can be loaded in time."

"Make it two days," said the grand master. "Better to keep everything together than strung out along the road because the wagons aren't ready."

"I would offer a suggestion," said Sir Hugo. "We can shave off some time by cutting across the countryside and avoiding Lidenbach altogether."

"It would also allow us to avoid the gaze of the king's general," said Lord Erskin. "I like it."

"Then we are agreed?"

They all nodded.

"It seems your mission here has succeeded," offered Sir Hugo. "We shall meet you on the battlefield. How will we know when we've arrived?"

Charlaine chuckled. "I should think that the least of your worries, Sir Hugo. You must trust me when I say the terrain is unmistakable."

Early the following day, Charlaine and Marlena headed back to Braunfel.

"It's nice to see something go our way for a change," said Marlena.

"Indeed."

"Do you think it'll be enough?"

"It will have to suffice. At the very least, we now know what we're dealing with."

"Well," added her aide, "we know the quantity, not necessarily the quality. Those farmers weren't too impressive with their pitchforks."

"True, but put them behind a fortified position, and they'll stand."

"How can you be so sure?"

"They fight for their land and their loved ones. What greater motivation does one need?"

"I wasn't questioning their motivation, merely their ability. It's not unreasonable to see them as the weak link in our lines."

"Then I shall be sure to use them sparingly."

"And how do you do that?"

"That's simple," said Charlaine. "I'll place each group between more experienced warriors. After that, all we can do is pray it is enough."

31

DISCOVERY

SUMMER 1103 SR

The bow of the *Fearless* hit the bottom of the trough, then dug into the next wave, sending water cascading over the deck. Danica hung on to the railing as she searched the area. *Illustrious* was off the port side, struggling with the wind, much like her own ship, while *Valiant* and *Sprite* followed in their wake, having a better time of it.

Anya stumbled across the deck before she, too, grasped the railing. "Perhaps we should make for the coast," she said. "This wind could take us too far north."

"No. Hugging the coast would only alert the empire to our presence. Our objective is to sail deeper into Halvarian waters to spy out their ports."

"We're too far out to sea for any hope of spotting a harbour, let alone enemy ships."

"You forget about Laldor, the sailing master from the Vindicator. He's been of great use these past few months, drawing up charts of the region."

"Are you sure we can trust him?"

"He's prospered in our service," replied Danica, "and I gather he'd like to continue doing so, so yes, I trust him."

"And what do his charts tell us?"

"There are two major ports east of the Scattered Isles. The closest to Arnsfeld is Noordmacht, but the larger one is farther west, in a place called Thansalay. You might recall we captured the governor of that city at Temple Bay."

"Ah, yes. Lord Augustus Conwyn, I remember him now. If I recall, you almost strangled him to death?"

"That was Charlaine, not me. I was busy with other things at the time."

"Whatever happened to him?"

"I heard a fellow prisoner killed him a few weeks after their defeat. Apparently, he was a cruel taskmaster."

"A fitting end for a tyrant," said Anya. "So, what do we know about Noordmacht?"

Danica braced as *Fearless* topped another wave, waiting as the bow struck bottom again before continuing the conversation. "It's a small anchorage, not as protected as Lidenbach, but the shore drops off precipitously, allowing even large ships to get close to the docks with little problem. There's a town there as well, although nowhere near the size of Lidenbach." She glanced skyward, but the clouds still covered the sun. "I can give you a better idea of how much farther there is to travel once we can view the stars."

"Then I shall pray for the wind to clear the sky by nightfall."

Evening found them in Danica's cabin, with charts spread out on the table. "By my reckoning, we should be here." Danica stabbed her finger down.

"I thought us farther west," said Anya. "The wind's certainly strong enough."

"True, but the current in these parts heads eastward, making the calculation a little more difficult. We'll turn south come morning and look for one of these landmarks."

The sailing master had made detailed notes concerning the coastline, even pointing out distinctive rock formations and trees. Once they sighted land, it wouldn't take long to determine their location.

"Do we bring in all our ships or only *Fearless*?"

"Neither. The *Sprite* will go in."

"Surely the *Valiant* is faster?"

"It is," said Danica, "but it's far likelier to be recognized because of its triangular sail. The last thing we need right now is a Halvarian squadron trying to hunt us down."

"I'm not sure I like the idea of sending in such a small ship."

"If the *Sprite* runs into any trouble, she has orders to return."

"And if the enemy is too numerous?"

"Then she'll sail eastward, hugging the coast until she's out of Halvarian waters. I intend to keep *Valiant* to the north, just within sight of *Sprite's* sails, thus maintaining contact without the chance of being spotted from shore."

"And if *Sprite* has to flee?"

"I already thought of that," said Danica. "They'll hoist a series of flags denoting the enemy's strength."

"How many flags?"

"One red flag for each warship and yellow for each merchant. So, even if they flee, we'll know their numbers. I doubt it will come to that, though."

"You sound confident."

"It's unlikely they'd expect us to risk ships sailing this far into their territory."

"You realize," said Anya, "this will only work once."

"True, but I have other tricks up my sleeve."

"Such as?"

Danica smiled, but before she said more, the cabin door swung open, and Sister Grace entered bearing a tray of food.

"Time to eat, Admiral."

"Perfect timing," said Anya. "The admiral was about to tell me all her secrets?"

"Truly?"

"No," said Danica. "You'll just have to wait like everyone else." She looked down at the platter placed before her. "Is that lamb?"

"It is. We picked some up in Lidenbach, and I was saving it for a special occasion."

"Which is?"

"We turned south. Naturally, I assumed that meant we're about to take some sort of action against the empire."

"And so we are," replied Danica, "although we're not engaging them in battle just yet, not unless there's no other choice."

"I am curious about one thing," said Anya. "What happens if we encounter only one or two warships when we get to Noordmacht? Do we attack them?"

"As tempting as that might be, our most important job is to find the enemy fleet, and while we could handily best such a small force, there's always the risk of damage to our ships. I shouldn't need to tell you how disastrous that would be."

"Understood. I'll leave you to your meal, Admiral."

Sister Grace waited until the captain left before speaking. "Some wine, Admiral?"

"Water will do fine, thank you. I need to keep a clear head."

"Do you really think they'll have ships in Noordmacht?"

"Most assuredly. The question is, how many?"

Streaks of red filled the dawn sky as the *Sprite* made its way towards shore. It was a small ship, almost as small as the open-topped *Cygnet*, but it was a handy sailer. The crew numbered only six, yet its previous owner had crammed over twenty pirates aboard.

Today, the ship carried one extra person, Danica, who stood at the bow, as was her usual want. They sliced through the waves with little effort, reducing bow spray to a fine mist.

As they neared the coast, the tiny vessel turned westward, paralleling the shore. This was the most dangerous part of the trip, for if they stumbled across a large fleet, they would be hard-pressed to escape, especially with the wind coming from the east.

Danica stared up at the cloudless sky, and despite the ominous early morning sun, part of her knew it would remain clear. She looked back at the crew.

Blasco Dorhaven had once served aboard the *Lydia*. He'd remained with the ship when it was sold to the order, eventually becoming the helmsman. After years of exemplary service, Danica had awarded him command of the *Sprite*. The ship had proven its worth on multiple occasions, carrying messages back and forth between Arnsfeld and Reinwick. Now, it's undertaking a far more perilous mission, that of spying on the enemy.

The shoreline next drew Danica's attention. A gnarled oak tree with a distinctive lower branch stood out from the otherwise barren coast. "The hanging tree."

"It's well-named," said Blasco, "although it doesn't look like any bodies are dangling from it at this particular moment."

"How much farther, do you think?"

"Assuming the charts are accurate, we should soon see Noordmacht. How close do you want to get?"

"That largely depends on what the place looks like," said Danica. "Ideally, I want to count how many ships are in port. If we could identify the individual ships, that would be even better."

"What if we sailed right up to the docks?"

"I doubt we could get that close."

"Oh, I don't know," said Blasco. "You're not wearing anything identifying you as a Temple Knight, and it'd be easy enough to lower that flag." His gaze drifted to the top of the mast, where the distinctive pennant of the Temple fleet flew. "Of course, it's entirely your decision. I have no idea where the order stands on subterfuge."

"Because we've sworn to always tell the truth?"

"Precisely."

"Then why suggest it?" she asked.

"It wouldn't be the first time a ship flew someone else's flag to avoid trouble."

"Very well. Bring it down."

Blasco gave the order, watching as one of his crew climbed up to retrieve the pennant. "What would you like in its place?"

"Are you suggesting you have multiple flags to choose from?"

The captain laughed. "You'd be surprised what the previous owner kept aboard. Mind you, there are no Halvarian flags, but I could offer you Burgemont's, if you wish, or perhaps Reinwick?"

"I'll leave that decision entirely up to you."

"Thus, absolving you of the need to lie?"

"Don't worry," said Danica. "We'll raise our true flag if things go sour. Remember, we're only here for a look, not to provoke anyone."

"Fair enough." He turned to the west. "Well, well. It appears the port was closer than we expected."

Danica followed his gaze. Towards the shore, the land rose in a white-faced cliff where it met the water. A gaggle of ships lay beneath, tied to a long wooden dock running along its base.

"A dozen," said Blasco, "but most look like small fishing vessels."

Danica strained to make out details, but the captain's eyesight was better than hers. "How many warships?"

"Three, assuming the larger ones are ships of war and not some sort of merchant."

The wind in these parts was fickle, and they soon found themselves sailing directly against it. The *Sprite* altered course, taking them farther out to sea, but now the distance was too great to make out ship names.

"A three-master," said Blasco. "That's new."

"I wonder if it's the *Glorious*," replied Danica. "It visited Lidenbach some time ago, but we lost track of it."

"Let's find out, shall we?" He ordered the ship to adjust its course, turning south to get closer. "I'm going in. We'll sail the *Sprite* right past that thing. If you can't read the name at that range, you might as well hang up your admiral's hat."

Danica chuckled. "I didn't know there was such a thing, but I concede the point."

"You should probably pick up some rope and look busy so you don't stand out. Say, do you think anyone might recognize you?"

"I'm not in armour, and I'm dressed like a deckhand. What do you think?"

He nodded. "You're probably right. Just to be on the safe side, though, leave the talking to me."

"You intend to get close enough to talk?"

"Of course," said Blasco. "We're all fellow travellers. After all, it's only common courtesy. Were we to do otherwise, it might invite scrutiny."

"And what will you say?"

"We'll exchange pleasantries, I'm sure. Mind you, it won't last long. Once they see we're heading back out to sea, they'll become suspicious."

"You think they'll follow?"

"No. Their sails are furled. We'll be long gone by the time they get their canvas out. We might not have the wind on our approach, but we'll surely have it when we escape. This ship is fast; I doubt even the *Valiant* could catch her."

"Perhaps one day, when all this conflict is over, we'll have a race. It would be interesting to find out if you're right."

"I am, trust me. I spent a lifetime at sea and know a fast ship when I see it. *Sprite* is one of the fastest ships afloat. That's why she was such a successful pirate."

"I might remind you we still captured her."

The captain grinned. "Point well made. We'll exercise caution."

The town of Noordmacht sat high atop the cliffs, dominated by a large tower overlooking the sea. Even from this range, Danica could see people atop it, the object of their attention the *Sprite*.

Three sets of steps went from the top of the cliff down to the docks. The longest of these ran back and forth across the rock face, enabling a slower climb, presumably for those bearing goods. The other two, on either side, were narrower and more direct, useful for individuals who wanted to get down to the water as quickly as possible.

The Halvarian ships were lined up facing east, the better to enable them to put out to sea, considering the prevailing wind. The *Sprite* came close to the shore, then turned to port, resulting in a course that would take them down the line of warships.

The first of these had *Courageous* embossed in gold letters, indicating it was no ordinary vessel and certainly not a provincial.

Danica stood there, watching as they passed, the *Sprite* slowing its speed slightly. Several men watched them, but no one thought to challenge the small ship.

"Interesting," muttered Danica. "None of these appear to be provincials."

"Is that unusual?" asked the captain.

"It's been our experience that the empire's ships sail in threes, usually one Imperial accompanied by two provincials, but they appear to have done something different here."

"Are you familiar with *Courageous*?"

"No," she replied. "You?"

He shook his head. "Then again, I'm an expert at sailing ships, not identifying them. I'll leave that to you tacticians." He lowered his voice. "Here's the next one."

They sailed up alongside another warship, this one similarly marked. "The *Zealous*," said Danica. "Hardly a surprising name." She looked farther down the line to the three-master, eager to see what name it claimed, but a voice interrupted her.

"Ahoy there," called out a richly dressed man from the deck of the *Zealous*. "From where do you hail?"

"Vilnitz," replied Blasco, waving up at the fellow. "You have an impressive ship."

The man waved back, then the arrival of one of his men diverted his attention. They exchanged a few quiet words before they both disappeared.

"Trouble?" asked Danica.

"Let's hope not."

They finally came up alongside the largest ship. Danica thought the enemy flagship at Temple Bay gaudy, but this ship pushed the bounds of good taste to extremes.

"*Victorious*," said Blasco. "They certainly intend to inspire awe, don't they?"

"The gold leaf on that ship could fund our fleet for months."

"Months? I'd say more like years. How in the name of the Saints can they afford such displays?"

"They have the resources of an entire empire," replied Danica. "It also projects power. Who would dare stand against it?"

"I can think of a few," said the captain, breaking into a grin. He suddenly straightened. "Here comes trouble."

The *Sprite's* deck was considerably lower than the *Victorious*, giving the Halvarians an excellent view of the smaller vessel's deck. A few men gathered on the larger ship, looking down upon their unexpected visitor.

"You there," called out a thin individual. "By whose permission do you sail these waters?"

"I am a simple wine merchant," shouted back Blasco. "Come from Vilnitz bearing some of the finest vintages."

"Pull up in front of us and tie off. You're required to submit to a search."

"For what, may I ask?"

"We must ensure you're not carrying contraband."

"A likely story," Blasco muttered under his breath, then returned to speaking loudly. "I would be delighted." He ordered men about, ostensibly to ready them to tie the ship up once they docked, but everyone knew this was not their ultimate objective. "Stand by," he said. "This is going to be a hard turn."

They eased past the *Victorious* and then turned, not towards the dock as their challenger expected, but away from it. Moments later, they unfurled the sail to its fullest extent, and the wind, perhaps sensing their dire straits, picked up, filling the canvas. The *Sprite* leaped forward, almost toppling Danica.

Shouts came from behind them, and then a roar. Danica instinctively ducked as a streak of flame flew overhead. Thankfully, it was cast in haste and missed them, sizzling as it hit the water.

"Oh great," she said. "They have a Fire Mage!"

The enemy mage ran towards the bow, but by the time he climbed onto the forecastle, the *Sprite* was even farther away. Another streak of flame shot across the water but fell short, kicking up nought but steam.

Blasco looked ahead, but Danica, little more than a passenger, kept her attention on the *Victorious*, where sailors scrambled along the decks, looking like an angry anthill. Shouted orders carried across the water, and then the men swarmed up the mast to set the sails. The enemy flagship crawled forward, but there was no danger of overtaking the *Sprite*.

"Well done, Captain," she said, finally taking a breath. "Your crew has earned its pay today."

He took time to glance at the Halvarian vessels. "Nothing like taunting the enemy with our backsides, is there?" He suddenly realized to whom he was talking and blushed. "Sorry, Admiral. I didn't mean to imply anything."

She laughed. "It's quite all right, Captain. You earned the right to speak your mind."

By nightfall, they'd rejoined the rest of the squadron, and Danica gathered her captains aboard the *Fearless* to discuss their next steps.

"Three ships," she said, "and no signs of any merchants to carry warriors. If the empire intends on a naval expedition, it won't come from Noordmacht."

"Perhaps they have yet to mass their ships?" offered Zivka, captain of the *Illustrious*.

"The port is small," countered Blasco, "and incapable of handling over ten ships of any consequence."

"Then we must sail farther west," said Danica, "to Thansalay."

"That's a major port," said Vivian, "and likely well-guarded. You can't just sail in there like you did today."

"Then we need to try something different."

"What do you have in mind?"

"The farther west we go, the lower the likelihood of encountering ships from outside the empire."

"I'm not sure what you're proposing."

"Nor I," added Anya. "And that squadron back there could cut off any chance of retreat."

"They'd have to know who we were," said Blasco. "The name *Sprite* means nothing in these waters. They likely took us for smugglers."

"Be that as it may," replied Anya, "we cannot dismiss the danger. We know the Halvarians use magic. Your account of today's little adventure confirms that."

"We knew that long ago," said Danica.

"We did, but we didn't know how widespread it was. We should also not be so quick to dismiss the ramifications."

"Which are?"

"What if they can use their magic to communicate over long distances?"

"You're worried if they spot us in Thansalay, they'll send word to Noordmacht?"

"It makes sense, doesn't it?"

Sister Grace held up her hand. "May I speak?"

"Of course," replied Danica.

"Do we know how far away Thansalay is?"

"Not precisely, but likely fifty or sixty miles. Why?"

"Isn't it possible they could contact Noordmacht using more traditional methods? Riders, perhaps?"

"They'd have a hard time outpacing a ship," said Blasco.

"Still," replied Danica. "It's worth consideration. We should try to keep our existence here as quiet as possible."

"But," said Anya, "we can't get close enough to count ships without revealing our presence."

Danica smiled. "Then we shall trust in our faith."

"But the Saints only advise, not control."

"I'm referring to faith in our crew."

32

SKIRMISH

SUMMER 1103 SR

Charlaine stared across the river. "That's a lot of boats," she said, "and they're getting ready to cross."

"Is there nothing we can do?" asked Marlena.

"Not without siege engines. Even if we had crossbows, we'd find it difficult hitting anything at this range."

"But once they start crossing, they'll be vulnerable, won't they?"

"The baron only has one company of archers, which won't make much difference against that many vessels. Besides, the empire will likely place their own archers in the bow of each boat to dissuade us from such a course of action."

"So, we just watch them cross?"

"We are Temple Knights," said Charlaine. "Our strength is in our ability to manoeuvre in formation. How do you propose we do that along a shoreline?"

"Wait until they land, then hit them on the riverbank?"

"The terrain here is too unfavourable. We'll skirmish with them, but I'm afraid it'll be little more than a delaying action. Although our main objective will be to withdraw, I'd like to inflict some losses on them first to slow them down." She turned to Marlena, expecting more discussion, but her aide stared back at the town. "Something wrong?"

"Is that Orlina Day?"

Charlaine noted the old woman's approach. "It is." She raised her voice. "Orlina, I'm surprised to see you here. Is everything all right?"

"Of course! I come bearing good news for a change."

"Which is?"

She smiled but said nothing until she was closer. "My apologies, but my throat is hoarse after so much talking."

"I don't understand."

"I mentioned some time ago I would secure the woods to the south of your intended battlefield. I'm pleased to announce I finalized the arrangements."

"That's excellent news. Might I enquire as to the details?"

"Most certainly," said Orlina. "It occurred to me that—"

She didn't have time to finish her sentence, for at that precise moment, Marlena grabbed Charlaine's arm. "It's started," was all she said, but her meaning was clear.

Hundreds of men had appeared across the river, all armed for battle. They made their way to the bank, their voices echoing off the trees as they dragged the boats into the water and climbed in.

Charlaine looked upriver, where her mounted knights stood ready to engage, but they could do little until the enemy drew closer.

"It's so frustrating," said Marlena. "All we can do is watch as they cross unopposed."

Orlina smiled. "It will not be as easy as you might think."

Charlaine noticed the sly look on the old woman's face. "Meaning?"

"Right now, lots of them are splashing around in the water. It's only a matter of time before something takes notice."

"Something? You mean the serpent? That's miles away, surely?"

"The creature lives in these waters. As such, it is aware of what transpires."

"Can you call it?"

"No," said Orlina. "Were it a woodland creature, it would be a different matter, but my powers end where the water is concerned. I have no doubt, however, that all that noise will attract its attention."

"That's all well and good," said Marlena, "but how long would it take to get here?"

"That largely depends on where it's been of late."

"It was closer to the mouth of the Stillwater when we saw it," said Charlaine. "And that's miles away."

"True, but they've been preparing their boats for days now, and that's likely garnered its attention."

"I'm not an expert on serpents, but will it be enough to halt their advance?"

"Halt it? Likely not, though I suppose it depends more on the courage of those men rather than their numbers. I would find it difficult to enter a river with a creature such as that lurking about, wouldn't you?"

The first few boats rowed out into the middle of the water, where the current caught them, pushing them slightly downstream, but the rowers soon got the better of it and adjusted their course.

"I admire their courage," said Marlena. "They're heading right for us."

Charlaine stared across the river as they dragged more boats from hiding. The Halvarians had planned this attack well, and the execution was proceeding at a fast pace.

"There," said Orlina, pointing. "Do you see it?"

A ripple appeared downstream. At first, Charlaine took it for a shallow spot, but then it moved left and right as it travelled up the river.

"It's the serpent," she said at last.

"We're saved," added Marlena.

With the enemy focused on their target, it wasn't until their first boat overturned that they took notice. Shouts of triumph soon turned to panic as crossbow bolts flew across the water, trying to keep the unseen menace at bay.

The panicked response led to the first casualties when the enemy loosed bolts with such abandon that their own men fell victim.

A massive maw rose out of the water, plucking a man from one of the boats. He let out a scream before being dragged beneath the surface, his anguished cries cut short by the water.

"By the Saints," said Marlena. "I can't watch this." She turned away, sickened by the sight.

Charlaine, however, watched in fascination. The attack stalled as many of the boat crews frantically tried to return to the western bank, but the boats were so tightly packed together, they got in each other's way.

The serpent's coil lifted a boat, with all but one of the men jumping out of the tiny craft. The creature ignored the remaining occupant and, one by one pulled those in the water beneath the surface.

It looked as though they might abandon the entire attack until a trio of women appeared, calm despite the terror surrounding them. They stood on the bank, surveying all that had occurred. Charlaine wondered if they might be military commanders or agents of the emperor, but as they began moving their hands around in what could only be magical gestures, she realized their true nature.

Streaks of flame arched out, splashing off the water's surface, causing steam to rise. The serpent raised its head to see what had caused this strange effect, and they cast again, sending more flames to strike the beast's neck. A terrible wailing echoed across the water, and then it disappeared beneath the surface, the smell of burned flesh drifting to where Charlaine stood.

Any hope the creature would repeat its offensive was put to rest when the telltale wake reappeared, heading north. In the aftermath of the attack, the Halvarians rushed to the safety of their own side of the river.

"It worked!" said Marlena. "We've beaten them without even unsheathing our swords."

"This is only a lull," replied Charlaine. "A chance to catch their breath before they resume the offensive."

"I should go," said Orlina. "You will need someone at the field of battle to explain things. Is your army on its way?"

"I certainly hope so," replied Charlaine. "I'm a little surprised they haven't already arrived."

"I wish you luck here, Commander. The Gods know you'll need it." The old woman turned, making her way back towards town with surprising speed for someone her age.

"What now?" asked Marlena. "Do we withdraw up the road?"

"Not yet. I want to see what their next move is."

"Surely they'll just attempt another crossing?"

"Would you climb back into a boat after seeing that serpent?"

"But they drove it off, didn't they?"

"They most assuredly did," replied Charlaine, "but you can't discount their fear of its return or that there might be a second one lurking somewhere nearby."

"So that's it? They just give up?"

"I doubt they'd make it that easy for us."

"Then how do they cross?"

"Perhaps they have Earth Mages at their disposal. If Orlina Day can pull stones forth from the ground, wouldn't it be possible for them to construct a crude bridge using the very same technique?"

"You're right," said Marlena. "We must be on the lookout for an Earth Mage."

A quiet descended over the river. They'd recovered a few bodies, but other than that, there was very little activity. Charlaine wondered if the serpent's attack had indeed broken the back of the Halvarian's will. However, the appearance on the far bank of warriors formed up in columns, marching straight for the water's edge, dispelled her hopes. She struggled to understand what they were doing, and then she saw a few men and women casting spells down by the riverbank.

"Something's up," said Marlena.

"Yes," agreed Charlaine, "but what? Surely, they don't think they can evaporate liquid using Fire Magic?"

Marlena stared, open-mouthed, as the water's surface rippled and the river level dipped down.

"What's happening?" she finally asked.

Charlaine immediately grasped the consequences of the magic. "They're making their own ford."

Sure enough, the water receded until only a trickle was visible, then the columns entered the river, their boots only ankle-deep.

"To horse," called out Charlaine. "We may not get another chance."

They climbed into their saddles and rejoined the rest of the companies.

"The enemy will soon be on our shore," said Charlaine. "Our task this day is not to defeat them but to hit them, then withdraw. If we cause them to fear our blades, they will hesitate when next we meet."

"We're ready," said Captain Bernelle.

"Then let it begin." Charlaine drew her sword, holding it on high. "For Saint Agnes!" she shouted, the call echoed by all the Temple Knights. The first company advanced, keeping their formation despite the uneven ground. They slowed as they neared the riverbank, allowing their horses to navigate what was now a significant drop. After some twenty paces, they dressed their ranks, readying for contact.

The Halvarians sent their footmen first, three companies of provincials by the look of them. They started off at a fast pace, but as they hit what used to be the bottom of the river, their boots sank into the thick silt, slowing them and making it difficult to maintain their formation.

Charlaine released her knights, and they plunged ahead, their own lines held in check by the legendary discipline only Temple Knights were capable of. The ground thundered, water splashing everywhere as the first line of sister knights struck the Halvarian companies.

The initial impact drove deep into the enemy before the attack quickly lost all order, degenerating into a series of deadly skirmishes. Charlaine swung, staving in a helmet and sending her opponent to the ground. Stormcloud pushed forward, knocking aside two men who were trampled beneath the hooves of other knights.

Charlaine's entire experience came down to a series of thrusts and counterthrusts as she lost sight of the rest of the battle. Blood flew, splashing across her visor, and yet more men stood ahead of her, reaching out with swords and axes, trying to bring her down.

Something careened off her pauldron, and a searing heat encompassed her shoulder. Their Fire Mages had joined the fray.

"Back!" she screamed. "Return and regroup!"

Others took up her call as she turned Stormcloud around, heading for the eastern bank. She glanced over her shoulder to see the river floor awash with blood, bodies scattered everywhere. She saw no horses or knights amongst the fallen and gave thanks they'd come through unscathed.

She spotted Temple Captain Miranda's company waiting for the first attack to clear out of the way. She guided Stormcloud to one side before turning to watch the next stage unfold.

The second company advanced, maintaining its line. The damage the first attack had inflicted was still fresh in the enemy's minds, so much so that they turned and fled, rushing for the safety of the western bank, some even throwing down their weapons in panic.

Miranda urged her command forward, and the familiar battle cry rang out. "For Saint Agnes!"

They rode through the survivors as if they were no more than ghosts. Then, as Miranda turned in her saddle, ready to order the withdrawal, flames engulfed her.

Crossbowmen moved up on the far bank, loosing volleys into the fray, most only rattling off the knights' plate armour, but the horses suffered greatly. Charlaine spotted a knight pulling a fellow sister up behind her, but as they turned to ride away, a bolt slammed into the new passenger, and she fell to the riverbed.

Charlaine looked to the last of her companies, where Florence readied her attack, preparing to rush into the fray. Disaster threatened to unfold before her. Charlaine galloped over, blocking the way.

"Hold!" she ordered. "There will be no more charges this day."

What remained of Miranda's company climbed up the eastern bank. Charlaine turned, looking for Marlena, only to see her directing the survivors to take up positions behind those of Florence.

The Halvarians ignored their own dead, sending a new wave of men marching across the ford as if it were the most mundane of tasks. However, their Imperial companies came this time instead of provincials, their armour glinting in the sun.

Charlaine calculated the speed of their march, then turned to face her dwindling command. "Marlena, you take command of Miranda's company. Withdraw them towards the keep and send word to the baron of what has transpired. Bernelle, take your company into the village in small groups and ambush the enemy as they advance. They are to hit quickly, then withdraw. And no heroics. Understood? Florence, I want you one hundred yards that way." Charlaine pointed eastward. "You are to allow the Halvarians to climb this riverbank before engaging them. One charge, and one charge only. Once you've done that, you withdraw to the keep in good order."

The Temple Knights moved quickly, all save for Marlena. Charlaine rode over, seeing the look of panic on her aide's face.

"I can't do this," said Marlena. "I'm not trained for this."

"Nonsense. You're more than ready, and the knights know what to do."

"There's got to be someone else more qualified."

Charlaine's gaze swept over the reduced command. "Most of these knights were untested before today. You've seen battle, Marlena. You've faced the Halvarians on land and at sea. I have every confidence in you. Your order needs you… I need you."

"Yes, Commander. Of course. Sorry."

"Don't apologize. Now, get your knights moving while you still have time."

She watched Marlena give her orders tentatively at first but then with growing confidence. The reformed company rode off as a disciplined column once more.

Charlaine moved aside as Florence directed her knights to form into two lines, facing the river, ready to charge on the captain's command. Their visors were down, hiding the faces of the Temple Knights, but Charlaine could well imagine their fear. Most of them possessed little experience, especially against an enemy who came in such overwhelming numbers.

Riding into battle was one thing, but the coming skirmish required much greater discipline, that of withdrawing afterwards. Many an order of knighthood had been ruined by staying too long, and she fretted the same fate might befall this group.

Halvarian arrows rained down from above, a prelude to the melee about to commence. Moments later, the leading companies began climbing the bank, their formations breaking apart as they navigated the uneven ground.

Florence waited, biding her time as the enemy reformed. She counted to ten before raising her sword, signalling the advance. The warhorses spurred forward, keeping a tight line, their pace increasing until they were in a full gallop.

The Halvarians, seeing the approaching horses, tried to organize a defence, but it was too late by the time their captains recognized the danger.

The Temple Knights of Saint Agnes smashed into the lead company, their mighty chargers trampling men beneath their hooves even as the sister knights reached out with swords and axes.

The centre company completely disintegrated, sending a flood of warriors west towards the safety of the far bank. These panicked souls made matters worse for the Halvarians, halting the advance of those companies next in line.

Florence drove through the centre company, but now those on either flank threatened to cut off any chance of the knights retreating. Thankfully, a horn blast sounded the retreat, and the Temple Knights wheeled about, trotting back eastward as though on parade. The moment of danger passed as they withdrew, reforming into a line some hundred yards to the east.

More Imperial companies surged over the eastern bank, signalling that such an attack wouldn't work again. The time for withdrawal was at hand, so Charlaine gave the order. Florence turned her knights to the right, filing into the town of Braunfel to start the next stage of the fight.

Charlaine watched the enemy as they secured their hold of this side of the river by spreading archers on either side of their footmen. More troubling, however, were the horsemen who now made their way across, not the dreaded Emperor's Own, but lightly armoured men on relatively small horses, the perfect instrument for scouting and harassing a retreating foe.

There was little she could do about it, so she turned Stormcloud and rode off to catch up with the rest of her command.

33

THE FLEET

SUMMER 1103 SR

The port of Thansalay lay safely hidden within two jetties reaching out into the Great Northern Sea like enormous arms. A small tower stood on the tip of each from which archers could rain down arrows on unwanted visitors. A wall ran along the jetties, making it difficult for those out at sea to see inside the bay.

From Danica's point of view, there were plenty of masts, but with no sight of the hulls, it was difficult to take stock of what ships might be present.

"That's inconvenient," said Anya. "You'd think the empire's fleet would want to boast of its prowess, not hide behind walls."

"It's unfortunate, to be sure," replied Danica, "but I should've foreseen this possibility."

"Could we not simply sail into the harbour? We're not flying our own flag, and *Fearless* is clearly of Halvarian design. I should think entering would be relatively easy."

"And if they ask us to identify ourselves? You forget, we stripped the old *Devastator* of all its gold leaf and painted the upper hull to match our tabards. They might mistake us for an empire vessel at this range, but I'm afraid any closer and our true allegiance would become quite obvious."

"Then what do we do?"

"What indeed?" said Danica. "Unlike our last port of call, Thansalay lies on a flat coastline."

"So, we land down the coast and go overland?"

"That's certainly one possibility."

"Are you suggesting there's an alternative?" asked Anya.

"We could send in small boats under cover of darkness."

"You think they could get past those towers unnoticed?"

"I'm not suggesting we row them right into the harbour, merely close to the sea walls."

"I'm afraid you'll have to explain that to me."

"We sail to the outer walls and use grapnels to get a couple of our people to the top. Once there, they do a quick count, then return."

"What about guards? Surely you don't think they'd leave the wall empty?"

"We're deep in Halvarian waters. Who would dare sail this far into the empire?"

"And if there are warriors on that wall?" pressed Anya.

"Our knights will have a use for their crossbows."

"It's risky."

"I never said it wasn't, but we have to see what's in that harbour. If the fleet truly is massing, we need to know."

"Could there be more harbours to the west?"

"Anything's possible," said Danica. "We know very little about these waters other than what Laldor told us. He seemed to think Thansalay the most logical port to assemble their fleet, and I see no reason to doubt him."

Anya looked towards the distant walls. "That's a long way to row."

"We could shorten that by having the *Sprite* tow the boats a little closer."

"Just how many boats do you intend to send?"

"Two, each rowed by crewmen and carrying half a dozen knights, ensuring we have sufficient numbers to deal with anything that might threaten us atop the wall."

"And who will command the expedition?"

"I will," said Danica. She held up her hand to cut off any argument. "I know you don't like it, but you must admit I'm best suited to evaluate their strength."

"You're also the one we can least afford to lose."

"Sister Grace will be there to keep me safe."

"This is no laughing matter, Admiral."

"Of that, I'm well aware, but if we are to stand any hope of stopping the empire, we need to know what ships are there."

"And once you've ascertained their numbers?"

"That largely depends on how many we see," replied Danica. "At the very least, we'll send the *Sprite* to take word to the rest of our fleet."

"And will we engage the enemy?"

"If the numbers are in our favour, yes, but I doubt we'd be so lucky. We know they typically employ their ships in squadrons of threes. I'm reasonably confident they'd have more than one of those groups escorting any military expedition they might be considering. That, alone, suggests they badly outnumber us."

"That didn't stop us at Temple Bay."

"True," said Danica, "but our priority here is to prevent an army from landing, not defeating a fleet."

"But they're one and the same, aren't they?"

"In this case, no. Chances are they'll employ merchant ships to transport their warriors instead of placing them aboard their warships. Ideally, we'd strike when they're at their most vulnerable."

"Which is?"

"When their loaded boats are rowing into shore."

"I can't see their fleet letting us sail amongst them."

"Nor can I," said Danica, "but that is for future consideration. Of more immediate concern is determining their numbers."

"We don't even know if they're contemplating a naval expedition. What if we're wrong?"

"Then we've wasted our time. Better that than being surprised by a large fleet, don't you think?"

"I suppose I didn't look at it quite that way." Anya glanced skyward. "We've still some time before the sun sets."

"Have the sisters rest. It's likely to be a long night."

The darkness lent an air of danger to the proceedings as they lowered the boats over the side. *Fearless* and *Illustrious*, each provided six knights while *Sprite* stood nearby, ready to take the small vessels under tow to save everyone's strength until they were closer.

"I don't like this," said Anya. "It's a cloudy night, which makes the task all the more difficult."

"There is little choice," replied Danica. "If we don't act soon, they may set sail before we're ready."

"Perhaps you could call on one of those sea unicorns you saw and ask him for help?"

"It wasn't a unicorn," replied the admiral, "and even if it were friendly, we'd have no way of communicating with it."

Danica climbed over the railing, making her way down the side of the *Fearless* to where the boat waited. She took a seat at the bow, then nodded to the sailor at the tiller. Those manning the oars pushed off and began manoeuvring over to the *Sprite*.

A lantern marked the location of the boat from *Illustrious*, aft of the

Sprite, and tying a rope to their bow. Danica dipped her fingers into the water, judging the temperature. The Great Northern Sea was not a hospitable place, and even in summer, the waters were cold. She glanced at the knights who wore their plate armour. For them, drowning was far more likely than freezing to death if they happened to fall overboard.

Her thoughts turned dark as she imagined bodies floating in the grey depths of the sea. She tried to shake it off, but something about the chilly air and the dark night filled her with a sense of foreboding.

A call from above broke through her fears, and then the *Sprite* tossed a line down. She dutifully tied off the rope and resumed her seat. It felt like an eternity before it went taut and yanked the boat through the water.

"Admiral?" said Sister Grace. "Perhaps you'd honour us with a prayer before we get too close?"

"Yes," said Danica, glad for the distraction. "Let me see, now." She searched her mind, trying to come up with something inspiring. "Saint Agnes," she finally began, "give us strength that we might carry out your will and the wisdom to succeed in the face of adversity. Guide our swords this night so we can overcome our enemies and triumph over those who would do harm to innocents." She paused, considering her words. To her mind, they sounded inadequate, but the looks on the faces of her knights said otherwise. "Saints be with us."

"Saints be with us all," came the reply.

The trip inshore felt like it was taking half the night before a voice finally called out. Danica untied the rope and watched it disappear into the darkness. The crew took up the oars, rowing while the tillerman steered them towards the distant harbour, its location marked by the light of its two towers. The *Sprite* had covered half the distance, but any closer, and it risked discovery. Now it was up to the oarsmen from *Fearless* and *Illustrious* to close the range.

Her gaze drifted to the distant sea wall. From their current position, it was little more than a dark smear, the only light the odd patrol walking along the top, their lanterns illuminating the area. As she watched, the lights blinked. She sat up, ignoring the chill in the air.

"Something wrong?" asked Grace.

"Still your oars," she called out, her voice urgent.

She stared at the distant walls of the harbour. Again, the light blinked, and then she realized the ramifications.

"Get that lantern lit and signal the *Sprite*! You men, turn this boat around and row with all your strength."

"What is it?" asked Sister Grace.

"The Halvarians have put to sea."

"Are you certain?"

She pointed. "Watch those lights upon the wall. As ships pass in front of them, their masts block the light for but a moment."

"It appears we wasted our time."

"Not so," said Danica. "If we hadn't come this close, we would've never spotted them."

Sister Margo lit the lantern, waving it towards the last known position of the *Sprite*.

A voice called out from the darkness, "Admiral, what's happening?"

"The enemy fleet is coming out of the harbour," she shouted. "Can you still see the *Sprite*?"

"Aye."

"Call them back. We must return to our ships with all haste."

Voices called out in the darkness, then the bulk of the *Sprite* loomed over them. Danica wasted no time, calling for the rope as their escort sailed past. She finished tying it to the bow, and then the line grew taut. The boat slewed around, picking up speed, following in the wake of the *Sprite*.

Danica climbed back aboard the *Fearless*, stumbling in the darkness as she set foot upon the deck.

"Anya," she called out. "Prepare to get underway. The enemy is on the move."

"Aye, Admiral."

"Signal the rest of the fleet. We'll set sail and head inshore once both boats are back aboard."

"Won't that be dangerous?"

"It will, but if we are to have any hope of spotting them, it's our only choice."

"Have we any idea how many ships?"

"I'm afraid not. I wouldn't even have noticed had it not been for them blocking our view of the lights."

"Could it be a merchant ship you saw?"

"Not unless there were several of them." Danica watched as the rest of the knights came aboard, then the crew hauled up the boat, storing it on the deck.

"*Illustrious* signals all ready, Admiral."

"Have them fall behind us. *Valiant* to the north but close enough we can still spot their lanterns, *Sprite* as well. I don't want the enemy to identify them."

"You mean to sail right into their fleet?"

"In the dark, *Fearless* and *Illustrious* both look like Halvarian vessels."

"And once dawn comes?"

Danica grinned. "We'll take a quick tally of their numbers before heading farther out to sea." She moved to the bow, climbing up into the forecastle and straining to look south. Only the lights of Thansalay were visible, and even then, they were distant and faint. Had she waited too long? Was the enemy already farther up the coast? Doubt nagged at her, but then she heard an explosion of water, the telltale sound of a whale. Such creatures were said to be good luck, and the thought pleased her. Perhaps things hadn't gone so badly after all?

The *Fearless* plowed through the water, making good speed, but the lookouts could see little with the clouds blocking the moon. The good news was the Halvarian fleet was under the same hindrance, which meant they needed to proceed cautiously or risk running aground. Danica knew her ships must eventually slow but hoped there might be some sight of the enemy before she had to make that decision.

Anya came up to stand beside her. "This darkness could mean the ruin of us all. Why in the name of the Saints would they sail under such conditions?"

"I can think of two reasons. Either they spotted us and wanted to avoid us, or they have a timetable they can't change, which I suspect is more likely. I think they intend to coincide this expedition's arrival with the march of their army."

The captain was about to respond, but something to the south drew her attention. "Did you see that?"

Danica followed her gaze.

"The briefest of lights," added Anya.

"They must be using hooded lanterns to avoid collisions. We should emulate them. Have we any below?"

"We do."

"Then have them fetched and readied."

"Do you want them unhooded?"

"Not yet," replied Danica. "We haven't determined how they're employed. If we use them incorrectly, it might give away our ruse."

As the *Fearless* sailed on, more lights appeared, this time coloured red.

"How in the name of the Saints are they doing that?" asked Anya.

"I imagine they're using tinted glass."

"But why red?"

"It's harder to see at long distances." A thought crossed Danica's mind. "They must know we're in the area. Why else take such precautions?" Behind her, some of her knights had come up on deck, using a taper to light their lanterns. "Bring one of those here," she called out. "I have an idea."

Sister Grace made her way up to the forecastle to the strange sight of Danica using her dagger to cut her own tabard. "What are you doing, Admiral?"

"We need a red light, but we have no coloured glass. I'm betting the scarlet of our order will suffice." She tore off a large square. "Here. Put this over it. Careful though, we don't want to set it alight." She waited, looking on in anticipation as Grace raised the lantern.

"It worked," said the knight.

"It did, but that's only the first step."

"Ship to port," hissed Anya.

Danica peered into the darkness. A large shadow loomed off to the left as they passed a ship. It suddenly occurred to her they might be moving too fast.

"Reduce sail," she whispered. "And get a crewman up here."

"To what end?"

"If we're hailed, replying in a woman's voice would give us away."

As if summoned by her remarks, a man called out from the darkness, "Show your light!"

Grace swivelled the lantern so that her body wasn't blocking it.

"Are you the *Courageous*?" asked the voice.

They remained silent until a crewman clambered up to their position.

"I say, again," came the voice, "are you *Courageous*?"

"Aye," replied the crewman, taking his cue from the admiral.

"Then move to starboard, you fool, else you'll risk tangling the yardarms."

"Give the order," whispered Anya.

The fellow fled aft to inform the person manning the rudder.

"Ship to starboard," called out another crewman.

Danica looked around them. The *Fearless* had manoeuvred directly into the enemy fleet.

"What do we do now?" asked Anya.

"Maintain our course and position. As far as they're concerned, we're a part of one big, happy fleet."

"And if they discover our true identity?"

"Then there is no option but to fight. Have the knights go below and don their armour, then tell them to rest."

"Rest? In armour?"

"It can't be helped. If any of those ships realize what we're up to, they'll swarm us. Better to be prepared to fight at any moment."

The night wore on. The *Fearless* partially furled her sail, allowing it to more or less match the speed of the rest of the ships, but the man at the rudder made constant adjustments to avoid wandering too far to either side.

Danica prowled the deck, alternating sides, trying to make out as much as possible in the dark. The ship portside was similar in size to their own, but in the brief moment they'd gotten close to starboard, she spotted no forecastle aboard the vessel on that side, indicating it was more like *Illustrious*. The thought made her go to the stern for fear that her command sailed too close, but they were following her lead and maintaining enough distance to keep them in sight.

Anya adjusted the sail halfway through the night, for the wind picked up. *Fearless* was a fast ship, much faster than her Halvarian counterparts, and finding the right speed was a case of constant trial and error.

An early morning fog rolled in, making visibility even worse. Danica finally ordered the sails furled, and the ship slowed to a halt. She was disappointed to give up the chase, but she put the safety of her crew first. They dropped anchor, but then, echoing off in the distance, came the sound of other ships doing the same.

"Saints preserve us," said Anya. "We're surrounded."

"Not quite," replied Danica. "*Illustrious* is behind us, or at least was before this fog came up."

"And the rest of our ships?"

"Hopefully farther out to sea."

"I don't like this. We're trapped like rats."

"Heavily armoured rats," corrected Danica. "Steel your resolve, Anya. We're going to be here awhile." She looked around the ship, but the fog was so thick now she couldn't even see the top of her mast.

Danica fought off exhaustion. She'd been awake for many hours, and while the danger of the moment initially kept her alert and ready for action, that feeling had faded. Grace appeared at her side, a steaming tankard in hand.

Danica took the drink, sipping it. "Soup?"

"You have to eat something, Admiral."

"Yes, I suppose I do. Thank you."

Her aide moved to the side railing. "Is it my imagination, or is this fog getting lighter?"

"Dawn must be coming. Can you see anything of interest?"

"I think so, a shadow off to the south." She paused a moment. "No. Make that two."

A slight wind came up, clearing away some of the fog. Two ships anchored off their starboard side, one of them a three-master. "That's *Glorious*," said Grace. "Or at least a ship of the same design."

Danica moved aft, her aide following. They climbed up into the sterncastle and looked behind them. "Any sign of *Illustrious*?"

"Not that I can see, Admiral. No, wait, there's something off to one side."

They both stared, willing the fog to thin. There was definitely a ship there, but whose was it?

"All knights up on deck," said Danica. "And get word to the captain. I want the crew ready to unfurl the sail at a moment's notice."

"Aye, Admiral." Grace raced off to pass on the word.

Danica continued to stare. The fog lessened as the sun rose, burning it off. With visibility improving, she could now see the ship to the rear, but the gold leaf decorating its bow was not welcome news.

"It appears," she said, more to herself than anyone else, "we are surrounded."

34

WITHDRAWAL

SUMMER 1103 SR

The Halvarians flooded through the streets of Braunfel. The townsfolk, most having abandoned the place, took care to lock doors where they could, but it did nothing to stop the plundering. Several people, determined to protect what little they owned, chose to remain, thinking their presence alone might dissuade the enemy from taking their property. The Halvarians dragged them out into the streets, killing them after a prolonged and cruel beating.

The blood of the empire's warriors was up. They'd taken casualties crossing the river and now vented their anger on whatever was at hand. It didn't take long for fires to start, and the flames spread quickly, sending thick smoke curling into the air.

Charlaine watched the enemy march past the alleyway where she and a dozen Temple Knights waited, each itching to strike back.

"Forward," she called, urging Stormcloud into the street. They'd been at it all morning, using alleys and back roads to hit the Halvarians from the flanks. She'd worried the tactics would prove troublesome, that the enemy would learn and adapt to them, but whoever commanded the provincial Halvarians cared little for such thoughts.

The strike was swift and sent the enemy rushing for cover. The Temple Knights retired, once more seeking the alleys and disappearing from their foes' sight.

"That's five more," said Enna. "Do they learn nothing?"

"They break their legions into cohorts," explained Charlaine, "with a captain-general commanding each. I suspect the leader of this group is far to the rear, likely resting while his men do the dirty work."

"Does he care nothing for their lives?"

"No, and why would he? These are provincial troops. As such, they see them as expendable."

"So, he simply throws them away?"

"Can we say the nobles of the Petty Kingdoms are any different?"

"That's ghastly," said Enna. "How can you condone such a thing?"

"Do not confuse understanding with absolution. Saint Agnes teaches us every life has meaning, but we are not in a position to dictate the morality of war to the nobility."

"This sickens me. All we're doing is killing five men at a time. Surely there is more we can do?"

"Do not discount our actions," said Charlaine. "What we're doing here might do little damage to their numbers, but it will have a pronounced effect on their morale."

They turned onto a back street, heading towards the keep.

"But surely," said Enna, "it would be better to attack in larger numbers?"

"You might think so, but this is more effective. Our plan here is to slow them down. The more we carry out raids like that, the more cautious they'll become. With luck, they'll slow to a crawl, convinced we'll appear from nowhere to ravage their ranks."

"Thank the Saints I'm only a knight," said Enna. "I have no head for such strategies."

Braunfel Keep sat upon a hill overlooking the town, and from that vantage point, it was easy to see the enemy's progress. Charlaine led her small group up the hill, onto the field that lay in front of the keep, where the rest of her Temple Knights waited. They'd been harassing the enemy all morning, but now the horses were tired. Soon, they would begin the long trek eastward to the battlefield.

She rode over to Marlena. "Any losses to report?"

"Two wounded," her aide replied, "though they're still capable of riding." She paused, noticing the smoke rising from the town. "Will we return to raiding?"

"No," replied Charlaine. "You're to take your company up the Lidenbach road to the battlefield. Hopefully, the Royal Army has arrived."

"And if they haven't?"

"You must make what preparations you can. In the meantime, we'll continue with our delaying tactics here."

"How much time can you buy us?"

"Difficult to say," said Charlaine. "It depends on the legion's commander.

At the moment, the provincials are running rampant, and though it means the town suffers, it works to our advantage." She noted the baron's approach. "You'd best be on your way, Captain. It seems I have other things to attend to."

Marlena gave the order, and her company turned to the left and was soon trotting up the Lidenbach road in twos.

"Good morning, Commander," said Lord Handrik. "I see you've been busy."

"I have indeed, my lord." Her gaze flicked to the burning buildings. "I only wish I bore better news."

The baron shrugged. "Burning the town was inevitable. At least some of the townsfolk made it to safety, although I suspect they're clogging the road by now, which won't make your withdrawal any easier."

"We shall manage. What of you? Are you prepared for a siege?"

"I am, though I doubt it will come to that for some time. I've yet to see any evidence of siege equipment within the enemy's army."

"All the better for us," said Charlaine. "It means they'll have to dig in to prevent you from counterattacking. The more men you keep busy here, the better."

"Don't worry about me. There are enough stores to last months. I do, however, have a request."

"Speak freely, my lord. Now is not the time to talk in circles."

"I ask that you take my wife with you."

"Surely she'd be safer in the keep?"

"Perhaps," said the baron, "but if you're unable to defeat the empire on the battlefield, it'll only be a matter of time before they turn on my stronghold. Should that happen, we'll fight on, but I have no doubt they'd eventually breach our walls. I shouldn't need to remind you of the fate awaiting those inside."

"There's no guarantee I can defeat them in battle."

"True, but she could flee, perhaps even as far east as Reinwick. I'm sure she'd find sanctuary there."

"I shall do what I can for her," said Charlaine, "but I have much to occupy my time. She'll need to fend for herself."

"I'll ensure others are there to take on that burden." He paused a moment, his cheeks reddening slightly. "There is a real possibility we shall not meet again, Commander. I wanted you to know how much I appreciate all you've done for my barony and our kingdom."

"It is my honour and my privilege, but all is not lost. Take heart, my lord, for the matter is yet to be decided."

"I wish I had your faith."

"I will do everything I can to stop the empire," said Charlaine, "but if you give up hope, all is lost. Your very presence here is the key to facing off against the might of the Halvarian Empire. Every warrior needed to hold you inside that keep is one less my knights must face in battle."

The baron straightened. "Of course. I shall do all I can. Any advice?"

"As a matter of fact, yes. Use your archers to keep the enemy on their toes. The farther back from the walls they stay, the more men they'll need to surround the place."

"Good, for I have arrows in abundance. Now, you must excuse me while I see to my wife's preparations."

"I suggest haste, my lord, for the enemy grows nearer with each passing breath."

The baron rode back to the keep. Charlaine spied Captain Bernelle coming up the hill, knights trailing behind her.

"What news?" she called out.

"Another twenty down," replied the captain, "but we're now seeing signs of well-armoured footmen. I fear the Imperials are marching through Braunfel."

"Take your company east. In about five miles, you'll come across some nice open farmland, an ideal place for a charge or two."

"And yourself?"

"We'll remain here until the enemy begins climbing this hill. Florence and I will slow them down, then join you."

"Are you sure you don't want us to stay?"

"As much as I admire the offer, you'll only get in the way. The road is narrow, with barely enough room for one company, let alone two. No, you'll be more effective preparing a countercharge."

"Aye, Commander. That being the case, we'd best be on our way."

"Very well. You are dismissed."

Bernelle rode off, and Charlaine watched her exchange words with members of her company. Would Bernelle survive the coming battle? Would any of her captains? Like as not, the battle would be a bloody one, with every possibility that none of them would survive. She hardened her heart. If they were all to die, then at least it would be in the service of Saint Agnes. What more could a Temple Knight ask for?

It was late in the afternoon when the enemy finally attempted to claim the keep. The first sign was a group of horsemen ascending the hill only to see the Temple Knights waiting for them. Rather than dawdle, they quickly turned around and returned to the relative safety of the town's streets.

Charlaine strode to the edge of the hill, giving her a clear view of a group of warriors waiting at the bottom, ready to climb up the road. A dragon decorated the top of their dark-green standard, marking them as Imperials instead of provincial troops, and if that weren't enough, their heavy metal armour made it even more apparent.

Charlaine had fought Imperials before, but those were seaborne troops with shirts of mail. These, on the other hand, wore metal plates, giving them the appearance of dismounted knights. The thought gave her pause to consider whether these might not be the Emperor's Own, but then a group of horsemen came into view, driving all such notions from her.

They rode magnificent chargers, large horses that would be the envy of Temple Knights were they to profess such feelings. Their armour sparkled with gold and silver adornments in abundance. Even their standard was more ornate, a riot of green and gold that captured the sunlight and reflected it back tenfold. The very sight of them filled Charlaine with dread, for there was more of them than she'd expected. Were they to strike now, she had no doubt they'd drive her Temple Knights from the hill.

The longer she stared, the more that reason took hold. These ornate warriors remained at the rear, doing nothing to prepare for battle. However, the footmen formed into a dense column, with the crossbowmen moving to their flanks.

The first bolts flew forth, doing little damage. No doubt they were there to impress the footmen, the intent being to fill their comrades with courage at the notion that they supported the advance.

Charlaine wished for archers of her own. Perhaps the use of auxiliaries would be of benefit to her order? She quickly dismissed the thought. There were too few women warriors, and mixing men and women within a Temple Order would only lead to bigger issues. Better to leave such things to their allies.

The thought of allies had her looking to the east. She couldn't see the field she'd picked to make her stand, but something made her think of Orlina Day. The Earth Mage had been about to tell her of her 'arrangements', but the attack commenced, cutting off all possibility of further discussion.

Drums sounded, then horns echoed throughout the town of Braunfel. The Imperial footmen now advanced up the road towards the keep.

"Time to go," she said, directing her comments to Florence.

"Are we not to counterattack?" asked the captain.

"I think not. There are too many men down there, and the road too constricting. We are mounted knights and need room to manoeuvre."

"So, we just surrender the road?"

"The baron will keep them busy," said Charlaine, "but we'll arrange a surprise or two once we get into the countryside." She paused as Florence rode on with her knights, falling in behind them and risking one last glance at the keep. There she spotted Lady Rebecca riding across the field, six men escorting her.

"Sorry I'm late," she called out. "I needed to gather a few things."

Charlaine slowed, waiting for her to catch up. "I hope whatever delayed you was worth it?"

"My husband insisted I take letters for the king. Is he to meet us in Lidenbach?"

"We're not heading to Lidenbach, at least not yet we're not, although you're more than welcome to ride on if that's your intent."

"I shall await the Royal Army's arrival, if that's all right with you."

"By all means, but we must hurry if we are to avoid that army." Charlaine nodded at the column now reaching the top of the hill.

"Then let us be on our way!"

The army of Arnsfeld gathered. A thousand men had marched from Dubrow, and now, two days after the Halvarians crossed the Stillwater, they rested, pickets out to watch for any signs of the enemy.

Charlaine arrived that evening, her horse lathered. She made her way to the grand master's tent, finding them in the midst of a discussion.

"Well?" the grand master was saying. "Where is she?"

Marlena's voice was easy to make out. "She will be here, Your Grace. I promise you."

"That's easy enough for you to say, but we need to deploy the men. Are we to have no notion of how to defend this place?"

"I am here," Charlaine announced, scanning the room as she entered. "The king didn't make it?"

"I wasn't aware we were expecting him," said Lord Austin. "However, it matters not. In his absence, command falls to His Grace, Grand Master Rudd."

"That's not entirely true."

"I beg your pardon."

"Yes," said His Grace. "What do you mean by that?"

"His Majesty gave me strict instructions to assume command in his absence."

"What nonsense is this? I'm the senior noble here; you're not even from Arnsfeld!"

"And yet that was his wish."

"I assume," said Lord Erskin, "you have some way to verify this claim?"

"I do." Charlaine produced a sealed letter, carefully folded and adorned with the Royal Seal.

Sir Hugo stepped forward to take it, breaking it open, and reading its contents. "This is definitely from His Majesty. I recognize the handwriting. It makes it quite clear we are to follow the commander's orders."

The grand master held out his hand. "Let me see that."

Sir Hugo gave him the note, and Charlaine feared he might rip it up, but his face softened.

"My apologies, Commander. We place ourselves at your disposal, as His Majesty wishes."

"Thank you, Your Grace."

"Might I ask how you wish to utilize us?"

"I have some ideas, but I would appreciate hearing your thoughts on the matter."

"Our strength is in our horse, so I suggest we combine your Temple Knights with the Silver Spurs."

"And where would you have us place them, Your Grace? Do we mass them in the north or south, or perhaps we locate them centrally?"

"Any of those would do."

"I disagree," said Sir Hugo, resulting in a look of disapproval from his grand master. "The knights are best used to take advantage of any weaknesses we detect in the enemy's attack. We can't do that if they're all in one place. Better to split them up into smaller groups, as individual companies."

"And what of our footmen?" said Lord Austin. "Not to mention our archers. Are they to be massed as well?" He turned his gaze on Charlaine. "What are your thoughts, Commander?"

"We could spread the foot along the top of the hill with the levy between companies, placing archers to the rear to rain arrows on the enemy as they approached. With any luck, we'd catch them as they're crossing the stream."

"Clever," said Sir Hugo. "It would break up the attack."

Outside, a guard challenged a new arrival, then an exhausted Brother Gatan stepped into the tent, his distinctive brown tabard marking him as a Temple Knight of Saint Mathew. Although covered from head to foot in dust and dirt, his smile indicated he bore good tidings.

"Commander," he said, nodding in recognition. "I'm afraid I don't know the rest of you, save for Sir Hugo, but I come bearing good news."

"Which is?" asked the grand master.

"I come from Lidenbach, and behind me follow three companies of sister knights, as well as one of my own order."

"This is good news indeed," said Charlaine. "Thank you, Brother. Your help is much appreciated. How long until they arrive?"

"They shall be here first thing in the morning. I thought it best they arrive rested rather than push on in the dark."

"A wise decision," said the grand master. "What say you, Commander? Shall we get down to details?"

"Yes," said Charlaine. "The Knights of the Silver Spurs are to be stationed to the north behind the footmen. I shall also place the cavalry of the barons under your command, provided there are no objections?" She looked around but saw only approval. "My Temple Knights will deploy to the south, once more just behind the line of foot. In both cases, we'll hold back the cavalry and utilize them only if an opportunity presents itself."

"And my order?" asked Gatan.

"In the centre, if you would be so kind, in case the enemy breaks through."

"And when are we to move into position?"

"First thing tomorrow," replied Charlaine. "I'll send word to our reinforcements to let them know where we want them."

"How do you know the attack will come tomorrow?" asked Lord Austin.

"I don't know for certain, but my knights have been harassing and delaying the enemy throughout the day. We bloodied their noses, and I suspect they'll be eager to bring us to task."

"One moment," said the grand master. "We talked of forming on the hill, but what about our flanks?"

"The Brinwald lies to our north," said Charlaine, "and the undergrowth is far too dense to allow easy passage."

"And the woods to the south? Are they similarly thick?"

"No, but I was assured we have help on the way."

"More help?" said Sir Hugo. "Care to share what form that might take?"

"I'm afraid I know little of its nature."

"Then how do you know it's safe?"

"Because I have faith."

The grand master shrugged. "That's to be expected, isn't it? You're a Temple Knight after all."

"I speak not of faith in my Saint, rather my faith in my fellow Humans."

"Now you're talking in riddles. If you don't know what type of help is coming, how do you know it exists? Surely even you must realize that faith alone can't save us."

"No," said Charlaine, "but we don't have the resources to man it ourselves. Thus, it falls on the shoulders of our ally, Orlina Day."

"The Earth Mage?" said the grand master. "Are you certain that's wise? She worships the Old Gods!"

"This invasion is against all the people of Arnsfeld, Your Grace, not only those who follow the teachings of the Saints."

He shook his head. "I only hope you know what you're doing."

35

FEARLESS

SUMMER 1103 SR

The fog finally lifted, revealing the precarious position in which the *Fearless* now found itself. Two enemy ships stood off the port side, three off the starboard, while more were in front. To make matters worse, there was little room to manoeuvre, and even if they could miraculously turn around, another ship stood off their stern. The Temple Knights rushed up on deck, grabbing their crossbows from the weapons chests.

"Hoist our colours," ordered Danica. "If we are to die this day, best we do it under the flag of our Saint." She sought out Anya. "Raise the anchor, get the sail unfurled, Captain, and have the sisters prepare to repel boarders."

"Aye, Admiral." As she issued the orders, the *Fearless* began moving.

Only now discovering their true identity, the ships surrounding *Fearless* raised the alarm. Men rushed around on their decks while archers scrambled to take up positions on the fighting castles mounted fore and aft. A couple of the large three-masters stood on either side of them, but the real prize was in front, for there lay four immense cogs resembling the *Leviathan*.

Danica noticed someone pulling the cover off the arbalest. "Break out the flame bolt, and don't loose till you're guaranteed a hit."

The cog immediately in front of them was still anchored, its crew running around in a panic. Warriors crowded its deck, waiting to be offloaded somewhere along the coast. The enemy vessel reacted slowly, as the passengers hampered the crew's efforts while, at the same time, weighed down the ship.

The range closed quickly, and then *Fearless* turned to port, its bowsprit narrowly missing the back of one of the cogs.

"Let fly!" shouted Anya.

The arbalest bolt sailed over the narrow gap, striking the cog's mast, its head breaking open and discharging an orange liquid. An instant later, a spark erupted into an explosion, flames spreading across the deck and igniting several warriors before the sail caught fire. Crossbow bolts followed, the Temple Knights taking down five or six men.

Danica focused her attention on her own ship. "Grace," she called out. "Count as many of those ships as you can. The rest of you reload."

All around her, the Halvarian fleet reacted. One of the large three-masters behind them turned to follow while to the north, a vessel similar in size to her own prepared to intercept.

Anya moved up beside her. "Orders, Admiral?"

"Keep us straight."

"If that ship rams us, we're finished."

"I'm open to suggestions."

"We build up speed, then make a sudden shift to port, just enough to pass in front of that ship."

"It's your command, Captain."

Danica looked aft. Flames engulfed the cog they'd hit, the crew jumping into the sea to avoid a fiery death. She looked around, desperate for any sign of the *Illustrious*, but all she saw were empire warships.

Fearless turned into the wind, its speed dropping precipitously, while the enemy ship that had been in front now sat off the starboard bow, picking up speed as their sails filled. Arrows flew forth, most splashing harmlessly into the sea, while only a few carried on the entire distance, the closest lodging into the railing by Danica's hand.

"*Majestic* looks as if she's following us," called out Anya.

A glance aft confirmed the gold lettering proclaiming the ship's name, and then she looked to port. "I'm more worried about that." She noted the name of the vessel. "*Glorious*. We've seen her before."

A call came back from the arbalest. "More fire, Captain?"

"No," said Anya. "There's only one left. Best to save it for the merchants. Load regular bolts."

Danica ignored the chaos behind them. *Fearless* was fast enough to outrun the *Majestic*, provided nothing slowed them. "Concentrate on the *Glorious*," she shouted.

The Temple Knights moved to the port side and took aim. The *Glorious* was still some distance off, but with the wind at its back, it was closing quickly.

The other vessel, bearing the name *Righteous*, moved swiftly, but their captain had made an error, for she carried on past them and must now sail back towards the wind to catch them. All *Fearless* needed to do was clear the bow of the *Glorious* and then turn to starboard, filling her sails.

With her nose close to the wind, *Fearless* slowed even as the enemy vessels sped up. *Glorious* was coming straight for them, and as the larger ship, a collision would work to their advantage. Danica braced for impact, but at the last moment, the Halvarian turned to starboard, its bowsprit scraping along the side of *Fearless*, tearing off part of the railing and snagging the rope leading to the foremast. Despite her preparations, Danica fell to the deck as the ship lurched.

Grace, however, had the presence of mind to grab an axe and hack away at the entangled line. Three times she hit, and then the strands parted, releasing the tangled ships from their death grip. Now loose, the bowsprit of the Halvarian careened past, striking her and knocking her across the deck.

For a moment, *Glorious* and *Fearless* lay alongside each other, facing opposite directions. Bolts flew from both ships but to little effect. Aboard the enemy ship, a man garbed in silver and gold gesticulated, then flames leaped across the distance, striking the deck near the arbalest on *Fearless*.

Sister Margo took aim and let fly with a bolt of her own. Even though it missed the enemy mage, it convinced him to keep his head down.

Behind them, the *Righteous* completed its turn. In the confusion of battle, its captain failed to account for the actions of his allies and ran straight into *Glorious*. Before he grasped the gravity of his situation, the *Majestic*, which had been following the Temple ship, crashed into *Righteous*. The three ships, now entangled, ceased all movement.

The *Fearless*, finally clearing the mass of enemy vessels, turned to starboard, wind filling her sails. A few random bolts flew from the Halvarians, but the immediate danger was over.

Danica took a deep breath, finally starting to relax, only to be surprised by a warning of another ship approaching from the north. She rushed forward to get a better view, but it turned out to be *Valiant*, sailing south to locate them.

By mid-morning, they remained within sight of the enemy fleet, paralleling its course. After being knocked unconscious, they'd carried Sister Grace below. Thankfully, besides bruising and a dent in her armour, she was intact, and only three crew were injured, none of them severely. Danica led them all in a prayer of gratitude.

The *Sprite*, escorted by *Valiant*, was on its way to alert the fleet at Cape

Maralan. Meanwhile, the *Fearless* and *Illustrious* would continue to monitor the Halvarian's progress, though at a discreet distance.

Anya stepped into Danica's cabin. "You called me, Admiral?"

"I did. You did well today."

"Thank you. Though, I honestly didn't think we'd get out of that one."

"*Fearless* is a fine ship."

"She is, and faster than her sisters. Thank the Saints they only had one Fire Mage."

"Yes," said Danica. "I've been thinking about that. When we ran across them at Temple Bay, the only mage there was aboard the *Devastator*, the very ship we now call *Fearless*."

"And?"

"I don't think they employ as many mages as we imagine. Don't get me wrong, we know they have a great many of them, but the empire is large, and they can't be everywhere. This expedition, though, is important to them."

"So, are you saying we can expect more mages or not?"

"I think it's safe to assume they'll have more. I imagine all the larger vessels will have at least one."

"And by larger, you mean?"

"The three-masted warships," said Danica. "Did we get an accurate accounting of their fleet?"

"I talked to everyone. We can't be certain, but accounts vary from a low of ten to a high of fifteen, possibly more. Even if the lower number is accurate, it's worrisome."

"Is that including the merchants?"

"No, though in that regard, we damaged one. It's sailing west as we speak, no doubt returning to the safety of Thansalay."

"Did they dispatch any ships to escort it home?"

"Not that we could see," replied Anya. "Had we the *Valiant*, we could have sent it to intercept."

"There would be little point. Our objective here is to prevent a landing, not capture prizes."

"What's your strategy once we catch up with the rest of our fleet?"

"Our priority must be those cogs. Destroy them, and the invasion fails."

"But there are still warriors aboard their warships."

"Yes," said Danica, "but I doubt there's sufficient to take the Royal Castle in Lidenbach. I believe they mean to land behind Charlaine's forces while the Halvarian army keeps them busy. The loss to our side would be catastrophic."

All colour fled Anya's face. "What can we do? We haven't the numbers to take on their entire fleet."

"We have little choice; to do nothing will ensure their victory. What we need is the rest of our ships."

"Can we call on those back at Temple Bay?"

"No. They'd never get here in time. By now, the *Sprite* will be well on its way to Cape Maralan. From there, they'll proceed directly to Lidenbach, then sail west, following the coast. What *Fearless* and *Illustrious* need to do is rendezvous with them so we can plan our attack."

"But the enemy is already sailing east. Can we outrun them?"

"I think so," said Danica. "Those cogs might be able to carry lots of men, but they're slow. The rest of their ships will reduce sail to protect them, giving us the time to make our plans. Signal the *Illustrious* to come alongside, and we'll let them know our intentions."

"Aye, Admiral." Anya left, leaving Danica deep in thought. She dragged out the few charts she possessed of the area and poured over them. If the Halvarians were preparing to attack from behind Charlaine, there were only a few places they could land. The Brinwald was far too thick to allow men to move inland, meaning they'd need to go farther east in search of a spot. That left only a twenty-mile stretch of coastline between the woods and the capital.

The other problem the enemy faced was getting their people ashore. A large cog like the *Leviathan* could hold a lot, but a ship's boat could only take so many at a once. If she were in command, she would use all the boats from the fleet to ferry the men, thus speeding up the transfer.

Of course, there was also the possibility each warship's complement of warriors might be sent ashore, leading to further delays. She smiled at the thought, for it occurred to her, if that were the case, the Halvarian warships would divest themselves of the only men they had to counter boarding actions by her Temple Knights.

Fearless and *Illustrious* plowed through the waves, the wind filling their sails. They'd left the Halvarians behind yesterday, and now Danica looked ahead, seeking any sign of the Temple fleet. Finally, as the sun sank on the horizon, she spotted a cluster of masts in the distance.

It was dark by the time they dropped anchor, but there was no time for rest. She sent word for her captains to come aboard her flagship, then began planning the attack.

Sister Laurel, captain of the *Invincible*, was the last to arrive, squeezing into the admiral's cramped cabin just after midnight.

"Welcome all," began Danica. "As you are no doubt aware, the enemy fleet is heading up the coast. I believe they'll land east of the Brinwald in preparation for moving against the Army of Arnsfeld and, in so doing, will surround them. Our job is to prevent that from happening."

"Do we know the size of their fleet?" asked Laurel.

"We think there's at least twelve warships, possibly eighteen. Against that, we have only eight, nine if you include the *Sprite*. The priority for us, though, isn't the warships, it's the cogs or, if they've begun unloading, the ship's boats ferrying men ashore."

"Our strategy is to tie down the warships with our larger ships while *Valiant* and *Valour* sail in amongst the boats to wreak as much damage as possible."

"Might I ask a question?" said Vivian.

"By all means."

"You say we are to take out the boats, but how do we do that? Surely, you're not suggesting we try to board rowboats?"

"No. You'll use your arbalest, along with crossbows. If that proves ineffective, you are to take more drastic action."

"Which is?"

"Ramming. I know that could damage your ships, but in my opinion, it's worth the risk. Also, thanks to Barbek, each ship is equipped with two fire bolts, save for *Fearless*."

"What happened to those aboard *Fearless*?"

"We ended up using one against a cog, to great effect I might add. The other, we'll pass on to *Valiant*."

"What of the *Sprite*?" asked Zivka.

"She has no arbalest or fighting complement, so she'll stand by to help evacuate any ships of ours that may be lost."

"Lost?" said Vivian. "Do you mean captured or sunk?"

"We're dealing with Halvarians here, and we know they employ Fire Mages. There is the threat they could set some of our ships alight. Should that happen, you are to abandon ship and take to the boats."

"Might it not be wiser to put our knights ashore and defeat the enemy as they land?"

"We'd find ourselves quickly outnumbered, and without horses, we'd have no advantage. We can do more damage to them on the water."

She looked around at the faces before her. They all knew what she was asking of them. Now, all that remained was to give them their individual assignments.

"The ships are to operate in pairs, much as they have for the past few months. For *Valiant* and *Valour*, the main target is the landing boats, but the rest of us are to concentrate on the three-masters."

"How many are there?" asked Zivka.

"We counted four. We fought *Glorious* yesterday, and they had a Fire Mage aboard. Treat the others as if they are similarly equipped. My plan calls for each pair to pick a target, placing themselves along either side. With any luck, they'll have sent the bulk of their warriors ashore to help in the assault, leaving them vulnerable, but even if they didn't, they'll be hard-pressed to fight two boarding actions simultaneously. Remember, they outnumber us significantly, so you'll need to be quick or risk a counterattack by other enemy ships."

"Do they have a flagship?" asked Zivka.

"I believe so," said Danica. "The *Glorious* flew an ornate flag when last we saw it, and I'm guessing it belongs to whoever is in charge."

"Couldn't the same be said of us?"

"Now that you mention it, I suppose it could."

"Should we lower your pennant?" asked Anya.

"I'll consider it, but it might work to our advantage."

"In what way?"

"As bait."

"You can't be serious?"

"Actually," added Vivian, "it makes sense. We know the Halvarians have heard of the admiral's reputation. If we let *Fearless* and *Illustrious* go in first, it might tempt their whole fleet to chase after them."

Danica smiled. "Precisely, and that's when the rest of you can pick your targets. We'll approach in a line, two ships abreast, but leave enough room to manoeuvre."

"And if we capture any of them?"

"As I said earlier, the main objective is to destroy their ability to land men. While capturing ships is certainly worth considering, we must also take into account that each prize will require knights to occupy it."

"So, we sink them?"

"Cripple them if you can. Even the best sailors won't get far without sails. If you can't spare a prize crew, consider sinking them."

"Why not burn them?" asked Vivian.

"Fire can be capricious, and we can't risk the flames spreading to our own ships." She looked around the room one last time. "This will be a bloody affair that's been building for some time. The empire has a lot depending on this, and they may turn desperate."

"Meaning?"

"We cannot dismiss the possibility they might sacrifice their ships to destroy us."

"I'm sorry," said Anya. "What are you suggesting?"

"They have Fire Mages, and we know from past experiences that Imperial troops can be fanatics. There's a chance they may set their own ships alight once we've grappled with them."

"Surely not?" said Zivka.

"It's simply a matter of numbers," replied Danica. "They have enough ships that they can afford to sacrifice some. There is some good news, though. The provincials are likely unwilling to do such a thing. Unfortunately, the same can't be said for the rest."

"Just how many provincials are there?"

"We're not entirely sure," replied Anya. "We counted three, but there could be more."

"The important thing," said Danica, "is to keep a cool head. If you trust your training and experience, we have a good chance of blunting their attack. Now, you'd best return to your ships and get some sleep. Tomorrow will be a busy day."

They filed out without another word. Danica sat on the edge of her bed only to hear a knock. "Come."

A Temple Knight opened the door, bearing a tray. "I brought you some food, Admiral."

"Grace? You should be below deck, recuperating."

"I'm bruised, Admiral, not dead, and if I don't feed you, who will?"

Danica wanted to order her out, but the smell of food got the better of her. "What have you got there?"

"Some leftover stew and a cup of mead."

"Where in the name of the Saints did you get mead?"

"I'm afraid I'm not at liberty to reveal my sources, Admiral."

"Well, I'd hate to see it go to waste."

Her aide set the tray on the end of the bed, and Danica picked up the spoon.

"We're going into battle tomorrow, Grace, but I don't want you fighting unless absolutely necessary." She pointed at her makeshift desk. "You see those papers?"

"Yes."

"Should the *Fearless* find itself in danger of capture, you are to toss them overboard in a weighted bag. You understand?"

"Yes, Admiral."

Danica reached over and picked up a sealed letter. "I want you to have this."

"What is it?"

"A letter of recommendation. You've only been my aide for a short time, but you've proven yourself of immense value. This letter ensures you get the recognition you deserve."

"You keep it, Admiral. You can give it to me once the battle's over."

At her look of complete trust, a lump formed in Danica's throat. How many of her fellow sisters would die in tomorrow's fighting? The sentiment stole any words she might have uttered. Instead, she nodded, placing the letter back amongst the other papers.

36

THE BATTLE BEGINS

SUMMER 1103 SR

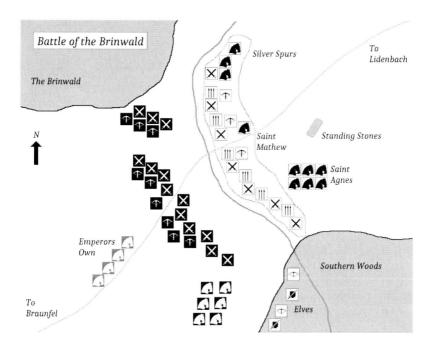

The he Halvarian legion marched onto the battlefield shortly after dawn, the provincials moving up the road in a rough line, archers behind the footmen, with companies of horse to the south.

It would be some time until they posed a threat to Charlaine's well-ordered defence, and the enemy would likely array its entire army before taking up the mantle of attack. Her interest lay not in the provincials but in the Imperial footmen following behind.

"By the Saints, there's a lot of them," said the grand master.

Charlaine estimated their numbers, then smiled.

"You find something amusing, Commander?"

"It seems our strategy has worked."

"They still outnumber us."

"True, but it could've been far worse."

"Worse?"

"What you see arrayed before us is, by my estimate, roughly three-quarters of a legion rather than a whole one."

"Where are the rest?" asked the grand master.

"Likely surrounding Braunfel Keep."

"While I'm happy they're not at full strength, I might remind you they still significantly outnumber us."

Charlaine looked behind her at the Temple Knight companies who'd arrived in the wee hours of the morning.

"Have faith," she said. "We have the advantage of position."

"I doubt that will make much difference against such numbers."

She spotted Orlina Day walking towards her. "If you will excuse me, Your Grace. There are things I must attend to."

"Yes, of course. I should make my way back to my order, anyway." The grand master trotted off.

The Earth Mage halted before her. "It seems the hour is upon us."

"So it is," said Charlaine. "Is our southern flank safe?"

Orlina smiled. "No enemy shall march beneath its boughs."

"Might I ask by what means you accomplished this?"

"I called upon some old allies to come to our aid."

"Allies? Can you be more specific?"

The old woman merely glanced to the southern end of the Halvarian lines. "Watch those horsemen, and you'll understand."

The enemy riders moved closer to the woods but halted shy of the trees.

"Ah," said Orlina. "It appears I was a little premature in my expectations."

The leading companies of the legion came to a halt, waiting as the rest of their forces moved up.

"It is as I suspected," said Charlaine. "They're keeping their cavalry to the south. I trust our friends in the woods won't be too hard-pressed to keep them at bay?"

"I hope not, but then again, I didn't expect quite so many of them."

"If there is a danger to my southern flank, I need to know."

"They will not fail us."

"I might find that easier to accept if you'd tell me who 'they' are?"

Orlina turned and looked directly at Charlaine. "They are the Elder Race."

"You mean Elves? Aren't they pretty much extinct?"

"Not at all. They merely withdrew from the realms of men. Oh, you can still find the odd one in the cities of the Petty Kingdoms, but most keep to the deeper woodlands these days."

"Where did you find them?"

"They live in the very woods they now defend."

"Astounding," said Charlaine. "Although I do wonder, if they remained hidden for all these years, why reveal their presence now?"

"The empire threatens their way of life as much as it threatens ours. I'm told Halvaria has taken steps to eradicate such folk from the Continent. This is the last chance for the Elves of Mythanos to fight back against them."

"Mythanos?"

"Their name for the woods they call home."

"Do they have a city?"

"They have," said Orlina, "although perhaps the term 'city' doesn't quite do it justice. You could walk beneath it without even being aware of its presence. It lies miles to the south, where the woods thicken, much like the Brinwald."

"The only Elf I've ever met was a fellow named Gwalinor," said Charlaine, "and he was a Sea Elf."

"You should consider yourself lucky, for those who travel the seas are said to be the rarest of all." She nodded towards the south. "Their leader, Bethiel, will do all in her power to hold those woods, but I won't lie; the numbers arrayed against us are far worse than I imagined."

"Then we shall endeavour to assist where possible."

The enemy formed a long line just out of range of Charlaine's archers. So many warriors gathered in one place was an impressive sight, and for a moment, panic threatened to overwhelm her.

Unconsciously, she ran three fingers across her chest, the sign of Saint Agnes, and then a calmness settled over her. With battle about to be joined, she realized the stage was set. She could do little now to alter the destiny unfolding this day; she must hold on and do her duty.

Her thoughts moved to the princess, and she turned east to see Rebecca sitting on her horse, far to the rear. Should things go badly, her guards' orders were to take her to Lidenbach. Charlaine only hoped it was enough to keep her safe.

Marlena appeared at her side. "Impressive, aren't they?"

"They are," agreed Charlaine, shaken from her reverie. "I read somewhere that the empire has many legions like this. Thank the Saints they only invaded with one." Her gaze swept over the knights of her order. "How is your company?"

"Eager to do their part, though I doubt it will be for some time. Should I return to them?"

"You might as well remain here. It'll save me from sending a messenger when the time comes. What do you make of the enemy's tactics?"

"I notice they put the provincials in the middle."

"What does that tell you?"

"That they'll likely take the brunt of the fighting."

"What else have you noted?"

"Imperial footmen on either flank, with their horsemen massed to the south. I assume that means they intend a flanking manoeuvre. Should I take my Temple Knights to intercept?"

"No," replied Charlaine. "We have allies in those woods. Elves, to be precise." She noted the look of surprise. "I know. I was as shocked as you."

"Can they hold?"

"Only time will tell. In any case, I need our knights right where they are. If our defence wavers, I'll move them up to reinforce the king's men."

A few arrows flew from the Halvarians but fell woefully short.

"It won't be long now," said Charlaine. "The battle is about to commence."

The empire's warriors advanced into the stream, and the archers of Arnsfeld launched their first volleys, arrows dropping on the enemy ranks from on high. It would have been an impressive sight had she more of them, but the tactic proved ineffective, doing little sign of damage.

A roar erupted before her as the enemy advanced up the hill. A horn sounded, announcing the assault, and then others chimed in, spreading out on either side of her position. They aimed their initial attack at the centre of her line, but of more concern were events in the south where the massed horsemen of Halvaria waited to enter the woods.

"I must trust in the Elves," said Charlaine, mostly to herself, "and concentrate on the rest of the battle." Her vantage point atop the hill gave her a commanding view of the assault unfolding before her.

"There," said Marlena, pointing. "Do you see them?"

Charlaine saw the Emperor's Own in all their glory. From this distance, they looked like knights, their armour sparkling in the bright sunlight.

They moved with precision, much as the Temple Knights did, and she knew, in that instant, they held the future of kingdoms in their hands. If the Emperor's Own broke through her line, the battle would be lost, sealing the fate of Arnsfeld and that of the Petty Kingdoms.

"That's your target," said Charlaine.

"I don't understand. Are you suggesting we charge now?"

"No, but you should seize the moment if an opportunity presents itself."

"How will I know when it's time?"

"You must trust your instincts," said Charlaine. "But it won't be for some time yet." Her attention turned back to the enemy foot when another cheer went up as the Halvarians crashed into the Arnsfeld line.

The sounds of battle drifted to her. She wanted to help, to send in her Temple Knights, but knew she had to wait. This line must hold—all their hopes depended on it. She closed her eyes, praying to Saint Agnes.

With a shock, she forced them open as she realized she hadn't led the army in a prayer. It unsettled her, but then reason took hold. She must stay focused on the battle lest she fail to see any unexpected threats.

An arrow flew past her, and Marlena flipped down her visor. Charlaine followed suit, although it restricted her view of the field. The action proved most fortuitous, for moments later, an arrow bounced off her helmet. "It appears their archers are better than we thought."

"It's a pity we don't have more of our own," said Marlena. "It would go a long way to keeping them at bay."

The fighting intensified, but the Halvarians' cheers changed to cries of alarm as they streamed back down the hill, seeking safety from the axes and swords of the king's warriors.

"It worked!" said Marlena.

"It's not over yet," replied Charlaine. "Far from it." Horns sounded to the north, and she strained to see what was happening, then spotted horsemen flooding down the hill, rushing headlong into the enemy lines.

"The Knights of the Silver Spur are charging," said Marlena. "Was that your idea?"

"It most certainly was not. Fools! They risk everything."

"I don't understand."

"They launched their attack too early, and the very same terrain that works to our advantage only serves to break up their attack."

"What can we do?"

"Nothing. We must hold fast and hope they win through. Let's get closer, shall we? I need to see what's happening."

They rode north, keeping behind their own warriors. The fighting in the north intensified while the rest of the battlefield lay quiet as both sides licked their wounds.

At first, the Knights of the Silver Spur sliced through the opposition, but their horses tired and lost their impetus as they advanced. The empire moved a wall of crossbowmen forward to unleash a rain of death, catching the spent knights off guard.

The bolts did little damage to the armoured knights, but their mounts fared much worse. Horses tumbled, crushing their riders, and the empire sent forth heavily armoured men to finish them off, quickly reducing the Knights of the Silver Spur to less than twenty.

The rest of the cavalry, overcome with the zeal of battle, followed the knight's example and charged, but they suffered from the volleys of death, their lighter armour providing little protection against such a tactic. By the time it was all over, the entire complement of cavalry was destroyed and, with it, her northern flank, for there was now a considerable gap between the Brinwald and her army. The enemy quickly took the offensive, sending companies north to exploit the opening.

Marlena gave voice to her fears. "Saints alive, they'll turn our flank."

Charlaine stared at the rear of her line. Could she get her Temple Knights north in time? She was about to give the order when she spotted distinctive brown-surcoated riders heading north. The Mathewites crashed into the enemy, ignoring the heavier footmen and concentrating instead on their crossbowmen. The Order of the Silver Spur's auxiliaries followed, eager to salvage the honour of their order.

She held her breath, fearing calamity, but the Saints were with them as they drove deep into the enemy lines, destroying any chance the empire had of turning the flank.

"Look!" said Marlena. "To the south."

Hundreds of Halvarian horsemen charged towards the southern woods, but as they advanced, arrows flew forth, wreaking fearful damage. Horses went down with riders thrown from their mounts. Those behind were too tightly packed to avoid the carnage and only added to the misery. The attack stalled, but the death of so many steeds horrified Charlaine.

There was no way of knowing how many of the Elder race opposed the charge, but if the casualties were any indication, there must have been a significant number. Then, as the empire's cavalry withdrew, the Elves emerged, clad in green surcoats and silver mail. Most held long shields that fell past their knees, while a third bore strange-looking bows as tall as those wielding them. More arrows flew forth, finding their marks and staining the ground red.

A lull fell over the battlefield as the Temple Knights of Saint Mathew in the north halted, returning to the safety of the Arnsfeld line to recover. They'd suffered fearful damage, losing over half their number, but had averted a catastrophe. To the south, the Elves stood at the edge of the woods, wary of the Emperor's Own waiting in reserve.

Charlaine took stock of the situation. The battle would continue, but for the moment, the man in charge of the Halvarian Legion seemed content to send only small groups forward to collect the dead and wounded.

She turned to Marlena. "Gather what volunteers you can to bring the injured to safety."

"And the dead?"

"We can't afford to bury them just yet. Leave them where they lie but be careful; the enemy could end this truce at any moment."

Marlena rode off, leaving Charlaine to contemplate her next moves. The empire had suffered more losses than her command, yet the near annihilation of the Silver Spurs had done irreparable damage. Even worse, it forced the Temple Knights of Saint Mathew to intervene, dwindling their already small numbers. The Temple Knights of Saint Agnes were the only reserve she had left, many of whom were relatively inexperienced.

Thanks to their distinctive standard, the Emperor's Own were easy to locate, positioned behind the massed ranks of footmen. Were they to charge south into the Elven ranks, would their superior armour allow them to push back the woodland folk? It occurred to her that she could counterattack with her sister knights, but she held no illusions that such a tactic would work to her advantage.

For the other temple orders, recruits were trained knights, men who'd spent a lifetime preparing for war, whereas her order excelled at close-order tactics, where they could put their numbers and discipline to best use. To take advantage of that strength, she needed an open field, not a forest that would make such tactics impossible.

She sought the enemy commander's standard only to find it in amongst the Emperor's Own, now forming into two long lines. It could only mean one thing; the next phase of the battle was about to commence.

People from both sides still ran around rescuing the wounded, but that didn't stop the empire as their footmen advanced, scattering those caught between the two armies.

Arak Thorn, the Halvarian Commander-General, had decided to finish things by sending his entire army forward in one bold manoeuvre. Charlaine struggled to grasp it, her attention pulled from the north to the south.

Warriors climbed the hills once more, this time preceded by a devastating volley of arrows. The enemy had learned their lesson and concentrated their archers on the levy wherever possible. Not used to such punishment, the farmers of Arnsfeld took frightful losses before they broke, dropping their weapons and fleeing towards safety. Their flight opened up holes in the defender's lines, holes which the empire was quick to exploit.

Charlaine rode for her life, seeking the safety of a nearby company of footmen as the provincial troops swarmed the top of the hill, engulfing the tiny formation. Cut off from the rest of her command, she could do little but draw her weapon and prepare for the worst.

Arrows flew into the company's ranks, taking down at least five men and creating a gap in the formation. Charlaine rushed forward, using her horse to knock over an axe wielder. She struck out, slicing into a helmet, forcing another back. Something scraped along her leg, but her armour kept her from harm. Stormcloud reared up and kicked out, hitting someone in the chest and sending him flying into those behind.

Charlaine resisted the urge to advance, opting to remain in place to hold the line until more of her own footmen rushed to fill the gap. A spear tip struck her leg, but her greave absorbed the impact. She, in turn, stabbed out, the tip of her sword hitting a shield. An Arnsfeld footman appeared at her side, sinking his spear into the fellow while his comrades struggled to restore their line.

Unable to see the rest of the battle, the fear that they'd all failed gripped Charlaine. The empire would win this, then march up the coast and take the capital!

37

SKIRMISH AT SEA

SUMMER 1103 SR

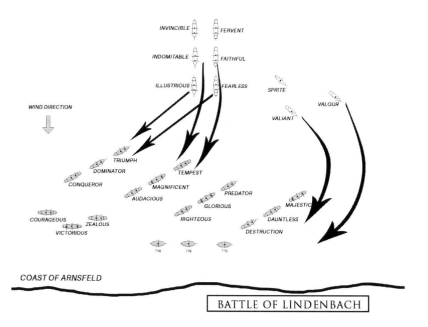

INVINCIBLE · FERVENT

INDOMITABLE · FAITHFUL

ILLUSTRIOUS · FEARLESS · SPRITE

VALOUR

VALIANT

WIND DIRECTION

TRIUMPH

DOMINATOR · TEMPEST

CONQUEROR

MAGNIFICENT · PREDATOR

AUDACIOUS

GLORIOUS · MAJESTIC

COURAGEOUS · ZEALOUS · RIGHTEOUS · DAUNTLESS

VICTORIOUS · DESTRUCTION

Cog · Cog · Cog

COAST OF ARNSFELD

BATTLE OF LINDENBACH

From her position on *Fearless*, Danica looked aft to *Faithful* and *Fervent*, strung out in a line behind her, then starboard where the *Indomitable* and *Invincible* followed in the wake of *Illustrious*, just as planned. The *Valiant* and *Valour* sat farther out to port, ready to join in once they made contact.

The wind had shifted shortly after sunrise and now blew in from the north, the perfect weather for the order's attack. Ahead of them sat the Halvarian fleet, warriors climbing into boats, ready to row to the beach. From the look of it, they had yet to set any ashore, but Danica knew it was only a matter of time. They must get in amongst the enemy ships while the smaller vessels remained vulnerable.

Illustrious turned to starboard. She would sail past a provincial ship, the *Triumph*, sending a volley of crossbow bolts into its hull, while *Fearless* did the same from the other side. They would board if needed, but Danica hoped it would prove unnecessary.

Faithful and *Indomitable* continued farther south, aiming for one of the three-masted ships busy disgorging warriors into smaller boats. After that, each captain bore the responsibility of making her own decisions, for the nature of war was chaotic and ever-shifting.

Danica was armoured, head to toe, but kept her visor up for the moment, the better to take in the view. *Illustrious* released an arbalest bolt, then its hull disappeared behind the *Triumph* as *Fearless* began turning to starboard. Her knights stood, swords in hand, ready to board and disable the Halvarian vessel.

The lack of response on the enemy ship was surprising. Someone loosed a bolt from its forward-mounted ballista, but the projectile went wide, splashing into the sea.

Standing at the arbalest, Margo loosed a grapnel shot straight at the enemy ship, striking the railing, then digging into the deck. The Temple Knights began winching them closer.

From her vantage point, Danica watched Zivka drop a boarding ramp from *Illustrious* onto the enemy vessel and charge across, followed by twelve Temple Knights. The *Triumph's* crew tried to stop them, but without a complement of warriors, it was a foregone conclusion.

"Leave this ship to *Illustrious*," she called out. "We'll make our way down the line." Rather than retrieve the grapnel, her knights cut the rope, readying another for the arbalest. The *Fearless* continued alongside *Triumph*, past Zivka's Temple Knights as they hacked at the ropes holding the ship's sails in place. Once they fell to the deck, the knights tossed the canvas overboard, then climbed back aboard the *Illustrious*, eager to move farther down the line of enemy ships.

The small boats of the Halvarian fleet were easy to spot. While a few of them had reached the shore and were disgorging their passengers, the vast majority were still rowing, spurred on by the presence of the Temple ships.

Danica tried to remain calm. The *Triumph* had fallen quickly, but it was still early. The *Magnificent* lay to port, its golden letters proclaiming its identity to all. *Faithful* and *Indomitable* headed straight for it, a good sign, but she glimpsed a ship beyond it—*Glorious*, the enemy's flagship.

Anchored behind *Triumph* was another provincial, and she strained to make out the name. *Dominator*, the same ship they'd met at the mouth of the Stillwater. She tried to imagine the surprise on Captain Douglas's face, then remembered his dark-clothed companion.

"Careful," she called out. "There may be a mage aboard the next ship."

The knights finished loading the arbalest, and then Margo swivelled it, aiming for the *Dominator*. Danica pushed the rest of the battle from her mind, concentrating instead on her own fight. A slight gust of wind blew across her face, and she realized she'd neglected to pull down her visor. She rectified the fault, moving to the forecastle for a better view.

What she saw brought a smile to her lips. The *Dominator* had loaded its boat with men, and that vessel now sat directly in the path of *Fearless*.

"Stand by," said Danica. "Don't loose until you're sure of the target. We don't want to miss them."

"*Dominator*. Our hull will take care of the other."

She looked aft, only to see Anya at the ship's rudder, having taken control herself. Scraping up along the length of an enemy ship was tricky business, and the captain was concerned for the safety of her command.

The arbalest released its bolt, the rope playing out as it sailed across to *Dominator*, striking the ship just in front of the forward mast. Then *Fearless* shuddered as its bow sailed through a boat, full of warriors.

A volley of arrows flew from the enemy warship, one glancing off Danica's helmet. Her knights released their own volley, which proved far more accurate, and a trio of Halvarian archers went down, but the rest kept loosing arrow after arrow.

With their volley discharged, the Temple Knights aboard *Fearless* turned to the winch. The rope went taut, and the two ships moved closer, now side to side.

Danica hoped all the enemy's warriors were aboard the ship's boat, but it appeared Captain Douglas had kept some in reserve. Those men now rushed along the deck, ready to repel boarders.

The two ships crashed into each other, knocking people from their feet. One poor, unfortunate soul fell from the crow's nest, hitting the deck with a gut-wrenching thud.

Danica drew her sword, running to the midships, where six sisters prepared to drop a boarding ramp. Arrows clattered off their armour, but they ignored them, concentrating on getting the spiked board into place. Once it was secured in the *Dominator's* deck, the first Temple Knight rushed across.

She couldn't tell who was underneath all the armour, but as the woman reached the enemy railing, a sword smashed into her leg, toppling her to one side, a spear thrust sending the knight tumbling into the sea.

More Temple Knights surged across, overwhelming the opposition and pushing them back to the sterncastle, but then a streak of fire flew in amongst them, striking a sister in the chest while splattering those nearby.

A man clad in black stood on the aft deck, the same individual who'd shown himself at the mouth of the Stillwater. With a quick movement of his hands, he flung something the size of an acorn into the melee. There was scarcely enough time to register the attack, let alone react to it, before a loud crack released a rush of flames, engulfing both attackers and defenders alike.

It was a tactical error, for the Temple Knights' plate armour lessened its effects, while the provincial's lighter armour did little to protect them. The explosion cleared the deck of any opposition, and then Sister Margo led the knights up the ladder to the sterncastle.

She set foot on the upper deck as the mage unleashed his next spell, flames shooting out from his fingertips, closing the distance, then swirling around her. Sparks flew off, making a sputtering noise as it held Margo's arms in place, her weapon clattering to the deck.

Danica moved to the mainmast and reached into a weapons chest, setting down her sword and pulling forth a crossbow. Practiced hands drew back the string, locking it in place. She slid the bolt in, raised it, and let fly towards the Fire Mage as Margo screamed in agony.

The Fire Mage stiffened as the bolt penetrated his chest, interrupting his concentration. The pillar of flame dissipated as the villain stumbled back, allowing Margo to retrieve her sword. The Halvarian stared down at the bolt protruding from his chest. He opened his mouth, but Margo sliced open his neck before any words escaped. He fell to the deck, his head tilted at an obscene angle.

Danica retrieved her sword and crossed the boarding plank as Sister Grace appeared, prodding Captain Douglas with the tip of her blade.

"I surrender this ship," he said, "and place my crew under your protection."

The Fire Mage's death signalled the end of the struggle. What few men remained tossed their weapons to the deck and were quickly rounded up.

"I claim this ship in the name of the Temple Knights of Saint Agnes," said Danica. "Take the crew below and see them secured. We'll bring the captain aboard *Fearless*." She turned to Grace. "I thought I told you to stay in my cabin?"

"You did, but I couldn't stand by and do nothing while my sisters risked their lives."

"You may have captured the *Dominator*," said Captain Douglas, "but you've yet to face our flagship."

"A fleet is more than one ship, Captain. And fear not. We'll get to it eventually. Your part in this battle, however, has come to an end. Take him away, Grace."

Douglas offered no resistance as she led him across the boarding plank.

Anya soon reported in. "Only one casualty, Admiral. I'm afraid we lost Sister Zara to the sea."

"And Margo? I saw her engulfed in flames."

"Shaken but uninjured. I understand they tried the same spell on Commander Charlaine back at Temple Bay. Unusual to see a Fire Mage aboard a provincial ship."

"Indeed," replied Danica. "I wonder what other surprises await us." She noted the *Illustrious* sailing past to engage *Conqueror*. From her perspective, things had gone according to plan, but she worried how her other ships fared. Crossing back to the *Fearless*, she made her way aft to get a better view of the rest of the battle. *Faithful* and *Indomitable* lay alongside a three-masted Halvarian ship, but judging from its flags, this wasn't their flagship. *Invincible* and *Fervent* were likewise engaged, although with a smaller vessel, likely a provincial.

Valiant and *Valour* were out there somewhere, but the intervening ships blocked her view of them. Off to the south sat the three cogs, so far undamaged, and that's when she found inspiration.

"Captain Anya," she called out. "I changed my mind. Bring all the prisoners aboard *Fearless*."

"Admiral?"

"You heard me. Send six knights searching for anything flammable. The rest are to return to our ship as quickly as possible."

To her credit, the captain didn't question her admiral. Instead, she barked out orders, sending knights scurrying back across the boarding plank. They threw down another plank to facilitate the transfer of *Dominator's* crew. Margo returned from below deck, carrying a barrel.

"We found oil, Admiral," she called out.

"Spread it on the deck but be careful. We don't want it lit just yet. I need two volunteers. One to steer *Dominator*, the other to light the oil right before impact."

"I volunteer," said Margo, "but we'll need someone to set the sails for us."

"I'm well aware. I'll get a few men from *Fearless* to do that, but then you're on your own."

"And our target?"

Danica waved her over, pointing to the south. "Those cogs are your target. Even if you can set one of them alight, it'll be worth it. You'll need to get out of your armour before you go unless you fancy sinking to the sea floor."

Grace rushed across the deck. "Did I hear you're looking for volunteers?"

"Are you sure you're up to it?"

"Working a tiller doesn't sound too strenuous."

"It's likely not," said Danica, "but you're not going down with the ship; that means you'll need to swim."

"I'll manage it, Admiral."

"Very well. Margo, you'll be in charge. Get that oil into place as quickly as you can. The crewmen will set the sails, then use the boat from the *Fearless* to evacuate. After that, you're on your own."

"Any advice?" asked Grace.

"Yes. Don't light the fire until you're almost touching the enemy. We don't want the flames spreading to our own ships."

Danica stood there waiting, something that was not easy for her to do.

Anya finally reported all was ready. "Orders, Admiral?"

"Remove the boarding planks and stand by on sails. We're going to give the *Illustrious* a hand. Once the crew sets the sails on *Dominator*, have them row back to us; we won't be going far."

"Aye, Admiral."

With the planks raised, the *Fearless* now floated free. Men scrambled up the mast, letting down the canvas. The wind, still coming from the north, filled them quickly, and the ship moved forward.

"Stand by on the arbalest," called out Anya.

Danica turned aft, watching as the *Dominator's* sails unfurled and the ship moved away, albeit at a much slower pace than her own flagship. Would her plan work?

The release of *Fearless's* arbalest interrupted her thoughts. The sound of fighting drifted towards them, proof Zivka's ship had engaged with the enemy. However, instead of waiting for the coming attack, the Halvarians launched an assault of their own. Imperial warriors now pushed across the boarding ramps, eager to take the fight to the *Illustrious*.

The arbalest bolt slammed into the Halvarian's hull, and the *Fearless* winched themselves closer. A woman stood on the *Conqueror's* aft deck, her hands working magic as a streak of flame flew across the water, striking one of the yardarms of the *Fearless* and setting it ablaze.

Crew members rushed to fill buckets with water, but a quicker solution was required. "Cut it loose," shouted Danica, "before the rigging catches."

Axes chopped down, freeing the ropes, and then the yardarm crashed to the deck, splintering the railing on both sides of the ship, the sudden impact extinguishing the fire.

"Crossbows!" Danica called out as another flame shot overhead.

One of her knights, nimble of foot, ran across the downed yardarm, for one end had struck the *Conqueror's* railing and become lodged in place. She landed mid-deck, sword at the ready, only to be hit by yet another streak of flame, this time from the bow of the Halvarian ship.

A smattering of bolts flew from *Fearless*, directed at the Fire Mage on the aft deck, but the woman ducked below the railing.

Danica sheathed her sword and rushed onto the yardarm, using her outstretched arms to help keep her balance. Her hands instinctively drew her twin daggers as soon as she was across, and then she hit the deck and rolled, avoiding another streak of flame that splashed against the railing.

The second Fire Mage stood in the sterncastle, his hands conjuring more flames. Danica jumped to her feet, rushing towards him, ignoring the crewmen scrambling around her. Heat brushed past her face as another blast came her way. She took the steps two at a time, launching herself at the fellow. Hit halfway through his casting, she drove him to the deck, falling atop him. Her daggers punched out, piercing his chest and sending blood spraying upwards. The body went limp beneath her, and she rose, drawn by the sounds of feet running towards her.

Two Halvarian warriors approached, Imperial troops, if their armour was any indication. The first struck out with an axe, a high swing she easily avoided, then she stepped in close, driving a dagger into an arm. His comrade, likely more experienced, stabbed out, but the blade tip scraped off her breastplate.

She pivoted, striking out with her second dagger and did no damage, but it drove him backwards. In his rush to avoid another attack, he tripped on the steps, tumbling down them to lie still on the deck below.

Danica threw up her visor to get a better view of the fight. Six Temple Knights had followed her example and were now securing the main deck of the *Conqueror*. Another group, still on the *Fearless*, dropped a boarding plank and were preparing to rush to their aid.

She looked to the *Illustrious*; the enemy had initially gained the main deck but had been driven back across their ramps. The presence of Temple Knights aboard their own vessel caused many of the Halvarians to surrender their weapons.

Though the battle still raged around them, her knights had done well. Danica moved to the top step, ready to join them, but a strike from behind almost toppled her from her perch.

As she fell forward, she had the presence of mind to grab the railing. Quick as she could, she twisted, turning around to face her attacker. The impressively tall fellow was encased in an immaculate mail suit, save his head, exposing his neatly trimmed beard and hair.

"So," he snarled. "We meet at last." He muttered something else, and his blade ignited.

Danica used the delay to move away from the steps, tightly gripping her daggers as she watched for any signs of further casting.

"This will be an absolute pleasure," the mage continued. "For too long, you've interfered in the empire's affairs. It's time you pay the price."

"You have the advantage of me," she said, trying to buy some time. "Might I know the name of the man determined to vanquish me?"

"Gallio," he replied. "Gallio Sartellian." He smiled, which only made him look more menacing.

"I'm—"

"I know exactly who you are, Admiral. Now, prepare to die."

She didn't wait, charging him instead to get in close where she could use her daggers to maximum effect. This was no dance of blades but a sudden rush with twin daggers of destruction stabbing out in rapid succession. Her first attack scraped off his breastplate, the second off his arm, but her third struck his gorget before sliding upwards into his chin. Danica drove it forward with all her strength and had the satisfaction of feeling it sink in to the hilt. Gallio's eyes opened wide for only a moment before the light went out of them, and he fell to the deck with a thud, pulling the dagger from her grasp.

A hand grabbed her arm, and she wheeled around only to see Anya. "The ship is ours, Admiral." She peered down at the body. "Who's that?"

"A Fire Mage by the name of Gallio Sartellian. Does that mean anything to you?"

"Aren't the Sartellians found across the courts of the Petty Kingdoms?"

"It appears they, like the Stormwinds, have connections within the empire. Remind me to bring this to the commander's attention."

"Of course, Admiral, but shouldn't we see to the fleet first?"

Danica looked out across the water, trying to make sense of the confusion. Vessels were scattered everywhere, making any assessment difficult. It took a moment to find *Dominator*. She was heading south, towards the cogs, her timbers not yet alight. Beyond her, a couple of Temple ships fought over an Imperial warship. More lay beyond, although thanks to the intervening ships, she could see little other than masts.

"Disable *Conqueror*," said the admiral, "then inform *Illustrious* we'll be turning about. It's time we found that Halvarian flagship."

38

THE BATTLE CONTINUES

SUMMER 1103 SR

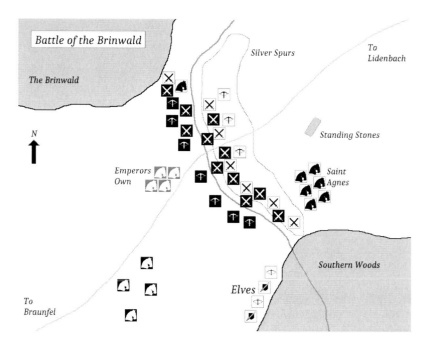

The Emperor's Own began their advance, heading directly for the centre of the Arnsfeld line, which was already overwhelmed, their line cut into small pockets of resistance. All that remained was to deal the death blow.

Horns sounded, and then the finest warriors in the Halvarian Empire crested the hill, pushing aside their provincial troops, ready to bring the king's army to its knees.

Charlaine spotted the banner of Arak Thorn, proudly waving amidst the empire's elite warriors. Had she the ability, she would've ordered her Temple Knights to counter the charge, but here, cut off from her command, she could do little but watch. The noise of battle drowned out all else as her footmen strove to hold on to their tenuous position.

A Halvarian horseman broke through, then another, and Charlaine rushed forward to stem the attack. She struck out, slicing across a breast-plate, but the thick armour protected the rider. An axe crashed against her sword arm, numbing it and knocking her blade aside. Only years of training enabled her to keep hold of it, but her attacker wasn't finished, raising his weapon for a heavier blow.

She flinched, expecting the attack, but it never came. Instead, a roar erupted as the man's horse was flung to the side, its rider crushed beneath its weight.

Charlaine stared in disbelief as a massive bear stood on its hind legs, letting out a roar that shook the very air. It lumbered past, swatting aside warriors as if they were gnats. She shook her arm to get feeling back in it, then manoeuvred Stormcloud to follow in the great bear's wake.

Marlena stood in the stirrups, raising her sword on high, the other captains mimicking her actions. Now was the time for action before it was too late.

Three hundred Temple Knights advanced. They started at a trot, but as they closed the distance, their speed increased, the ground shaking with the weight of their hooves.

Hitting the southern end of the Halvarian line, they cleaved through the Imperial troops who'd gained the heights. The clash was brief, the sisters continuing down the hill, leaving the enemy's blood flowing into the stream.

With nothing standing in their way, the Temple Knights rode through the enemy line into the field to the south. At the sight of their ferocity, the remaining Halvarian cavalry, already weakened by the stubborn resistance of the Elves, turned and fled.

Marlena paid them no heed, instead tearing around the bottom of the legion and coming up in its rear. Upon seeing the advance, the Elves of Mythanos moved out of the woods, forming into a line of their own, their deadly Elven Bows taking up positions behind their armoured foot.

. . .

Knowing nothing of the events to the south, Charlaine focused on following the strange beast tearing through the Emperor's Own. Horns sounded behind her, and she glanced back to spot knights in brown surcoats coming to the rescue. The remaining brothers of Saint Mathew cut through the surrounding provincials and now spread out, engaging the Emperor's Own.

The bear slashed out, its claws digging through a breastplate with little effort. Someone tried to slice the beast, but it caught the man's arm in its jaws and clamped down. Blood spurted over rough fur, and the limb snapped loose, falling to the ground.

A spear jab took the thing in the chest, but the beast snapped off the tip, knocking its wielder off balance. The bear's roar of pain cut through the din of battle, and then the creature pitched forward, its lifeblood flowing from its wound.

Those around it backed up, fearful lest it be some sort of ruse. Charlaine watched as the bear glowed slightly, the fur shimmering before the entire thing shrank, becoming the inert form of Orlina Day.

Brown-clad knights rode past her, driving farther into the ranks of the Emperor's Own. Now out of the fray, Charlaine dismounted and knelt to examine the old woman. Her breath came faintly, her body bleeding from her wounded chest, yet her eyes remained clear.

"It is done," said Orlina. "You defeated the empire. Now finish the job."

"They are retreating," replied Charlaine. "The battle is over."

Orlina grabbed her arm, pulling her closer. "You must not let their leader escape, or they will be back."

A horse came alongside them, and Charlaine looked up to see Brother Gatan. "We have them surrounded, Commander."

"I don't understand. How?"

"Your Temple Knights broke through in the south, and even now, they are pressing in from the rear. There's also the matter of the men in green and silver cutting off the road."

"They are Elves," said Orlina, her breath rasping.

"Elves? Surely not?"

"Do I look like I jest?"

He noticed the blood staining the Earth Mage's chest. "You're wounded," he said, dismounting. "Let me see if I can stem the flow of blood."

"You're wounded yourself," said Charlaine.

"Few are not this day. Resume command of the battle, Commander, and I shall see to the care of this woman."

Charlaine climbed back into the saddle and looked around. The provincials had thrown down their weapons and were surrendering in droves, but more than a hundred Emperor's Own remained, half of them now afoot, clustered into a tight group, and while there was a lull in the battle, they clearly expected to fight on.

Charlaine rode forward, placing herself between her own army and what remained of the empire's finest.

"Surrender," she called out. "There is no need for further bloodshed this day."

She spotted movement amongst the enemy, and then someone wearing a winged helm rode forward and removed it, exposing a blood-soaked face beneath. "The Emperor's Own does not surrender!"

"Would you rather I bring up our crossbows and finish you off?"

"Only a Temple Knight would eschew the honour of the melee."

"Do not speak to me of honour," said Charlaine. "Honour didn't bring you here—greed did. Your emperor covets the land of others. That is no noble cause."

"It is our destiny to rule over the entire Continent. You may have defeated us here, but your precious kingdom will still fall." He smiled, and something in his manner alarmed her. Even in the face of certain death, he appeared content, as if more were at play here. Her thoughts turned to Danica, and she wondered if the admiral had suffered a loss.

"Brother Gatan," she called out. "Have the crossbows form up. Any man who refuses to throw down their arms is a fair target." She turned to the Halvarian commander. "I assume you are Arak Thorn, Commander-General of this legion?"

He sat up even straighter. "Yes, I have that honour. And who might you be?"

"Charlaine deShandria, Regional Commander of the Temple Knights of Saint Agnes."

His face suddenly paled. At first, Charlaine assumed he recognized her name, but then he slumped forward in the saddle. The man to his left raised his visor even as Arak Thorn fell, lifeless, from the saddle.

"My apologies, Commander. The commander-general exceeded his authority by invading this land. As his second-in-command, my duty is to assume command of this legion. In my new capacity as acting commander-general, I humbly ask for a truce."

"A truce? To what end?"

"Should you agree, what remains of our legion will return to Halvarian soil. I, in turn, can give you my solemn promise the empire's army will not return."

"You don't have the authority to speak for your emperor," said Charlaine.

"True, but my death here accomplishes nothing. Let us end this conflict."

"And why should I trust you?"

"What have you got to lose? At the very least, you avoid further bloodshed, or is peace not the ultimate goal of your order?"

Charlaine mulled it over. If they'd destroyed the fleet, she must return to Lidenbach with all haste, yet the continued resistance of the Halvarians here made that difficult.

"I will allow you to retreat, provided you agree to lay down your arms. As a gesture of goodwill, we shall permit you to keep your armour and mounts."

"To this, I humbly agree," the fellow replied.

"Might I know your name, General, so that I can inform my superiors?"

"Captain-General Malik Thorn."

"Thorn?"

"Yes, Commander. The commander-general was my father."

"And you killed him?"

Malik shrugged. "What else was I to do? He disobeyed orders and brought the empire to the brink of war. As such, he got precisely what he deserved."

"And you, as a consequence, became the new commander-general."

He smiled. "I see you understand how the empire works."

"And you can guarantee your men will obey your orders?"

"Of course, providing you promise us protection from any reprisals?"

"Most certainly."

He nodded to his men, and they began divesting themselves of weapons.

All the Temple Captains gathered around a fire, including Brother Gatan, who'd assumed the position upon his superior's demise.

"So much for the vaunted Emperor's Own," said Marlena. "What I don't understand, is why they didn't fight to the end? Aren't they fanatics?"

"No more so than us," replied Charlaine. "But this wasn't about honour or bravery; it was about power. Malik Thorn killed his father to take command of the legion, an action I can only assume their emperor will approve. It also allowed the empire to save face."

"Save face?" said Marlena. "How?"

"He blamed the entire attack on a superior who overstepped the bounds of his authority, thus absolving the emperor of any guilt in the matter."

"We all know their armies don't move without the emperor's say-so."

"There's a world of difference between knowing and proving."

"So, what happens now?" asked Marlena.

"Some of us escort the Halvarians across the river while the rest ride for Lidenbach."

"Why the rush?"

"The Halvarians are not trustworthy," replied Charlaine, "and are not above taking whatever methods they deem necessary to achieve their objectives. I think they knew we'd make a stand and hoped to cut us off from behind."

"Surely you're not suggesting they knew about all our preparations?"

"Likely not, but the empire likes to ensure their success wherever they go. I suspect they had several contingency plans."

"Such as?"

"A landing by sea, for one. Have we any news from our fleet?"

"I'm afraid not," said Bernelle. "Could they have been defeated?"

"Anything's possible, but even if they weren't, that still leaves Lord Corbin and a ship full of Halvarians in the capital. Who knows what mischief they could get into?"

"How many companies shall ride for the capital?"

"I'll take two. That should be sufficient to deal with the men aboard *Conqueror*."

"You're assuming they didn't send reinforcements," offered Brother Gatan. "You may return to find the place under the empire's rule."

"What do you suggest instead?"

"Take all the Temple Knights, my own included."

"Will that leave enough warriors to escort the Halvarians back to their territory?"

"I think so," replied the Mathewite. "Don't forget. We disarmed them."

Charlaine nodded. "Very well. I'll take your company and those of Bernelle, Marlena, and Florence. The rest can assist in the relief of Braunfel Keep."

"Are you sure you won't take more?"

"I doubt another company or two would make much of a difference, and I don't want to slow us down by the need for a supply line. It will be a long ride, and we must complete it as quickly as possible."

"What of our losses?" asked Marlena.

"Replace them with sisters from the remaining companies. We'll sort out more permanent assignments once we return to Lidenbach." She looked around. "I know you're all tired, and I hate to be the bearer of bad news, but there's more to do. Our success here will all be undone if Lord Corbin has seized the Throne in our absence. Get some food into your charges and water the horses. We need to be on the road as soon as possible. Now, off you go, all except for Captain Marlena. I want a word."

They returned to their companies, spurred on by the urgency in Charlaine's voice.

"What is it?" asked Marlena.

"Were you the one who ordered the charge?"

"I was. You told me I'd know when it was the right moment. Should I have done otherwise?"

"No. You did well. I just wanted to congratulate you. That charge of yours was the attack that broke the empire."

"Hardly that."

"It was decisive."

"I couldn't have done it without the other captains."

"Also true, but I shall write to the Antonine of your actions. Such initiative is a rare thing."

"Thank you, Commander. I appreciate your words of encouragement."

"You have a bright future ahead of you, Marlena. I'm sure you'll flourish in your next command."

"My next command? Am I not to return to service as your aide?"

"Much as I'd like that, you're too valuable an asset to our order. You'll do well as a Temple Captain, and who knows, perhaps one day you'll even make Temple Commander? You certainly deserve it."

"But who is to act as your aide?"

"I'll manage well enough now we don't have an invasion to deal with."

"I might remind you we still don't know the fate of our fleet."

Charlaine smiled. "Don't we? I know Danica, and she's not the sort to give up easily. If she found herself up against the might of the Halvarian Navy, she wouldn't go down without a fight."

"How can you be so callous about it?"

"Callous? Nonsense. I have faith that she will win through. Of course, they may still be fighting even as we speak, but the end result will be a victory. Of that, I'm certain."

"I wish I had your faith," said Marlena. "The Saints truly do guide you."

"No more so than you. And it's not faith in the Saints that wins through in the end; it's faith in our friends."

"Words to live by."

"I'm glad you understand. Now, see to your new company. They need guidance."

"My new company? Wasn't that temporary?"

"Someone needs to take over from Florence," said Charlaine, "and you're more than deserving of that honour. As regional commander, I'm making it official. As soon as we get back to Lidenbach, I'll send confirmation to the Antonine."

. . .

Charlaine sat atop Stormcloud, watching her Temple Knights ride past, when she spotted a familiar horse.

"Your Highness," she said. "I thought you'd be returning to Braunfel."

"I considered it," the princess replied, "but my duty to the king takes precedence. I hear you're marching for the capital?"

"We are?"

"May I accompany you?"

"It will be a hard ride," said Charlaine, "and we can't afford to wait for stragglers."

"Then I shall forgive you if you fall behind."

"In that case, perhaps you'd care to join me at the head of the column?"

"I'd be delighted."

They trotted farther up the road to take their place.

"You did remarkably well today," said Rebecca. "My father will be most pleased. Tell me, why did you command and not the Grand Master of the Silver Spurs? Surely he had seniority?"

"Perhaps, but I had the authorization of your father to command the army."

"And why would he do that?"

"He felt my previous experience battling the Halvarians would prove advantageous."

"And so it did," said Rebecca.

"The battle was close, Highness, far closer than I hoped, if truth be told. One wrong move and it could easily have spelled the end of us."

"Yet the Battle of Braunfel will now be remembered as one of our greatest victories."

"I only hope that when the story is retold, they give credit to Orlina Day and the Elves. Without their intervention, we wouldn't have stood a ghost of a chance."

"Now you're being modest. Accept the acclaim, Commander. You well deserve it."

"I do not serve the order to receive accolades. I do it to help others live better lives."

Rebecca glanced over her shoulder but could no longer see the Army of Arnsfeld. "There are some who would gladly take the credit for you."

"No one in my order, of that, I'm sure."

"I referred to the barons or perhaps even the grand master. He's always been one to tout his accomplishments."

"I'm afraid the grand master is no longer with us. He died leading the Silver Spurs."

"I'm sorry to hear that. Did he die well?"

"You would need to ask the men with whom he served. I was too busy trying not to be overwhelmed by Halvarians. If you want to know who was really responsible for winning this battle, talk to Temple Captain Marlena. She led the charge that broke the enemy's back."

"It appears your entire order is blessed with exceptional leaders. Perhaps you could teach my father's army a thing or two about such things?"

They rode on in silence for a little while, then Charlaine led the column off the road and north towards the coast.

"Where are we going?" asked Rebecca.

"Unless I miss my guess, the empire landed men somewhere along this coastline."

"To what end?"

"I would have thought to take us from behind, but since that didn't happen, it's more likely they intended to march to Lidenbach."

"But if that's true, it makes getting back to the capital even more urgent."

"A visit to the coast will give us some indication of whether or not they landed successfully. After all, you can't simply beach a few hundred men and not leave some sign."

39

GLORIOUS

SUMMER 1103 SR

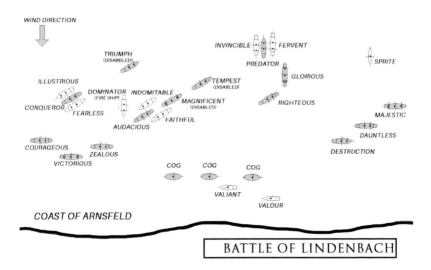

WIND DIRECTION

INVINCIBLE ◆ FERVENT

TRIUMPH
(DISABLED)

PREDATOR

SPRITE

GLORIOUS

ILLUSTRIOUS

TEMPEST
(DISABLED)

DOMINATOR   INDOMITABLE
(FIRE SHIP)

RIGHTEOUS

CONQUEROR

MAGNIFICENT
(DISABLED)

FEARLESS

FAITHFUL

MAJESTIC

AUDACIOUS

DAUNTLESS

COURAGEOUS

DESTRUCTION

ZEALOUS

VICTORIOUS

COG   COG   COG

VALIANT

VALOUR

COAST OF ARNSFELD

BATTLE OF LINDENBACH

The *Conqueror* fell behind, and the *Fearless* turned east, the deck pitching to starboard as the wind threatened to pull her over.

Danica clung to the railing, staring at the surrounding battle. The *Dominator* was smoking now, and Grace and Margo braced for impact as the vessel struck the side of one of the massive cogs. Beyond that, another ship was alight. Presumably, the *Valiant* or *Valour* had used their flaming bolts to some success.

The battle was no longer under her control. Instead, she must rely on the fortitude and courage of her sister knights and their brave crews.

Anya appeared at her side. "We're being pursued, Admiral."

The Halvarian ships were on the move, and one similar to hers now followed them. Just south were two more, including a three-master. In front of her, the *Indomitable* was in trouble, enemy warriors swarming her deck. If she turned about to face the threat from the rear, she condemned one of her own to capture or destruction.

"Orders, Admiral?"

She resigned herself to the necessity of turning about once more, but then *Illustrious* altered course, crossing the bow of the Imperial ship and preventing any further pursuit. "Continue on to *Indomitable* and prepare to board. Any sign of the *Glorious*?"

"Not at the moment, but something's burning." She pointed to a trail of smoke to the east. "Unfortunately, there's no way to tell if it's ours or theirs."

Danica fought down her panic. Everything was a jumble of masts, making identification difficult, if not impossible. Then she caught sight of a flag atop the burning ship, the unmistakable waves of Saint Agnes. One of her ships burned, but she couldn't tell which. Moments later, the bow of a Halvarian warship came around the hull of a disabled vessel, revealing the enemy flagship.

The upper decks of the *Glorious* were awash with gold, its masts topped with banners proclaiming it the glory of the Halvarian Empire. Even from this range, she could see the warriors packed in aboard its deck, ready to bring death to their enemies.

"We're coming alongside the *Indomitable* now," said Anya. "Shall we board?"

"No. They need to fend for themselves. We must get to the *Glorious* before she wreaks havoc with any more of our ships."

"There's another one behind it, Admiral."

"Then the *Fearless* must take on two. Are you up to the challenge, Captain?"

A look of indignation crossed Anya's face. "Need you ask?"

They sailed past *Indomitable,* the fighting on its deck intense. Just as they passed its bow, they spotted *Faithful* coming to the ship's rescue, boarding the Halvarian from the other side.

The knights aboard *Fearless* gave a cheer, the sound echoing across the water. Their elation was short-lived, for *Glorious* bore down on them, its forecastle brimming with archers, its main deck awash with armoured warriors. There was no longer time to worry about the fleet's other ships, for *Fearless* was about to be in the fight of its life.

. . .

Temple Knights crouched below the walls of the forecastle, crossbows loaded and ready. Danica stood behind the loaded arbalest, taking over the duty from the absent Margo. By mutual consent, they'd ignored the enemy archers, trusting in their armour to keep them safe. Being unarmoured, the crewmen elected to remain behind cover during the approach, at least as much as possible. Thankfully, the archers targeted the Temple Knights, seeing them as the bigger threat.

A storm of arrows flew across the water, many sinking into the forecastle. Danica stared up at the crow's nest, waiting for the lookout to signal the start of the attack. When the shout came, the Temple Knights rose, picked their targets, and loosed bolts.

Danica aimed at a gaudily dressed fellow directing the readying of a boarding ramp. The arbalest bolt hit true, taking him in the chest and punching clean through into another behind. The knights discarded their spent crossbows, drawing axes and hammers, far better weapons for penetrating heavy armour.

Danica led them down from the forecastle, rushing to the main deck as Halvarians swung across on ropes. They were easily dispatched, but the effort gave the enemy time to deploy the boarding ramps. Two spiked planks thudded into *Fearless*, and the initial wave of Imperial footmen crossed over.

The first rank had their legs cut out from beneath them, sending them tumbling into the sea. The next rank pushed on, forcing the Temple Knights back from the end of the plank. With a foothold established, more flowed across, their triumphant voices screaming out.

The fight grew into a massive melee, the scarlet tunics of the Temple Knights mixed in amongst the green of the empire. The men of the *Glorious* were well-armed and heavily armoured but lacked the discipline of the Temple Knights. Danica pulled her own small group back to the forecastle while Anya led hers to the stern. The enemy, outnumbering the knights by almost two to one, saw victory within their grasp.

Danica, now free of the melee, assessed the situation. The only thing preventing the complete loss of her flagship was that they commanded the fighting castles at either end. She dispatched two knights to hold the steps while the others took up their crossbows, loosing off bolts. The enemy archers aboard *Glorious* withheld their volleys, too concerned lest they hit their own men. Danica glanced up to see the lookout crawling out along at the yardarm of the *Fearless*, knife in hand. She realized his intention to cut loose the sail.

"Stand by," yelled Danica. "They're about to get the surprise of their lives."

A group of Halvarian warriors tried rushing up the stairs, but a well-placed volley tore into them, knocking them back into their companions.

Danica kept an eye on the lookout, watching the sail droop slightly when the knife cut through the first ropes. Then it fell to the deck, smothering both the men of the empire and their advance.

She screamed out in defiance, jumping over the forecastle, and landed amongst the bewildered enemy on the main deck, striking through the canvas and taking down two men.

Emboldened by her actions, the rest of the Temple Knights followed suit, rushing onto the deck in any manner they could. At least one went down, the victim of a bad jump, and then the fight began in earnest.

A familiar calm settled over Danica as she took the battle to the enemy. Years of practice had honed her skills, taught her body how to kill, and now it did so without conscious thought. The fury of the Temple Knights was released in full, pushing the Halvarians back in disarray.

The sisters fought their way to the mainmast only to find their fellow sisters advancing from the rear. They soon cleared the deck of all opposition and crossed onto the *Glorious*, their weapons dripping with blood. They were the vengeance of Agnes, come to punish those who would oppress!

Danica found herself caught amidst a press of men, but they retreated as her axe carved a path through them. A wall of flame suddenly shot up, burning several Halvarian footmen. She fell back, dodging the fire while looking for its source.

A woman stood on the aft deck, its height allowing her to pick her targets. Beside her, a man dressed in green-and-gold robes gesticulated, flames leaping from his fingertips as he picked out his target. The woman, less dramatically, pointed her finger at Danica and laughed as she released a spear of ice.

The admiral dove to the side, shards of ice bouncing off her armour. She quickly rose and rushed forward, jumping through the wall of fire.

The heat was tremendous, and she emerged on the other side to discover her the edges of her tabard aflame. Rather than take the time to extinguish the fire, she kept running, taking the steps to the sterncastle two at a time, reaching the top as the Fire Mage released his spell. Smoke billowed from his hands, obscuring her view and penetrating her visor. While her eyes watered and her throat constricted, her mind remained clear. The enemy stood before her, and nothing was going to stop her. She continued her charge, barrelling into the fellow and driving him to the deck. A quick thrust of her dagger finished him off, and then she rolled to one side as a streak of ice shot through the smoke.

She rose to a crouch. Her eyes still watered, making it difficult to see much of anything, but with the Fire Mage dead, the smoke cleared as the wind blew it away.

Danica rubbed her eyes, then launched her attack, swinging with all her strength, the axe sinking into the mage's bicep, slicing through and continuing into the woman's chest. The mage's agonized scream abruptly stopped as she fell to lie motionless.

More Temple Knights joined Danica as she seized control of the rudder, the ship's steersman having backed away at the point of a dagger. She turned them to starboard, the deck shuddering beneath her as the movement ripped the boarding planks from *Fearless*, and then a gap appeared between the two ships.

As her knights cut the lines to the sails, the crew of *Glorious* looked on in dismay. The ship now floated out of control, wallowing in the wind. Two others burned to the east, and then the wind shifted, pushing them closer. The sea is a harsh mistress, but death by fire is every sailor's worst nightmare. Most of the Halvarians tossed their weapons overboard and raised their hands in surrender, while two forced a man to his knees.

Danica handed over the tiller, then went down to the main deck. The warriors of Halvaria backed away, the fear on their faces evident for all to see.

"Who have we here?" she asked.

The fellow glared back. "I am Commander-General Yarel Parth, Admiral of the North Halvarian Fleet."

"Do you yield your ship?"

He spat in her face. Suddenly, a dagger took him from behind, driving into his neck. Danica looked on in shock as the body slumped forward.

"My name is Numaris Lechnor, Captain of the *Glorious*. On behalf of the emperor, I surrender this ship."

"And the rest of your fleet?"

"I cannot answer for them, and even if I could, how would I contact them?"

Danica was about to respond, then remembered the other ship following behind the *Glorious*. She looked aft, but the sterncastle blocked her view.

"You're looking for *Righteous*," said Captain Lechnor. "She likely fled when you cut down our flag."

His statement caused her to look up. A single knight perched in the lookout, the flag of the enemy still clutched in her hand. "Who is that?"

"Sister Braelynn," replied Anya. "She joined the crew in Vilnitz."

"We must make sure to thank her for her efforts. Without her quick thinking, we'd have yet another ship to face."

"Should we pursue, Admiral?"

Danica scanned the deck of the *Glorious*. "No, we've done enough. See to the wounded and send the signal to regroup away from those burning hulks."

Blood still stained the decks as Danica returned to her flagship. It was late in the day, and her surviving captains assembled aboard *Fearless*. She took in their faces—elation of a sort, yet also exhaustion.

"Losses?" she asked.

Anya looked up with sorrow in her eyes. "I'm afraid we lost the *Invincible* with all hands, Admiral, the result of fire. As for the rest of the fleet, losses were minimal. Twenty-seven knights were slain, with twelve more wounded. The crews fared better, losing only six, although twenty-three received wounds of varying degrees."

"And the enemy?"

"Not surprisingly," replied Vivian, "those who made it ashore surrendered once it was clear there would be no further landings."

"As to ships," continued Anya, "the enemy lost six vessels to fire, two of which were cogs, and we captured a further seven warships, although not without damage. It'll be some time before the empire can threaten anyone in these waters."

"Actually," added Vivian, "*Valour* captured the last cog, although what we'll do with her is anyone's guess. She's not the most seaworthy of ships. I recommend scuttling her."

"I will take it under advisement," said Danica. "How many actually escaped?"

"Only four. A tremendous victory by any measurement. Thanks to prisoners, we now have an accurate count of their fleet."

"Which is?"

"They sailed with fifteen warships, almost double our number, yet we were victorious."

"We're not done," said Danica. "We must get word of our victory to Commander Charlaine. I only hope she was able to hold off the empire."

"Should we sail back to Lidenbach?"

"We can't, at least not yet. We have wounded to deal with, not to mention prisoners. There's also the matter of finding enough men to crew all those captured ships. We must make efforts to keep our hard-won prizes. We're only one storm away from losing everything."

"Shall we send *Sprite* to Lidenbach to inform the king of our victory?"

"No. I want to learn how the land battle went before we worry about politics."

"And if the commander lost?" asked Vivian.

"We burn the captured ships and make sail for Lidenbach. Let's not get ahead of ourselves, though. Send knights ashore to keep an eye on the Braunfel road."

"There are already knights ashore, Admiral."

"For dealing with prisoners, but their hands are full at the moment." An idea struck Danica. "How many of those captured ships were provincials?"

"Only two," replied Anya. "Why?"

"See if you can recruit any of their crews to serve us, at least until we make port."

"Aye, Admiral."

The sun was low on the horizon as Danica stepped ashore. The wrecks of the burned ships drifted into the shallow waters before sinking, leaving their charred bones protruding out of the sea like some ancient creatures sent from the Underworld.

"The prisoners are over there," said Anya, pointing. "We estimate about two hundred made it to shore."

"It doesn't look like that many."

"That's because we only have seventy or so in custody. The others fled, likely more concerned they'd be put into slavery."

"Arnsfeld doesn't support slavery," said Danica, "but the Halvarians do, so much so they think others do the same.

"I considered sending out knights to search for them, but it would prove difficult without horses."

"But you set watches?"

"Yes," replied Anya. "That is the standard procedure."

"We made some progress in repairing the fleet, but it'll still be a couple of days before we can leave this place. In the meantime, I should like to send some people to seek out Commander Charlaine."

"I'll dispatch them first thing in the morning, Admiral." Anya nodded towards the prisoners. "What do we do with them?"

"That captured cog carried a lot of food; have some sent ashore. As for their ultimate fate, that's entirely in the hands of King Stefan. We'll load them back aboard ship, but I suspect that won't be for a few days. In the meantime, keep them fed and watered, and let's try not to let any more of them escape."

"Aye, Admiral."

"Anything else I should know about?"

"I sent a couple of scouts south," said Anya, "with orders to search the road and report back on anything unusual."

"And?"

"They returned with nothing to report."

"That's good," said Danica. "It means the enemy failed to march on Lidenbach."

"Wouldn't they be there by now?"

"And leave no trace on the road? I assume our people looked for any signs of traffic?"

"They did. As I said, there was nothing to report except a quiet road."

Danica pondered this information. There was the chance Charlaine was still fighting or had been forced to make a stand elsewhere, but the absence of any road traffic suggested otherwise.

"Have them check again come morning. As for me, I'll return to the *Fearless*. If there are any further developments, you can find me there."

"Aye, Admiral."

Danica made her way back to the boat, and she'd just sat down when a knight came running towards her.

"Admiral!"

"What is it?"

"Riders approaching from the south."

She jumped from the boat, her boots sinking into the sand. "Assemble what knights we already have ashore, then send word back to *Fearless*."

"Is that wise, Admiral? If the enemy is advancing up the road, we stand little chance of stopping them in our present state."

She stared south, waiting for signs of movement, and it didn't take long. The column rode four abreast, led by two individuals, while the tight formation left no doubt about their identity. She drew a deep breath, letting it out slowly. "Well, that's a relief."

Charlaine slowed the column, riding ahead to the beach where the burned-out boats lay. She soon caught sight of Danica and altered course.

"Well, Admiral. You have been busy!"

A smile came to her oldest friend. "Charlaine! Good to see you. I assume you were successful?"

"As were you, it seems. You remember the princess?"

"Yes, of course. Pleased to see you, Your Highness."

Rebecca nodded. "The kingdom has been doubly blessed this day. Is this all that remains of the empire's fleet?"

"A few escaped," replied Danica, "but I doubt they'll show their faces in these waters for some time."

"Perhaps you might do us a favour," said Charlaine.

"Name it."

"We need to return to Lidenbach, and your ships would be much faster and safer than going overland."

"I'm afraid my fleet is not in very good shape. I could send the *Sprite*, or perhaps the *Valiant* or *Valour*, but I need the rest to safeguard the damaged vessels. How many do you want to transport?"

"Only about ten. Your destruction of their fleet has lessened the chance of an assault, but I fear there may still be some subterfuge at work."

"Then *Valiant*, it is, and I shall be pleased to accompany you."

"Shouldn't you remain here with the fleet?"

"Lidenbach is only a short distance from here by sea. I can return well before this time tomorrow."

"How soon can we leave?"

Danica smiled. "It just so happens a boat is waiting. We'll be underway within the hour."

40

LIDENBACH

SUMMER 1103 SR

The *Valiant* slipped into Lidenbach Bay as the sun rose over the horizon, the light flooding the harbour and revealing the surprising presence of a Halvarian warship.

"That's not the *Conqueror*," said Charlaine.

"No," replied Danica. "We captured her during the battle. That one's a three-master, likely the *Majestic*. It fled when it looked like they were going to lose."

"What's it doing here?"

"That's a good question. Perhaps it came to collect Lord Corbin? Or to bring word of their defeat?"

"It's the height of arrogance to sail into a hostile bay in the middle of a war. Then again, it's not as if King Stefan has any men left to stop them."

"Vivian's taking us right up to the dock. No sense in delaying this any more than absolutely necessary."

"I see warriors aboard the empire's ship," noted Rebecca.

"Good," said Charlaine. "That means they haven't tried to storm the Royal Castle yet."

"Should we take action against the *Majestic*?" asked Danica. "*Valiant* still has some of those flaming bolts."

"No," said Charlaine, "not unless it proves troublesome. We don't want to risk setting the entire dock alight."

The ship slowed before bumping up against the wharf. The sailors leaped onto the dock and began tying off.

"Come on," said Charlaine. "There's no time to waste." She stepped onto the wooden planks, only for one of them to give way, leaving her ankle deep in water. "Ah, yes. I forgot about that. Watch your step."

Danica was soon ashore, helping her to extricate herself. Rebecca, meanwhile, took a more cautious approach, testing her footing before setting her full weight down on the wooden beams.

"We best leave the knights here," said Charlaine, "in case the Halvarians prove troublesome."

"Agreed," said Danica. "Though I must admit it looks very peaceful here. Perhaps we rushed back for nothing?"

"Hardly nothing," replied Rebecca. "Lord Corbin needs to atone for the actions of his kingdom. At the very least, we can tell my father of our victory."

"Victories," corrected Charlaine. "We won on land and at sea. As for the Halvarians, they're an empire, not a kingdom. Expecting them to apologize for anything is a waste of time. It wouldn't surprise me if their ship was here to kill their own envoy. It seems to be the way they reward failure."

They proceeded up the hill, past the shop that had been their first introduction to the streets of Lidenbach.

"It's strange how this all turned out," said Danica. "We arrived on the *Valiant* all those months ago, and now here we are, walking the exact same route."

"Yes," agreed Charlaine, "except we've turned the tables. Rather than fearing the Halvarians, we swept them aside. I know it won't last, but at least we have some breathing room. It'll be years before they try that again."

"You bought us time," said Rebecca, "but there is an old saying, 'the empire never forgets.' The next time they come, it will be in even greater numbers."

"Well," said Danica, "at least they won't have a fleet."

"Is it really so hard to build ships?"

"It is when we're out hunting them. I intend to enlarge our fleet and blockade their ports."

"And how will you pay for that?"

Danica smiled. "There's a lot of gold leaf on those ships we captured."

"Coins won't be the problem," said Charlaine, "manpower will. We lack the Temple Knights for that many, not to mention the men to sail them."

"Let me worry about that," said Danica. "I have a few ideas."

The road bent north, and the castle gate came into view. A solitary guard stood ready to challenge them, but upon recognizing the princess, he waved them through.

Charlaine halted, looking closely at the fellow. "Who commands here?" she asked.

"The king, of course. Who else?"

"Have you heard any disturbances?"

"Such as?"

"The sound of fighting, for example?"

"No," the guard replied. "All's been quiet. In fact, it's been that way since Lord Corbin left."

"Left?" said Charlaine. "When was that?"

"Yesterday evening, just after dusk. Why? Is it important?"

"It could be." She turned to her companions. "Come, we must hurry. You lead, Highness. You're more familiar with this place."

The guard wasn't finished. "Are you here for the gathering?"

"What gathering?" asked Rebecca.

"The king called on all important folk to gather in the great hall. Were you not told?"

"We only just arrived by boat."

"Then you best hurry. They've likely started by now."

They passed through the gate, making their way to the inner keep, where ten warriors stood in front of the double doors leading to the great hall.

"What's this now?" said Rebecca.

A burly guard bowed. "Merely an honour guard for His Majesty, Highness. Are you here for the announcement?"

"What announcement?"

The guard shrugged. "I'm afraid I don't know. Perhaps something about the war?" His gaze flicked to the two Temple Knights. "Did we win?"

Charlaine growled with impatience. "We wouldn't be here otherwise. May we enter?"

"Of course." He nodded to one of his men, who, in turn, opened a door.

They stepped into a room packed full of people. Someone had even gone to great lengths to hang banners from the walls. Many of the guests appeared to be in a festive mood.

"I don't understand," said Rebecca. "There's no way they could have heard of our success."

"I agree," added Charlaine. "It seems unlikely the *Majestic* would trumpet word of the empire's defeat." She paused and sniffed. "There's a strange smell in here."

"It's probably all the people," said Danica. "Their perfume is assaulting my nostrils."

"I don't see any sign of the king."

"He's likely still dressing," said Rebecca. "It takes considerable effort to don the official robes of state, and it's relatively early."

"Something's not right here," said Charlaine. "If they were celebrating our victory, I'd expect people to be cheering in the streets." She spotted a familiar face. "Master Skellen, I'm surprised to see you here."

The smith turned around, his cheeks breaking into a smile. "Commander Charlaine, this is a surprise. I thought you'd be in the field with the army."

"I just returned."

"Are things well?"

"Quite well, actually."

"She's being modest," said Rebecca. "We defeated the Halvarians on land and at sea."

All conversations around her stopped at her words, then came whispers as people repeated the news. It didn't take long for those gathered to break into spontaneous applause.

"This is marvellous, Highness," said Master Skellen. "Though I must admit to some surprise His Majesty didn't tell us himself. Is that why the king gathered us here in the great hall?"

"I couldn't say, but it seems unlikely."

Charlaine noted the confused look on the smith's face. "It appears before our arrival, no one knew of our victory."

"Perhaps he has another announcement?" offered the smith.

"When is he to speak?"

"We've been expecting him for some time. He's usually very punctual."

"I don't like this," said Charlaine. "It smells of a Halvarian plot."

"Let us seek out my father," replied Rebecca. "Come. I'll take you to him." She pushed her way through the crowd, exiting the room through a side door. They went down a short corridor, then she paused, knocking on a door. "Father? It's me, Rebecca. Are you in there?"

No answer came forth.

"I smell smoke," said Danica. "Stand back." She rammed her shoulder against the door, but it refused to budge. In desperation, she tried another approach, standing back slightly and kicking it open, the door banging against the wall.

A body lay on the floor, a pool of blood expanding beneath it. Rebecca rushed forward, and as she bent to examine it, she looked up in shock. "It's Lord Corbin!"

"Impossible," said Danica. "He left last night."

"The guard lied!" exclaimed Charlaine. "That can mean only one thing. He's working for the Halvarians."

"But why?" said Rebecca. "I don't understand."

"Corbin failed and had to pay the price."

"And my father?"

Danica pointed to where smoke seeped from under another door. "What's through there?"

"A study. My father often uses it to prepare himself for special occasions."

"There's light flickering behind it."

Charlaine rushed the door, and as she hit, it gave way immediately, sending her tumbling into the room. Flames licked the walls, and she leaped to her feet, trying to take in her surroundings before the smoke blinded her.

Two bodies were on the floor. One, most likely a servant, lay in a pool of blood, while the other still burned fiercely, a blackened crown upon his head. She staggered from the room, sucking in air, trying to clear her lungs.

"I'm afraid your father is dead," she announced. "Burned to death, by the look of it, and I'm pretty sure I know who was responsible."

Rebecca fell to her knees, tears coming to her eyes.

"I'll call the guards," said Danica.

"No, wait. General Falthorn controls them, and we suspect he's in the pay of the empire."

"Are you suggesting he did this?"

"No. Someone incinerated that body, yet the rest of the room was only recently set alight. There's only one thing that explains it."

"Fire Magic," said Danica. "I'm really beginning to dislike that entire branch of magic. Do you think he came aboard the *Majestic*?"

"No. He had to be here already, waiting to pounce. It explains how he got close to both Corbin and the king. I think it was Ashan."

"Where is he now?"

"I've seen enough Fire Magic these last few years to know this attack was recent. He's probably still in the inner keep somewhere."

"The great hall," said Rebecca, fighting back her grief. "He has to go through it to leave."

"But we would've passed him, surely?"

"There's a hidden door behind that mirror. It leads out into the great hall, behind the throne."

Charlaine moved swiftly, grasping the edge and swinging it to one side, revealing a small alcove and another door set into the stone. She grabbed the handle, pulling it towards her to peek out, but the back of the throne blocked her view of the great hall. She knew from previous visits it stood upon a raised platform, so she entered the room and stepped around the throne, searching for the Fire Mage.

Those closest noticed her sudden appearance, leading many to turn in expectation, which made it easier to spot Ashan pushing his way through the crowd to reach the exit.

"Stop that man!" she shouted, pointing at the fleeing mage.

Ashan stopped and turned, calling up his magic to conjure flames. Those around him immediately backed up, cowed by his display of raw power.

Charlaine, expecting him to launch a streak of fire towards her, was taken aback, when he instead turned to the row of banners. The fire surged from his hands, striking the wall and splashing against a banner which burst into flames. And then Charlaine remembered the strange smell—it had to be oil. With an escape this well-orchestrated, someone must have helped him.

The crowd panicked, pushing against the far wall. Charlaine leaped off the stage, rushing towards Ashan, but the fellow had a commanding lead and ran out the main doors, which slammed shut behind him.

Smoke began filling the room, drifting up to the high ceilings. The fire spread to another banner as Danica and Rebecca appeared from behind the throne.

"Get out!" the princess shouted. "The entire place is going up in flames!"

Charlaine reached the double doors, grabbing a handle and pulling, but as the door came open, a pile of furniture on the other side blocked her exit. Ashan, rushing towards the gatehouse, turned, casually sending out a spark that sank into the obstruction. A slight popping sound echoed through the courtyard before it burst into flames.

The soldiers in the courtyard lowered spears and rushed forward, not to attack but to prevent anyone from attempting to escape. Charlaine spotted General Falthorn watching from outside, a smug look on his face.

"Move aside," came a voice from behind. Boris Skellen and three others bearing an upside-down table burst through the crowd. They reached the doorway and used the table like a plough to push the flaming wood aside.

A spear jabbed forward, taking the smith in the arm, and he fell back. Charlaine rushed through the gap, her sword already in hand. Spears thrust out, one catching on her tabard, but she ignored it, trusting in her armour to keep her safe. She sliced out, digging into a hand, and the guard retreated.

Two more jabbed their spears at her, unwilling to close with the Temple Knight. She parried the first, but the second struck her pauldron, pushing her left arm back and putting her off balance. She fell to one knee as the spear came at her again.

Danica flew past, jumping between the two guards, her daggers slashing around in a frenzy, overwhelming the spearmen. The first fell, laying there unmoving, while the second dropped his weapon and raised his hands in surrender.

General Falthorn cursed, then turned and ran, his men forgotten. Without his presence, three surrendered, while the rest fled through the gatehouse as fast as their feet could carry them.

Charlaine rose, turning to Master Skellen. "Clear out that debris and get those people out of there. Danica, you're with me."

"That Fire Mage is long gone by now," replied Danica.

"I don't think so. Unless I miss my guess, he's making for the *Majestic*."

"I'll take charge here," called out Rebecca. "You go find my father's murderer."

They reached the docks as *Majestic* pushed off. Charlaine had thought to rush aboard, but the presence of so many Halvarian warriors made success unlikely. She halted, her breath coming in ragged gasps.

"They're getting away!" she shouted.

Danica came up beside her, struggling to speak. Instead, she pointed at the *Valiant*. They gathered what little strength remained and climbed aboard the Temple ship, collapsing on the deck.

Vivian had been watching the Halvarian vessel with great interest and knew exactly what was required. She called out orders, and the crew sprang into action, untying the ship and pushing her away from the dock.

Now free of her mooring, the *Majestic* unfurled her sails, and the great ship headed towards the sea, archers moving to the sterncastle to let loose with an ineffective volley.

Temple Knights rushed onto the deck, donning armour as the *Valiant* made headway. Charlaine, finding her breath, moved up to the bow, watching helplessly as the enemy vessel headed west.

"We'll catch her," said Danica.

"Let's hope so. Though I don't like the idea of closing with a Fire Mage again."

"We've fought them before."

"We have, but if he's capable of incinerating the king with his magic, he's more powerful than anyone else we've ever encountered."

"I don't understand this at all," said Danica. "Lord Corbin is one thing, he failed the empire, but the king? What could they possibly hope to achieve?"

"Who knows? Perhaps it's their way of proving that even in defeat, they still have teeth."

The *Valiant's* sails caught the wind, the ship moving towards the harbour entrance, picking up speed as it went.

"This won't be much of a race," said Danica. "The *Valiant* is a faster ship."

"It is, but this is no ordinary battle. I doubt the *Majestic* will turn around and allow us to board. Why would they when they can simply keep their distance while Ashan sends streaks of fire our way?"

"We still have some of those flame bolts Barbek gave us," said Danica. "Though admittedly, we need to be close if we want any chance of hitting them."

"So, we've lost them?"

"I've sailed the Great Northern Sea for some time now," said Danica, "and if there's one thing I've discovered, it's that the winds can be fickle. We'll maintain our position, bide our time, and hope the wind shifts to our advantage?"

"And if it does?"

"We'll be in for the fight of our lives."

Charlaine examined her tiny command. A dozen Temple Knights stood on *Valiant*, ready to answer the call when needed, but would that be enough? The *Majestic* was a much larger vessel, and though there was more to a ship than simply size, their main deck sat higher in the water than *Valiant's*. Boarding would be a difficult endeavour, and that didn't even take into consideration the warriors aboard the enemy ship.

"You took *Glorious*," she said. "What were its fighting men like?"

"They were heavily armoured," replied Danica, "much as knights are. It was a difficult fight, and we had the entire complement of *Fearless*. Why? Do you mean to board her?"

"It crossed my mind."

"We'd be better to stand off and use fire."

"Ordinarily, I'd agree, but I saw Ashan cast that streak of fire in the great hall. I suspect he has the advantage in terms of range, not to mention he can cast spells far faster than we can send bolts. An arbalest is a fine weapon but pales compared to a well-trained mage."

"Are you suggesting we recruit mages of our own?"

Charlaine chuckled. "It would certainly help, but I don't see anyone lining up to volunteer, do you?" She looked over at the Temple Knights. "You might as well let them rest. By the look of it, it'll be a long chase."

"You should get some rest yourself," said Danica. "No offence, but you look worn out."

"I could say the same for you. I suppose that's what comes from fighting off hordes of enemies."

"Aside from this fellow Ashan, do you think these troubles are really over?"

"I certainly hope so. I'd hate to do this all over again in a few years."

"So, we halted the empire?"

"I don't think they'll invade Arnsfeld again, if that's what you're asking. However, that doesn't mean they won't try elsewhere. This is only one of four kingdoms in the north that border the Empire of Halvaria. I imagine next time, they'll try crossing farther to the south and likely in much greater numbers. The prisoner Marlena and I captured across the border believed something called 'the great dream' was being readied."

"The great dream?" said Danica.

"Yes, the subjugation of the Petty Kingdoms."

"Which ones?"

"All of them."

"Is that even possible?"

"Not if I have anything to say about it."

"They would need an immense army," said Danica. "Possibly many."

"True," replied Charlaine, "but they've spent centuries conquering kingdoms. Imagine the population base they have to draw on. They could field dozens of legions if they put their minds to it. They only attacked with one this time. Next time, I doubt we'll be so lucky."

41

PURSUIT

SUMMER 1103 SR

Danica stood on *Valiant's* foredeck, a breeze caressing her hair. Off in the distance, the *Majestic* sailed as if it didn't have a care in the world. They'd followed it all morning, unable to catch up, but now, with the sun nearing its zenith, the wind looked like it was about to shift.

The first sign was the occasional breeze from the north, but as they marked midday, the sails slackened, forcing both ships to turn to the northwest, giving the *Valiant* the advantage. Rigged with a triangular sail, she could sail closer to the wind, whereas the square-rigged Halvarian had to tack, constantly adjusting its position relative to the wind to make headway.

"We're gaining on them," said Vivian. "It won't be long before we come within range of that mage of theirs. I want to get the knights back on deck, if it's all right with you, Admiral?"

"It's your ship, Captain," said Danica.

"Have you any suggestions about how we might deal with them?"

"I would avoid boarding at all costs. Their deck is higher than ours, giving them the advantage. They also significantly outnumber us."

"I thought of that," said Vivian, "but I'm more concerned with running into other ships. If you recall, four of them escaped that battle. The last thing we want is to run into them out here."

"What if we could slow them down?"

"How would we do that?"

"When the *Fearless* escorted the merchant ships, a trio of Halvarians attacked us. Sister Margo used one of those blunt-headed bolts to punch a hole into a ship's hull. It didn't sink them but was enough to convince them to slow down."

"Yes," said Vivian. "I heard of that. But the water was choppy, wasn't it? I doubt this weather would present us with a clean target."

"Not for the lower hull, no, but there are other, more vulnerable targets we could take advantage of."

"Such as?"

"The rudder. It's also convenient," said Danica, "especially considering we'd be approaching from their rear."

"I don't know. Hitting a hull is one thing; it's a large target, but a rudder? That requires a great degree of skill."

"Or very close range. I'm not saying it's not without its risks. We'd have to contend with archers on their sterncastle, not to mention that Fire Mage of theirs."

"What about putting fire to their sails? Those, at least, would be bigger targets, and we still have those fire bolts."

"I like the idea, Vivian. You may commence the attack at your discretion."

Sister Amelia came up from below. "Captain? We have a problem."

"What is it?" replied Vivian.

"We're leaking."

"You're damaged?" said Danica. "How did that happen?"

"We rammed a few boats during the battle," replied Vivian. "That likely weakened the hull. I'll go and take a look." She made her way to the hatch, disappearing below with Sister Amelia.

"That's unfortunate. We may have to call off the chase."

"Yes," said Charlaine, "and right when we were making progress. Assuming we sprang a leak, how much time do we have?"

"That depends on how badly damaged we are. All ships leak to a certain extent, but when the water comes in faster than we can get rid of it, there's a problem." Danica looked around, her gaze resting on the coast. "I wouldn't worry too much. Even if we were taking on water by the bucket load, there's still time to get to shore or at least climb into the ship's boat."

"That doesn't exactly fill me with confidence. It's bad enough we're about to go into battle. Now you're telling me we're essentially sinking?"

"Let's see what Vivian has to report. She knows this ship better than anyone."

Charlaine tried to keep busy by putting herself in the enemy's boots. Were she their captain, what would she do? The *Majestic* was a larger ship, likely with a corresponding increase in crewmen. It also employed a bigger fighting complement, along with a Fire Mage.

The more she thought about it, the more certain she became that the enemy's best option was to turn around and engage the *Valiant*. That being the case, why hadn't they already done so? Since leaving Lidenbach, they'd sailed west, turning northwest only when the wind shifted.

The only explanation she could think of was more enemy vessels were in the area. If that were the case, they'd turn on *Valiant* as soon as their comrades were in sight.

It was a sobering thought, and even worse, the wind coming from the west gave the incoming Halvarian ships the advantage. *Valiant* was a handy sailer, but they could only do so much with the wind against them. Would it be better to turn around now before they came into sight?

Captain Vivian returned. "Good news and bad, I'm afraid."

"Let's have it," said Danica.

"There's too much pressure on the bow. The hull is showing signs of fatigue."

"Fatigue?" said Charlaine.

"Yes. Some of the planks are split at the seams, letting water leak in."

"Can you repair it?"

"Eventually, but we'll need to steady the ship to do that, and sailing along at this speed isn't doing us any favours."

"And the good news?"

"There's still some time before we're forced to abandon ship."

"Very well," said Danica. "Raise the sails and lower the anchor." She turned to Charlaine. "I'm afraid we'll have to let them get away."

A shout from the crow's nest demanded their attention. "Sails to the west, Captain!"

They all leaned forward, straining to see what approached. It took some time before they could make out the masts, their sails full.

Charlaine stomach dropped as her worst fears came true. A trio of Halvarian ships were coming to the *Majestic's* aid, with *Valiant* unable to escape.

Danica remained calm, her eyes locked on the distant vessels. "I know those sails," she said. "It's *Fearless*. She's escorting the captured ships back to Lidenbach."

"Thank the Saints for that," said Vivian. "I worried we might have to fight with a wounded vessel."

"That could still be a possibility. Look!"

The *Majestic* turned about, setting an intercept course for the *Valiant*.

"Now they want to fight?" said Charlaine. "They could have saved us a headache and faced us this morning!"

"Knights to arms," called out Vivian, "and ready the arbalest."

"What kind of bolt?" asked Amelia.

"Fire. And aim for their sails. If we're to survive the encounter, it'll be by out-manoeuvring them."

The dance began as the Halvarian bore down on the smaller Temple ship. Danica watched the enemy like a hawk. "Those three-masted ships looked big from *Fearless*; from *Valiant*, they look positively gargantuan."

"They're making straight for us," said Vivian. "I think they intend to ram."

"That would be a big mistake. It would sink us, but they'd likely do irreparable damage to their own hull, and with *Fearless* coming from the west, well… you can imagine the outcome."

"I might remind you," said Charlaine, "the empire is not above making sacrifices to achieve their objectives."

"Yes, but to destroy one of their largest ships just to take out *Valiant*? That seems a little excessive to me."

"And killing Corbin wasn't?"

"All right," said Danica. "I concede the point. Captain, I'm afraid we need that sail of yours unfurled again."

To her credit, Vivian didn't complain. "Aye, Admiral." Once again, she gave the orders to get the ship moving.

Sister Amelia pulled the cover off the arbalest and wound it, pulling the cable back to its fullest extent. She reached into the box at its base, drawing forth a strange-looking bolt with a bulbous end.

"If I'm ever back in Reinwick," said Charlaine, "remind me to ask Barbek what's in those things."

"Better not to know," replied Danica. "In any case, it's probably a secret, and he'd have to kill you to keep it from getting out."

Sister Amelia looked shocked, while Charlaine stifled a giggle, then turned away to hide her mirth.

The *Majestic* sliced through the waves, the wind behind her, her fore-castle crammed with archers. They let loose with a volley of arrows, but the attack was premature and struck nought but seawater. A ballista bolt sailed forth, but they released too early as well, the wave action against the Halvarian ship causing it to fire at too steep an angle.

The Fire Mage was somewhere in amongst the archers and only gave away his position when a streak of flame flew across the water, striking *Valiant* amidships just in front of the mast, singeing the railing and sending a spatter of fire over the deck.

A crewman rushed forward, water bucket at the ready, sloshing it over the flames and extinguishing them with a hiss.

The *Valiant's* rudder turned hard to starboard, attempting to avoid the collision, but her movements were sluggish. The ship tilted to the left, and Charlaine struggled to hang on.

Unfazed, Danica stood, her feet firmly planted on the deck, her knees bent to account for the angle. "Loose as we come alongside!"

Amelia waited as the ship steadied. The *Majestic* lay portside, its crew straining to turn at the last minute to strike the Temple ship.

The arbalest made a thunk as the bolt released, sailing up at a steep angle, striking the *Majestic's* mainmast and breaking open to send flames all along the yardarm.

A cheer went up from *Valiant* as the fire spread to the sails, but then they were snuffed out as if an invisible hand swatted them away. Ashan apparently had more than one spell up his sleeve.

"He's good," said Danica as the enemy sailed past. "Bring *Valiant* back around, and we'll try again." She turned to Amelia. "Do you think you can hit the rudder?"

"Get me that close again, and I guarantee it."

The enemy kept heading south, ready to turn east as soon as it was out of *Valiant's* range. Charlaine knew the *Valiant* as a nimble ship, but the next manoeuvre surprised her. The deck tilted, then the vessel whipped around, the wind pushing the ship over at an obscene angle. Water rushed across her feet as the starboard railing briefly submerged before righting itself.

The *Majestic* was moving fast, the *Valiant* having lost speed with the turn. Amelia released the bolt, this time one with a regular tip. Danica would have preferred it was blunt like the one *Fearless* used to punch through a hull, but this one seemed blessed, for it struck the stern of the *Majestic*, close to the rudder, jamming it.

The Halvarian captain didn't realize his dilemma until they tried to turn to port. When the ship didn't respond, they peered over the stern, but from that angle, they couldn't see the problem.

Someone thought to reduce sail, but it was too late. The ship was in the shallows now, and the *Majestic*, with a deeper draft than the Temple ship, struck a submerged rock and jammed fast, sending men tumbling across the deck. The *Valiant* slowed, its crew watching as the enemy vessel began taking on water.

"Prepare the ship's boat," ordered Vivian. She looked at Danica. "Permission to rescue survivors, Admiral?"

"Granted."

Charlaine watched as the *Majestic* set its own boat into the water. A few men climbed into it, and then she spotted Ashan taking up an oar.

"There's that mage," she warned.

"Stop that boat," shouted Danica. "Take us in, Captain."

"Admiral?"

"Destroy it before the Fire Mage makes it ashore!"

The *Valiant* turned south, its sails straining as it picked up speed. Ashan's boat cleared the collision sight and was moving towards a sandy stretch of the coastline.

The *Valiant* advanced, its bow now heavy with water. Charlaine leaned over the railing, watching the enemy boat disappear as it passed beneath the bow, and then a sickening crunch followed, and the ship came to a sudden halt, almost tipping her overboard.

"Abandon ship," called out Vivian. "Get that boat into the water."

The crew knew their business, and it didn't take long before they were aboard and rowing to shore. Several Halvarian survivors floundered in the water, and the Temple boat assisted where it could. By the time they reached the beach, more than ten of the enemy were clinging to the sides in desperation.

The knights climbed out first, eager to take the Halvarians into custody. The crew of the *Valiant* took the boat back out to bring others to safety.

It was late afternoon when Rebecca arrived. She'd ridden out of the capital at the head of a company of men. She found Charlaine and Danica looking over a body as the *Fearless* dropped its anchor offshore.

"What have you there?" she called out.

"We found the body of Ashan, the Fire Mage," replied Charlaine.

"Drowned?"

"Well, crushed and then drowned. In the end, I suppose it amounts to the same thing."

"And your ship?"

"I'm afraid the *Valiant* is lost."

"Oh, I don't know," said Danica. "We might be able to repair her now the empire's not breathing down our necks."

"What of you?" asked Charlaine. "What brings you out here?"

"I was hoping to find General Falthorn. We had reports he was heading down the Braunfel road. Unfortunately, that wasn't the case."

"You would have had a better chance of catching him with horsemen."

"Agreed," said Rebecca, "but we sent all our cavalry to help stem the invasion." She dismounted, coming closer. "So much for Ashan. I don't understand why he would do such a thing? It's especially perplexing, considering his family."

"His family? I thought he was a mage of little prestige. He certainly gave me no indication of having connections."

"Little prestige? Did you not recognize his family name?"

"No," said Charlaine. "He never told me. Why? Who was he?"

"He's Ashan Sartellian. He's from one of the most powerful magical families on the Continent."

"Sartellian?" said Danica. "Hold on a moment. We met a Sartellian aboard the *Conqueror*. With all that's happened, I forgot to tell you."

"I know that name too," said Charlaine. "Larissa Stormwind mentioned it back at the court of Reinwick."

"Of course," said Rebecca. "The two families have very close ties. Didn't you know?"

"No, I didn't, but I shan't make that mistake again."

"You must warn the others," replied Danica.

"Others?" said the princess. "What others?"

"Colleagues of ours," offered Charlaine, "spread throughout the Continent. If the Sartellians are working closely with the empire, it puts them in the same basket as the Stormwinds."

"You think both families serve the emperor?"

"We already discovered collusion amongst the Stormwinds, and if the two families are as close as you infer, the Sartellians must also be involved."

"You'll have a hard time convincing the courts of the Petty Kingdoms of that," said Rebecca.

"Still, we must do what we can. What of Arnsfeld? Will you ban the presence of Sartellians at court?"

"I believe my husband will agree to that once he's aware of all that has transpired. The Stormwinds, too, if what you say is true." She considered her words for a moment. "My pardon, Commander. Of course you're telling the truth; you are a Temple Knight after all."

"My deepest condolences on the loss of your father," said Charlaine. "With all that has happened, we've had little time to consider the implications. You must be devastated."

"If truth be told, I've expected his death for some time now, although I thought it would be due to ill health rather than murder. I can only hope it was quick."

Charlaine said nothing on the matter. She'd read of people being burned by magic, which was said to be painful, not something she thought she should share with the princess. Instead, she turned to other topics. "What of the general?"

"He is a traitor, to be sure. I've sent word throughout the kingdom that he is to be arrested on sight. Once Handrik hears of it, he'll take a more active approach to finding him, but at the moment, there is only so much a princess can do."

"He didn't act alone. Those guards ran away too."

"The full extent of his treachery has yet to be determined, but we'll learn of it nonetheless. I shall avenge my father's death, no matter how long it takes. I assume we can count on your support in the coming months?"

"Of course, Highness."

"I wonder if you might leave your companies here in Arnsfeld? I understand some of them came from neighbouring realms?"

"They did, but a decision like that requires the permission of the grand mistress. I shall write to her about what has happened here, but I must warn you, it will be months before I receive a reply." She smiled apologetically. "In the meantime, it might be prudent to leave a couple of companies in Braunfel, if only to ensure no Halvarian stragglers create problems. I assume the rest of the king's army will return to their homes?"

"You'll need to ask my husband that, but I wouldn't bet on it. He has always been of the opinion a large army acts as a strong deterrent. The problem, however, is the cost. The barons can only shoulder so much of the expense." The princess looked around. "It appears there is little I can do here save to take some prisoners into custody. If you don't mind, I shall return to Lidenbach."

Danica looked out at the Temple ships. "Can I offer you and your men a ride? The *Fearless* has plenty of space."

"I should like that very much, thank you."

"I'll take care of it," said Vivian. "It's not as if I have a ship to worry about anymore."

Danica chuckled. "Don't worry. I'm sure I can find you another one without too much effort. Next time you want a bigger ship, though, just ask."

Vivian shook her head as she led the princess to the ship's boat, leaving Danica and Charlaine on the beach.

"Well?" said Danica. "Was it all worth it?"

"This wouldn't be the first time I considered the cost of peace, nor do I believe it will be the last. Our order doesn't seek to make war, but by the Saints, we won't stand by and see the rights of others trampled. So, to answer your question, yes, it was worth it. What do you think?"

"We asked a lot of our people, and they rewarded us with success. I just wish the price hadn't been so high."

"High? We inflicted far more casualties than we suffered."

"We did," agreed Danica, "but how many of those individuals would still be alive today if the Cunars had remained in Arnsfeld? Their withdrawal precipitated this war. How many more times must we pay the price for their treachery?"

42

CORONATION
AUTUMN 1103 SR

The Temple Knights of Saint Agnes stood rigid, their swords raised in salute as King Handrik led his queen from the Temple of Saint Mathew. A carriage waited at the bottom of the steps, guarded by Brother Gatan and three fellow knights.

The king paused as he reached the street, turning to face Charlaine. "You were instrumental in securing my kingdom," he said. "I thank you most heartily for your support. I promise you I will take great efforts to secure this realm from further Halvarian incursions."

"Now is hardly the place to speak of such things," replied Charlaine. "You've just been crowned, Your Majesty, and your people wait impatiently to celebrate your coronation."

"Yet I wouldn't be here today were it not for your efforts. Or perhaps I should say the kingdom wouldn't be here for me to rule? Either way, we owe you a great debt."

"There is no debt, sire. I merely did what my order demanded of me."

The king barked out a laugh. "I'm sure you did far more than they expected, but I'll honour your humility. And you…" He looked at Danica, who stood next to her commander. "Without the protection of your ships, they would have decimated our sea trade. Ask me anything as a boon, and I shall grant it if it is within my power."

"Might you consider building your own warships?"

"I've given it much consideration, but I think it a wiser investment to donate funds to yours, don't you? From this day forward, I will supply a yearly stipend to help defray your costs. I also offer you the unrestricted use of our harbour and permission to recruit crews."

"Your Majesty is most generous."

"I don't blame my predecessor for his mistakes, but I promise you, I shall not make the same errors. From this day forward, Arnsfeld will be strong in the face of Halvarian aggression."

"One day," said Charlaine, "the empire will attempt to return to your court, sire."

"They already tried, and I refused their overtures. I've also taken pains to spread word of what transpired within our borders, including their treachery at court. It will, I think, be many years before a vessel of theirs finds shelter in any Petty Kingdom."

"And the Fire Mage, Ashan Sartellian?"

"I shared word of his betrayal, but I fear the story fell on deaf ears. My neighbours still value the counsel of his family and are quick to blame everything on one lone individual. Fear not, however. I banned them from my court, along with the Stormwinds."

"Tell us," chimed in Rebecca. "How else can we show our gratitude, Commander?"

"The kingdom's safety is reward enough for me, Majesties."

The king nodded. "Well spoken. I trust we will see you up at the celebration?"

"Of course."

"Then I shall leave you to it." King Handrik continued to the carriage, waiting as the queen entered first, then stepped inside and closed the door.

Charlaine watched the carriage pull away before turning to her dearest friend. "The king is in a generous spirit."

"Yes," said Danica. "Much more so than Stefan when we first met him. Then again, the kingdom was under the threat of invasion at the time, which would sour anyone's mood. What do you suppose happens now?"

"We dismiss the Temple Knights and ready ourselves for the celebration. What else?"

"I was referring to the current state of affairs, not today's events. When will you send the companies back to Burgemont, Angvil, and Rudor?"

"I'll wait until the king is ready to replace them with his own men. I shouldn't like to leave this place weakened. What about you?"

"Me? What have I got to do with any of this?"

Charlaine laughed. "You're the admiral of the fleet, Danica. Are you sailing back to Temple Bay or remaining here?"

"Well, it seems that with Marlena now a captain, you might need some help from time to time. In any case, I'll leave a fleet here to keep an eye on the empire. We wouldn't want them trying to flex their muscles again."

"Do you intend to blockade their ports?"

"I'd love to, but we need to get those captured ships into operation first. At the moment, we're still a little short of sailors."

"Well, you'll always be welcome at the commandery."

"Speaking of which," said Danica, "I hear the Temple Knights of Saint Mathew made their increase in numbers more permanent?"

"They have, and they've promoted Brother Gatan to Temple Captain. A fitting reward, considering his role in the Battle of the Brinwald."

"Oh, is that what we're calling it now?"

"Yes," replied Charlaine. "It was Bethiel's idea."

"The Elf you told me about?"

"Indeed. Orlina Day convinced her to come and meet Arnsfeld's new king."

"And how does His Majesty feel about having an Elven city in the middle of his kingdom?" Danica's right eyebrow raised slightly. "Is it a city or a bunch of Elves living in the woods?"

"Orlina said it was a city unlike any I'd seen before, but she was very light on details. In any event, I believe Handrik will see the wisdom in an alliance, especially after the part they played halting the empire."

"You know, with the kingdom finally at peace, I might take it upon myself to do a little exploration."

"Exploration?"

"Yes," replied Danica. "You remember the ice floes I told you about up north?"

"You mean that place where you saw the unicorn whale?"

"That's the one. I want to return there with a trio of ships and map the area."

"A trio? Why three?"

"Only a precaution," said Danica, "in case of damage from the ice floe s. Care to join us?"

"No, thank you. I'm content to stay ashore for the foreseeable future. I'll leave all that excitement to you, but I'll expect a first-hand recounting of whatever you find up there."

"Agreed, although I wonder what you'll get up to while I'm gone. It's not as if there's much to demand your attention here."

"That's where you're wrong," replied Charlaine. "There's still the matter of corruption within the Church, especially with the Cunars' attempt to block our reinforcements. I fear it won't be long before they are emboldened to take more direct action against us, and when that happens, it could well spell the end of the Church as we know it."

EPILOGUE
AUTUMN 1103 SR

K aylene Gantzmann, Grand Mistress of the Temple Knights of Saint Agnes, entered the room, throwing her gloves onto her desk.

"The fools!" she hissed. "Have they no idea what they're doing?"

Her aide, Temple Captain Nicola, entered from the other door. "Trouble, Mistress?"

"I just returned from a meeting with the Matriarch of Saint Agnes."

"I'm well aware. I was the one who made the arrangements at your request. I assume it did not go well?"

"That's putting it mildly," said Kaylene. "The Council of Peers is in a frightful state, the orders squabbling amongst themselves over who has supremacy, and now the Patriarch of the Cunars is pushing to disband the other fighting orders." She slumped down into her seat, despair etched into her face. "I fear my time here will soon come to an end."

"Surely not," said Nicola. "You've served the order faithfully for years."

"Our matriarch is quickly coming to the conclusion that the time has come to consider my successor." She saw the look of shock on her aide. "Don't panic just yet. The process is extensive and will take months."

"Is there nothing we can do to stop this?"

"What would you have me do? Revolt against our own matriarch?"

"The Temple Knights are sworn to you, Mistress, not her."

"A fact of which I'm sure has not escaped her attention." She took a deep breath and looked around the room, stopping at the wooden model of a ship sitting on her shelf. She stood, moving towards it and taking it in hand, a smile breaking out.

Nicola noted her interest. "Isn't that the *Valiant*?"

"You know full well it is."

"How does that help us?"

"It is not the ship but those who sailed aboard her. I speak of our most celebrated member, Temple Commander Charlaine. If there is anyone who might be able to save the order, it's her. Send word for her to report to the Antonine."

"And the admiral? You know those two are thick as thieves."

The grand mistress winced. "Not your best analogy, to be sure, but you are correct. Summon hers too. Together, they might pull this off."

"This?" said Nicola. "You have a plan?"

"I do, but it will demand sacrifice. I only hope I'm not too late."

<<<<>>>>

PLEASE REVIEW TEMPLE COMMANDER

READ WARRIOR PRINCE

If you liked *Temple Commander* then *Servant of the Crown*, the first book in the *Heir to the Crown* series awaits.

START SERVANT OF THE CROWN

CAST OF CHARACTERS
PEOPLE AND PLACES

The Main Characters
Anya - Temple Knight, Captain of *Fearless*
Ashan - Kurathian, Fire Mage, court of King Stefan
Charlaine deShandria - Temple Commander of Saint Agnes
Danica Meer - Admiral, Temple Captain of Saint Agnes
Florence - Temple Captain, Arnsfeld
Grace - Temple Knight, *Fearless*
Marlena Falkenberg - Temple Knight of Saint Agnes, aide to Charlaine
Orlina Day - Sacred Mother of Tauril, Earth Mage, near Braunfel
Rebecca Stoltz- Princess of Arnsfeld, Daughter of Stefan
Stefan - King of Arnsfeld
Vivian - Temple Knight, assigned to *Valiant*
Zivka - Temple Knight, assigned to *Valiant*

Temple Knights of Saint Agnes
Grand Mistress
Kaylene Gantzmann - Head of the Temple Knights of Saint Agnes, the Antonine

Temple Commanders
Charlaine deShandria - Regional Commander, Arnsfeld
Nina - Arnsfeld

Temple Captains
Bernelle - Lidenbach
Danica Meer - Admiral of the Temple Fleet
Florence - served with Charlaine and Danica in Ilea, Arnsfeld
Giselle - Ilea, Commanded Charlaine and Danica in Ilea
Leona - Reinwick
Miranda - Lidenbach, served with Charlaine and Danica in Ilea
Nicola - Aide to the Grand Mistress, the Antonine

Temple Knights
Amelia - Assigned to *Valiant*
Anya - Captain of *Fearless*
Ava - Assigned to *Vanguard*

Braelynn - Assigned to *Fearless*
Celine - Assigned to *Valiant*
Enna - Lidenbach
Grace - Assigned to *Fearless*
Grazynia - Captain of *Vigilant*
Johanna - Lidenbach
Laurel - Captain of *Invincible*
Margo - Assigned to *Fearless*
Marlena Falkenberg - Aide to Charlaine, Lidenbach
Nadia - Captain of *Vanguard*
Octavia - Aide to Temple Captain Bernelle, Lidenbach
Samara - Assigned to Fearless
Teresa - Served with Charlaine and Danica in Ilea
Vivian - Assigned to *Valiant*
Zara - Assigned to *Fearless*
Zivka - Assigned to *Valiant*

HALVARIANS
Arak Thorn - Commander-general of an Imperial Legion
Aramar - Fire Mage, *Dominator*
Augustus Conwyn - Governor of Thansalay
Corbin - Envoy, Lidenbach
Douglas - Captain, *Dominator*
Hadmar - Aide to Captain Nargrun
Lucius - Servant to Captain Narak Juran
Malik Thorn - Son of Arak Thorn
Narak Juran - Captain, Fifth Company, Emperor's Own
Nargrun - Captain
Numaris Lechnor - Captain, *Glorious*
Yarel Parth - Admiral of the North Halvarian Fleet

LIDENBACH
Alpen - Owner, *Antoine*, a large cog
Ansel Dulworth - Merchant Captain, *Barlowe*
Ashan - Kurathian, Fire Mage, Court of King Stefan
Asmirius - Scholar, adviser to King Stefan
Bethiel - Elf Leader of Mythanos
Blasco Dorhaven - Captain, Temple Ship *Sprite*
Boris Skellen - Guild smith
Brendan Gantz - Crewman, *Valiant*
Elgar Booker - Captain, pirate ship *Sprite*

Gatan - Temple Knight of Saint Mathew
Jules Morel - Smith
Wallis Falthorn - General of the Royal Army of Arnsfeld

Arnsfeld

Austin Renholt - Baron of Agenhoff
Erskin Gerrit - Baron of Dubrow
Grier Burke - Sergeant, Braunfel
Guillermo Carvahlen - Captain, *Sapphire*
Handrik Sommer - Baron of Braunfel, Husband of Rebecca
Hugo - Knight of the Silver Spur
Kheymar Rudd - Grand Master, Knights of the Silver Spur
Luca Day- Grandson of Orlina Day
Nadine Ripley - Co-owner of the Cygnet, small merchant ship
Orlina Day - Sacred Mother of Tauril, Earth Mage
Randal Norwin - Baron of Kurtzenberg
Rebecca Stoltz- Princess of Arnsfeld, Daughter to King Stefan
Sandro Ripley - Co-owner of the *Cygnet*, small merchant ship
Stefan - King of Arnsfeld
Stormcloud - Charlaine's horse

Others

Akosia - Goddess of Water
Barbek Stoutarm - Dwarven smith, Korvoran
Elsbeth Fel - Sacred Mother of Akosia, Reinwick
Frederick Altenburg - Son of the Baron of Altenburg, Hadenfeld
Gallio Sartellion - Fire Mage in the employ of Halvaria
Gwalinor - Life Mage, Sea Elf, Ilea
Laldor Morningstone - Sailing master, *Vindicator*
Larissa Stormwind - Water Mage, Korvoran
Ludwig Altenburg - Son of Baron of Verfeld
Marcellus - Cunar Temple Captain
Tauril - Goddess of the Forest
Tomas deShandria - Master smith, father to Charlaine, Malburg
Wilfhelm Brondecker - Duke of Reinwick

Places

Petty Kingdoms

Abelard - Kingdom, Northern Coast
Andover - Kingdom, Northern Coast, birthplace of Danica
Angvil - Kingdom, south of Arnsfeld

Arnsfeld - Kingdom, Northern coast, adjacent to Halvaria
Burgemont - Kingdom, Northern Coast, east of Arnsfeld
Corassus - City State, Southern Coast of the Continent, home to the Holy Fleet
Erlingen - Duchy, south of Andover
Hadenfeld - Central Kingdom, birthplace of Charlaine
Ilea - Kingdom, Southern Coast
Langwal - Kingdom, Northern coast
Reinwick - Duchy, northern Petty Kingdom
Rudor - Kingdom, southeast of Arnsfeld
Talyria - Middle kingdom lying in the western reaches of the Continent

CITIES/TOWNS
Agenhoff - Town/Barony, Arnsfeld
Alantra - Capital, Calabria
Braunfel - Town/Barony, Arnsfeld
Brecken - Town/Barony, Arnsfeld
Dubrow - Town/Barony, Arnsfeld
Gossenveldt - City, Duchy of Reinwick
Korvoran - Capital city, Duchy of Reinwick
Kronberg - Town/Barony, Arnsfeld
Kurtzenberg - Town/Barony, Arnsfeld
Lidenbach - Port, Capital of Arnsfeld
Malburg - City, Hadenfeld
Meirshoff - Town/Barony, Arnsfeld
Mythanos - Hidden Elven city, Arnsfeld
Nausig - Town/Barony, Arnsfeld
Niederbeck - Town/Barony, Arnsfeld
Noordmacht - Small town, Northern coast of Halvaria
Thansalay - City, Northern coast of Halvaria
The Antonine - The Holy City, within the city of Reichendorf
Vilnitz - Major port, Burgemont

OTHER PLACES
Amity - Smallest of the Five Sisters Islands
Calabria - Kingdom, western coast of Shimmering Sea, occupied by Halvaria
Constance - One of the Five Sisters Islands
Cyrellia - Former Petty Kingdom subjugated by Halvaria in 1070 SR
Cape Maralan - Landmark, Burgemont
Great Northern Sea - North of the Petty Kingdoms

Halvaria - Large empire west of the Petty Kingdoms
Kouras - One of the Kurathian Islands
Kurathia - Series of Southern Islands ruled by princes
Patience - Largest of the Five Sisters Islands
Scattered Isles - Series of islands north of Halvaria
Shimmering Sea - Large sea, south of the Petty Kingdoms
Stillwater River - River separating Halvaria and Arnsfeld
Temple Bay - Home of the Temple Fleet, Island of Patience
Thansalay - City/Province of Halvaria
The Barking Hound - Inn between Braunfel and Lidenbach
The Brinwald - Heavy forest north of Braunfel
The Broken Oar - Tavern, Lidenbach
The Eyes - Two islands north of Langwal
The Five Sisters - A series of five islands, northeast of Reinwick
The Skrill - Tavern, Braunfel
Therengia(Old Kingdom) - Ancient kingdom, destroyed roughly 400 years ago

Battles
Battle of Alantra (1096 SR) - Sea Battle fought between Ilea/Holy fleet and Halvaria
Battle of Temple Bay (1097 SR) - Sea Battle fought between Halvaria and the Temple Fleet
Battle of the Braunfeld Brinwald (1103 SR) - Land Battle fought between Arnsfeld and Halvaria
Battle of Lidenbach (1103 SR) - Sea battle fought between Arnsfeld and Halvaria

The Church
Council of Peers - Ruling council of the Church of the Saints
Order of Saint Agnes - Protector of women
Order of Saint Ansgar - Internal investigators of the Church
Order of Saint Augustine - Guardians of the Holy Relics
Order of Saint Cunar - Primary warriors of the Church
Order of Saint Mathew - Protectors of the poor and sick
Order of Saint Ragnar - Dedicated to eradicating Death Magic
Temple Knight - Holy Warrior dedicated to one of the six military fighting orders of the Church
The Primus - Ultimate Church authority elected by the Council of Peers
Matriarch/Patriarch - The head of each of the six church orders and members of the Council of Peers

SHIPS

HALVARIAN SHIPS

Audacious - Imperial warship
Conqueror - Imperial warship
Courageous - Imperial warship
Dauntless - Imperial warship
Destruction - Provincial warship
Dominator - Provincial warship
Glorious - Three masted Imperial warship, Flagship of the North Halvarian
Leviathan - Large Halvarian merchant ship
Magnificent - Three masted Imperial warship
Majestic - Three masted Imperial warship
Predator - Provincial warship
Righteous - Imperial warship
Tempest - Imperial warship
Triumph - Provincial warship
Victorious - Three masted Imperial warship
Vindicator - Provincial warship
Zealous - Imperial warship

THE NORTHERN HOLY FLEET

Faithful - Large double-masted warship
Fearless - Large double-masted warship (Formerly *Devastator*), Temple Flagship
Fervent - Large double-masted warship
Furious - Large double-masted warship (Formerly *Annihilator*)
Illustrious - Double-masted warship (Formerly *Vindicator*)
Indomitable - Double-masted warship (Formerly *Terror*)
Invincible - Double-masted warship (Captured Halvarian ship of same name)
Sprite - Captured pirate ship taken into service with the Temple Fleet
Valiant - Flagship of the Northern Fleet
Valour - Sister ship to *Valiant*
Vanguard - Fast warship of the Order of Saint Agnes
Vigilant - Small Warship of the Order of Saint Agnes

OTHER SHIPS

Antoine - Merchant ship from Lidenbach, a cog
Barlowe - Merchant ship of Andover
Cygnet - Small merchant vessel, Great Northern Sea

Icewind - Small merchant ship, Great Northern Sea
Liddy - Small merchant ship, Great Northern Sea
Moonfish - Small merchant ship, Great Northern Sea
Pelican - Small merchant ship, Great Northern Sea
Sapphire - Merchant vessel captained by Guillermo Carvahlen
Triumphant - Flagship of Holy Fleet in Corassus, Shimmering Sea

THINGS

Holy Fleet - Church fleet based in Corassus
Knights of the Silver Spur - Order of knighthood based in Arnsfeld
Shadowbark - Heavy dark-coloured wood
Temple Fleet - Ships under the command of the Temple Knights of Saint Agnes
The Emporer's Own - Elite imperial guard companies serving the Empire of Halvaria
The Stillwater - River forming the border between Arnsfeld and Halvaria
The Valiant Six - The six Temple Knights that originally served aboard the *Valiant*
Sartellian - Last name given to Fire Mages trained in Korascajan
Water Serpent (Skrill) - Large aquatic creature with a dragon-like head

A FEW WORDS FROM PAUL

Charlaine doesn't lack for courage, but becoming a Temple Commander puts her to the test, not as a warrior, but as a strategist. She is thrust into the unenviable position of having to fill a void left by the Cunars, who abandoned their responsibility to defend the land from Halvarian aggression. Unable to strike back, she must cobble together a strategy to weaken her opponent while assembling an army to halt their invasion.

Meanwhile, Danica leads the Temple Fleet into even more dangerous waters, where the enemy significantly outnumbers them. The combination of these two sister knights and their faith in each other will ultimately destroy the threat.

More importantly, they uncover the connection between the Sartellians and the Empire, which will have lasting repercussions for Ludwig, who struggles with his own issues in Hadenfeld, that come to the fore in Warrior Prince, the next book in the Power Ascending series.

Rest assured, Charlaine and Danica will march again, this time to the very heart of their order, in Temple General.

I could not have completed Temple Commander without the outstanding contributions of my wife, Carol, who has acted as both editor and supporter of the entire series. In addition, I would like to thank Christie Bennett, Amanda Bennett, and Stephanie Sandrock for their support and encouragement.

I also owe a debt of gratitude to my BETA team for their valuable feedback. So thank you, Rachel Deibler, Michael Rhew, Phyllis Simpson, Don Hinckley, Charles Mohapel, Debra Reeves, Mitchell Schneidkraut, Susan Young, Joanna Smith, Keven Hutchinson, and Anna Ostberg.

Lastly, I must thank you, the reader, without whom these books would never see the light of day. Your reviews inspire me to continue writing, and independent authors like myself appreciate you taking the time to leave a comment or review on your favourite retailer's website.

ABOUT THE AUTHOR

Paul J Bennett (b. 1961) emigrated from England to Canada in 1967. His father served in the British Royal Navy, and his mother worked for the BBC in London. As a young man, Paul followed in his father's footsteps, joining the Canadian Armed Forces in 1983. He is married to Carol Bennett and has three daughters who are all creative in their own right.

Paul's interest in writing started in his teen years when he discovered the roleplaying game, Dungeons & Dragons (D & D). What attracted him to this new hobby was the creativity it required; the need to create realms, worlds and adventures that pulled the gamers into his stories.

In his 30's, Paul started to dabble in designing his own roleplaying system, using the Peninsular War in Portugal as his backdrop. His regular gaming group were willing victims, er, participants in helping to playtest this new system. A few years later, he added additional settings to his game, including Science Fiction, Post-Apocalyptic, World War II, and the all-important Fantasy Realm where his stories take place.

The beginnings of his first book 'Servant to the Crown' originated over five years ago when he began running a new fantasy campaign. For the world that the Kingdom of Merceria is in, he ran his adventures like a TV show, with seasons that each had twelve episodes, and an overarching plot. When the campaign ended, he knew all the characters, what they had to accomplish, what needed to happen to move the plot along, and it was this that inspired to sit down to write his first novel.

Paul now has four series based in his fantasy world of Eiddenwerthe, and is looking forward to sharing many more books with his readers over the coming years.

Manufactured by Amazon.ca
Acheson, AB

10758979R00233